UNDERTOW

B.C. BLUES CRIME NOVELS

Cold Girl

UNDERTOW

A B.C. BLUES CRIME NOVEL

R.M. GREENAWAY

DUNDURN
TORONTO

Cover image: GlebStock/Shutterstock
Printer: Webcom

Library and Archives Canada Cataloguing in Publication

Greenaway, R. M., author
    Undertow / R.M. Greenaway.

(A B.C. blues crime novel)
Issued in print and electronic formats.
ISBN 978-1-4597-3558-3 (paperback).--ISBN 978-1-4597-3559-0 (pdf).--
ISBN 978-1-4597-3560-6 (epub)

    I. Title. II. Series: Greenaway, R. M. B.C. blues crime novel.

PS8613.R4285U53 2017   C813'.6   C2016-905290-7
                                           C2016-905291-5

1   2   3   4   5   21   20   19   18   17

We acknowledge the support of the Canada Council for the Arts and the Ontario Arts Council for our publishing program. We also acknowledge the financial support of the Government of Ontario, through the Ontario Book Publishing Tax Credit and the Ontario Media Development Corporation, and the Government of Canada.

Care has been taken to trace the ownership of copyright material used in this book. The author and the publisher welcome any information enabling them to rectify any references or credits in subsequent editions.

— J. Kirk Howard, President

VISIT US AT

dundurn.com | @dundurnpress | dundurnpress | dundurnpress

Dundurn
3 Church Street, Suite 500
Toronto, Ontario, Canada
M5E 1M2

To Chaz

One

BITTER END

LANCE LIU WAS BEGINNING to believe he wasn't dead after all. He hurt all over, couldn't see too well, couldn't seem to move. But if he was dead, he would be pain-free, wouldn't he? And probably serene, and looking down a tunnel of warm, bright light. He was distinctly being or doing none of that.

So he had survived. He blew out a shaky breath. He blinked at the murk above, all dark and dribbly, spattering erratic raindrops on his face. The tree was pissing on him, like it hadn't done enough already. All around was tall grass, bushes. The bushes made him nervous. Would sure be nice to have his vision back. Damned shenanigans.

What had his mom always said?

Coming events cast their shadows before them.

Or *I told you so.*

After tonight, he was going to make some major changes in his life. Maybe return to church. He wanted to bring a hand to the side of his head and feel the damage, but couldn't. Tried to shift his legs and couldn't. Just needed to calm himself a bit. He tried to pray, stretched out under the giant tree that had smacked him twice. "Dear God ..." he whispered, doing his best, because his best was all God required. "Forgive me my —" but a noise stopped him. He listened hard.

A car sped past above, wet tires on wet road. Was that the noise he had heard? He struggled to turn that way. He shouted out, "Hey! Help!"

The car was gone. Didn't see his vehicle down here, didn't see trouble, wouldn't come to his rescue. Nobody would come to his rescue. The panic surged through him like a low-grade electric shock. He couldn't keep lying here. He needed to get back to the family, make sure they were safe. He managed to flop a knee, up and down, and up again. Good. Not paralyzed.

He made more resolutions as he worked his other leg back to life and flexed his hands. Never rise to a taunt again.

That was what put him in this ditch. Taunts. The SUV dripped privilege, just *glared* cash, a big, boxy black-and-chrome Hummer telling him *I'm rich; you're a blue-collar shithead.* All he had wanted was to level the field, make a buck, and take that guy down a notch. No face-to-face confrontation. No bloodshed. No harm done.

Didn't happen that way.

* * *

How *did* it happen? Lance picked up the tail in Deep Cove, as instructed. He was led around town a bit, stopping at the liquor store and a KFC, and finally hitting the Upper Levels. All good, just two trucks tootling along the highway. Where it went wrong was the Hummer taking an off-ramp up a sparsely trafficked two-laner, leaving Lance exposed and vulnerable. Which would have been a really good time to back off. And he didn't.

The Hummer sprinted away, topping a hundred in a sixty zone. Lance did his best to keep the vehicle in sight, trying to tail without looking like a tail. The Hummer swerved hard through a hairpin. Lance took the curve more cautiously, but his tires still squealed. At which point he was hit by an epiphany. "I don't need this," he declared. He dropped back so the Hummer's wide-ass tail lights ahead shrank and converged into the darkness. "*We* don't need this. *Nobody* needs this. I'm calling it off. Not just this, but all of it. Pack it in, moving back to Cowtown, with or without you, man."

The *you, man* was Sig, the Sig Blatt in his mind, his business partner and pal. Moving west was Sig's idea, just like this Hummer business. The Sig in his mind was peeved, a pale, blotchy face telling him to stay on that Hummer's ass. Lance switched him off and spoke to Cheryl instead, the other reason for this move.

Cheryl's pressure was more a passive insistence. A prairie girl who thought it would be so cool to live on the very edge of the Pacific Rim. "See what I'm doing here?" he told her. "Never had this kind of baloney in Calgary, did we?" He'd been based in Airdrie, not Calgary, but from this distance, way over here on the west coast, Calgary and Airdrie pretty well converged to a point on the map.

"And all this so you could wade in the waves. Well, you waded, didn't you? Then you said it was cold and dirty and you wanted to go home. One flippin' day at the beach. Big moves like this don't come for free. D'you have any idea what that walk on the beach cost us?" He made up a number. "Five hundred dollars a millisecond's worth of walk on the beach. No way, princess. I've had it. I'm gonna beg Ray for the job back, and we're outta here tomorrow."

Sig popped back into view, still griping. But in the end Sig would pull up stakes, too. He would follow Lance back to Morice & Bros. Electric (1997) and their cheapskate boss Ray Duhammond. Sig would get it, eventually. They just weren't cut out to be businessmen.

The tail lights were back in sight, for some reason, and growing larger. The Hummer had slowed right down. Lance did, too. He slapped at his jacket pockets, then the seat beside him piled with receipts, grubby boxes of connectors, a tangle of hand tools. He found his iPhone and thumbed the home button. A colourful, glowing line indicated his phone servant was listening. He snarled at her: "Siri. Call fucking Sig."

Red blazed at the side of the road ahead and to his right, smeared by rain and darkness. The Hummer had pulled over and was parked on the shoulder. Lance drove past, not giving a fig anymore who was in that Hummer or what he, she, they, or it was up to. Siri apologized and said she didn't understand his request. He started to repeat, "Call Sig," without the F-word, but headlights popped up in his rear-view mirror, pitched and straightened and expanded.

The Hummer was beginning to scare him.

It was now coming up on his rear, and by the way those headlights were spreading like a couple of supernovas, it was coming fast. He sighed in relief as the Hummer pulled into the oncoming lane and tore past. Passed on a solid line, it was in such a hurry. Why the rush? There was nothing up here but forest, rock wall, and more forest.

He didn't care. He was off the case. He slowed further, on the lookout for a good place to pull a U-ey, and in the distance, red dots flared. The fickle-hearted Hummer had put on its brakes. Again. A knot tightened in Lance's gut. White lights glared. The Hummer had thrown itself into reverse and was moving. Seemed to be moving fast, too.

Lance swore aloud. He flashed his high beams. He leaned on his horn. He tried steering forward into the oncoming lane, but the road was narrow here, and the SUV was wigwagging, hogging the centre, blocking him.

This wasn't a freak accident. It was an attack.

He shifted into reverse and pressed the gas, scudding backward into the night, but the Hummer came at him fast and straight. Lance veered toward the shoulder, but the white lights followed. A car's length, half — "My God!" They were going to connect. Or he would be sandwiched by somebody coming around the dark curve behind him. He was looking ahead, behind, over his shoulder. On one side the road fell away steeply; on the other he sensed the slope would be milder, and aimed in that direction. He crossed into the oncoming lanes, felt tires hit gravel, and gravity took him.

Tall grasses scraped the chassis as he slid to a stop, spiking the brakes and twisting the wheel. The truck swung to face downslope and rocked to a standstill.

Lance's headlights shone on dark woods. He was tilted awkwardly to the right, boots pushed against the manifold to keep him upright. Getting the driver's door open would be tough, and getting the truck back on the road tougher still.

But the fate of his vehicle was the least of his worries. He had two options now: reach for the knife in the glovebox or get out and run.

In the end, his usual half-assed indecision lost the day for him. He opened the driver's door when he should have left it locked, leaned across the centre console, wedging his elbows among slithering junk, and grappled for the glove compartment hatch, when a soft voice behind him made him jump. The man from the SUV was here — who else could it be? — standing close. He had stepped up onto the running board and pulled the door wide open, letting in the wet, chilly night. The man leaned in, asking Lance in a kind voice if everything was all right. But it wasn't kindness, really. It was sugar-coated sarcasm, and Lance redoubled his efforts to get his buck knife.

The glovebox hatch flipped open, but too late. He felt the weight of the man leaning in as though to climb on top of him, felt fists grab the leather of his jacket and tug. Lance gave up on the knife and flipped around with a rough idea of kicking the man off, shouting, "What the fuck d'you want, man, wha'd I do?"

He was dragged out into the night and released. He staggered upright.

"I was about to ask you the same thing," the man said. He stood too close, eyes fixed and intense. "What's with the follow?"

He was a stocky white guy, a few inches shorter than Lance. But a bull. A fine drizzle touched Lance's face. His truck was idling at his back, and up the bank and across the road the Hummer was, too. He could smell the drift of exhaust, could see the confusion of headlights and tail lights, and the SUV's hazards blinking. He could hear his own door alarm pinging. The lights lit up the forest downslope behind them. The trees stood about like a crowd of cold-hearted onlookers, tall, dark figures topped with shuddering leaves.

There was a third person here, he realized, giving her a double take. She stood just up the bank. He couldn't see her face, but her presence lifted his spirits. Women always kept the peace. She wouldn't let anything bad happen. He gave her a weak smile. He flagged her a signal to say he was innocent, that he really could use some help down here.

She didn't move.

He tried for a chummy tone with the guy. "I'm new in town, man. Electrician, just starting up. I was heading out to Horseshoe Bay to meet buddies, right? Took the wrong turnoff." He forced a laugh. "It's a friggin' maze, this town. All these ramps look the same. Figured we'd loop back down to the highway soon enough. Latched onto your tail lights, hoping you'd lead me out. Can't blame you thinking I was following you, bud. Just a misunderstanding."

"Except I seen you before," the man said. "Didn't I, now?" He was older than Lance, in his mid-forties, probably, and carried a big gut. He had a round, buzz-cut head and fussily groomed beard. The fat gold chain around his neck, the diamond in his ear, and the glossy black SUV up on the road said he was over-the-top flush. He was also angry, and maybe stoned, too. Eyes fierce but empty, like an overdosed gamer after an all-night binge. But it wasn't games he was whacked on. Definitely some chemical worming through his brain. And that was bad news.

Lance looked at the woman in the shadows, about as helpful as a hood ornament. He said to the man with the diamond in his ear, "No way, man. Wasn't me you saw, or if it was, I sure wasn't following you. Company I work for, we got a huge fleet."

In truth, it was a fleet of two: the canopied Chev he drove and Sig's Ford.

He slapped at the logo on the door of his truck — *L&S Electric,* which stood for Lance and Sig, two prairie guys trying to break into the big-city market — and made up a number. "Yup, twenty-four of us out there on a slow day."

The man said, "Give me your phone."

"Why?"

"'Cause mine's dead, and we gotta call you a tow truck, don't we?"

His manner had changed, relaxed, lost the sarcastic edge. He sounded amused, and it dawned on Lance that he was just another shit-for-brains bully, pushy but harmless, playing mind games. Even the spooky-eye thing was an act.

"Hey, not necessary." Lance tried for a chuckle as he straightened from what he only now realized was a cower.

He adjusted his twisted jacket. "Was a huge misunderstanding, man. You guys go on your way, and I'll call me a tow."

"Yeah, but listen, I'd feel a whole lot better if you did it now. Don't want to leave you in the lurch down here."

The guy sounded apologetic now, smiling. Maybe he was afraid of a lawsuit, wanted to leave things at a no-hard-feelings level. Lance gave an uneasy shrug. He pulled out his iPhone and keyed in the code. The phone unlocked, and he opened his contact list for the BCAA number, to call for road service — and only then it occurred to him that no man with a diamond in his ear, driving a top-of-the-line Hummer, would let his cellphone die. Guy would have it hooked to a charger like life support. And the girlfriend would have a phone on her too, wouldn't she? Pink, studded with rhinestones. These were not phoneless people. The thought came simultaneously with the grab. The phone was taken from him, and he couldn't grab it back. "No," he moaned, understanding the enormity of what had just happened. He had surrendered all his contacts to this freaky bastard, handed Sig over on a platter. Worse, much worse, his home address, Cheryl and the kids. His darling Cheryl, his beautiful tot Rosalie, and his little boy, Joseph.

The man was waving the phone overhead like a winning ticket, looking up at his girlfriend. She shouted something, and it sounded like either *go on* or *don't*.

Lance received a rough shove and stumbled away from his vehicle.

Another shove, and he was careening through tall shrubs, low weeds, down on his knees, up on his feet.

Pushed again, and he was into the trees. He fought back, swung loose and hit nothing. He turned to flee, but all too late. He wasn't a fighter or a planner, and this guy was. The guy was telling him as he dogged after him that this was what he got for messing with people's lives. Lance tried to bellow, but it came out a whimper: "What? I don't know what you're talking about." He was backed up beside one of the huge trees, straight as a telephone pole. No branches within reach to grasp for leverage, nowhere to hide. "You gotta believe me, mister. I'm from Airdrie. I'm an electrician. I don't know you from a hole in the wall, I swear."

The man reached out, grabbed him by the ear, and shoved his head sideways into the tree.

Stars showered against crimson. Lance heard himself scream out in pain and terror. He flailed his arms, tried to kick or step back, but he was dazed, and the man had that hellish grip on his ear, and was saying again this was all his fault. Lance cried out to be left alone and instead was pushed again into the tree, hard. His right ear and scalp were hot and wet, beyond pain now, and he knew the man was going to slam him till his skull cracked open and his brains spattered like a melon against the corrugated iron of the tree trunk. His legs buckled. He felt himself sag, his body parts thud to earth, and sprawl. He lay a moment on the sloping ground, trying to curl into himself, to protect his body from whatever would land next, a boot or fist or rock. His thoughts raced and scattered. He was done for.

The impact didn't come. Just a pattering of words. The man leaned over him, a dark shape without definition.

He was saying something low and complicated, almost conversational. Lance could make no sense of it. He closed his eyes, and now there was silence, a nothingness. Then the swish and crunch of feet wading through weeds, uphill and away. The man was leaving.

Maybe to grab a gun, to finish this off.

Lance blinked furiously to clear the blur, but the blur remained. He heard two car doors slam. And, God, he heard the SUV drive away. Hope flowed over him like a cool tide.

He gave himself a minute to lie still, reflecting on this clean slate, his mistakes and resolutions, and how fiercely he would be hugging his family tonight.

But what was that? Again he held his breath, tilting his head to listen. There, a new noise that didn't fit with the shush of grasses and leaves rustling in the wind. Not close, but not far, a furtive crunching heading this way. He became stone still. Something was down here with him. A creature, a killer dog released by the man in the Hummer? He blinked again. He could make out nothing but a blue-grey haze criss-crossed with grass blades, and the shapes of bushes. The thing came slowly, snapping branches underfoot, and it wasn't a dog. By the sound he knew it was big as a rhino. Bigger. It was a mastodon, and he lay in its sights. Maybe it was harmless. Maybe if he yelled, he would scare it off. He tried to scrabble his legs, but couldn't. Couldn't roll over or curl a hand into a protective fist. Couldn't shout. It was near now, wasn't slowing. The bushes were thrashing. He had pissed his jeans.

He managed to cry out to the one who always made things right. She gathered him up when he fell and fixed all his screw-ups, and he needed her now so badly. "*Mama.*" But she was back in Airdrie, so far away. He would have given all he had to see her smile right now, to feel her forgiving embrace.

A smile erases a million worries.

The creature was on top of him now, all black and oily and obliterating the sky. He reached out to touch it, and his heart, his pounding heart … He squeezed his eyes shut, bellowed, and was silent.

Two

LIGHT AND SHADOW

BLESSEDLY, THE LONSDALE barbershop had not changed at all in Dion's time away. He stood in the entrance and took it all in with a smile. Music, mirrors, posters, and Persian bric-a-brac. There was the strong scent of aftershave that he hadn't even realized he missed, till now. Nobody here but Hami in his white smock, busy tidying up his workstations.

Hami turned and saw him. He did a double take. "It can't be," he said, Hami the ham, so shocked he staggered. "My God. You're back. Long time no see!"

Dion said "*Salam*," about the only Farsi word he knew. "'Course I'm back, why wouldn't I be? I didn't make an appointment. Have time for a walk-in?"

"Of course. Come, come."

Dion hung his leather car coat on a hook and sat in one of three vinyl padded chairs before the wall-length mirror. He waited for the barber to clip the cape around his shoulders and tuck it in around his collar. With cape secured, he checked out his world in the mirror's reflection. Hami prepared scissors and razor and spray bottle, making small talk as if only a week or two had passed, not close to a year.

All of it was pleasant, yet something was out of place. Dion fixed on Hami's face and words, trying to ignore the slight skew.

"Was last July, yes?" Hami said, eying him up for the cut. "I read about it in the paper, saw your name, couldn't believe my eyes. They said there were fatalities, but said too that you survived. But me, I don't trust the news. Then you miss your next appointment, never come back again, and I'm thinking for sure, man, my best customer is dead. The same?" he said, talking style.

"Things happened," Dion said. "Yes, don't change a thing."

"So what things happened?"

"I took a transfer. Went north to work till I got back up to speed."

"Aha. And now you're back up to speed?"

"Totally. Better than ever. Passed the tests with flying colours." It was a white lie. There were no flying colours, but no signs of brain injury either, which meant no medical reason to shift him out of active duty. The initial diagnosis in layman's terms of "shook up" remained, as far as Dion understood. He pointed and fired a bullet at his own reflected self, made a *pewww* noise. "Hit the target dead-on, near-perfect bull's eye. BS'd with a shrink for a few hours, did the math, scenarios, memory tests. Whatever they threw at me, I passed, no sweat."

"Kudos," Hami said, but vaguely. He had paused to stare in the mirror, comb and scissors in hand, like he was thinking of something more important as he studied Dion's face. "Maybe you keep it long, eh? Such a good-looking guy, why you want the old fart look?"

Dion's dark hair wasn't long at all, but it had relaxed over his year away. It flipped in at the eyes now, curled about the collar, and made him look younger than his twenty-nine years. But whether it looked good or not wasn't the point. The point was to look exactly as he had the day before the crash that had nearly killed him. A hundred years ago, last summer.

"Same cut," he told Hami. "You remember, right?"

Hami said, "Hey, buddy, short back and sides, boring as hell. I could do this with my eyes closed."

The radio was tuned to a Western rock station, and it struck Dion that this was the difference that bothered him. It wasn't the usual upbeat Persian pop that his barber had always kept jangling. This was a U.S. band he should be able to name, but couldn't.

Didn't matter. Musically speaking, Hami was leaving his culture behind, but that was okay, too, for everything else here was timeless. He watched himself re-emerge, the cut neat and close with only the bangs allowed to follow their natural cowlick. Not seamless, because he had lost weight and was still working at getting it back. But it wasn't a bad likeness.

For the first time since stepping off the Greyhound last week, he felt hopeful. It had been a tough haul. He had sat through the two-day bus ride like an android tourist, watching the landscape rise and fall. There were a lot of canyons, forests, and small-town depot sandwiches to get through, but at last he landed at the Main Street terminal in downtown Vancouver, and was cabbing across the bridge to home, the North Shore, straight to the most economical room he could book, the Royal Arms.

On the day following his arrival came the tests and interviews, and he had done better than expected. But his first day back on the job would be the real test, and that was still to come.

Today he was fixing himself up for a comeback. He'd gotten himself new clothes that shouted *I'm the best*, and now the haircut, and tonight he would probably spend an unhealthy amount of time in front of the mirror, trying on expressions. Illusion was a big part of success, after all, and as long as he looked good, he would be fine.

A blur of motion caught his eye in the big barbershop window reflected behind him. Nothing specific, but an active chaos of light and shadow that thrilled him. Pigeons swooped and awnings flapped. Cars slid by or stopped, depending on the lights. But it was the people he watched. They walked past the glass and warped the spring sunshine, ducked through the fine, slanting rain, stood waiting for the bus. He knew now how vital they were to him, these perfect strangers who made up a city, and how vital he was to them.

He was going to prove how vital he was in the days to come. He had been summoned back to GIS, the General Investigations Section, by one of the NCOs, Sergeant Mike Bosko, which meant they had faith in him. So what could go wrong?

The cut was done. Perfect. He settled up, leaving the usual tip, and smiled at Hami, the smile and direct gaze all part of the plan. Smile at everybody, and smile big.

"You want me to put you down for two weeks here, bud?" Hami asked at the counter, his appointment book open. "Wednesday still best?"

Dion had forgotten that the trims were a standing order. They came at two-week intervals, and Wednesday had always been his day of preference. He had no idea why. He said, "Of course, Wednesday. Thanks, Hami. You've always got me covered."

Hami extended a fist, and Dion remembered this ritual, too. He bumped the barber's knuckles with his own, and Hami said, "Great to have you back, my friend."

"Great to be back.... You've changed your music."

Up now was an old Beach Boys classic about a miserable experience aboard a ship. Hami was grimacing and rolling his eyes at the speakers. "I'm assimilating, man. Godawful noise, this."

On Lonsdale the rain had fused with the sunshine to become a dazzling mist. Several blocks downhill, the giant Q marked the Quay market and the harbour. Dion had no urge to go down there and look at the water, which was strange. Wasn't that what he had been homesick for, the sound and smell, the magnetic pull of the sea?

Maybe not. There was an order to things. Get back to work, see the crew, confront Bosko, and then call up Kate. Then he would go and look at the water. He lit a cigarette and walked along 3rd, which became Marine Drive, where the traffic was heavy and endless. A used-car lot twinkled into view.

Cars and SUVs filled the lot, a variety pack of shiny metal. When he came to the bumper of the closest car, he stopped and took it in. A dark-blue coupe, a Honda Civic, poised at a dynamic angle, nosing into the sidewalk as though frozen in escape. A placard on its windshield advertised a price he recognized as decent. The windows were tinted. He peered inside and saw the interior was a handsome black, if not leather, then a good imitation.

He hadn't owned a car since the crash. In Smithers he had walked or cabbed anywhere he needed to go, except when on the job. The job demanded that he drive, sometimes at speed, occasionally on ice, so he had no choice but to get good at it again. Here on the Lower Mainland an off-duty vehicle was not optional. He needed a car, but he would never drive again just for the fun of it. No thanks.

He read the stat sheets on the car's window and saw the mileage wasn't so bad. He circled the Civic again, and already a salesman was approaching, hands in pockets. The salesman stopped and looked at the car, proud as a new dad. He remarked that Dion had great taste in wheels, and did he have any questions? Dion said no, he didn't right now, thanks. He stood and drew at his cigarette and looked at the car, while the salesman looked at the sky and talked about the weather. The salesman segued from weather into suggesting a test spin.

Dion smiled at the salesman. He wasn't born yesterday. He knew what used sporty-looking coupes with great price tags meant, and the kind of people who fell for them. He was about to say so, but the salesman spoke first. "Whatcha got to lose?"

He had a point. The man took his driver's licence to make a copy and went to get the key and demo plates, and Dion stood on the sidewalk to wait. He looked south along Marine Drive at the city skyline, then northward, at the mountains. He thought about the highway that wove through them, and the long drive between this point and that, North Vancouver and Smithers. Strange how a part of him wanted to go back there even after he had worked so hard to be here. This was where he belonged, not there.

The salesman brought the keys. It took a moment for Dion to remember why. "Thank you."

"You're ... all right?" the salesman said.

Dion smiled at him, and smiled big. "Absolutely."

Three

CRIME CURRENTS

EACH NEW DAY, DAVE LEITH had to look harder for that silver lining. For over a month now he had been living in a strange city, confined to a crappy little apartment that was costing him twelve hundred a month, plus utilities, and driving a rental car to an office full of strangers, none of whom he had managed to befriend. He asked himself now: when exactly in the recent past had this move to the metropolis struck him as a "great idea"?

Last night from Prince Rupert, his wife Alison had given yet another long-distance reassurance: "You just need time to adjust."

"It's not exactly what I thought it would be," he had told her.

"What ever is?" she asked.

Sure, he would adjust — what choice did he have? But Alison didn't get it, that adjustment for him was step two in a two-step process. First he had to get over the disappointment, and he had to do that in his own particular style, griping all the way.

At least the daily commute from his apartment to the North Van detachment had become routine by now; he no longer tilted an ear to the GPS delivering her robotic instructions. He merged onto Highway 1 and joined another vehicular lineup. North Vancouver hadn't failed in its promises in any big way; the bright lights were maybe not as bright as he'd imagined, but he had grown up in a small Saskatchewan city, and his thrill-meter was set fairly low. Really he was only disappointed in himself. Where was the handsomer, smarter, wittier Dave Leith that this move was supposed to have made him? A juvenile fantasy, of course, but still he would check the mirror as he shaved each morning and be chagrined to see no progress. He remained a tall, thickening, doubtful-looking forty-four-year-old with lumpy, blond hair beginning to recede, blue eyes too close set, nose and chin too big, mouth too thin and always clamped into a self-conscious smile.

There was no wild nightlife here, either, at least not for him. He had made the effort and gone out drinking twice with the rowdier set of his new workmates, but the situation — it was mostly the noisy atmosphere that got him down — only made him antsy. Not that he would quit trying.

He seemed to spend all his time commuting, burning frozen dinners in the apartment's quirky oven, and studying up on the procedures and protocols of his new office. In an effort to impress his new superior, Sergeant Mike Bosko — the man he'd met on a northern assignment and who had made this transfer happen — he also brought his caseload home with him to mull over as he ate his burned dinners.

He missed Prince Rupert. Missed his buddies and comfortable bungalow on its good-sized lot, which now had a big for-sale sign on the front lawn. He missed the morning fogs and the busy harbour, the locals and summer tourists. Alison was still up there, with the furniture and their two-year-old, Isabelle, waiting for Leith to get settled before coming to join him.

Their foolish expectation had been that he would find a great little house, put an offer on it — stretching the budget just a bit — and they would transition smoothly from one residence to another.

The expectation had hit a brick wall called the ridiculous price of real estate in North Vancouver. He was still reverberating from the shock. Some local staff were buying properties as far afield as Abbotsford, he heard. Which meant they spent half their lives commuting.

He was off Highway 1 and driving down the spine of North Vancouver, Lonsdale Avenue, a gauntlet of traffic lights that each turned sadistic yellow as he approached. He had learned that pulling faces and swearing at traffic lights didn't help. Didn't help at all.

Making it through the last light, he turned his car up 15th and down St. Georges and entered the underground parkade of his new detachment.

The North Vancouver RCMP HQ was a modern terraced monolith, three above-ground levels of concrete and glass that looked more like a beached ocean liner than a building. He left his car and rode the elevator up to Level 2, walked down the corridor, and swung into the briefing hall where "A" watch gathered to learn of the day's challenges.

North Van was a mill of hot files, unlike laid-back Rupert, City of Rainbows, up there on its rocky shore. Some crimes were bad, others worse. Today's was off the scale, horrific, and the point-form description, even without the graphic details, rattled Leith as Watch Commander Doug Paley laid it out. A mother and daughter found dead in their home, Paley was saying. Found by a concerned neighbour. Neighbour had seen lights on all night, heard music going, too, and no sign of the residents. She didn't know them personally, not even their names. But the lights and music had struck her as odd enough that she had gone up the back stairs this morning and peeked inside.

First-on-scene gave some details, describing the scene, the victims.

One of the dead was just a toddler. Like Leith's own little Izzy.

* * *

Leith rode in the passenger seat with Doug Paley. Paley was late-middle-aged, heavy set, and cynical. He didn't speak throughout the drive, and only as he pulled in to the curb and yanked on the handbrake did he tell Leith what was what. He would talk to the first responders outside, then join Leith inside the house.

The house was a modest one-storey with finished basement on the corner of 23rd and Mahon. Several squad cars and the crime-scene vans were ranged along the avenue. A crowd of the curious was gathering: neighbours and passersby. Constables kept traffic moving. At the back of a van, Leith zipped into anti-contamination coveralls. The home's front gate was propped open, the egress path marked with crime-scene tape. He climbed cement steps to the door, identified himself to the constable at the door, was given general directions, and entered the house.

Music played, soft rock. There was an unpleasant smell, but it wasn't the worst he had ever worked at not inhaling. Inside the front door a flight of stairs led down, and another led up. He took the flight up, and the music got louder and the smell got ranker. From the top of the stairs radiated a hallway to what might be bedrooms and a bathroom. The place looked neat and clean. Kitchen straight ahead and a combo living room/dining room to his left. The bodies were in the living room, along with the first signs of chaos: a lamp knocked over, dry flowers strewn willy-nilly, a toppled high chair.

Leith stood at the threshold and looked down on the strange tableau. The bodies. They were Asian, the child so like his own, but with downy black hair and ivory skin. She was on her stomach to Leith's left, next to the leg of a wood-and-glass coffee table. A young woman lay ten feet away, face up, before the fireplace. She was slim, wearing blue jeans and a short-sleeved sweater, bare feet. Her long, glossy black hair criss-crossed in swaths over her face, as though draped to hide her features.

The coroner moved in with his kit and an assistant, obscuring the view.

The clothing of both victims seemed intact on first sight. No visible trauma, and aside from the upset furniture, no signs of violence, even. But all it took was a little imagination to hear the screams, to see the struggle, to feel the fear. Violence had swept through this house and left no sound but the music playing, an absurdly hopped-up pop song Leith had heard before somewhere, sometime.

Mother and child had already been pronounced dead. They remained only to be studied, charted, photographed, and stared at by people like Leith, who should be doing his job and analyzing. But he wasn't there yet. He was thinking again of the gross error he had made in transferring his family to this city. His big responsibility in life was to keep them out of harm's way, and instead he was bringing them right into its embrace. The north wasn't crime-free, by any means, but the victimology was more predictable. Down here, high density brought out the weirdos and the guns, no doubt about it, which meant anybody could be mowed down, at any time.

This poor little thing was at the very same tottering age as Izzy, when the tiny legs were losing their baby fat and gaining muscle tone. She should have been learning to talk, too, stomping about with her eyes open to the wonders of the world. Leith looked sideways at Paley, who was done speaking with the coroner and now stood beside him, relaying the findings.

"Strangled, he's thinking." Paley was staring down at the adult victim. "Looks like bruising around the throat. There's that tea towel. Does that look like it's been twined into a rope, to you? That might have done it."

"The hair over her face …" Leith said.

"Yeah, yeah. The hair placement — that's remorse, right? Or apology, or something like that."

"Looks more like insult to me."

The coroner stood and moved away, leaving the assistant making notes.

"Or that," Paley agreed. "As for the baby, she might have fallen and hit her head on that coffee table, we're thinking."

"Do we have names yet?"

Paley didn't answer, too busy staring over Leith's shoulder. Leith turned to see why and watched a young man approach from the hallway, also in white coveralls, shirt collar and tie showing under the unzipped throat of his Tyvek. He looked familiar to Leith, and not in a happy, well-met kind of way.

This was someone he had worked with in the not-so-distant past, up north in the Hazeltons, for a few long weeks through the bitterness of February. So Dion had somehow made it back to North Van, just as he had promised, and instead of being demoted to janitor, as Leith had thought most likely, he had advanced from uniform to the suit-and-tie brigade. Which meant they would be working together again. Hoo-*ray*.

"Well, there you are," Paley exclaimed as Dion came to stand with them. "Heard you were back, you sneaky son-of-a-bitch, but wasn't expecting you today."

"All hands on deck on this one," Dion answered cheerfully. "So to hell with orientation, they just pushed me out the door." He glanced at the bodies, then glanced at Leith, and looked at Leith again, with surprise. Then a shockingly huge smile, as if this meeting really made his day. "I was wondering when I'd run into you! How are you doing? Got set up okay?"

As Leith recalled, their northern parting of ways had been unpleasant. But maybe it was all water under the bridge. He smiled, too, and shook Dion's extended hand, their first physical contact, barring one brief skirmish at the Hazelton detachment. "Getting by," he said. "How are you?"

"Great, great."

The reunion formalities over, Dion became business-like. He gestured at the two bodies and said to Paley, "Just talked to Dadd and got suspected cause of death and his timing estimate —"

The name Dadd — Jack Dadd, the coroner — threw Leith each time.

"— adult female died about twelve hours ago, so it happened last evening. But I guess you have the basics on this one, Doug?"

"The basics," Paley echoed flatly.

"Strangled," Dion said. "Petechiae and some edema visible. Damage to her tongue — she probably bit it — and narrow bruises on the neck, but no cutting. The child, at a guess, likely died of head trauma. TOD about six hours ago, he says — that's quite a bit later than the adult, so it was probably secondary TBI."

TOD, TBI. Time of death was common enough, but TBI made Leith think a moment. Traumatic brain injury. The new, improved Dion opened his notebook, found a page, and studied it. "The homeowner's name is King, and he's got it rented to Lance and Cheryl Liu," he told Paley, with glances at Leith to include him. "The Lius are new in town, out from Alberta. They took the place on March 1st. Lance Liu has just incorporated a company called L&S Electric. He's not been reached yet. I called the L&S number and got voice mail, so I'll follow up. The name *L&S* suggests there's a partner, so —"

"Hey," Paley cut in. "That's all very fuckin' fantastic, but did I ask for a report? Did I?"

"No," Dion said. "You want a report?"

"Too late, I already got it, didn't I?"

Leith suspected this was more a skit than a real conversation. In spite of the age gap, these two were friends from way back.

"Sorry, Doug," Dion said, not sounding sorry at all. "It was hairy at the office. Jim was buried, so I task-shared. You want me to follow up on this L&S thing?"

Paley rolled his eyes. Leith was glad that Dion was apparently okay now. The northern Dion he knew had been remote, unlikeable, and … well, *unsmart.* The new Dion was now outlining to Paley the task he had butted his way into. Probably the most important task on the board at the moment, hunting down their best and only suspect — the missing husband, Lance Liu.

The conversation between the two seemed snappy and efficient, and ended on a positive note. Paley moved off to supervise the removal of the bodies, and Dion remained by Leith's side, pointing down at something. Leith followed the line of his finger to the child's feet.

"One shoe on, one off," Dion said. "Where's the other shoe?"

Booties, not shoes, thought Leith, a bit of an expert. "I saw that," he lied.

"Probably under her body," Dion told him. "Keep an eye out. Also, I don't see a vase."

He turned and headed away, unzipping the bunny suit.

Leith watched him go, then looked at the child's feet, at the pink velvet bootie on one, a tiny striped sock on the other, green and yellow. *Vase,* he thought. *What?*

* * *

The Level 3 office had once been occupied by Staff Sergeant Tony Cleveland, now retired. Cleveland had kept the door shut and the screens closed. He hadn't liked drop-ins, so nobody had dropped in. Now the slats were open, and so was the door. Dion poked his head in and took in the view. He saw that Cleveland's classic etchings of famous bridges were gone, and modern posters were up instead, large photographs of this or that, mounted behind glass with minimalist steel frames. The new occupant, Sergeant Michael Bosko, sat at the desk, working at his computer and talking to himself. Or so it seemed.

With a nod toward the visitor's chair, Bosko acknowledged Dion, then carried on bashing his fingertips on a heavy-duty laptop and chatting via Bluetooth.

"Yes, of course," Bosko said, smiling. "They call it the acid test." He quit typing and peered at the laptop screen. "Just dropped a point. No, I am not kidding you. Absolutely. Yes, absolutely."

Without a sign-off, he tapped something near his ear and looked across at Dion. There was no recognition in his stare. Strange, since he knew Dion, at least remotely. They had met in the Hazeltons, working on the same case, though nowhere near in the same league. Had not exchanged a word, or even eye contact, much, which might explain the lack of *aha*. Still, it was Bosko who had gotten Dion back here, so ...

"Calvin Dion, hello." Recognition must have kicked in, for now Bosko was on his feet, smiling. "Or is it Cal?"

"Cal's good." Dion had risen too, reaching across the desk. This was another of the day's big challenges: the all-important first impression, the firm handshake, the confident smile. The smile had to reach the eyes, or it was worse than no smile at all. The reach and grip had to be solid, fluid, and of just the right duration — not so brief as to seem skittish, but releasing before being released, to show initiative. "Morning, sir."

They both resumed their seats. Reborn from the haircut to the silk-blend socks, Dion had been careful not to show up on Day One looking like a menswear mannequin. That would make him look insecure. He had knotted the tie properly but hadn't snugged it too tight, tucked the shirttails in, then did a few overhead stretches to slack off the tension. He was showered and shaved, but had skipped the cologne, and his short black hair was a tad mussed. According to the mirror, he was perfectly imperfect.

"So you didn't have time to set up your pencil jar before they sent you off to the field, I hear," Bosko said. He had a deep, easy voice, almost lazy. And controlled, as though nothing could fluster him. "I also understand you're already in the thick of it, so I won't keep you. I called you in just to welcome you back and have a one-minute face-to-face, since I don't believe we ever actually spoke, did we? How are you doing so far?"

"Great," Dion said. Seated straight, but not too straight, his expression enthused but not maniacal. "I'm stoked to be home. I wanted to thank you. For putting your trust in me, sir. You won't be disappointed."

"I don't expect I will be. Now, you've been away for a while, and things have been shuffled around a bit, so if you need any help with our setup here, procedure, fitting back in, or just need to talk something through, come on over and let me know. The door's open."

Dion nodded. "There is one thing. I was working on a file when the crash happened. It's still unsolved. Would I be able to get back on it?"

Bosko asked for the particulars, and Dion gave him the file name — written down and memorized before this meeting — and the basics. Last summer a young woman's body had been found washed ashore. Snagged in the boulders that formed a rampart down by the Neptune Terminals. He didn't give Bosko the fine details, how Jane Doe's face had been eroded by gasses, brine, and parasites, so a police artist had reconstructed her, as best she could, in pencil, to be followed up by a 3D model. Early twenties, short hair that was natural brown but dyed white-blond, wide-spaced eyes, rosebud mouth. Ancestry undetermined, but possibly Eurasian. Pink spandex bathing suit — a pricey brand — embedded in flesh, grotesque and slimy. And one earring, the other apparently lost. He had been trying before his departure to track down the jeweller who made the earring.

It was of characteristic design, a round, enamelled button, a yellow shape against a red background. The shape might have been a star, except it was cut off. Around the edges ran little beads of gold, fourteen-carat.

The bathing suit and the season — summertime — suggested she had come off a boat. The pathologist determined she had been strangled by a fine, hard ligature. Alternatively, it might have been a necklace that had cut into her bloating flesh before snapping and sinking to the ocean floor.

She would have been beautiful, once.

Nobody had come to claim her, and she had never been given a name, and like any unfinished job, she continued to haunt Dion.

"I'll tell you what," Bosko said, after calling the case up on the intranet. "You're free to look it over, but I'd like you on this Mahon case, hundred percent."

Mahon Avenue, murdered mother and child, missing husband. "Yes, sir. Thank you."

And just like that, they were done. Dion stood and smiled again. As he left the room and strode down the hall, he counted again the four possibilities of why he was back in North Vancouver. Possibility one was just what he'd been told, that Bosko was impressed with him for some reason — his excellent past record, say — and for that reason alone, he'd had him summoned. Possibility two: sheer error. Bosko was a busy man with lots on his mind, and maybe a wire had crossed, a typo or false memory, and he simply had someone else in mind. Three, Bosko was a manipulator. He considered Dion a liability and wanted him gone, but needed a good excuse, so he'd decided to place him in a stressful situation — the big-city crime scene — to watch him come apart.

The fourth possibility kept Dion awake nights: he was being investigated. Bosko was working a crime, had a theory, was putting his suspicion to the test, and to test it properly he needed his suspect close at hand.

Down on Level 2, at the desk he'd been given, Dion set aside his doubts and focussed on the Lius. He listed his thoughts on paper. First on the list, he made a call to the Justice Department for a telephone warrant, doing Jimmy Torr's job for him, then to the Corporate Registry of Companies, and fairly soon had the information he was looking for: the names of all partners in the company, which totalled two, each owning fifty percent of L&S Electric.

He guessed the "L" was Lance Liu. The "S," he knew now, would be a Sigmund Blatt. The company had been incorporated only three months ago. Its address was a PO box, and its phone number was the one he had tried earlier without luck. Now he made more calls, tracking down the unlisted contact information for the surviving partner.

Within the hour he took the information a few desks down to Jimmy Torr. He sat and waited for Torr to finish a call, then told him, "I've got a line on Sigmund Blatt, the missing man's partner. You want me to follow up?"

He had known Torr for years. Torr was in his middle thirties, built, irritable, and insecure. He had never liked Dion, and vice versa. But animosity felt good to Dion. It meant for a while he could drop the cheek-numbing smile.

"I'll take care of it," Torr said coldly, reaching for the note. "Thanks."

"It's priority. Lance Liu's our best bet right now, and he's missing. If you're not going to deal with it straight away, I will. Paley's given me the go-ahead."

Torr looked at the paper. He said, "Call him up, tell him I'll be there in twenty minutes."

"I tried. Got an answering machine."

"Did you leave a message? Tell him to get back to you A-SAP?"

"No. Better to cold-call him anyway," Dion said. "I could head over there now."

Torr said sourly, "What meds they got you on?" He didn't wait for an answer, but stood and grabbed his suit jacket, making a statement with the set of his shoulders that he was going alone. Dion followed.

Four

ECHOES

LEITH HAD SEEN WHAT HE had to see in the house on Mahon, and as the place filled with Ident members buckling down for an in-depth search, he thought he would leave, make himself useful back at the office. He was heading down the stairs toward the front door when he heard a commotion, a kind of collective gasp, then a murmuring of excited voices.

It was so unlike any other commotion he had heard at crime scenes over the years that he returned at a jog to the top of the stairs and followed the sound to the kitchen. Here he saw half a dozen white-clad Idents clustered about the lower corner cabinet next to the kitchen sink. All were peering into the darkness, and one was speaking gently to it.

Dog or cat, Leith thought.

"What's up?" he asked the member closest to him.

"There's a child in there," she said. "A boy, we're thinking. He's crouched way at the back. He won't come out."

A child, Leith thought. *Alive.* He added a mental *wow.* "Is he hurt? Is he stuck?"

Nobody thought the kid was hurt or stuck, but nobody knew for sure.

Leith told the group, "Everybody clear out. Except you," he told the female member, because women were nicer, and kids knew it. "What's your name?" he asked, as the others left the room.

"Constable Kim Tam, sir."

"Try to coax him out, okay? I'll wait over here."

He stood in the corner of the room and watched Tam crouch down by the open cabinet doors. She leaned over so her head almost touched the floor, and cooed in at the boy. *Must be a terrifically small human to fit in there, on the lower shelf, far back among pots and pans,* Leith marvelled.

"It's all good now," Tam was saying, in a warm, smiley voice. "The bad man is gone," she said, and Leith sighed. He'd have a talk with her later about planting false memories. But too late now; the bad man had come and gone. She nodded encouragement into the shadows. "We're going to take care of you now, okay? You must be so cold! I have a blanket here, and we'll get you a nice cup of cocoa, how about that?"

Finally there was movement and a shifting of cookware. A little face appeared, caught sight of Leith, who was working hard to look like safe harbour, and ducked back inside. Tam turned and glared at Leith, letting him know safe harbour was the last thing he looked like. He stepped further away, and she went about undoing the damage.

At last she had the little survivor gathered in her arms, hugging him tight. There were tears in her eyes as she stood and turned to Leith, and a flash of outrage, asking what kind of monster could tear this little darling's world apart like this.

Any decent person would feel that outrage. Children left parentless, parents left childless, families shredded. Leith knew the outrage most viscerally. In his line of work, anger was a valuable but delicate resource, possibly not renewable, not to be overused. He had learned the lesson maybe too late, because his anger these days felt like a worn tire, dulled by age and subject to bursting. As hers would, too, in time, if she didn't watch out.

"What's your name, little guy?" Tam was asking the child. He was somewhere between three and four years old. He wore flannel pyjamas that smelled of stale pee. He wouldn't talk. Nor did he cry or fuss; he just huddled in Tam's arms. Whatever he'd seen in this place last night had shocked him numb.

"Maybe he doesn't speak English," Leith suggested.

Tam said, "I'm sure he speaks perfect English."

Leith wasn't sure how she could know, but trusted she was right. He got on the phone, calling Paley to send in a female GIS member to help get the kid to the hospital. The one who showed up a few minutes later was a bit of a disappointment, not the kind of female he had in mind. He had worked with her before in a passing way. JD Temple was tall, about thirty years old, with short brown hair. Her face was marred by a birth defect, a cleft lip that had never been properly repaired. She had a skinny build, fierce dark eyes, and an air of macho impatience. Leith would have preferred the soft femininity of Kim Tam, but Tam was Ident, and her job was here at the scene, combing and picking up lint with her team like an OCD housemaid.

Problem? JD's stare asked him as she plucked the reluctant child from a reluctant Tam, reading the doubt on Leith's face and resenting it.

Yes, there was a problem, because right now this little survivor was Leith's best clue, and he wanted that clue to be as comfortable as possible. He wasn't sure JD was capable of giving that kind of comfort. "Great," he said. "Let's go."

* * *

Sigmund Blatt's stats said he lived on the fourth floor of a low-rise down near the industrial zone. Nobody at his unit number buzzed the door open, so Torr got the manager to open up. Torr asked the manager what he knew of Blatt, and the manager, a hard-eyed Asian — Vietnamese, Dion believed — only shrugged, signing that he wasn't up on his English. He was, however, able to explain that the elevator was out of order.

"See the way he looked at me?" Torr said as he and Dion climbed the stairs to four. "Looked at me like *I'm* the invasive species. Blatt won't be home, I guarantee you. We're doing ten miles of stairs for nothing. Fuck you."

The *fuck you* wasn't up to Torr's usual standard. Maybe it was the exertion of the climb. They arrived, damp and winded, at the door of apartment 416. Dion was out of shape from lack of exercise, and Torr was a body builder, not a mountaineer. Torr flapped his elbows to air the sweat, then knocked on the door, two loud thumps, predicting again that nobody would answer. Nobody did.

"It was worth a try," Dion said, as he and Torr exchanged angry looks. He got on his phone and called the number from his notebook. Again, nobody picked up. Was Sigmund Blatt missing along with Lance Liu? He let it ring, and heard a cellphone tweedling, a distant, eerie, echoey sound, as if from outer space. Torr walked down the hall and pushed open the fire door, looked down the stairwell, and held up a hand for silence. The tweedling was coming from below, rising slowly.

Dion disconnected, and the tweedling stopped. They waited on the landing, and a minute later, a man appeared, plodding up the stairs. He was burly and red-faced, with bristling blond hair. When he noticed their presence he didn't flinch, but kept climbing until he stood facing them on the landing. He wore jeans, a well-worn black leather jacket, and heavy-duty workman's boots. Torr said, "Sigmund Blatt?"

"That's me."

Torr showed his ID and said, "Why didn't you answer your phone?"

"Didn't recognize the number."

"Not a great business model, is it?"

"It's my personal cell. My partner does sales. What's the problem?"

Like the building manager, Blatt latched suspicious eyes on Torr and ignored Dion.

"Your partner *is* the problem," Torr answered. "Lance Liu. Where is he?"

"I've been wondering that myself. Trying to get a hold of him. No answer. No answer at his home, either. Weird."

Torr gave Blatt a heavy stare, maybe challenging him to figure it out, that something was terribly wrong; why else would two cops be standing here wanting to talk? The staring contest grew edgy, till Blatt brushed past them, out of the stairwell, and into the corridor. The two cops trailed after him. He stopped at 416 and fished for keys. "Guess you better come in," he said.

Dion followed Torr into the apartment. The place was messy and musty. Over by the window a big white bird, some kind of parrot, muttered and squawked from a cage. Unlike the apartment, the cage appeared to be clean and well tended. Sigmund Blatt flung clothes and shopping bags off a sofa set and indicated they should sit, if they cared to, but nobody was in the mood.

Dion watched Torr arranging his face to break the news, a professional blend of sympathy and suspicion. "Mr. Blatt," Torr said. "I'm sorry, but we're here because Mr. Liu's wife and daughter were found dead in their home this morning. You know Cheryl Liu, do you?"

Blatt had taken a step backward. His mouth dropped open. His eyes narrowed, then widened. "Oh no," he said, and to Dion the surprise seemed genuine. So did the shock, and then the slow surge of grief. This man knew the family well. He had maybe been there through weddings, births, Christmases, barbecues. They were dear to him.

"Cheryl?" Blatt said, hands to his face. "Rosie? Dead? No. Joey?"

Dion knew who Cheryl was and could assume who Rosie was, but the third was a mystery. Torr seemed to still be mentally counting off bodies, so he asked, "Who's Joey?"

"Their kid, the boy." Blatt's hands left his face, a face that was visibly paling. Dion watched for more subtle clues, maybe a telltale flash of fear, the sickness of guilt. Back when he'd been a keener, before the crash, he had been the detachment's go-to interrogator. Looking at Blatt now, he knew he was seeing something below the surface, a mystery emotion buried in shock and grief. He tried to put a name to it and couldn't. Just couldn't get a grip on the right words.

Blatt was back to answering Torr's questions. The sense of a clue almost within reach was gone, and Dion found himself looking at the parrot — if that's what it was — instead of the suspect. He noticed the white bird with its punk hairdo was bobbing its head to the conversation, trying to get a word in. A bit of a power struggle was being waged now between Torr and Blatt, with Torr fielding questions instead of asking his own. Dion lost the thread of their dialogue, and without the thread there was no fabric.

He focussed on Blatt again when Blatt swore on his grandmother's grave that he didn't know where Lance was. "All right, sir," Torr said, and finally Blatt was free to sink onto his sofa and bury his face in his arms.

Only on the stairs did it come to Dion, the perfect description for Blatt's reaction. Misplaced confusion.

He stopped to capture the words in his notebook. Torr kept stomping down, griping as he went. The stairwell was a vertical tower of concrete and iron, and every sound within it rang bell-like. Even Torr's griping had a musical resonance as it floated back. Dion stood with notebook open, startled off task by déjà vu. A different stairwell, but the same effect. Voices and boot thuds echoing up and down. The boom of Looch's laughter.

Out of sight now, Torr bellowed up, "Hey, what's up?"

It was a good question, and it brought Dion back to where he was, on somebody's stairwell, notebook open in his hands. He looked at what he'd scribbled there — *confusion* — and couldn't for the life of him think why.

Five

THE CRUMBLING SHORES

OVER THE LAST SEVERAL hours Leith had crossed the road from detachment to hospital more than once, anxious not to miss the cabinet kid's first words. The cabinet kid's name, he'd discovered through the team's research, was Joseph Liu. Joseph had suffered a panic attack in the examination room and had been given a mild sedative. Now he was asleep. Leith had posted JD Temple at the boy's bedside to be there when he woke.

But not knowing JD well enough to know how far he could trust her vigilance, he continued to check in from time to time. It irked her, he could tell. "What, you think I'll forget?" she said, looking up from some kind of pencil puzzle.

She was in an armchair, backlit by fuzzy spring sunlight. She wasn't only as snarky as a man, but dressed like one, too, in easy-fit canvas trousers and a fleece vest over a grey hoodie.

"You're looking at your magazine there," Leith pointed out. "Not Joseph here."

"I'm looking at both," she said. "People don't just pop awake and start chatting. I'll notice that he's stirring when he's stirring, if that's okay with you."

Leith felt like he'd just been peppered with rubber bullets. "Anyway, I was just passing by," he lied. He stood by the bed, looking down at his greatest hope right now, the living witness. Joseph seemed unharmed. His clothes had been bagged as evidence. Maybe he wasn't just asleep, but had sunken into a deep freeze to escape the horrors of what he'd seen and heard. Maybe the deep freeze would last for years.

The fact that Joseph had been hiding told Leith something. Joseph's mom had probably seen trouble brewing, and she'd pushed him inside the cabinet for safety. This implied that the intruder had burst in rather unexpectedly. Enough time to hide the son, but not enough time to protect the infant, Rosalie — or Rosie, another name he had since added to the file — or herself.

What had Joseph seen, heard? What would he forget and what would he remember for the rest of his life?

"Hey, Joseph," Leith tried.

Nothing.

From her chair, JD said, "Who calls their kid Joseph? He goes by Joey."

"You figure?"

"Sure."

"Hey, Joey," Leith said.

Still nothing.

"Let me try," JD said.

She switched places with him, and her voice softened as she leaned over the bed. "How are you feeling, Joey?"

Leith admired the simple tactic. Joseph was not only human, but Canadian, and as such he would feel obliged to answer if asked a direct question, even if that meant struggling out of a drugged sleep.

Leith was ready to give up and leave when Joseph's foot gave a kick. The boy's eyes flew open, now looking at the ceiling, and now at JD.

There was no fright in those eyes that Leith could see from where he sat. Just bleary astonishment. Leith could see JD's smile reflected in the pale-blue windows that spanned the room, and he marvelled again at her transformation from tomboy to angel.

"Are you hungry?" she was asking.

Joey nodded.

"What would you like?" she asked, and she took the extra step of touching his face, smoothing his hair. "You can have anything you want. You name it."

The boy considered. There would be a battle going on inside his soul, Leith knew. Memories and fear clashing with relief and hunger. Being human, he would suppress the bad and seek out the good. Damn, he'd spend the next however many years suppressing the bad.

"Taco," was the kid's first word, with a bit of a question mark on the end.

"Ooh, sounds lovely," JD said. "I'll get my assistant here to order some up, okay?"

She glanced around at Leith, and she wasn't quite smirking, but there was a mean glint in her eye. Leith was already making the call. One taco for Joey, one for

JD as a reward for good work. And two for himself, because he was suddenly ravenously hungry.

* * *

In the end, though, there were no breakthroughs. Joey — the name he responded to best — could tell them little they didn't already know. Except that, no, mom hadn't pushed him in the cabinet. He'd been playing hide-and-seek with her. Leith doubted mom and child had been playing hide-and-seek, at least not in the playful sense. Cheryl had probably only said so to make Joey hide. And fast.

And then — only a teaser — Joey said he had seen the man.

He couldn't say whether this man knocked or rang the bell first. He couldn't say where he had come from, either, the front door or back. Or whether he was admitted or barged in without invitation. He couldn't say how long the man was in the house before the violence began. He didn't know if his mom knew this man, or what they had said to one another, except the man was shouting at his mom. If she had addressed the man by name, he couldn't say. Joey had never seen him before, he didn't think. He couldn't describe him, except he was big. Between every answer, he had a question, piercing and plaintive: *Where's my mom?* Sometimes it switched to *Where's my dad?*

How do you tell a four-year-old that all he considers safe and forever is gone? JD explained that something had happened to his mom, and she couldn't be here with him, but she loved him very much. They would find his dad soon, she promised. She also reassured him — this time it wasn't a big white lie — that his grandmother Zan was on her way to see him. This news seemed to ease his heart a bit. Just a bit, though his chin wobbled and his eyes filled with tears.

When JD asked what colour the man's hair was, he couldn't say. If he had a beard or not, couldn't say. Joey didn't see anybody else except the big man shouting at his mom. Rosie was crying. He heard his mom screaming. Joey demonstrated how he had covered his ears so as not to hear.

JD asked Joey if he'd been hiding before the man came, or after. Again, he couldn't say. He was beginning to withdraw again, softly sobbing, and Leith decided it was enough for now.

He returned to the house on Mahon with JD, and they looked at the cabinet where the boy had hidden. JD squatted down and looked inside. "This is the kind of useless space where things get lost, so people end up installing those spinny rack things."

Leith knew what she referred to, a circular wire shelf unit that rotates, just like he had in his own home back in Rupert. He shivered to think what would have happened if the Mahon homeowners had stuck one of those contraptions in here. There would have been no room for a four-year-old to hide, in that case. And then maybe there'd be a third victim in this attack. With gloved hands he tried the door, opening and closing it. The door was split down the middle, hinged for its corner configuration. It had been shut tight when Ident discovered the little boy five hours ago.

He said, "Get in there and see if you can shut it from inside."

JD said, "You're joking."

He was, and like all his attempts at humour, it fell flat. He said, "Wouldn't be easy, though, would it?"

JD agreed, it would be a hell of a job, shutting that door from inside. Especially if you were four, squished into the lower shelf, and scared out of your wits. "Someone shut it," she suggested. "Mom, I guess."

Except Joey said he had seen the man. Leith and JD looked from the cabinet door to the living room, visible from here but some distance away. Leith didn't think Cheryl had been close enough to shut the cabinet door. She was over there, dealing with her assailant. An assailant who had wrestled her child from her arms. Rosalie had fallen or been thrown, banged her head on the coffee table. Blood had seeped through her brain, eventually killing her.

Leith said, "Or how about it was the killer himself? How about it was the dad? Loved his son too much to harm him. Shut him in here so he wouldn't witness what he was about to do to Mom?"

JD didn't answer right away, but studied him so pointedly he thought he had the remains of a taco on his chin. He swiped at it with his palm. She said, "If it was his dad, he would say it was his dad. The kid's shocked, but he's grounded. I think he saw a stranger in his house. Not his dad, and not somebody he knows. If it was someone he knew, he'd say so. Lance Liu didn't do this."

So who shut the cabinet door, and where was Lance Liu? Leith wondered. He checked his watch and realized it was getting close to quitting time. His phone rang as he and JD left the murder house — Doug Paley calling him back for the debrief.

* * *

The late afternoon debriefing had gone well, and Dion was pleased with himself. He drove away from the office in his new used Honda Civic, replaying it in his mind. He had dazzled everyone with his performance. He'd dazzled himself! Nervous, but hadn't shown it. He had stood and delivered a strong, stammer-free report on Sigmund Blatt, reciting Blatt's criminal record: some assault, some drugs, some theft, but all fairly minor and dated, going back to his younger years. He had finished with his opinion that Blatt needed further observation. And Sergeant Bosko had been there to see this great performance, which meant an "A" for his comeback report card.

Public speaking had never been a problem for Dion, before the crash. He had enjoyed having the floor, sometimes to the point of having things thrown at him, pens and balled-up sandwich wrappers. After the crash, talking one-on-one was a challenge. The words didn't flow. Talking to a group never happened, because he avoided groups altogether.

But today he had no choice, and he had tackled it head-on, and he had succeeded. Now his shirt was soaked like he'd been dunked in a tub, but he was okay.

The success thrilled him. Proof that he worked well under pressure, and since this job was all about pressure, he would do well at the job.

After a long walk and a meal downtown, he returned to the Royal Arms. The hotel stood like a cinderblock battalion on Lynn Valley Road, with its three storeys of rooms to let, its pub off the lobby to one side, restaurant on the other. He looked at the face of the building as he pocketed his keys. Something niggled at him, a task forgotten or a call he had failed to make. Whatever it was, he hadn't written it down, and that was a mistake.

He entered the lobby, still frowning at whatever it was he had forgotten. He nodded hello to the desk clerk and climbed the stairs. In his room on the second floor he hung up his car coat and sat on the bed to remove his shoes. The curtains of the one large window were open, and city lights glared in.

The room wasn't great. Painted in murky tans and browns, with accents of olive green, the colouring alone could make a man reach for the bottle. But right now, as he sat on the bed with his brand-new personal iPhone in hand, he didn't care. He had a mission, and he needed to do it now, as he sailed the updraft of success.

Kate's contact info wasn't programmed into the phone, but it was imprinted in his memory, right down to the postal code. He entered her phone number, touched the connect icon. Four rings, each one jangling his nerves like a taser zap, before her voice came on the line. "Hello?"

He gasped. She sounded sexier and huskier than he remembered. "Kate," he said. "It's me, Cal. I'm back in North Van. Can we meet?"

Abrupt, but positively spoken, with a gloss of an- ticipation. He almost believed, even after burning his bridges with her, that there was a chance they would pick up where they had left off.

"Cal," she said. The sexiness was gone. Still husky, but it was more the gritty rasp of someone just woken. "I was wondering if you'd call. How are you?"

Her matter-of-factness disturbed him. He was ready for anger, had his answers lined up, apologies and promises and declarations. He said, "You knew I was back?"

"Of course. Doug told me. And I'm really glad you called. I really am, Cal. Just the timing isn't great."

Kate Ballantyne was an artist and instructor. She worked at Emily Carr over on Granville Island, and lived in her own artist-instructor world, so different from his own. It had never occurred to him that she would stay in touch with the crew once he was gone, talking about him behind his back, exchanging news. "So where and when would you like to meet?" she said. "Tomorrow night? Eight o'clock, at the Quay?"

Already, his courage was banking. "I thought now, actually. I really need to see you. I could drive by. You're still at the same place in Kitsilano? Because I could totally —"

"I am, yeah, but you can't. Not tonight. For one thing, it's really late."

"Sure, but —"

"For another, my boyfriend will be home soon, so it's probably not the best time to come rushing over. A little awkward."

His thumb hit the disconnect button. He stared at the phone for a moment and then stood and threw it at the nearest wall. The phone dinged the drywall and thumped to the carpet. The TV mumbling in the next room went quiet.

Shame kicked in fast. Taking his disappointment out on the phone was childish. It was what hotheads did in the movies when their lives unravelled. He inspected the damage to the wall. Maybe the hotel would charge him for it, but probably not, because this was the Royal Arms, one of the last affordable inns in North Vancouver. Doomed, in fact. The waitress downstairs had told him demolition was set for next year. To make way for another five-star franchise hotel, she said. Because that's what the world needs, another Hilton.

He leaned his forehead against the ding. Kate had a new boyfriend. Why was he surprised? She was a gorgeous, sociable woman, and he had stonewalled her. He felt dinner curdling in his gut. He felt socked by a terrible loneliness, and he understood what the feeling was. Homesickness.

Which made no sense. He *was* home.

No, he *wasn't*. Home was that way. North. He had been in denial, believing he wanted to come back here. He didn't really want to be back, wasn't ready, and never would be. He hated it here.

He had hated it up north, but he had adjusted. Trouble was, he hadn't realized he had adjusted until it was too late, and he had transported himself back to a city where he no longer clicked.

Now he understood. The north was different from anything he had known before. The northern people had let him in, and the northern air worked through his blood, and the northern trees could speak. He had been almost there when he left. Almost ready to learn the language of the northern trees.

Six

A MOODY BREEZE

THERE IS NOTHING LIKE the fresh chill of a spring morning to set a man up with new hope. Leith stepped into the big, busy restaurant he had discovered on 2nd Avenue just off Lonsdale that provided a hearty breakfast for a decent price and catered to a mixed crowd of bums and businessmen. He felt oddly happy, but maybe it was just the prospect of sizzling, buttery bacon and eggs.

It was a split-level restaurant, and he favoured the upper section, featuring several back-to-back booths. He stepped up and walked toward an available seat, but froze as he heard a familiar voice, low and leisurely, saying, "But I happen to like Cal, and that's a problem. It's too bad. You might say a lose-lose proposition. Anyway, hold fire, till I let you know. For now, just …"

The words cut off cold. From where Leith stood, he could not see the speaker, but he could see the listener, a white male in his forties, slim and slight and neatly dressed, with such close-cropped hair he might have been bald, a goatee, and cold, wide-open eyes. The stranger had possibly noted Leith's piqued interest and lifted a discreet finger, which was maybe why the voice — it was definitely Bosko's — had stopped in its tracks. The stranger said something, and Bosko looked around the edge of the booth and saw Leith. Leith grinned. Bosko seemed pleased to see him and said, "Hey, Dave. You've found my favourite breakfast joint."

"I thought I heard your voice," Leith said. "Sorry. Didn't mean to interrupt."

"No, come and join me," Bosko said, beaming. "Parker is actually just leaving."

"Morning," Leith said, as the man called Parker shifted over and stood.

"Morning," Parker said. He nodded at Bosko, saying, "Give you a call next week." Then he nodded at Leith and walked out.

Leith sat in Parker's vacated spot, wishing to hell he had stopped at McDonald's for a McMuffin, his original plan. Instead he had unwittingly intercepted a secretive conversation about somebody named Cal, and he knew of only one Cal in the neighbourhood. Worse, the conversation had aborted midsentence, and a wary-eyed stranger named Parker had all but flown off in cloak-and-dagger haste. All of which added up to a big question mark in Leith's mind. Enough that he said, "Thought I overheard you talking about Dion here. What's up?"

Before Bosko could answer, the waitress came by. Bosko asked for a refill, and Leith ordered breakfast. The waitress filled their cups and left.

Bosko's phone was buzzing, but he ignored it. He seemed to be considering Leith, not like someone caught in the act, but in a calm, good-natured way. He wore the usual white shirt, dark suit, and broad, dented-looking tie, solid colour, no pattern. Today the tie was mauve. He said, "Parker's an old friend of mine. We're both psychology nuts. We were talking about head injury, case studies, the DSM, all that. I was telling him about Dion's remarkable recovery."

"Uh," Leith said, meaning to say *ah*.

Bosko's low voice, which usually carried undertones of inexplicable delight, had come across as oddly flat. Also, Bosko liked to tarry over subjects that interested him, sometimes in a maddening way, but now he hustled the talk away from Parker and the DSM to the lesser topics of weather, traffic, and family.

Which wasn't too bright, for a cop.

Leith's breakfast arrived, and Bosko looked as though he would head out. But not quite. He watched Leith trying to knock ketchup from the bottle and said, "I hope things are going well for you, Dave. I'm still congratulating myself for having snagged you away from Prince Rupert. I knew I liked you the day we shook hands. It was just one of those trust-at-first-sight things, you could say. That's in large part why I got you down here and onto my team. You've got solid values."

"Well, thank you," Leith said, expecting all this flattery was a lead-in to bad news, compensation in advance.

But it wasn't. Bosko stood to pull on his coat. He smiled once more, then walked between tables, an oversized figure, out into the little foyer. On his way he checked his cell for all the messages he'd missed, pulled change from a trouser pocket to pay the woman at the till, had a word with her that made her laugh. Then he was out the door, phone to his ear.

Bosko would be checking messages and returning calls as he lay on his deathbed, Leith reflected. A multitasker to the last breath. But what had this all been about?

Alone, he worked on finishing his breakfast. Afterward, his gut ached as if he'd eaten too fast, which he probably had. He had a funny feeling that he had known all along, back in February, those strange days in the Hazeltons. He had seen the nonrelationship between Bosko and Dion progress from very little to nothing at all. As far as Leith could see, the two men had barely looked at or spoken to one another during those two weeks. To the point that it became just a bit weird.

Now he was sure. It wasn't all in his head. Something was amiss. Dion was in trouble, in a big way, and Bosko was onto it.

His own phone buzzed now, the RCMP-issued BlackBerry. The dispatcher wanted him on the scene of an MVA, which meant either she'd got the wrong Leith or he'd been demoted. He told her he was with GIS, not traffic control. She told him the vehicle was registered to Lance Liu, and there was a fatality involved. It was all she knew. She gave him the coordinates and left him to figure the rest out for himself.

* * *

At 6:45, Dion left the hotel to head in to work. The skies were rosy and clear, and already the temperature was rising toward T-shirt weather. He was not in a T-shirt, but a suit and tie. He worried that the beery stench of the Royal Arms would stick to his clothes. He lifted forearm to nose and sniffed. He could smell nothing nasty in the fabric, but maybe that was because he was immersed in it.

Arriving at work, he learned that Lance Liu's truck had been found nose-down on the road up to Cypress Bowl. A man matching the description of Liu himself was pinned under the wheels of the truck. Deceased. Doug Paley was on location, and he wanted Dion out there right away.

* * *

Leith's GPS had got him stuck in traffic, and he didn't arrive at the scene until sometime past eight. Already the spot on the forested road that climbed up to Cypress Bowl was clogged with emergency vehicles, and officers were directing tourists to slow down but keep moving. Leith drove through the bottleneck, adding his car to the traffic jam.

He found the designated footpath and made his way down a fairly steep slope. It levelled out into a milder incline of long grasses and bushes, ending at a stand of trees — a mix of conifers and deciduous — and the truck in question, a dark-blue Silverado lodged nose-first against a tree. Forensics members searched the grasses in a wide perimeter, or took photographs, or stood in consultation. The truck was barricaded off by tape, and standing somewhat by its rear were Doug Paley and Cal Dion. Leith had a feeling as he approached that much had happened in his absence, that the party was winding down, that he was a fifth wheel rolling up a tad too late to matter.

Paley confirmed it with a twitch of his moustache. "You with Cold Cases now, Dave? Ha. What happened? Get lost?"

"There was an accident on the Upper Levels just inches before the ramp," Leith said. It was a wild exaggeration, and only half the answer, but he wasn't about to admit the worst of it — the fifteen minutes of going the wrong way on the wrong ramp, and the fifteen minutes to correct the mistake.

"Could have taken Chippendale," Dion said. "A few twists and turns, but you cut some clicks."

"Never go that route," Paley countered. "Probably get stuck behind some church lady doing ten under the limit."

"So what, just hit the lights and pass," Dion said. "The highway's fine when it goes, deadly when it stops. Chippendale is a good alternate route, is all I'm saying."

Leith was looking at the tilted Silverado, the gathering of forensic people at its front bumper, and what he could see of the victim. With the body's position, the tall weeds, the mass of the truck, and so many professionals in the way, about all he could see down on the ground was an outstretched leg in faded denims. "Lance Liu?" he asked Paley.

"That's what his ID says, and he fits the photo," Dion answered, faster, sharper, and more on-the-ball than anybody on the planet, apparently.

Leith looked at him. "He was run over by his own truck?"

Dion beckoned, then tramped down to the rear of the Silverado. Leith joined him. Dion gestured up the hill, toward the road some distance away. Here and there forensic members bent and crouched like they'd lost something small but vital in the grasses. "Seems he reversed off the road at quite an angle, overcorrected, and ended up there, where the flag is," Dion said. "There's drag marks through the soil like he braked hard and slid, and we think there's footprints around where the cab would have ended up, but it's hard to make out with the weeds. We're thinking he lost control of the vehicle, got out, came down here to the treeline and either sat down or collapsed. There's no blood trail. Key's in the ignition, switched to battery mode, truck's in neutral, brakes off, so it could actually have rolled down and pinned him. He's suffered some head trauma that doesn't fit with the vehicle going into the ditch, and like I say, there's no blood trail, but the injury does look recent enough to fit the timeline. The vehicle shows no sign of rollover, no body damage, anything like that, except where the bumper hit the tree, and that's minor. A low-speed impact. If it hadn't hit the tree, it would have likely continued over the body. Far as the injuries, Doug thinks maybe Liu fell, hit his head on a rock, but to me it looks more like a flat kind of impact, like abrasions, like he struck a branch.

I don't see any branches around here low enough that he could have run into them in the dark, so maybe he tripped and slammed into the tree trunk — except he's quite pulped."

He indicated a large area around his own right temple in illustration before carrying on. "I don't think it's even possible to hurt yourself that bad with a trip and fall. I think he was clubbed, left to die, and his attacker put the truck in neutral and let it roll down. Maybe to crush him, but probably not, 'cause what kind of luck would it take for that truck to roll downslope at this angle, nearly sixty-five feet, and land right on the guy where he lay?"

"Or maybe that attacker got in and drove it down," Leith said, thinking this far more likely.

Dion seemed not to hear, and pointed in a travelling line from roadside to truck. "Probably he just wanted the truck to disappear into the forest, which worked out pretty well, right? From the road you can't see it at all down here 'cause of the bushes, and in fact we might not have found him for days, except a guy cycling uphill had to fix his bike when the chain came off, and while he was doing that he looked down. He saw metal, went to investigate, called us."

He seemed to be finished, so Leith thanked him. He went around the truck to look at the body from the far side. Coroner Jack Dadd had done his inspection and was clearing up his gear. Paley joined Leith and they both crouched by the crime-scene tape for a better squint. Paley said, "Well, this is weird. Dadd got in close and says the truck didn't kill him. See that tire that's pressed up against his chest? Barely a touch, Dadd says.

Not enough pressure to break ribs. Not even to bend 'em. Wouldn't have prevented him from breathing."

So what had killed Lance Liu? The wounds to the right side of his head were a literal bloody mess, but Paley told him the injuries weren't as bad as they looked. Actually fairly superficial, according to Dadd. Not a killing blow, anyway. As hard as Leith peered to gather detail, he couldn't hazard a guess as to whether a rock or a branch or whatever else on earth had done the damage.

Dion joined them. Leith stood and looked around. A playful breeze buffeted the hillside. Some small dark birds, starlings maybe, dashed about the skies. The three men watched the RCMP-contracted tow truck arrive and begin its careful descent to hook up the Silverado. The tow truck idled, and Dion went to talk to the driver. The conversation was out of earshot but seemed to be earnest and energetic.

Leith was again sizing up the distance between road and body, puzzling over the logistics. Paley was still looking at the tow truck. He said, "Fucking dick."

"Who, what?" Leith said, looking up.

"Ever seen *Invasion of the Body Snatchers*? If you ask me, my friend Cal has definitely been snatched. I'm kidding. I love the guy. He's only been back a day, so he's trying too hard. And so what that we asked him out for beer last night post-briefing, and he said yes most definitely, and then didn't show up? So what if we reserved an extra-big table, and ended up having to drink our Fireball shooters without him? We soldiered on. It'll take him a while to get back up to speed, that's all."

Leith looked at Paley, then at Dion in the distance, arguing with the tow truck driver, and then Paley again, hurt. "How come I didn't hear about this extra-big table and Fireball shooters?"

"Oh, hey. Sorry about that, Dave."

Paley didn't look sorry. He gave his hands a back-to-work clap. "Liu's phone's still missing. We couldn't get a ping yesterday, but maybe whoever's got it had it turned off, and maybe it's on now, so we'll keep trying. And you're going to talk to the kid again — Joey, right? The grand-mom's still with him?"

Leith nodded, thinking of the terrible task ahead of him: breaking the news to Zan Liu.

Paley's moustache contracted, maybe in sympa-thy. "The body will be there for ID in an hour. I'll be talking to the Chens myself again, meanwhile. They're Edmonton people."

The Chens were Cheryl Liu's parents, Leith knew. They had flown over last night but were too emotional to interview. Eventually they would have to pull them-selves together enough to talk. He had little faith that they could offer anything meaningful. He left the breezy field with its starlings and its corpse, making a call to JD Temple as he returned to his car, destination Joey.

* * *

He met JD at the hospital. She was seated in the waiting room and talking with Joey Liu's paternal grandmother, Zan Liu. Leith introduced himself and took a chair as well. He could see that Mrs. Liu, a widow who had just lost a daughter-in-law and granddaughter to some face-less bastard, and who didn't know where her son was, was working on keeping the shock and grief bottled. Maybe because she had one precious four-year-old sur-vivor to look after now and couldn't afford to fall apart. Pretty soon she would learn she had lost a son as well.

Leith told her. And maybe she had suspected all along because, although the tears creeked down her face, she didn't break down. Nor did she when he took her to the morgue. She laid a hand gently on Lance Liu's chest, in-spected his face with concern as though maybe banda-ges would solve the problem, and whispered something to him in Chinese.

* * *

Leith asked Zan if she could tell him a bit about Lance and Cheryl, just anything she cared to say. Zan told him how Lance and Cheryl had met, courted, married. Nothing she said seemed to progress the case forward, but he let her talk, as she seemed to wish to do. Food was brought in, which she didn't consume. And Jasmine tea, which she did.

Cheryl was a good girl, she said. A fine wife and moth-er, had no enemies. Lance had been her only serious relationship. They were a happy couple, in love, never separated even for a day. Lance was a really good boy. Hard-working, took care of his family.

"If there was something seriously wrong, do you feel either of them would have talked to you about it?" Leith asked.

"Yes, I am sure Lance would have told me."

Joey slept, on and off. When awake, he snivelled and sucked his thumb. JD asked him more about the closed cabinet door, whether he could recall anything further, but instead of opening up, he seemed to be shutting them out.

Leith nodded at JD; there would be no more questions tonight.

Down on the street a wind was gusting litter about. People walked by at slants and seemed to be battling their own clothes. JD's short hair fluttered, and her squinting eyes had that fierce warrior look Leith had noticed before. She said, "Did you see that?"

"See what?"

"Joey, the way he curled up, squeezed his eyes shut."

"Sure, I could see that. What of it?"

"It comes in waves," she said. "Memories. He wants to think about his mom but doesn't want to think about his mom. But he's working through it. I think he'll have something to tell us about what he saw. Sometime."

"Sometime soon, I hope."

"Sometime," JD repeated. And after a pause, added, "I hate this job. I really do."

Seven

SHELTER

WITHIN THE TEAM AT LARGE was an amorphous clique that Leith was coming to think of as *the crew*, those who hung about post-debrief and went out pubbing, sometimes into the small hours, as if they couldn't let go of the blues. Leith knew the feeling.

Tonight he joined them.

The crew was male-centric, probably because after-hours conferences like this were loaded with bad language and political incorrectness, and women had more sense than to put up with that kind of bullshit. JD Temple was the only female who seemed to tag along regularly. Maybe because she was accepted as just another guy. Maybe because she didn't have any other life to live.

The crew's hangout of choice was Rainey's Bar & Grill down near the Quay, walking distance from the detachment. Rainey's was a dark and classy joint, a good-time pub geared toward aging rockers. Lots of loud music,

CCR and Doors and Rolling Stones, to make guys of Leith's age feel right at home.

"Gimme Shelter." Rape, murder — like they didn't hear enough of it on the job. Leith took off his suit jacket, loosened his tie, and ordered whatever draft was on special. He phoned Alison in Prince Rupert to let her know he had made it through another day. Her voice was far away and not quite real in his ear. He told her it was too noisy here to talk, that he'd call again later.

Membership in the crew was self-regulated, and the rules were loose. Joining in the conversation — not mandatory. To Leith's right sat Doug Paley, letting out a beery belch. To his left was JD, leaning across him to tell Paley what she thought of his manners. On the far side of the table were the big bruiser, Constable Jimmy Torr, and the handsome Viking-type, Sean Urbanski, scruffy because he was pitching to get into Special "E," undercover ops.

There were two others here Leith hadn't met before, general duty members Ricky something and Tara something else.

To everyone's surprise, Dion showed up, too, taking a seat between Urbanski and Tara and joining in the conversation like one of the regulars.

Snacks were ordered and came, crowding the cluttered table with plates of hot, greasy calories. Leith couldn't catch much of anything being said, amidst the noise of "Fortunate Son" and "Pour Some Sugar on Me" and "New Sensation." Mostly he talked with JD. He asked her what "JD" stood for, but she wouldn't say. Paley overheard the question and supplied the answer: *Joan Deirdre*.

Somewhere on Leith's third beer, he was thinking JD would have been pretty if she'd put some effort into it, but she interrupted the dangerous drift of his thoughts by crying out that if they didn't play something from this fucking century, she'd shoot out the speakers.

Paley, Torr, and Dion were debating case notes, the missing bootie, the missing cellphone, and other developments. Ricky and Tara reminisced about today's messy takedown at the Quay. Tara showed everyone the stitches on her elbow.

JD's patience ran out in her usual showy way; she stood and pointed at the speakers, saying, "Fuck this pole-dance shit." The pole-dance shit was a love song by Foreigner that took Leith back to many floorshows he had watched in his younger years. JD said she was going to catch a cab back to her flat to listen to the Hidden Cameras — if Leith heard right. She danced both middle fingers at Torr's nose as she left. Torr made obscene motions at her back with his tongue until Tara lobbed something at him, a deep-fried zucchini stick.

The tossed zucchini stick was funny, apparently. There was a lot of laughter at this table of cops. "She's kind of touchy, isn't she?" Leith asked Doug Paley.

"JD?" Paley snorted. "You should see her on a bad day."

Leith's eardrums were going numb, and he was tiring of the fun. He had finished his third pint and was considering a fourth — because sometimes fun could catch a second wind — when Mike Bosko arrived. He sauntered up with a frothy stein in hand and was greeted warmly by the crew. Warm, Leith thought, but holding back, like they all felt, as he did himself, that this NCO was a little too good to be true, and maybe not *really* on their level.

Bosko took a chair. He nodded hello at Leith, then broadcast, "How's it going?" to anyone who cared to answer.

"Not good," Doug Paley said. "We've just debunked Locard's principle. The killer took a bunch of evidence but left none behind."

"Remind me, what did he take?"

"One of the baby's shoes," Dion said. "And Lance Liu's cellphone."

"Trophies," Jimmy Torr offered, too drunk to hold his tongue in the presence of a superior. "Fucking baby-shoe trophy."

Bosko was interested. "Well, at least they found the possible murder weapon, I hear, in the case of Lance Liu. I hear it's big."

Leith raised his brows, until he got it. The autopsy had shown that Lance Liu had been struck fairly hard by a tree. Or against a tree. Blood, skin, and hair had been found smeared about head-height on the pine that Lance Liu lay below. Leith now knew it wasn't actually a pine, like everybody was calling it. It was a mature Douglas Fir, which was actually a spruce, or *Pseudotsuga menziesii,* none of which mattered. What mattered was the bark was dark and gnarly and held plenty of physical evidence. Ident members had searched for such evidence and found it. They had photographed and taken samples from the area of the tree in question, but hadn't stopped there. A great slab of its trunk had been cut out with a chainsaw to preserve the smear for posterity.

Then there was the truck that had rammed the tree, its chassis covering its owner, its tires just touching Lance Liu's chest. Neither head trauma nor truck had killed him, as Paley went on to inform Bosko. If not for the heart attack, the poor guy would be now sitting with a head swathed in bandages, telling them what the hell had happened out there.

The truck had been searched, of course, thoroughly. Nothing of great interest, except for a couple items in the glove box: a buck knife and a camera. The buck knife tested negative for blood. The camera was a little point-and-shoot Kodak. It looked brand new, and there was nothing on its memory card except three amazingly uninteresting street shots. JD suggested they weren't photos, really; they were experiments, an owner trying out an unfamiliar gadget for the first time.

Leith said yes to that fourth pint as the waitress stopped by. He would worry about the calorie overload tomorrow. Bosko sat back and smiled around the table like these were his children. His eyes passed over Ricky and Tara, Dion with a phone to his ear, Jimmy Torr and Doug Paley in conversation.

But there was nothing abstract about Mike Bosko, Leith believed. He could seem spaced-out at times, and could drone on about matters nobody wanted to hear, and was too free with the smiles and compliments, which sometimes struck Leith as dishonest. But he was sharper than he looked. Like a heron in the reeds, Mike Bosko was patient, somewhat camouflaged, and probably deadly, too, when it came time to strike.

* * *

Dion covered one ear with his palm and listened to Kate with the other. "You disconnected me last night," she said. "In the middle of a conversation. Kind of juvenile, isn't it?"

He was happy that she'd called. It gave him hope, and already he was rewriting her back into his life. The boyfriend was just a stand-in, and she would now drop him. She would understand the crash was just a test, one they would have to work together to pass.

He told her he was sorry — trying for soft but failing in this impossible environment, and had to repeat himself in a near roar: "I'm sorry."

"No, I'm sorry," she said. "I didn't mean to be so ... mean. Where are you? What's the noise? At a club?"

He told her he was at Rainey's and was leaving soon. She asked if he wanted to meet up. She was at the beach, at Cates Park. He listened, and now with a lull in the bar music he heard it, the waves and the ruckus of wind. He said, "What are you doing at Cates this time of night?"

"It's stormy. Nice. Dramatic. I'm getting inspired."

"You'll get yourself murdered, that's what," he told her. He glanced around the table and saw Leith watching him. He stood ungracefully, clambering out of the tight-knit chairs. He walked away from the group, out to the foyer, where heavy doors would block the noise.

"Where's your boyfriend?" he asked her.

"We're not getting together tonight," she said. "That's why I thought you and I could meet."

He checked his face in the glass of the doors. He hadn't drunk much, not even a full pint, but he was tired, and looked it. "Where?"

* * *

She wore a loose black parka, pale jeans, hiking boots. Her long blond hair was loose and windblown. She wasn't air-brushed perfection, as she had become in his mind. She was real, a solid physical form with a smudge of kohl under one eye, and the reality of her left him speechless.

Her arms were open. He hugged her, but briefly. They took a table in the back of the fast-food restaurant and told each other they looked great. She had a paper cup wafting steam. Tea. He went to buy a decaf, and finally they were seated, facing each other.

He said, "I started that off really bad last night. I'm sorry. And I'm sorry for not writing."

"Not writing ever, you mean," she said. "It's okay. You did what you felt you had to do. You were in serious pain. Everything changed. Looch was gone, and I was a reminder of all you'd lost. So you disconnected. I understand why. I was part of the problem. But did it help? Are you back?"

He didn't like the control in her voice or the steadiness of her gaze, and he especially didn't like her sympathy. Already his plan began to fall apart. "I'm not perfect. You know what would make me perfect? If I could fix what I broke, between you and me, and have you back in my life. That's what."

She didn't answer right off. He watched her beautiful, oval face for clues. Other than the smudged eyeliner, she wore no makeup, and her skin wasn't as flawless as he recalled. There was a crinkliness around the eyes and a brown sunspot on her cheek, freckles spattered across her nose. And one eye was slightly narrower than the other, unless it was just a tension squint. She didn't seem tense, but she'd always been better than him at masking the subtler feelings.

She said, "I've got a boyfriend, Cal."

A reflection in the window caught his eye: the best-looking couple on the planet, but their faces were shadowed. He thought of her in bed. With him. He said, "I know. So dump him."

She said, "Tell me about the north."

He stared at her hands, the way they encircled her cup, soaking up its warmth. Those artsy silver rings she wore, fingernails unpainted and not so clean. He tried to recall the pleasant things he should be saying to her now, but all he could think of was that man in her life. He needed details, name, occupation. Description.

"Cal?" Kate said.

He looked at her face and recalled the question. "What d'you mean, tell you about the north? That's like saying tell me about life. It's a big place. Anything specific you want to know?"

She was silent.

He said, "No? Tell me about your boyfriend, then. What's he all about?"

Her answer, when it came after a long pause, was unresponsive. "About me, yes, I'm still at Emily Carr. I'm full time now, in the photography department. I love it. Love my students. Well, most of them. You should see the montage I'm working on, though. It would blow your mind. I'm preparing for a show —"

"I wasn't asking about you," he said.

Another pause, this time with analytical stare attached. "I noticed. So you want to know about Patrick. Why? Are you thinking of hunting him down and beating him up?"

Patrick. He crossed his arms. Already the beautiful couple in the reflection were backing into their corners. The light in here was bleak. He could see tonight ending in the coldest way. "What? No."

"Like you did to Jake."

Jake was an old incident, long forgotten, at least in his books. Fidelity had never been the strong point of their relationship, and their fights had been epic. "I didn't hunt him down. And I didn't beat him up."

She took a last sip of tea and pushed the cup away. She said, "I'm glad you're doing well, Cal. It was good to see you again. I hope you find your way back."

Dion slapped the tabletop as she started to rise, bringing her back down. "I *never* loved you," he said. Leaning forward, he saw surprise darken her eyes. "I tried. I watched all the movies, practically read the rule books. But it didn't work. But that's just because I wasn't ready. Get this. I'm ready now. I'm really, really ready now, and you just have to tell me when I'm doing things right or when I'm doing things wrong, and I'll listen. I'll figure it out, but I need you with me."

Her face was pinkening. She said, "I'm happy where I am. You're just going to have to learn to be happy where you are. Oh, I almost forgot." She leaned to dig into her backpack, and he realized she was shakier than he thought. She placed an object — black, squarish, and elegant, about an inch thick, tied with a silver ribbon — on the table before him. "It's a present. Maybe you'll hate me for it, but I put it together for you."

He could see without opening it what it was. An album. He untied the ribbon, opened the cover and saw the first photograph, black and white. A group shot, him and Kate, Looch and Brooke, downtown, in front of a Vancouver nightclub, a loose line of friends smiling at the camera. *What a genius fucking gift*, he thought. Great memories. Kate was abandoning him, Looch was dead, and Brooke had never liked him much, frankly. There were more photos within, bulking out the pages. He glanced through a few, then closed the cover and put the book on the seat beside him. "Nice. Thanks."

"You probably know most of those shots. One day you may want them."

He was thinking he wanted to take this elegant black photo album full of moments he could never relive and pitch it at Patrick's face. "I didn't get you anything," he said.

Kate said, "Happiness finds its level, you know. Just give yourself time."

They discarded their cups and walked out into the illuminated plateau where the buses congregated. They parted ways at her parked car on Esplanade with no plans to meet again.

An hour later he was in bed, sleeping meds working through his bloodstream, and he remembered the gift.

He had left it on the seat beside him. Hadn't meant to forget it. She must have picked it up and kept it, instead of forcing it on him. She must have known he couldn't stomach it.

He wished he hadn't done that to her, reject her gift. He rolled over in bed and wrapped his arms around himself. He should have wrapped his arms around her, at McDonald's, when he'd had the chance. Should have asked her all about herself, every last detail, and even blessed her new relationship. Should have sworn he'd never disappoint her again.

That had been the heart of the plan. So where had it gone wrong?

Eight

FROM AFAR

THE FIRST FORTY-EIGHT was long gone. In fact, this was day six, which meant they were halfway through their third forty-eight. Not good. Leith sat with the core team in the smaller case room, gathered about the conference table and working over the game plan. Doug Paley was present, Cal Dion, Jimmy Torr, Sean Urbanski, and JD Temple.

Paley and Torr looked hungover — much like Leith felt — from last night at Rainey's. Only Dion had shown up clean and sharp as a fresh-pressed suit, and brimming with elaborations to his thoughts at last night's debrief. "So going with our theory that there were two people there," he was saying, speaking of the Liu murder scene on Mahon Avenue, the death of Cheryl and Rosalie, "I'm saying the same person who hid Joey in the cabinet took the baby's shoe — for proof if it came to blackmail, or insurance if it came to threats. It's time to get 'em to do another press release, include the missing shoe this time. And post a reward for any information that leads to an arrest. Because that second person is on the edge of her seat, and that might tip her our way. And it should have an immunity package attached, if we want her talking. Maybe she'll stick with her blackmail gamble, but probably not. Probably she'll go for the reward and some guarantee of protection. It's more reliable, and it's got the added bonus for her that the guy will be thrown in jail. Because she's afraid of him, right? Flash that ad and I bet we'll get a call the same day. She'd be putting herself in trouble with him, but it's better than what she's already facing. The money's going to catch her attention, and the immunity will pull her in. Unless, like I say, she was under duress and she only grabbed the evidence as insurance. But the results could be the same, she'll come forward to get herself out of a hole."

A lot of ifs and buts. Leith rested chin on knuckles and tried to look one step ahead of all this instead of two steps behind.

Paley, too, seemed to be lagging, but he wasn't shy about saying so. "So unlike the rest of us, Mighty Mouse, you've got it all worked out."

"Unless it's retribution," Dion said. "In which case it'll be coming our way, anyhow."

Leith didn't understand the last remark at all. He jotted down the word so he could mull it over. *Retribution*. Torr scowled at Dion across the table. "You're still saying 'she' like it's a fact. Who says it's a 'she'?"

"Nine to one she is," Dion told him shortly, not so crisp as Leith first thought. Feverish-looking, like he was fuelled by uppers.

"And I said, says who it's a *she*?" Torr repeated.

But Dion had run out of words and sat staring across at Torr in blank silence.

Leith used the opportunity to air his own objections to posting a press release or Crime Stoppers spot about the missing bootie. "For one thing, it's holdback info. For another, if there was a second person, I doubt he or she would put themselves in peril at any price, and I'm sure as hell not willing to offer immunity up front. Rosalie was still alive when those two — if there were two of them — left the scene. I'm damned if whoever could have saved that child but didn't cuts a deal and walks."

"It's lousy holdback," Dion said. "We've got better. And sure it's iffy, but say it works, it's better than the alternative."

"The alternative is …?" Torr said.

"She keeps quiet and stays with the killer, and he gets her next."

Earlier this morning, Bosko had pulled Leith aside for a mysterious chat. "I'm sure you get the drift that I've got a bit of an informal investigation underway," Bosko had said. He spoke with more gravity than Leith was accustomed to, which made him sit up and listen. "But it's purely at this level right now." Bosko pointed at his own temple as he said it, making clear the level he meant. "So not a concern for you right now. A'right?"

"Sure," Leith said, though he wasn't sure at all. "Yes, sir."

But Bosko wasn't done. "I'm actually glad we're talking about this. Because everything aside, you know, I'm worried about his welfare, and he doesn't seem to have much of a support system. In the most general sense, I'd like you to keep an eye on him for me, would you?"

Leith had walked away from the meeting with one eye shut. He was being locked out, and then invited in, no names named. Odd.

"Right?" Dion was saying to Paley, still on the track Leith had somewhat lost. "A lot better than she puts her life on the line in a blackmail plot that's going to end up getting her killed."

Torr said something about men with crystal balls. Paley said, "I'll put it to Bosko, see what he thinks."

He did, and later that morning Leith learned that Bosko, in consultation with other arms of the law, thought the offer of immunity wasn't a great plan, but true, time was of the essence, and right now dangling carrots was their best bet at catching the man behind the horrific killings. Go for it.

* * *

Dion made lists till his head ached. So far no evidence collected from the Liu home or Lance Liu's truck had jumped out as being useful. Sigmund Blatt had been researched hard, interviewed again, and all but disqualified as a person of interest. Blatt had nothing to gain from the deaths. He had no apparent grievance with his partner. They were good friends, in fact. Had met at work in Alberta as novices and remained pals ever since. Blatt had a minor criminal record, but stupidity-related, nothing violent, and nothing to do with Liu or the partnership.

During the investigation, Blatt left the province. Following his second interview he had called in and talked to Torr, letting him know he was shutting down the L&S business, now that the L was gone, and moving back to Alberta. Torr had asked him why. Blatt admitted that he was spooked. Maybe whoever had killed Lance would be after him, too. Torr asked him how he figured that might happen. Blatt said he didn't know and didn't want to stick around to find out. So he went, with strict orders to remain reachable.

Dion was paired up with Jimmy Torr on this case, and it was hardly the ideal working relationship, but together they chipped away at the personal lives of Lance and Cheryl. They talked at some length to Lance's extended family members, often by teleconference with the States. They contacted the couple's friends and relations in B.C. and Alberta, and previous employers, and even talked to Joey's preschool teachers, in case there was some bizarre connection with the surviving child. No connection was made. They went through computers, bank records, phone data. They used documents found in the truck to backtrack through Lance Liu's last living day, from invoices written to receipts for a Tim Hortons lunch, speaking to the two clients he'd dealt with, and looking at video footage from the gas station where he'd filled up for the last time in his life. By the end they had a patchy timeline and a better sense of who he was, but not much else.

They dug deep into the business itself, L&S Electric. Traced it back to its inception, checking for conflict along the way: displaced competitors, disgruntled clients. Finally they googled any keywords they could think of, hoping it would spit out some snippet of news or a blog bit or whatever else might be floating out there that might give some insight into what had happened.

Nothing emerged. The Liu marriage seemed solid enough, with no jealous lovers in the wings. L&S seemed ethically run. Both electricians, Lance and Sig, had their tickets, and had sunk their savings into the enterprise, coming at it debt-free. Cheryl Liu did the books, and if Lance was busy, she answered the phone for the company. She booked appointments and even offered advice to callers. The electricians hadn't been making money hand over fist, but they had just gotten started and seemed like sensible, ordinary men running a sensible, ordinary business.

Altogether it felt like three wasted days. Dion was about to start wasting Day Four on this line of inquiry, which was the seventh day following the murders, when he heard the breaking news: they had a suspect, and it had nothing to do with his hard work. It was a hot tip fresh in from Calgary. He dropped what he was doing and followed Torr down the hall to where the case room was set up like a shrine to the murdered Liu family.

Paley was at the computer, setting it up for his presentation. The news was big enough that Mike Bosko had come to listen in, standing next to Leith. Dion and others gathered around.

"It came in at just before five this morning," Paley said. "Which is just before six Mountain Time. A CPS officer named Brinkley got a recorded message on his work cell number. He passed the message to Calgary Serious Crimes, who forwarded it on to us. Dave and

I just spent the last half hour listening to the call. It's a blocked number, but Calgary sourced it by the background PA noises to Rockyview General. Oh, and it's *anonymous*," he said, putting air quotes around the word. "But, hey, let's not spoil it for you. Have a listen. Enjoy."

He dragged the mouse to start an audio file. There was a sound shift as the recording service kicked in, then a breathy huffing sound. Finally a hoarse female voice said, "Hiya. I'm calling about that murder of, uh, Lance Loo and his wifey and kid over in B.C. there."

The speaker paused, maybe to puff on a cigarette, then spent a while coughing. She sounded to Dion like a skinny woman in her thirties, if anything could be drawn from a voice twice removed. She said, "I'm calling from a blocked phone so you can't track me, 'cause I don't want to get in no trouble. I got two kids to look after, eh? So yeah, I know who did it, and his name's Philly Prince, and he lives at the brown duplex on 11th Ave. He took off on his hog two days before the murders happened, which I saw in the news, and I ain't seen 'im since, though I hear he's around. And he has a thing against that guy, and always said he was going to kill 'im. And Philly doesn't kid around, I should know 'cause I was married to the creep for one too many — aw *shhhhit*."

More noisy breathing as the caller considered what to do now that she'd blown her cover. Without another word, she disconnected. Some of the team laughed. Doug Paley twirled his hands like an MC following a great act. Dion jotted the information into his notebook, the name Philly Prince, and address. None of it rang any bells from his three days of talking to Liu contacts.

JD said, "Why'd she call this CPS Brinkley personally?"

Paley shrugged. "He does community patrols. Maybe she had some contact with him in the past, had his card for whatever reason. But we'll know soon enough. They're pulling her in as we speak."

The caller was a Maggie Boland, no doubt about it, known to the CPS (Calgary Police Service), ex-wife of Phillip Prince. The fact that Ms. Boland had two kids and worked in housekeeping at Rockyview Hospital, with a shift starting at 6:00 a.m. Mountain Time, fairly clinched it. Philly was Phillip H. Prince, member of the Calgarian chapter of the Outlaws, a biker gang based out of Edmonton. He had served time for assaults, and been charged with murder a few years back, along with a bunch of confederates, but was acquitted when the Crown's star witness turned. Calgary police were working along with the "K" division RCMP to track Prince down, but wouldn't collar him till they got instructions from the coast.

Paley said, "Which is what we have to decide right now. Pretty simple, right? We'll get him pulled in, and somebody here's got to fly out and talk to the little shit. And I've got the unlucky candidate already picked out. Right, Dave?"

Leith seemed to have been forewarned, Dion noticed. Glum, but not surprised. "I'd love to go to Calgary and tell a biker I think he killed someone, sure," Leith said, arms crossed.

"Let's have a big hand for Dave," Paley said, still the MC, and clapped. Others clapped, too. Dion clapped, though he was halfway out the door. Curiosity about the Philly Prince angle might have kept him on board a while longer, but he already had it figured Prince wasn't the killer they wanted. And for good reason. He saw Bosko slipping out. He followed, stopped him in the corridor, asked if they could have a word.

In Bosko's office he took the visitor's chair, just like a week earlier, but today it was with a twist. The last time he sat here he had been convinced he could get back to where he'd left off. He was fast discovering it wasn't working out. Losing Kate was not the worst of it; he could accept the downgrade. What he couldn't take was the feeling of being a bad fit. He could chime in and smile and join the gang at Rainey's, but he knew they saw through him. He was odd, and they knew it.

He had also killed a man. Criminally. Any moment now, somebody would find out. He didn't want to be around when it happened.

Putting physical distance between himself and the crime wasn't the only option open to him, and last night he had contemplated a more radical resolution: he could get it over with and confess. But that took nerve he didn't have. This morning he had made up his mind to go with Plan A. "I'm leaving the area. I know you need people up north, and I'd be happy to take any posting in the region. I'd waive the financial assistance, if that's any help. Barring that, I'll have to resign."

Bosko's brows were up. Then they screwed into a wince. He leaned forward, resting on his forearms, and spoke calmly. "I'm shocked. The last time we talked you seemed happy to be back. And confident. What's changed? Something I can help you through?"

"No, sir. I'm just not ready for the city. Prefer an outpost. That's all."

Dion looked at a wall of filing cabinets, more or less northward, and could almost feel it, cold wind raking his face, ruffling his hair. Canyons and rivers and rubbly roads jetting off into the wilds.

"It's barely been a week," Bosko pointed out.

Dion nodded. "A week is enough. I'm done. One way or another, I have to leave."

"Sure," Bosko said, after a moment's thought. "Okay." He clasped his hands on the desktop and twiddled his thumbs. "But let's think about this. Could it be you're being too self-critical? In my experience ..."

He went on, rolling out his advice. He told a story of his own inner conflicts. Then spoke about the inherent pressures of the job, and Dion's excellent service record, the tests he had passed, the need to give himself some slack. Dion didn't listen much until Bosko seemed to be wrapping up. "... and I'd very much like to keep you on. Of course there are things we need to work out —"

"There are also things that I *can't* work out, and that's the problem."

"But minor things." Bosko ploughed on. "Your last report on Liu, for instance. You've got good thoughts, Cal, but you do need to lay them out on paper better, so the reader knows what you're driving at. Obscure reports aren't fatal, but they don't help you, either. So let's deal with it. Let's coordinate with SRR and think about getting you some help. With writing and composition, for instance. In fact, what I'd suggest ..."

Dion sat straighter. He had thought that his writing and composition were excellent. *Obscure*?

"… in the end if you're still unsure, I can see what we can do about relocation or reassignment. But I whole-heartedly encourage you to give it some time." Bosko patted the air as though soothing a dog. "So lower your expectations a notch, give it a month, then we'll talk again. A'right?"

Dion felt more committed than ever to departure and shook his head. "Even if you look into transferring me, it'll take too long to happen. I'm going to have to quit."

Bosko sat back in his chair and gently swivelled. Finally he sat forward again with a new idea. "Dave's heading over to Calgary tomorrow morning, and he could probably use some company. How about you go with him? Use the time away to think it through. And talk to him. He's got a good ear and a good heart. I'm saying think twice, Cal. I'd really hate to lose you. Is that a deal?"

It wasn't a deal, but it wasn't a choice, either. Dion could refuse to go, but that would be cowardly. He could quit on the spot, but he wasn't ready for such a precipitous drop. Or he could get on the plane and delay ripping his heart out, at least for a day or two. He chose the plane.

Nine

AWEIGH

FIRST THING IN THE MORNING Dion climbed on the midsized jet to Calgary. He sat next to his travel companion. Leith had the window seat and didn't seem to want to chat, from the way he exchanged a few lines about the weather, then opened his *Maclean's* magazine and stuck his nose in it.

Dion reclined the aisle seat and closed his eyes. Sitting next to David Leith forced him to think about David Leith. They had known each other only months, not the years it felt like. February, in New Hazelton. The Catalina Café was their first introduction, getting briefed on a missing woman as the world outside was muffled in snow. Dion had been posted in Smithers, was new to the north, a stranger in the Hazeltons sent to help in the search. He was in bad shape then, worse than now, and his first interactions with Leith had not gone off well.

He didn't blame Leith for disliking him. If anything, it was a break. Like Torr's attitude, it spared them both from having to expend energy on being chummy. But unlike Torr, there were gears turning in Leith's mind. And he was perceptive. Dion could tell by Leith's occasional moody and penetrating stares, shot at him like lasers, that he could see through disguises. Which was unsettling.

"Afraid of flying?" Leith asked, still reading.

"No. Are you?"

"No."

An hour later, as they soared toward the jagged rip line of the Rockies, Leith shut the magazine. He said, "I've never lived in biker territory. Started out in Slave Lake, did time in Fort St. John. Didn't face much big-time gang action. Maybe these days Hells Angels are trying to set up shop there, but not so much back then. Spent the last seven years in Prince Rupert, where we had some HA port crimes, but it wasn't my department. And that's it. So not much experience with the two-wheeled species. What about you?"

"I've dealt with a few bike gangs. Never head-on. They're more a Surrey problem, Abbotsford. They seem to like wide open spaces."

"Huh," Leith said, after a moment's thought. Then, "I'm thinking I'll go at this one straight up, what d'you say? Hell with the friendly approach."

"Sure," Dion said. "What did you do before you became a cop?"

Leith looked at him with some mistrust. "Who says I did anything? Maybe I joined the force straight out of school."

"Maybe you did. But I doubt it."

"Okay, sure. I worked a few years first."

"In construction," Dion said.

Leith lowered a brow. "That's pretty much it."

"Till you were thirty, then joined up."

"Twenty-eight. Also pretty close. How d'you figure?"

"It's easy. I did the math. Two postings, averaging four years each, then seven in Prince Rupert, that's fifteen years. And you're about forty-five, so you joined up around thirty. Which is kind of late."

"I'm forty-four. But how do you figure construction? For all you know I was an accountant."

Dion laughed. "No way you were an accountant. You're like me, not the academic type. But you're hard working, so you probably got a job straight out of school. Best job guys can get straight out of school is in the construction industry. But you felt there was more to life than bending nails. You wanted to make the world a better place. So you joined up."

Leith gave him a smile, then looked out the window and downward. "Look at all that range," he said, but more to himself. Then he went back to his magazine.

* * *

They had lunch with some Calgarian police officers, more social than business. Dion enjoyed the neutrality of it, and wondered if he should try for a transfer eastward instead of north. He and Leith then spent the afternoon in an interview room talking to Phillip Prince. Physically, Prince wasn't overwhelming, but he was a bully, complete with bully tattoos, bully facial hair, and bully attitude. Leith started out by asking him what he had against Lance Liu.

"What d'you mean?" Prince said.

"People have been telling me you wanted to kill the guy. What was the gripe? How'd he step on your toes?"

Prince's face knotted defensively. "The fuck you talking about?"

Dion saw it coming, the usual let's-get-acquainted song and dance, and zoned out. It went on for about an hour, as he noted on his watch, before the talk became substantive, and in bits and pieces dense with obscenities, Prince told the story.

It turned out that in Prince's mind, Lance Liu was a clumsy motherfucking spark plug whose truck, while backing out of the driveway, had knocked over Prince's custom Harley Wide Glide. Liu and Prince weren't friends or associates, had never met before that day, were just thrown together by that one twist of bad fucking luck. Liu had been hired for an electric panel upgrade at the Prince home, that's all. He'd put in his hours and was done for the day, and departed. Prince was popping a Budweiser, heard a crash, ran outside, and after a bit of a fistfight, the two men had settled, off the books. Liu went away with a bunch of death threats thrown at his back, but he got off lucky. Prince used the settlement to repair his bike, but he was never happy with the machine after that. "It's just not fuckin' the same," he said. "When you fuckin' go over one fuckin' ten, something fuckin' rattles."

"So stay under one ten," Leith said. "Anything over, you're breaking the fuckin' limit."

"You're a fuckin' cunt," Prince said.

Next Leith put to Prince that Prince had hopped on his bike last week, driven to B.C., and wiped out the whole Liu family, all over one damned rattle. The accusation nearly popped a vein in Prince's temple, and on that note the interview ended.

* * *

They were put up in two rooms on the fourth floor of the Holiday Inn. Dion unloaded his travel bag. He had a shower, then took time by the big window to admire the view. He saw a flattened version of urban sprawl, lit up as far as the eye could see, and imagined living here, not as an RCMP officer, but a city detective. Because that was definitely an option.

When his watch beeped nine, he closed the blinds. He went downstairs, as agreed, and found Leith in the bar, waiting for him. They had dined separately because Leith had accepted an invitation by a few of the Calgary officers who wanted to hear the coastal perspective on crime, and Dion hadn't. Now they were here to talk over the Prince interrogation, compare notes, and kill some time before the flight home tomorrow.

The Holiday Inn's idea of a bar was fairly minimal. Leith was at a tall table, getting a head start on the drinking. The server brought Dion's order for a glass of beer and promised Leith the nachos were on their way. Leith thanked her, then said to Dion, "So what d'you think?"

Dion had gone into the interrogation knowing what he thought, and nothing of what he had seen or heard of Phillip Prince changed his mind. He shrugged and sucked the froth off his beer.

"I'm thinking he's not our bunny, and you know why?" Leith said. From what Dion knew, Leith was a beer-drinker, but tonight he was enjoying a Scotch. By the looks of it, he'd enjoyed a few already. "'Cause I'm gonna tell you why."

"Why?" Dion said.

"I have a two-year-old," Leith said. One eyelid hung slightly lower than the other, and his focal point seemed to drift in and out. "Well, she's about to turn two. And when she breaks something, and you go, Izzy, did you break that? she says no, like this. Nooo. I mean, since when do two-year-olds lie? What's the matter with this world? I thought you don't learn to lie till you're, what, five, six? Anyway, this is my point ..."

But the nachos came just then, and he forgot his point. Once the waitress was gone, Dion prompted him back on track. "He's not our bunny *why?*"

Leith munched on a glob of chips, melted cheese, and hot peppers. "My point is, when you accuse her of doing something that she actually *didn't* do — my kid Izzy I'm talking about — she'll flip out. I mean, she'll crawl the walls screaming, she'll be that mad. There's something about being falsely accused, it's like a deploy button. And it's the same with Prince. He's kind of at your two-year-old level, and he flipped out, too, when I put it to him he'd killed the Lius, right? You saw that, right? Kind of more subtle with him than with Izzy, but I caught it. Yup, I'd bank on it, he's a bad apple, but he didn't kill those people."

Leith was finished with his reasoning, and his mood seemed to dip. "But you haven't told me what you think."

"I totally agree," Dion said. He sat forward, glad they were now on the same page, and he could share his thoughts, which had been punching at his brain on and off all day. "'Course he didn't do it. It felt wrong from the start, because of the missing phone, right? Why would Prince take Liu's phone? Doesn't fit. So Lance Liu got attacked first, then whoever did it got the info off the phone — and he'd need the passcode to access it, Sig Blatt confirms Lance used a passcode — and then went after his family on a follow-up basis. Doesn't matter the pathologist says they died around the same time, Lance and Cheryl. Doesn't say anything about the time of the attack. Fact is, Lance Liu was lying there for a while before he died. If it was Phillip Prince who went over there to kill him in revenge for wrecking his bike — which, give me a break, even Prince isn't that shallow — it would be the other way around. He'd get to the family first and *then* carry on with his mission of finding Lance. At worst, and it's even more unlikely, he'd kill the wife in *looking* for Liu. I don't believe it. If you work through the whole thing backward, there's loads of information there, but it's like it's just out of reach. This guy was looking for something. How did he get the phone passcode? Did Liu give it to him? Was it forced out of him? And who's the woman who shut the kid in the cabinet? It's bizarre."

"Huh," Leith said, setting down his empty glass. He rubbed his gut and winced. "You know what? I should go to bed. G'night." He tapped his watch face. "Early tomorrow, right?"

"Right. See you," Dion said.

He watched Leith rise unsteadily to his feet and make his way to the till, pay with a credit card, nearly forget to collect a receipt, then leave. Alone, Dion stayed another ten minutes, finishing his beer. People came and went around him. He said no thanks to a second drink when the server came by. She took away the plate, the barely touched heap of nachos under its layer of congealed cheese not much touched by anyone.

* * *

On the flight home Dion had the window seat. He watched the dusty-green foothills fall away as the plane lifted, and observed aloud that they were going the wrong way. Leith said they were looping around to gain altitude, which was preferable to driving nose-first into the mountains. Leith seemed nicer today, but maybe depressed. He was clean shaven and reeked of aftershave. Over breakfast he had chatted some, get-to-know-you type stuff, but just filling time. Dion had mostly focussed on eating.

Now, buckled into his airplane seat, Leith apologized for last night. "I think you were trying to tell me something, and I couldn't follow. Had a bit to drink over dinner, and a few more in the lounge. Sorry about that. Want to try again?"

"No. I typed it up in a full report."

Dion thought about the report glowing on his laptop late last night. He had sat on the bed, referring to the online dictionary for every word he had doubts about. Even ran a few through the thesaurus, for variety.

Worked extra hard on the thing, to make it readable, almost poetic, still trying to impress Bosko. He thought of Bosko's advice to stick it out for a month. He thought of Bosko saying *I'd hate to lose you.*

He tried to imagine sitting here next to Leith on this one-point-five-hour flight, telling him everything. He shook his head and looked out the window. Now he saw clouds and the planet far below, squares of green and grey, snaking rivers, as their aircraft drifted toward the Pacific.

When he was twenty, he had gone autumn hiking with friends up at Hollyburn. High on the trails he had argued with someone, which led to him getting separated from the group, which left him lost on the mountain, walking half a day and into the evening, shouting and stumbling through wilderness. By nightfall he was cold, wet, tired, and sure he was going to die up there alone. When he found his friends, or when they found him, he sat in the car, somebody's arm around him, and dropped into the deepest, happiest sleep he'd ever known.

Would telling Leith be something like that? Would he disclose, and then fall into a dreamless sleep? No, it wouldn't be like that. Maybe at first there would be relief, but it wouldn't last. Wouldn't last beyond the snap of the handcuffs.

* * *

Leith, never a great fan of flying, was glad to be back on terra firma. He and Dion arrived at the detachment midafternoon, walking into a hubbub of exciting news. The excitement seemed to centre around a suntanned, white-haired couple who were trying in a frenetic way to tell Doug Paley something obviously important. Before Leith could get a sense of what it was, Paley began to usher the couple out of the GIS office and away to an interview room.

"Nance spotted it to starboard," the white-haired man was saying, and Leith saw him gesture at the ratty-looking plastic shopping bag Paley held. "We were drifting. She grabbed the long net, nearly fell in fetching it up."

"Bombay Sapphire," the woman said. "But I didn't know that at the time, did I? With the cap on, of course. Or not a cap. A cork. Like a funny little homemade cork."

"Great," Paley said, for the third time. "This way, folks."

"Floating out in the middle of the Burrard Inlet," the man put in.

The three turned the corner and disappeared from Leith's view, but the woman's shrill voice floated back. "Like a message in a bottle!"

Then there was silence as a door down the hallway clicked shut.

Leith asked anyone within earshot, "What was the message?"

JD Temple said, "A baby bootie, that's what."

Ten

HURRICANE

A LONG NIGHT OF HEAVY rain had washed the city clean, and the morning air was warm and humid, with mist lifting from the pavement and awnings. At 9:00 a.m., when Bosko arrived, Leith visited him in his office, first to give him the good news, then the bad. "It's definitely the bootie we're looking for, sir. No obvious evidence on it, but it's gone in for analysis. Unfortunately, the only prints on the bottle belong to the Stubbs. The couple who found it."

"And why did they fish it in?"

"Nancy Stubbs did that," Leith said. "She says it was pretty, bobbing in the waves. So she scooped it out, and saw there was something inside, and, you know, if it was me, I'd think twice about opening up a mysterious gin bottle, but the Stubbs did just that. They chucked the cork in the water — unfortunately — and used a wire bent into a hook to pull out the bootie. It didn't click right away, but then Ernie Stubbs recalled the newsflash, and so they brought it in. Not before handling the thing, though. Bet all the DNA we'll get off it belongs to them and Rosalie Liu."

"We can always hope," Bosko said. "Without prints or DNA, does it advance us at all?"

"Far as I can see, it's just an extra bit of weirdness to add to the file. The Lius weren't drinkers, so unless they kept a stock for guests, it doesn't seem it came from their place."

Bosko thanked him for the update, and since they were talking, asked about the Alberta lead. "Doug tells me it didn't quite pan out."

"Not quite written off, but not promising," Leith agreed, and gave a rundown of his interview with the biker Prince, Prince's hot denials, and the consensus between himself and Dion that Prince had not killed the Lius.

"Yes, I actually read Cal's report," Bosko said, grinning. "Did you see it? It's amazing. Reads like a runaway haiku. But in the end, when you step back, it's quite thorough."

"He's definitely running circles around me," Leith admitted.

"Anyway, so Mr. Prince is a dead end. At least you got a bit of a field trip out of it. The prairies revisited. Suffer any pangs of homesickness, seeing that boundless horizon?"

From earlier conversations, Bosko knew of Leith's prairie upbringing. Leith's feelings for flatness were ambivalent. Maybe when he reached the end of his life cycle he'd start hankering to go back to his roots, but right now topography didn't affect him much one way or the other. Except as it affected the price of housing.

"No, sir, I'm not there yet. I'm wondering about something, though. I realize you said it's at a certain level — your investigation — but has it got anything to do with the crash? I'm just not sure where it's going. I can't look out for him, if I don't know what I'm looking out for."

Bosko smiled. "There's not much to know about the crash, since the only witness has total localized amnesia around the event."

Leith crossed an ankle over a knee. "Wow. That bad, eh?"

"Though I expect he recalls more than he says."

"You think he's faking it?"

"Probably not," Bosko said. "There might be some genuine retrograde amnesia. Maybe simply to avoid dealing with the day of the crash. Which is understandable. He lost a good friend in the course of it, after all. If I have doubts, I mean about it being a genuine psychogenic condition, that is, an emotional response rather than a physical one. It's the fact he's been with the force his whole adult life. He's been at least partially shock-proofed. As for his post-crash cognitive hang-ups, the tests tell us he's competent, but in my opinion, he's working hard to cover a slight deficit. But I wouldn't go so far as to call it even the mildest anterograde amnesia."

Maybe Leith wouldn't, either, if he knew what that was. He chewed his lip and nodded.

He opened his mouth to apologize for being snoopy — but then his phone buzzed, and apparently Bosko's did, too. They both murmured "excuse me." Bosko put on his reading glasses to check his inbox, while Leith held the BlackBerry to his ear and said, "Leith."

The message was murder, and the meeting was over.

* * *

The call took them into the hills above Indian Arm, an area Leith didn't know. Looking at the aerial map on his phone, he saw the forests were thick and the residences few and far between. JD turned off the busy parkway and ascended their vehicle up a twisty and roughly paved road for another ten minutes before arriving at a lane opening that the GPS assured them was their destination.

The laneway curved uphill through trees, until a gateway announced they were at the threshold of the residence. Here a police vehicle was parked, and a constable stood guard. He nodded them through.

Within the gates, what looked like a compact country estate spread out. The broad asphalt parking area could easily accommodate a couple dozen vehicles. A border encircled a landscaped fountain, and a person could play minigolf on the rolling green lawn beyond. Or croquet. From the parking area, a driver could exit back to the laneway or pull into his choice of three jumbo-sized garages. One garage door, Leith saw, was rolled up.

He looked at the house, a modern version of an old-style manor, white siding with steely black trim. JD parked, and she and Leith stepped onto the tarmac and took in the scene. There were two civilian vehicles, high-end models — one a sports car, the other a black

SUV, and three police vehicles. Two of the cruisers were occupied, each with what had to be a civilian in the back seat. Witnesses, hopefully.

JD was talking to one of the constables as she flagged Leith over and confirmed it.

"Those are the witnesses who called it in," she said, indicating the two occupied cruisers. "Constable Johansson here got their basics and decided he'd better keep them apart for now."

Leith could make out the shapes of individuals in the two vehicles. Hard to say for sure, but both appeared co-operative, even subdued.

Young officer Johansson gestured at one cruiser. "Melanie York. She and the other lady found the body in the garage. Garage door was down when they arrived, and the car inside. Its engine was running. They said they didn't touch anything, just switched the engine off. Melanie York's the one that made the call. Oscar Roth is her brother." He looked across the parking area and added, "That's his Hummer."

"Oscar Roth is the dead guy," JD told Leith. "This is his house."

Dead guy's Hummer, dead guy's house, Leith thought. *Got it.* "Place is secured?"

"Yes, sir," Johansson said. "The other two garages are empty, except for a ride-on mower and a couple Ski-Doos and dirt bikes. And a fairly big boat trailer, no boat."

And no other dead bodies, Leith assumed. "And the women, have they been inside?"

"Yes, sir. They only found him after they went into the house. Heard the vehicle running through the interior access, went in, and found him lying there. You wouldn't believe what's in there, sir. A Boss 9."

Leith puffed out his breath. "Yes?"

"Only the rarest Mustang *ever*. Probably a '69, jet black, mint. Priceless." Johansson let the words settle. Then, "The victim's sister saw her brother, shut off the vehicle and opened the garage door, went back outside with the other lady, and called 911. Then Mackie, Bahari, Henson, and I arrived. We separated the ladies into two cars, then Mackie and I did a walk-around. Found forced entry at the back. French doors, window smashed. *Niiice* place. But a real mess inside."

JD shrugged at Leith. "Roth has no record, and this place isn't flagged in any way. No motive pops to mind."

Not flagged as a drug house, a guns house, an all-round trouble house, she meant. Leith nodded.

Johansson said, "The other lady there, I think she's the victim's girlfriend. Name's Jamie Paquette."

Leith said, "They all live here?"

"The girlfriend, yes, the sister, no. Sister lives in Deep Cove. That's her Nissan 350Z. Sharp car, excellent reviews."

Yes, it was indeed sharp, and probably ran well, too. Leith asked the constable, "So they found the body, the sister, and the girlfriend. Were they together at the time?"

"Yes. They had been in Deep Cove, at Ms. York's place. Ms. Paquette was visiting last night and ended up staying over. Ms. Paquette, she doesn't drive."

"Ah," Leith said.

"So this morning she was trying to call Mr. Roth to get a lift home. He wouldn't answer, so the two of them drove out here together. In the Nissan."

Leith had a look at both women in the two cruisers, and couldn't gather much from what he could see behind the sheen of glass. He saw pale, attractive faces staring ahead. The auburn-haired woman in one car — the victim's sister, identified as Melanie York — he gauged as about forty. The blonde in the other, the maybe girlfriend, was possibly in her mid-twenties.

He told Johansson to get both women to the detachment for a nonintrusive processing, with emphasis on their hands, and he'd be there in an hour and a bit to talk to them.

He and JD pulled on crime-scene suits from the kit in the trunk and walked over to the open garage door, which of the three sat adjacent to the house, the one with interior access. Paley had designated Leith team leader on this. His first time running the show on the North Shore, and it happened to be the death of a billionaire, just his luck.

This garage was walled off from the other two. Inside stood a constable, keeping watch, but doing little else. She made note of their entry and told them nothing had been touched since police arrival except the light switch.

Centred lovingly in the garage sat a muscle car, jet black, as Johansson promised, and mint, nosed toward the rear wall. Unlike Johansson, Leith was more interested in the body that lay face down on the cement. He looked as if he had tripped on his way down a couple risers from the interior entryway and crashed into the car's passenger-side door. Considering the head was hooded in some kind of sack, a trip or a push was quite possible.

The body was that of a chunky male dressed in designer jeans, lots of embroidery on the rear pockets. And a T-shirt, distressed black and factory frayed. He was barefoot. The sack on his head appeared to be a pillowcase, dark green, soiled, tightly bound around the throat with what looked like a man's necktie. JD said, "Don't know, sir, but if it was me finding him here like this, I'd have got that pillowcase off first thing. Then called 911."

The top of the head lay about eighteen inches from the side of the black car. The heavy arms lay spread out, and the knuckles were bloody. What looked like blood was smudged on the floor under his hands and seeped through the pillowcase fabric around the region of the lower face. Leith wondered what kind of horror they would find when they unwrapped the head.

"Check out the dent," JD said.

Leith followed her eyes up the side of the car, but saw nothing.

"It's shallow," she said. "You have to catch it in the light."

He moved around until he saw it, too, the slight cave on the passenger door. The damage matched quite nicely with how the body had fallen. "Quite a hit," he said. "He was shoved. Maybe got knocked out."

JD nodded. "Then they turned the car on to idle and left him to die. Vicious."

The coroner, Jack Dadd, arrived, along with the first of the Ident members, and got to work. Leith walked carefully around the vehicle, taking in what details he could. The Mustang was obviously beloved, a showpiece. Classic plush dice hung from the rear-view mirror. No debris on the seats within. He wondered if the owner ever drove it out and about, subjecting its finish to the elements. Probably not. On the right front-corner panel, just back of the wheel well, placed with all the thoughtfulness of a beauty mark on a woman's face, was the chrome word *BOSS*, with *429* underneath. And against all this loving care were crude letters scratched across the driver's door: *Die Ashole.*

Leith straightened from inspecting the vandalism and said to the Ident member closest to him, "Don't let Johansson see that. He might not get over it."

* * *

On the main floor of the big house, JD snugged her hood and joined Leith as he walked from lofty room to lofty room. The Ident photographer was having a field day, for it seemed a hurricane had been through here, household items flung, toppled, shattered. In the kitchen a knife rack had been upset, leaving pricey-looking cutlery scattered across the floor. This struck Leith as the eye of the storm. This was where the man had been taken down and hooded before being pushed into the garage. A bloody hand mark on the wall, smeared in that direction, told the grim tale of struggle and defeat.

Aside from the mayhem, it was a gorgeous place. Blocky but inviting leather furniture filled the living room, along with melodramatic flower arrangements. The floor was polished wood, scattered with ornate Indian carpets of rich gold and blue. From the stone-floored foyer two gently curved staircases led to the chambers above.

Did I just call them chambers? Leith thought. After doing the circuit of the main floor, he and JD went upstairs. Not much was disturbed up here, except for a linen closet in the hallway that had been pillaged, sheets and bedding flung to the floor.

"Matching set," JD said, looking at the dark-green bedding strewn about — it had been cleaned, pressed, and folded, but was now willy-nilly.

Four bedrooms were upstairs, and another room that might have been considered a lounge. Or reading room, except there were no books. And finally an office with a big desk, big leather chair, tacky posters, and dartboard.

One bedroom apparently belonged to a child, judging by the size of the bed, the colour scheme, and the toys. Where was the kid, then? Nobody had mentioned anything about an abduction. JD got on her phone to see if she could find a fast answer.

The last two rooms Leith saw were neatly made, as if reserved for guests.

The master bedroom — pretty near the size of his own apartment — was messy. The king-sized bed was unmade. Clothes lay discarded wherever: socks and underwear, men's jeans, ladies' slips. Newspapers and magazines were scattered on the floor by the bed and apparently stepped on. At first sight the room looked like another battleground, but it wasn't. It was simple laziness.

JD told him she had spoken to the dead man's sister, and the kid, Oscar Roth's daughter, was at her house with her housekeeper, and was safe. "Thank God,"

Leith said, thinking of little Rosalie Liu, who hadn't been so fortunate.

Downstairs, between kitchen and dining room, he and JD stood in a darkened nook where the homeowner had recreated a miniature English pub, complete with brass counter and three bar stools, beer taps, and all the fixings. Here French doors leading outside let in streams of pleasant morning light. The glass was modern, tough, double-pane, but had been smashed inward. The smashing tool lay outside on the patio, a five-foot-long iron pry bar.

Looking up, Leith saw a little white surveillance camera pointed at the smashed doorway. "Hallelujah!"

"Save your happy dance," JD said. "There's no feed. I checked."

He stared at her. "Why? *Why* is there no feed?"

But of course JD couldn't know any better than he did.

Eleven

A BLINDING FLASH

A NEW FLUSH OF INVESTIGATORS entered the area. Among them were Dion and Torr in their white suits. They stood in the garage, having a look at the body. Leith observed that while Torr squatted and peered, doing a good show of soaking up all visual indicia, Dion seemed less than interested.

Ident got to work. Leith and his investigators left the house and stood outside to hammer out a plan of action. Leith assigned out the tasks, exhibits, continuity of evidence, continuity of body. Someone to source the pry bar and someone else to speak to whoever dealt with the security system in this place. He also needed a couple of members to track down and interview the army of help he imagined must be running this show, the groundskeepers and cooks and scullery maids. And the butler, somebody suggested.

"Yes, the butler," he said. He told JD to stay and monitor the scene. To Dion he said, "Come and sit in on the witness interviews, would you?"

JD looked surprised, then disenchanted, then resentful, and Leith knew why. She was his right-hand man, not Dion. He would have to tell her, later. The new arrangement was by Bosko's decree.

* * *

This was Bosko's idea, Dion thought. Bosko was pulling strings to make him feel integral. Or else to ensnare him. He and Leith had taken chairs, and Leith was making the introductions to Melanie York. He asked her first about the child.

"My niece, Dallas," she told him. "I was babysitting her last night. She's with my housekeeper now. Don't worry, she's being well looked after."

Dion thought that on a better day, Melanie York was probably more aware of how attractive she was. She would know how to hold her head to best advantage, fold her legs, keep her shoulders back. But this wasn't a better day. Her brother had been murdered, and she had found him. Her facial muscles sagged, and her body was arranged on her chair in a rigid and graceless way. She wore jeans and a fine-weave cardigan over a plain white T-shirt, not much in the way of jewellery. She told Leith she was thirty-nine years old, childless, an ex-teacher of middle-school children, married for the last ten years to Jonathan York. She said the name with emphasis. "You must know him, right?"

Leith said he didn't, actually.

"Diamonds," she said, shortly. "He owns it. Or he's one principal. Oz — I mean Oscar — is the other."

Dion knew what Diamonds was. A new harbour-side nightclub that had been under construction and controversy last fall, when he had left the North Shore. A lot of people didn't want it built, but a lot of other people did, and those who did must have won, for the place was now up and running. He had seen a review in the paper written by a young person who thought it was kind of retro nineties, lame decor, music not great, cute bartenders, and she would give it three and a half stars for trying.

The other night he had pulled over as he was driving by to look it over. The building sprawled across the ex-shipyards at the foot of the Second Narrows bridge, far enough from downtown to lie cloaked in darkness. Blue-silver lights washed over the black exterior wall like stars, from eaves to entrance. The building was not as big as he'd expected, but stylish, the way its decks starfished out over the water. On hot summer nights, he imagined, clubbers would spill out with the music, visible to the world and advertising Diamonds as *the* place to be. On the night he had stopped to view the club from the street, there had been lineups at the entrance, with classic body-builder types allowing people through as space became available within.

He hadn't heard of any police callouts to Diamonds yet, but they would come. Fun like that always brought trouble, in one way or another.

Melanie told Leith that Diamonds had been running since New Year's, so not quite half a year. "Oz and Jon met at UBC. They were both Type T personalities and economics wizards, and best buddies, so that's how Diamonds was born."

"What's Type T?" Leith asked.

"Risk-takers. Entrepreneurs. Not happy unless they're walking the edge."

She described the paths Oz and Jon had taken after UBC — Jon at a trading company, Oz managing a night-club in Whistler. But they were always tossing bigger ideas around. And seven years ago, while they had all been out clubbing in downtown Vancouver — it had been Melanie's thirty-second birthday party — the two men knew their destiny. With Jon's talent for numbers and Oscar's hands-on experience, they would open a ground-breaking, twenty-four-seven dance-club and strip-bar combo on the North Shore.

"Type T," Leith said.

"Exactly," Melanie said.

"How's the business going?"

"They're kind of almost not really breaking even, I think. But it's only been, like I say, half a year. There's nothing like it on the North Shore, so they should find a niche, eventually. The twenty-four-seven idea didn't last long, but they are managing to attract businessmen for the strip shows, and youngish people for the club. But now with Oz gone ..."

She talked at length about her brother's death, but gave little away about how she felt about it. Then she went on about Oscar's failed marriage.

In the second hour, Dion's stamina began to slide. Lack of stamina was another secret he kept from the force. He hadn't expected Leith to bring him along, was the problem. He didn't like tasks unfinished, and a part of him was still processing what he had seen at the mansion — heavy dead man face down on the garage floor, dark-green pillowcase over his head tied with a necktie that was shiny grey on black. Evidence of a break-in, a main floor that looked like it had been turned inside out.

Melanie didn't take many breaks, which deprived him of catch-up time. Now she and Leith were talking about a car key for the Mustang, and now they were talking about Dallas, and Dion wondered how the discussion had gone stateside so suddenly.

"Brain damage," Melanie said.

But she wasn't talking about him, he realized as she returned his stare with an abstracted smile. Leith's questions plodded on. Dion gave up on notes, crossed his arms on the table and leaned forward to watch Melanie and do his best to listen.

"Cleo took a tumble when she was eight months pregnant," she was telling Leith. "They figure that's what did it, injury to the baby's cerebellum in the womb. Last I heard, they're calling it Autism Spectrum Disorder. ASD."

Cleo, Dion thought. *Who the hell was Cleo?*

"Born without much to say," Melanie said. "As I think I already told you, she's six, but she'll probably be three for the rest of her life."

"That's too bad," Leith said. "So Oscar and Cleo got divorced soon after Dallas was born, and you say the lawsuit's still ongoing? Big custody battle, was it?"

"Not custody. They both agreed Oz should keep Dallas. It's gone to appeal over the money. She secured a settlement, but Oz is fighting back. He thinks he should get child support. Cleo thinks otherwise." Melanie grimaced. "But don't get me started on those two. Anyway, it's moot now. She's won. She'll get the house, Oz's interest in Diamonds, and the kid to boot."

"And his interest is what, do you know?"

"I don't know the latest shareholder stats. Fifty percent of eighty, whatever that is, times wherever it's at right now."

"That's not too helpful," Leith said.

"I know. Sorry."

"And what about Jamie?" Leith asked.

Dion wrote it down and flipped back through his notes. Jamie was the dead man's girlfriend.

"She won't score anything from his death," Melanie said. "She's known him barely a year. Maybe another few months and they'd have gotten married, but as it is, she'll walk away with some nice clothes and jewellery, maybe a few bucks he put in her bank account, but that's about it. However, she's only twenty-six, and she's pretty. She'll find herself another rich guy to tow her along."

"Sounds like you're not too crazy about her?" Leith said.

"No, I like Jamie. I'm no better. I'm on a free ride myself."

Melanie's face twisted, then cleared. Her makeup was messy around the eyes. *Like Kate's the other night*, Dion thought. Also like Kate, there was a faint line of dirt under her nails, as though she had been lightly gardening and had forgotten to scrub out the soil.

Leith asked her to go over the events of the night and

day once more for him. Her response was sharp. "Oh my God, do I have to? I've already given it to the other fellow. In detail."

"Once more for the record, please."

She blew out a slow breath through pursed lips. "I was babysitting Dallas while Oz attended a house party somewhere out there in whatchamacallit. Lion's Bay. Jamie was elsewhere. She's a bit clingy, doesn't go anywhere without Oz, but she doesn't like house parties, and I guess she probably needed a shopping fix, so she cabbed over to Metrotown for the day. It was getting late. I expected Oz to call or come get Dally, but he didn't. Having too much fun, I guessed. Didn't matter to me. Dallas often stays over. Easiest kid in the world to care for. One toy, one stream of thought, no complaints. Food-wise, whatever you put in front of her, she'll eat." Melanie paused. "Where was I?"

"Oz and Jamie have left you babysitting Dallas. Was anyone with you?"

"No. Jon's on the Island. Business. About nine at night Jamie called. She said she couldn't reach Oz, had he come by to pick up Dallas, or what? I said no, he must be partying hard. She said she'd come wait with me, then. So she grabbed a cab and came over. We hung around, listened to music, drank cocktails."

"What time did she arrive?"

"Half hour or so after her call. There's a guest room downstairs she uses a lot, it's practically hers. She went to bed about twelve thirty, and I crashed about one, with Dally. In the morning, still no Oz. Tried his number, kept going to voice mail. So we left Dallas with my housekeeper, and I drove Jamie back to their place in Jon's car. He's got my truck on the Island."

The morning bits had already been confirmed by the housekeeper.

"It's not far to Oscar's," Melanie went on. "Fifteen to twenty minutes, depends on traffic. Traffic was light then, so probably took us fifteen at most. We walked inside, saw the mess. And the back door had been smashed. Heard the car running and ran into the garage. Found Oz. I tried to take that thing off his head, but couldn't untie the knot. He was dead. I knew it. And the fumes in there were awful. I went straight back outside and phoned 911. I called Jonathan too, in Victoria. He's grabbing the first flight back. He'll be here soon, I'm sure. He's devastated. Poor Jon." She stared into space, as if realizing for the first time that the death of her brother was just the first ripple of an expanding circle. "That's about it," she said. "If you want the unabridged version, it'll have to be another time. Sorry, but I need a break. Seriously."

Leith said, "So neither you or Jamie went out that night? Well, I suppose if Jamie went out while you were sleeping, you wouldn't know about it though, would you?"

Melanie studied him thoughtfully, almost smiling. "You think Jamie slipped out and killed him, then slipped back and put on this big act? Don't bother. She can't act. And she can't drive. Even if she could, I'd have heard her take the car. It's got a gutsy exhaust. I heard nothing."

"I'm not saying that," Leith said. "Just wondering if either of you went out."

"No. We were drunk. Too placid to kill anyone, promise."

"Okay." Leith's hand splayed on a manila folder that contained her first statement to the first-on-scene member. "We'll likely be talking again, but one last question for you. Who would want to kill your brother? Any ideas?"

She looked about to say no, but her eyes widened, and her body tensed, as if danger had just walked into the room. "He saw this coming!"

"What d'you mean?"

Her hand had clapped to the side of her face. "Oz made friends and enemies everywhere he turned. He's just impulsive. He can so easily say the wrong thing to the wrong person. It gets him in trouble sometimes. But lately, I think he mentioned he's being followed."

"Yes?" Leith said. "By who?"

"He didn't say." Melanie shrugged. "On the other hand, he's been a drama king ever since he was a little kid. Always seeing monsters in the shadows. He used to have night terrors and was easily spooked. Which went against his grain, because he was also reckless, and he craved attention. So he'd get in trouble wherever he went and whatever he did. So when he started talking about stalkers, I actually thought it was comical. We all did. He did himself, when he was sober. Until this morning I'd have said he was just trying to make life more colourful. But he was right," she said, and gazed at Dion. "My God, he was right."

Leith put more questions about this strange feeling of being followed to her, but she had nothing to add. He then asked if she had anything else to tell him, on any aspect of the case, and she said, "By all means, no." So he stood and escorted her out.

On his return he sat heavily. "Wow, our work's cut

out for us," he said. "We'll do Paquette next, and I'll get the guys to round up Cleo meanwhile."

Dion couldn't remember who Paquette was, and thought Cleo must be Oscar's daughter. He asked Leith why the child should be brought in. She was only six, and mentally challenged.

Leith said, "What child? Cleo, I'm talking about. Cleo Irvine, the angry ex. The one who gets it all. The one with motive written across her forehead. What page are you on?"

Fed up, Dion stood to say he wasn't feeling well, that he was calling it a day, and that Leith could find someone else to sit in — but a commotion down the hallway distracted them both.

He followed Leith to the doorway and watched Constable Sean Urbanski getting physical with a man who seemed intent on charging in. Urbanski wasn't putting his full weight into stopping the stranger, a tall, athletic-looking redhead. The man brushed past and approached Leith, putting a question to him in a voice ragged with emotion. "Are you in charge? What's going on? Who killed him? Why?"

The man was moving too fast for comfort. Dion readied himself to block a blow. Leith, more optimistically, had shot up a palm, instructions to stop right there. The man held back, as ordered, but seemed to levitate with angry energy.

Leith said, "Yes, I'm the one to talk to. Sean?"

Urbanski said, "Jon York. I was told to show him in."

Hearing his name seemed to sober the stranger. He stood gulping air. "Got a call from my wife this morning.

Got here soon as I could. From Victoria. Travel complications you wouldn't believe. What's going on? Is it true? Is Oz dead?"

He was the fair-skinned type whose complexion showed every emotion. He was mottled now, pink and white with frustration and shock. Dion knew that mangled look from his years of dealing with people who had just had the rug pulled from under them. He knew that look from the mirror. He had also dealt with people who tried to fake the mangled look and couldn't pull it off. He could tell this man Jonathan York was faking nothing. He was genuinely shattered, and that made him less interesting. Interesting enough, however, that he forgot his plan of storming out and leaving Leith in the lurch. He trailed after the two into the interview room.

Leith tried to encourage York to sit — a seated witness was easier to control — but York didn't want to. Dion wasn't worried. York looked physically fit but not aggressive. He was about forty-five, with a curly cap of dark-red hair and a casual three-day beard. He looked both rich and hip. He wore eyeglasses of a jetty shape, with clip-on shades he'd maybe forgotten to unclip. He carried a dark leather shoulder satchel and wore a lead-grey Gore-Tex jacket over a lead-grey mock turtleneck, dark-indigo jeans, and vintage long-toed boots.

Leith was giving him the basic facts, that Oscar Roth had been found dead in his own home this morning by York's wife, Melanie, and Oscar's girlfriend, Jamie.

"Yes, I know all that," York burst out, banging at his own forehead with a palm. "But who did it? Did you get him? Let me see the bastard. I'll kill the fuck."

Punch-drunk, Dion thought.

Leith told York to calm down, take a seat. He said they didn't have a suspect, but of course the investigation was in full swing, there was an Ident team all over the house and property, and every lead was being run into the ground. York finally took the chair. He sagged into it, took off his glasses and covered his face with both hands.

Leith summoned Dion out to the hallway and closed the door. "This is going to be like pulling teeth," he said. "I might as well talk to him alone. How about you go interview Ms. Paquette. Get Sean to sit in and take notes. And be thorough. Can you do that?"

"Yes, I can *do that,*" Dion said.

Leith went back to pulling teeth, and Dion, considering the assignment, stood riffling through his notebook pages, looking for a Ms. Paquette. The name escaped him, but by a process of elimination he worked it out. She was the dead man's girlfriend, Jamie.

Sean Urbanski was working on the Liu homicides, coordinating reports and maintaining a flowchart that was starting to stagnate. He was slouched at his desk, chatting on the phone. He was in jeans and a black button-down shirt, untucked, and he looked dishevelled, as he had every day since Dion's return. It was a change Dion found disturbing, like his old friend was suffering some kind of identity crisis. Or losing his beans.

Before the crash, Dion knew Sean as well groomed, a man who liked his colognes and cufflinks. But something had gone wrong. Now, if not for the computer monitor he sat before, he could have been some drug-dealing ape who had wandered his way into the office by mistake, blond hair hanging in tangles, chin unshaven, and a glittery rock in his earlobe.

Urbanski looked up. Dion told him about the interview and asked him to go set up Room 6 for video, get the witness in there with coffee or whatever, and he would be along himself in a few minutes. Urbanski grumbled something about short notice, but hoisted himself out of his chair and went to take care of it.

There was a set of washrooms on every level. Dion used the men's on Level 3, as it was usually empty, then confronted himself in the mirror, studying his eyes while he scrubbed his hands. This would be his first interview since the crash. He transmitted a warning to his reflection: *It's going to be on tape. People will be watching. Whole courtrooms might be watching. Don't screw up.*

His reflection said nothing. It looked ridiculously young, scared, and angry. His reflection seemed to understand more than he did what a long fall he was on the edge of.

He neutralized his face to a professional calm, dried his hands, straightened his tie knot, and checked his suit for lint. Then he took a deep breath and walked out, downstairs, and along the broad hallway to Interview Room 6.

It's not complicated, he told himself. He put the facts in order. Her name was Jamie Paquette. She was the girlfriend of the rich dead man whose head had been smashed into a flashy black Mustang. Paquette and Melanie York had found the body this morning. Other than that, he knew little else about her, and that was his job, to gather what he could, start filling in the blanks, something any third-rank GI member should be able to handle.

"No problem," he told the door. He pushed it open and stepped into the room. He went to the chair next to Urbanski, continuing to plot, compartmentalize, hold it together. He sat down, looked across the table at the most beautiful woman he had ever seen, and all his neatly aligned data points scattered.

Twelve

BREAKER ZONE

AFTER A NOT-SO-PRODUCTIVE interview, Leith released Jonathan York and returned to the GI office, where he found tempers flaring. Cal Dion and Sean Urbanski were facing off between the desks, calling each other names. A bit of a crowd had gathered to watch and egg them on. Leith could see as he waded through the onlookers that the fight was just at the shoulder-shoving stage, which meant it was about to escalate to fisticuffs if somebody didn't step in fast. He raised his arms referee-style, one for each combatant, and said, "Hey, guys, cool it. What's up?"

"That's what I want to know," Urbanski said from the end of Leith's right arm, not to Leith, but to Dion. "I didn't do nothin'. What's the matter with you?"

"You're what's the matter with me, you fucking chimp," Dion said from the end of Leith's left arm, not to Leith, but to Urbanski, poking at him with an angry finger. "You're not as smart as you think you are, Sean, in fact you never were, and now you look like shit to go with the IQ, so good for you, you finally got a matching set."

"Hey, hey," Urbanski shouted. "I was yanking your collar, man. I was fooling around. Jesus, what's up with that shit? You're gonna wanna work on that personality of yours, pal, what's left of it."

"Shut up, both of you," Leith told them.

"Brain-dead damaged fucking loser."

"And still two miles ahead of you."

"Oh really?" Both of Urbanski's hands went up, balled into fists, not to throw a punch but to give his ex-pal the classic double-bird *up yours* sign. "You sure could've fooled me in there just now. Think you're a genius? You're an amateur. You're worse than amateur, you're retarded. But hey, we got it on tape, right? Wanna rewind, retard? You wanna fuckin' rewind and watch it all and then tell me how many miles you are ahead of me?"

"Yeah, I do, and we will, and then you're going to shove it up your —"

"Shut the hell up, both of you," Leith bellowed, loud enough that they actually did.

* * *

Leith, the unsung mediator who really didn't have time for this garbage, listened to their stories, separate and apart.

In private, in the "soft" interview room, Sean Urbanski told Leith that Dion had botched the questioning of Jamie Paquette from beginning to end — which wasn't a big deal, we all have our bad days — but afterward Urbanski had cracked a joke, just between two red-blooded guys, something about the interviewee being a good-looking woman and Dion going zombie over it, which again is perfectly okay, perfectly natural, a guy sees a pretty woman and his nuts take over, happens all the time. Pressed further, Urbanski admitted his jokes were maybe off-colour, had maybe even verged on roughhouse, maybe kinda hardcore porn, and he'd expressed a criticism or two as well for the way Dion had run the show, which was worse than lame. But the jokes were just that, jokes, and the criticism was constructive, no cheap shots, nothing a pal couldn't handle, which, too bad, but Dion was obviously a pal no more, and what was wrong with him anyway?

"I thought he was cured," Urbanski finished, still rosy at the throat and temples. "I thought they fixed his head, and he's back with us. But he isn't. He's some kind of … Borg shit imposter with no sense of humour."

It was more or less what Doug Paley had said. Different monster but same idea.

"What was he like before?" Leith asked. He knew Dion as a walking grab-bag of trouble, but there were two sides to him, it seemed: before the crash and after. Not having known him before, he had to wonder about the personality split, and how deep it went. And more particularly, where it might go from here.

Urbanski said nothing but got up and walked out, to return a minute later with a single snapshot. "That's what he was before the crash. Two Christmases ago, at my place. A good dude."

In the colour photograph, Leith could see festive decorations and what appeared to be a bunch of drunks jeering at the camera. A house party. Urbanski was in there, raising a beer bottle, and fat, balding Doug Paley, and the skinny tomboy JD Temple in a green elf cap. And a hefty Italian-looking individual, maybe thirty-five or so, the loudmouth type, hand a blur caught mid-gesture and mouth working at getting some point across. That point was now buried in the sands of time. The words were directed at Dion, but Dion was looking straight into the lens, sweaty, exultant, and fully present.

"Who's this guy?" Leith asked of the loudmouth in the foreground, though he could guess.

"That's Looch," Urbanski said, quietly. He took the photo back, flicked at it and made a macho harrumphing noise, maybe to neutralize any sentimentality he might be betraying as he added, "Luciano Ferraro. He died in the crash. Which is totally fuckin' wrong. Miss him like hell. We all do."

"The guys around here, do they blame Cal for the crash? Do you?"

Urbanski shrugged. "The file says Cal was blindsided. He wasn't exactly taxiing along, though, the traffic guys say. But we'll never know exactly how fast he was doing it, will we? You gotta wonder, though."

"About what?"

"What they were doing out in Cloverdale, middle of the night, tearing up the fuckin' road. Smacks of something to me."

"Like what?"

Urbanski shrugged again, but this time didn't elaborate.

Leith finished up by advising him to keep a lid on his temper, and be patient with his coworkers. Especially

Dion, who was clearly struggling. And maybe tone down the language while on the job, okay? It's not good for the image. Urbanski promised to stop swearing.

To close off, Leith asked him for any impressions he'd formed of the sexy witness, Ms. Paquette, the source of all this trouble. Urbanski had only three words for her, spoken with passion: "Fuckin' spice, man."

* * *

Dion's version of the fight wasn't much different from Urbanski's, except he denied botching the interview. "I took it slow," he said. "I was thorough. I got what I needed from her."

"Well, I guess, like Sean says, we have it on tape. Want to see?"

Judging from the slant of Dion's mouth, it was the last thing he wanted. But he accompanied Leith to the case room, to the banks of computers along one wall. Leith sat down, brought a computer to life, and with some trial and error got the file uploaded off the in-house server. He told Dion to take a seat. Dion did so but kept his chair at a distance, watching the screen only occasionally.

The opening frames showed Jamie Paquette sitting alone on her side of the table, waiting to be grilled. Because she was seated it was hard to say, but Leith guessed her to be tall and lithe. Her skin was pale, her long hair golden blond and artfully tousled. Smudgy mascara only added to her charm. Her lower lip caught the light, a solemn mouth, attractively puffy. She looked frightened. Not surprising, considering she had just found her boyfriend bashed, head-bagged, and asphyxiated in her own home.

He saw her knuckle at her eyes, worsening the smudges, then sit hugging herself.

On the monitor, Urbanski entered the room and set a cup of something in front of her. He took a chair, introduced himself, and made the usual small talk, not too imaginatively. Something about the weather, and then something else about the weather. He pushed a box of Kleenex in front of her. She gave him a small smile as she swabbed her nose.

It wasn't a careful swabbing, Leith noticed. And considering how beautifully done-up she was, that lack of care meant something. It meant she had put vanity aside for the moment. It meant she had bigger things on her mind than ruined makeup or reddened nostrils.

After a delay Dion entered the room. He closed the door and took the chair next to Urbanski, and due to the camera angle remained more or less off-frame. Even so, as he checked out Ms. Paquette for the first time he was visibly a man transfixed.

He recovered his wits a moment later, but the interview that followed wasn't great. Not quite the botch-up Urbanski alleged, but definitely not prize-winning. Dion started unconventionally by asking Jamie where she'd grown up. Leith wondered why it mattered.

Jamie said, "John Oliver, mostly."

The high school? Leith thought.

"So South Vancouver?" Dion on the screen asked.

"Yeah. Forty-first."

Dion asked if she recalled how and when she had met Oscar Roth.

She lifted a hand to illustrate something twirling midair. "I was dancing. The Penthouse, I think. He bought me a drink."

So Jamie was a stripper. Or an ex-stripper. Interesting. Strippers tended to drag along in their wake criminals and drugs, and often the twisted, pimp-like mentality of their lovers. Was Oz a pimp?

"When was that?" Dion asked.

"After."

"After what?"

"What?"

"When did you meet Oz? What month, what year?"

"Oh, um." Her voice was almost too soft to pick up. "Last year." Her hands clutching the Kleenex seemed to be squeezing the life out of the thing. "It was springtime, like now. But hotter. They had no air conditioners in the rooms. We had to walk down, like, two flights of stairs. It was ..."

Leith couldn't catch the last word, but thought it was *horrible.*

Dion on the screen fidgeted with a pen he wasn't using. He said, "I understand you lived with Oscar Roth. When did you move in?"

"Soon as he got a day off to pick up my things. He's got a fabulous place. I've never seen anything like it. I'm from the other side of the tracks, right? It's nice living in a palace, all those faucets and things, but in the end, it's just another room, another window. And actually, you know what, I like the woods and birds and all, but you seen one tree, you seen 'em all, if you ask me. I miss Vancouver."

A chatterbox, Leith thought. A poor, uneducated, ravishing chatterbox with a smoker's rasp.

Dion asked her about Melanie and Jon York. "They're friends of yours?"

She nodded. "They're Oz's friends, really, but we hang out there a lot, in Deep Cove. They babysit Dally sometimes."

There was a long silence before Dion asked his next question. "Do you get along with Dallas?"

"Well, no, what's to get along with? She's just there. She's mental. She doesn't talk. Like, *ever*."

"Why's that?"

"Because she's mental."

Dion asked about Oscar's prize Mustang. She said it was a beautiful car and a waste of space, because he never drove it anywhere. She was hoping to learn to drive one day, and then she'd swipe the keys and put it to good use. She smiled as she said it. She had a pretty smile.

Dion went on to ask her in a fleeting way about Oscar's finances, his business dealings, his general health. She had nothing to offer on any front. He asked if she knew who had killed Oscar, or who might want him dead, or if Oscar knew he was in danger. She didn't.

Soon afterward he ended the interview.

Leith stopped the video and thought for a moment how to phrase his disappointment. He shifted his chair sideways so he and Dion could have a serious talk. Dion crossed his arms.

"You missed a whole whack of important stuff. What about Oscar's paranoia? Friends, enemies. Problems in his life that she may know of better than anybody, since she lived with the guy."

"I covered that off. I can get her back if you want me to ask it three different ways."

"Well, what was she doing all day? Was she with anyone? What time did she get a taxi to the Yorks'? What about her calls to Oscar, about the last time she was with him? What was he like? What was their relationship like? God, Cal. Are you not interested? I'm going to have to get her in for a rerun, and that's not exactly ideal. Get it?"

"Yes," Dion said. "I get it."

He didn't look as remorseful as he should. Leith changed tack. "So taking all this incredible lack of information into account, do we tentatively throw Paquette into our suspect pool? Seems to me she's viable. Any thoughts?"

Dion sat straighter, uncrossed his arms and looked stunned, which was incrementally better than looking sullen. "She can't drive. If she did it, you'd have to hook in Melanie York. If you think Melanie York's up to it, I guess you've got something. I don't, but maybe you do."

"Maybe if we had more information, we could rule her in or out."

Dion said, "Jamie Paquette didn't kill Oscar, because Melanie York says she didn't, because they were together, and I believe Melanie York. Jamie may know who's responsible, but you saw her when I put it to her. She wasn't going to give me a thing. Melanie York says Jamie can't act, but that's the irony of it. The sign of a good actor is people think they can't act. I think she can act very well, and I could see where it was going, and I wasn't going to flip her even if we sat there all night."

He was done. His logic seemed sketchy, and he looked ill, like someone in the throes of the hot-and-cold flu-sweats. More kindly, Leith said, "Anything else?"

"Yes. The ex-wife, Cleo. That's someone we should be looking at. There's the civil case, the money. This was a blitz attack. Robbery doesn't seem to be the motive, so Oscar's death was the end game. 'Die asshole' was scratched into the car door, spelled wrong. Someone with a grudge or someone pretending to be someone with a grudge, which is Cleo. She didn't do it, of course, but maybe she hired guns."

Leith said, "For a smart guy, you make a lot of assumptions."

"They're not assumptions."

"I think that's exactly what they are. Jamie Paquette could have given us a lot of background on our victim. Background we're now missing."

"*You* try, then. Get her in here. You're going to get reams of bullshit from her, and nothing else."

Leith looked at his phone and saw a message from JD Temple, something about — speak of the devil — Cleo Irvine. He rose and said, "Just got word the ex is in Seattle, and she's been there all week. I have to go make some calls. You look beat, Cal. You can sign out, and we'll talk again Monday. Some advice, though. Don't get into fights. If either of you two idiots landed a black eye you'd be up before a conduct hearing, explaining it all to them, not me. You realize that?"

"Yes. I'm sorry." On a physical level, Dion hadn't moved from his chair. In every other way, he seemed long gone.

Thirteen

AT SEA

IN THE HOUR BEFORE DAWN, Dion left the Royal Arms. He climbed into his Civic, lit a cigarette, and drove out onto the quiet city streets of North Vancouver. This being Sunday, and early, traffic would be sparse. He took the lower levels by the tracks and harbour, past Diamonds, the nightclub dozing in the morning mist, and joined bridge traffic over the Second Narrows. Over the waters he let Highway 1 carry him out of the city, going at a hundred kilometres an hour on cruise control. The limit rose to 110. The broad skies of the Fraser Valley opened before him, a band of clouds tinted pink by the rising sun.

For half an hour he stayed on Highway 1 before exiting onto the smaller Pacific Highway, which would beeline him into the floodplains of Surrey.

He wasn't familiar with the area. He had grown up in Vancouver, out on Knight Street. He knew his way around Richmond and Delta no problem, but the further-flung districts were uncharted territories in his mind, with the amorphous zone called Cloverdale sitting somewhere in between.

He knew the crash happened in Cloverdale. Hadn't known it at the time, of course. Hadn't cared. He didn't know the names of the roads, because he had never been in the frame of mind to ask, but he was confident as he set off this morning that he would recognize the spot when he saw it, even though that had been nighttime and this was day. He knew more or less the turns he had taken. He recalled an overpass. Not far past the overpass was the turnoff to what must have been a defunct gravel pit.

The crash site wasn't his target today. The defunct gravel pit was. He tried music but switched it off again. The landscape began to repeat itself: field and fencepost, a bunch of cows, a driveway marked with shrubs and a mailbox, another driveway marked by another shrub and another mailbox, a stretch of field, another bunch of cows. He found an overpass and travelled under it, but it was all wrong. Too many houses. He was on a different road altogether.

He began to see a problem forming. He needed a plan. Pulling to the shoulder, he shut off the engine and studied the map folded in advance to expose Cloverdale. Funny how tiny the area looked on paper, and how boundless it seemed in life. He found where he was on the map and looked out the windshield to correlate lines with reality. The pink clouds had evaporated, leaving nothing but pristine blue. The mountains were hazy grey humps in the distance. The traffic here was almost nonexistent. A truck barrelled past, and a car, and then nothing. He decided to grid search the most likely roads, starting with 68th, working his way down. Sooner or later he would hit it.

With no cars behind him and only a couple ahead, he drove slowly, looking from side to side. He had forgotten that south of the Fraser River the Lower Mainland levelled out into one gigantic plateau. He had forgotten how disorienting plateaus could be. He found a crossroad that looked a lot like the one where he'd been slammed into oblivion, but it wasn't.

After an hour of fruitless explorations, he pulled over once more, shut off the engine, and opened the window. He could smell mud. What seemed like silence at first became a chorus of bugs and birds. He sat and thought about all he'd lost, not because of his own righteous temper, but Looch's.

The killing night stayed with him in perfect detail — at least, the moments leading up to the crash did. He was back there now, standing on the abandoned flats in the dark, heart wildly beating. His knuckles stung raw and he could taste blood on his tongue. He looked across the expanse of land at a lit building, just a pinprick, too far off to pose a danger. All was dead still. There was the sour stink mingling with the heat that pulsed from the ground, drifting upward to burn in his throat. He was spent from shovelling, sweat-soaked, oddly disconnected, trying to think straight.

He remembered a ghostly line crossing the night sky, a jetliner leaving its trail of exhaust as it made its way from wherever to Richmond. He watched it form, realizing that those three hundred or so souls up there and himself down here were permanently parting ways. It hit him how one split-second decision had brought him here, and he looked across at Looch.

He found his voice and called out to him, some kind of reassurance. *Not a problem, man. We might as well be on the moon out here.* For once in his life Looch had stood speechless, staring at him through the gloom. Or not at him, but past him, toward the mounds of gravel and the rutted laneway where Dion's car sat, just minutes before that car was to become a death trap.

Dion turned and saw it, too, what Looch was staring at. Beyond the car and the mounds of gravel, a flicker of movement that shouldn't be there.

That was night and this was day. Almost a year had passed, and now he couldn't backtrack to the pit. He needed to find that pit. He would have to get the co-ordinates, but how to do it without raising eyebrows, was the question.

The online news. Why hadn't he thought to check that? A few keywords, and he would pull up an article that would start by naming the roads. Perfect.

With a fresh cigarette between his teeth, he sat working his phone and Googled in various combinations of words: *Ferraro, RCMP, Cloverdale, death.* Found the obituary, and some articles, but none naming roads, except one that said, "*... on 176th in Cloverdale.*"

He stared out the windshield. He had just driven that road, and that wasn't it, not even close. Somebody had got it wrong. Or somebody had tampered with the records. Could they do that, sabotage the news? His heart was banging just as it had that night, maybe harder, because now he was looking backward at his mistake, instead of forward at the unknown, and seeing just how hellish his life had become.

He stared into the rear-view mirror, expecting to catch a flash of light or a moving shadow, signs that somebody or something had followed him. He saw nothing but postcard serenity: green fields, grey asphalt, blue sky. It was an unreal stillness, a dead peace, and he was completely lost. He pulled a U-ey on the empty little road and headed back to the North Shore.

Fourteen

DEAD AHEAD

MONDAY MORNING, AFTER only one day off, Leith was steering the unmarked down Dollarton with a quiet Dion in the passenger seat, off to the York residence in Deep Cove for some follow-up interviews. The interviewees were Jonathan York and Jamie Paquette, with maybe a few questions for Melanie York thrown in as well. None of these characters sat hugely suspect in Leith's mind, except maybe Jamie — but he couldn't write her off just yet, thanks to Dion's underwhelming interview on Friday. He could have pulled them all into the office to talk, but he wanted to see them in their element. Check out how they played off against each other, too.

Deep Cove was another area Leith wasn't too familiar with. Dion could have probably directed him, but he was in a mopey mood, so Leith relied on his talking GPS. It had a young female voice. She sounded American, cool, efficient, patient. A better conversationalist than Dion, anyway. It occurred to Leith that these days he was having more conversations with his GPS than his wife. He resolved to call Alison tonight, pop a beer, stretch out on the bed in his furnished rental apartment, and spend some quality, long-distance time with her.

The York home was situated up a well-populated, woodsy hill. A narrow, winding road took them to a dead end and a nice-looking modern residence. Nowhere to park, really, so Leith pulled his car as far as he could to the side of the road. In the driveway sat a white Lexus SUV and a sporty Nissan, the silver bullet young constable Johansson had coveted.

Melanie York opened the door to them, wearing a simple black dress. She seemed more centred now, after having a few days to adjust to the new reality. Leith re-introduced himself and Dion. "Of course," she said. "Please come in."

The corridor inside was wide and clear of junk, naturally lit by skylights, adorned with driftwood and rocks. They stepped down into a good-sized living room. Jamie Paquette sat on the sofa, her legs tucked up. A child lay on the floor. Jon York stood by the window. It might have had a great view of Deep Cove's community, park, and harbour below, but the swooping branches of evergreens blotted out much of the light.

"Nice place," Leith said to Melanie. She smiled politely.

He looked again at Jamie Paquette, a woman he had so far only seen on a desaturated video monitor. She looked younger now, maybe because her face was not made up and her hair was tied back.

The child who lay on the brilliantly coloured rug before her would be the mentally challenged daughter of the dead man, he supposed. Dallas Roth.

Jon York, in casual cords and a loose silk shirt, had been on his phone. He pocketed it now and crossed the room to greet them. He shook Leith's hand emphatically, then Dion's. "I'm really sorry about the other day," he said. "I wasn't myself. I can't recall a single word I said, in fact. I hope I'll be more helpful today." He had a broad, attractive smile, now that he wasn't in shock, and Leith could see how he won his way through life, selling encyclopedia sets or nightclub shares, whatever came to hand. "We'll use the den, if that's okay?"

"Fine, thank you," Leith said.

They went along to a lower-level room almost as big as the living room above, with less natural light, only one floor-to-ceiling window panel, and a set of leather chairs. They took the armchairs near the window. Dion occupied himself making notes, and York left them to go fetch coffee.

"Great place," Leith said, sounding like a broken record. "Nice to have a view of the water."

The view from here was actually better than from upstairs. Leith could see yachts and what looked like houses stacked on houses. Deep Cove was a little holiday town, pretty and buzzing with life.

"For sure," Dion said, not looking at the pretty town or the dramatic cloud formations or the dazzling play of sunlight dancing on waves. He had run out of notes to jot down and was reviewing an email. He told Leith he was bringing himself up to speed on the latest tips that had been filtering in on the other big case, the Mahon Avenue homicides, Cheryl and Rosalie Liu, which was credible enough. Still, Leith thought it was more an avoidance manoeuvre.

York finally came back with a tray of coffee, cream, honey. York and Leith each had a cup, but Dion didn't. York talked about Arabicas and grinds. Leith was more of the drip-blend-whatever type, but made noises of appreciation.

With coffee in hand, they got to business. Leith wanted to know whatever York could tell him of his and Oscar Roth's relationship. York turned out to be a good speaker. Economical, with a bit of pitchman flare.

It wasn't the most interesting story, though, and a lot of it Leith already knew from Melanie York. How Jon and Oz had met, their education, first jobs, careers running parallel, then splitting off. Oz went into the night-club biz, York stuck with finance, but they'd remained close friends. He talked about Diamonds, its ups and downs, the big opening on January 1st, the bureaucratic tape that got so long and tangled it could choke a man.

"How's it doing now, the club?" Leith asked, the same question he had put to Melanie.

"Too soon to start making graphs," York said. "But it's looking positive."

"How will Oscar's death affect Diamonds?"

"Nothing extreme. I'm reefing the sails. Proceeding with caution. My big concern right now is dealing with the stakeholders. They've got questions, need comforting. Fair enough. Everybody knows Oz is the ideas man. I'm just the bookkeeper."

But a competent one, Leith thought. "Tough," he said sympathetically.

"Worst of all, I went straight from the shock of his death into damage-control mode. No time to think, let alone grieve. I'll wait for Sunday, then lock myself in my office and have a tantrum, I'm sure."

"You ever had any fights, you and Oscar?" Leith asked. "Arguments. Breakups?"

"No, nothing big. We were seriously good friends. Probably never had two days gone by where we didn't get together, business or pleasure, didn't matter. Never ran out of words. Argued, sure. But we were tight. Friends are ten a penny, but Oz and I were like this." He linked index fingers and pulled, and apparently couldn't break the grip. "Friendship like that, it's irreplaceable. I keep forgetting he's dead. Unreal."

He pressed thumb and fingers against his eyes. He inhaled and apologized with another smile, even more attractive with tears. "Sorry. What else d'you want to know?"

"Enemies," Leith said. It was a question he had asked at their last meeting, but York had been too distraught to answer.

Now the man nodded and pulled a folded paper from his breast pocket. "I made a list."

A list? Many people could name an enemy or two, but few needed to write them out. Leith took the note and looked at seven names neatly printed in a column. Two names were crossed off. He asked why.

"I did some checking up," York said. "They couldn't have done it. Opportunity."

Leith knew his team would be looking at the crossed-out names anyway. If he was an actuary he would be counting up the man-hours it would take to thoroughly investigate these seven names — well, six, anyway — and the rate of return, which would no doubt be zero. He asked for a synopsis on each, the six named gentlemen and one lady — the one lady being Cleo Irvine. He didn't tell York that he had already interviewed Cleo, and she was all but eliminated. Even her hypothetical hitman had been kicked off the case-room board. But he did want to hear York's take on it.

"It's more a harmless mud-slinging," York said. "Cleo's got everything she needs in life. She has nothing to do with this. You might as well take her off the list."

The other enemies were a couple of business deals that had gone wrong, and the jealous husband of a woman Oz had dated briefly before meeting Jamie. Then there was that oversensitive dude who got ousted from the club Oz had worked at in Whistler some time ago. The guy still wrote the occasional hate email, but he was probably more bark than bite. Finally, there was a libel suit related to the bidding process of the Diamonds development. Leith found none of it terribly exciting.

He said, "Who was your electrical contractor?"

"Bowen's."

"Ever hear of L&S, couple of independents?"

"Nope."

"Never worked for you?"

"Nope."

It had been a long shot. Leith flicked the piece of paper. "Was Oscar worried about any of these guys?"

"Hell, no. It's just you asked, so I racked my brains, and that's what I came up with."

"Last few months, did something change? He get worried about something?"

Jon York snapped his fingers. "You're talking about the stalker."

"Stalker ..."

"Oz has been antsy lately. He had the feeling he was being followed. We figured it's all in his head. He's a bit hyper."

Was, Leith mentally corrected. Because Oz had been permanently calmed down. Leith had studied photographs of the living Oz and seen a meaty guy with bristling dark-blond hair, a mean grin. Oz had a high-blood-pressure complexion. He was a joker, but he could be weepy, too, what might be called a loose cannon. After gathering info on him and looking into that solid face long enough, Leith felt he'd actually met him. It was the same with most murder victims he had to investigate; they would come alive. Too often they would step into his dreams and yell at him. Lance and Cheryl Liu had visited just last night. Lance was giving Joey a shoulder ride, Cheryl crying about a lost bootie.

He said, "Your wife says the same thing, that he was paranoid lately. Was he doing any kind of drugs that might explain it?"

York had dark-blue eyes, like sapphires. When he smiled they seemed to throw sparks. Lucky man, he had the ultimate house, the flashy car, and stunning eyes to boot. "Smoked pot, occasionally. Preferred his microbrews."

"Nothing harder than beer and dope? You're sure about that?"

"Far as I know." York shrugged. "He might have tried some harder stuff a time or two, I guess. I don't know." He turned to Dion. "Sure I can't get you something there?"

"No, thanks, I'm good," Dion said.

Next came Jamie Paquette, to be interviewed in the same room. She wore the antithesis of mourning attire, easy-fit denim shorts, bleached and frayed, flip-flops, and a filmy blue-green shirt tied above her flat stomach. Leith asked her how she was doing.

"Okay," she said. "Thanks. Still totally in fucking shock, but hey."

Now Leith almost got it, what had happened to Dion yesterday in the interview room as he first clapped eyes on her. Something about her gaze said she was not just with you, but inside you. Yesterday she had added tears to her arsenal, and who can resist a beautiful girl with wet eyes? Tougher than the average maiden in distress, though. Yet however rude she came across, it was an honest rude. Leith had the feeling she was as honest as any upstanding citizen he had ever interviewed, if not more so. Maybe too much so.

She said, "Do you know who killed Oz? I hope you find him fast, 'cause I'm scared."

"Why are you scared?" Leith asked.

"'Cause maybe they're after me now, don't you think?"

"I don't know. You have a reason to think they're after you?"

"I have no reason to think anything. I'm just scared. Wouldn't you be?"

"We're looking hard, Jamie. What are your plans now?"

"Stay with Mel and Jon a while. Then, I don't know."

In the end the interview was unprofitable, not much better than Dion's attempts. Yes, she agreed that Oz was a little paranoid lately, but he never gave her any specifics. She outlined for Leith her movements on the day of the killing. Shopping at Metrotown, cabbing back and forth. Tried Oscar's phone a couple times, then headed to Mel's place in the evening, after dinnertime. Showed Mel what she'd bought. They had a few drinks and crashed. In the morning, still couldn't get a hold of her doorknob of a boyfriend, so she and Mel drove up there.

"Must have been quite a scare," Leith said.

"Completely, totally, freaky scary," Jamie agreed. She was studying Dion now, and he was studying her back. "I ran the hell out of there. Melanie's way cooler, though, and she did whatever she did. I guess she shut off the car and opened the garage door. Then she came outside and called 911."

Leith tried to draw her attention back to him, without luck. "Neither of you had any idea what happened to Oscar?"

Jamie shook her head. "Not a clue. Sorry. Not a clue."

Leith thanked her, and she thanked him back. When she left the room, he and Dion discussed what they had, and agreed it was probably all they could get. They returned to the living room, and while Dion sat on the white leather sofa to complete his notes, Leith had a conversation with Melanie York on a more informal level, asking about Oscar's daughter, Dallas. They stood just out of earshot of the child, watching her. She was sprawled on her back now, playing with a plastic horse figurine, galloping it through the heavens of her imagination.

"She's sweet, mostly," Melanie said. "But she can have her tantrums. Vocabulary got to about a three-year-old's level. But she's stopped talking altogether lately, like she knows it's pointless. Goes to school half days, a special class. She'll always be in care."

"Does she know her father's gone?"

"Probably doesn't register."

"Were they close?"

"As close as he could be. Oz loved her, would do anything for her. But you can't get close to Dallas. We all hover over her, but she's in her bubble. In a way she's just become …" Melanie hesitated and dropped her voice to murmur, "… just part of the furniture. She's just *there*." Where had Leith heard those exact words, "just there," so recently? Jamie on the video screen, talking to Dion. Melanie was saying, "You go, hi, of course, call her sweetie, but you can't hug her — she doesn't like it. She doesn't look at you."

"Did she have caregivers, besides Oscar and Jamie?"

"Few hours a day hired help would usually go in. Jamie isn't what you'd call mother material."

Leith nodded. He had the complete inventory of the hired help. None of them were full time. Aside from the child's caregiver, there were weekly gardeners and house cleaners, the occasional pool man, and a housekeeper slash cook who put in about four hours a day, four days a week. There was no butler. After scrutiny by himself and the team, all the hired help had been cleared.

"What happens to Dallas now?"

"Cleo gets her," Melanie said coldly. "Though she never wanted her. Cleo's an art dealer, always off globe-trotting. I don't imagine she'll change course. She'll probably sell Oscar's house, buy herself a bigger condo, and stick the kid in a home. Which is probably for the best. Jon and I will keep tabs on it all, of course. Visit Dally, make sure it's a good place."

"Have you considered adopting her?"

Melanie's eyes seemed to drift. "I've suggested it. Jon's mulling it over. It's a lot to ask of him. Not financially. Oscar's estate will cover all expenses. But emotionally ..."

Leith said he understood. He saw that Dion was no longer working at his notebook but standing with Jon York by a liquor bar. The bar was more low-key than Oscar Roth's miniature reproduction of an English pub, merely a length of black marble in a corner, behind which could be found no doubt the usual sink and mini-fridge and spritzers. York and Dion were inspecting a small bottle. York was talking and Dion was listening, but they looked like buddies shooting the breeze.

Their apparent coziness surprised Leith and, in some way, hurt. He had tried to be nice to Dion, probably not so well, but for all his efforts, the distance between them only seemed to widen. Soon they would need mega-phones to communicate. Yet there he was, chatting and laughing with a perfect stranger.

He thanked Melanie for her time and signalled to Dion. Jon York walked them out to the driveway. By the car, York asked Leith about Oscar's body, funeral arrangements. Leith did his best to answer; sorry, the body wouldn't be released right away. He added that he hoped he wouldn't have to pester Jon and Melanie much further, but might need to come back.

"Of course," York said. "We all just want you to find whoever did this."

Because York was still a suspect, even with an alibi and tears, Leith looked him straight in the face and answered with a shade of challenge, "Oh, we will."

Fifteen

EBB

NEXT ON THE LIST WAS A visit to the Roth mansion. Since they were en route, they charted the course. As Melanie had suggested, it was a fifteen-minute drive, not so far in the scale of things, and Leith thought about Jamie Paquette leaving the house after everyone was in bed, making the significant hike, at least an hour, probably more, taking shortcut hiking trails, perhaps, killing her boyfriend, and walking back to the York house. Possible.

But even if it was conceivable that she could over-power a man like Roth, the timing was a really bad fit. Roth had died no later than 1:30 a.m., maybe as much as two hours earlier. Melanie York in her written state-ment said Jamie had gone to bed at half past midnight, and she herself had retired about 1:00 a.m. So for Jamie to squeeze a murder trip in there, Melanie would either have to be lying or mistaken. Or else Jamie was a swift-footed ninja. Or had access to a vehicle, or an accomplice. Or it just hadn't happened.

For now Leith bet on the latter.

Inside the Roth mansion, he and Dion walked from room to room. JD Temple had done her research, and Leith knew the home's background. Oscar had only bought the place two years ago, an estate sale through family connections, heavily discounted. Even with the discount he had leaned on a sizeable mortgage to get it, again with family assistance. The interior design was professional and cohesive. The house had come furnished, from draperies to kitchen utensils, and only in odd corners some garish thing or another had worked its way into the decor, revealing Oscar's boyish aesthetics. Maybe in time it would have devolved into a giant, messy, man-sized playpen, something Oz would now never accomplish.

As for who stood to gain from his death, that would be Cleo Irvine. She got the house and all its encumbrances. Oscar had defaulted somewhat, so when the dust settled she would walk away with possibly no more than the million he had put down. Not bad pocket change, but nothing to risk life in jail for either, especially for a woman with her own great career powering her along.

As they walked the halls, looking into rooms, trying to get a better sense of the dead man, Leith asked Dion what he and Jon York had been talking about over at the bar in York's Deep Cove home.

"Scorpions," Dion said. "Mostly."

"Scorpions?"

They were upstairs now, in Oscar Roth's office. A big bay window looked out over hill and dale, city and bridges, the straits. The closest hump of land that Leith could see would be some offshoot of Vancouver, probably. Maybe Burnaby.

He looked down at Oscar's desk. It was free of clutter, but only because the clutter had been collected as evidence. There was a stale smell of cigarettes and beer in the air, but the ashtray had been taken as well, along with its butts and contraband roaches. So the smell was probably soaked into the carpets and drapes.

Candy wrappers lay on the floor. For some reason one panel of plush gold curtain was missing, and Leith looked at the bare rod overhead, wondering if it was related to the murder but doubting it. There was nothing in the file about it being gathered as evidence. Probably a mishap. Oz had accidentally set fire to the curtain, or spilled wine all over it, and nobody had gotten around to replacing it.

Along with the ashtray and boxes of documents, Oscar Roth's computer had been seized. Nothing thrilling had been found on the hard drive. He had played a lot of games and looked at some porn, and there was a folder with the death-threat emails from that enemy of his — more bark than bite — but that was all.

There wasn't much left here to see. A dartboard and unframed posters of bikini babes on the wall, stuck up with pushpins. Both dartboard and babes had darts stuck in them.

Leith had all but forgotten the conversation about scorpions by the time Dion answered, leaning against the wall. "There's one called the deathstalker," he said. "But it's weird, because they think its venom can treat brain cancer. In Asia they drink scorpion wine to treat all kinds of things. It's also an aphrodisiac. York had a small bottle, this big, with a scorpion in it, but I don't think it's for anything more than showing off. I asked if he'd tried it. He said he had. He asked if I wanted a taste. I said no."

Leith sat in Oscar's office chair and looked at the open, polished surface of the desk, marred with a couple sticky rings where glasses of something had sat. The man didn't believe in coasters, and he also didn't let the house cleaners into this office much. Why? He said, "No hard drugs in this place, no paraphernalia either, and Jonathan York tells us Oscar was into nothing stronger than pot. Think that's true?"

"He also said maybe he had tried other stuff."

Leith looked at him. "Don't you think York, as his best pal, would know exactly what drugs Oscar tried? And that makes him a liar, right?"

Dion was looking at the poster of a popular South American actress/bombshell, at the dart stuck in her eye. He said, "I thought you don't like assumptions."

"Just something to look into."

Down the hall Leith observed that the spilled fabrics from the linen closet were gone now, and most of the bedding was back where it belonged, so neat that a housekeeper must have dealt with it. There was no sign of any dark-green bedding.

"Ident took it all?" Dion asked.

"I imagine so."

When they were in the car and on their way back to the detachment, Dion struck up a conversation from the passenger seat, but off topic. "I need to look at my file. Doug says to ask you about it."

"What file?"

"My MVA, in Cloverdale. I can't figure out where it happened. I need the coordinates. Why do I have to go through you?"

"Not sure," Leith said. "You don't know where it happened?"

"No, and the roads out there all look the same. So can I see it, the file?"

"We'll take a look, find out what you need. Why?"

Dion said nothing for a moment, maybe considering his choice of answers. *None of your business* was probably one of them. "Go pay my respects to Luciano Ferraro, is all. Why else?"

On that uninviting note, both men fell silent.

* * *

Leith's resolution to spend an hour on the phone with Alison that night didn't quite pan out. He had the bottle of beer and was stretched out on his bed with his head propped on a pillow. He missed her, and they did talk at more length than usual. But both had been born with reserved personalities, and they couldn't seem to get into the whole steamy phone sex thing. Instead they talked about the sale of the home in Prince Rupert.

"No bites at all?" Leith asked.

"We'll just have to lower the price, Dave. People drive by and keep going."

"It hasn't been long, babe. Let's hang in for another month. Anyway, I have a great idea. Lock up the house and get your ass down here. Just for a break. I'll go crazy if I have to go another week without you."

"What's wrong? You sound blue."

"Wish I'd never left," he confessed. He had told her this before, but never with such conviction. "Don't like it here. Today was not so good."

"Why? What happened?"

"Oh, just the planets out of whack," he lied. "Anyway, I've got a plan. We'll keep the proceeds and just rent till we sort things out. I'll put up with this place till a transfer op comes up."

He didn't tell her what he had in mind: a move to the prairies, to golden lands, a dome of sky choked with stars, and about half the stress. The trick was selling the idea to a girl from the coast. Alison had been born on the Island. She loved her ocean.

He and she said goodnight and disconnected. He lay thinking over Dion's words from earlier today, speaking of his Cloverdale disaster. *All the roads out there look the same.*

The statement made no sense. Dion maintained he remembered nothing of the day of the crash. Total, localized amnesia was credible enough, not uncommon in victims of head trauma. But then why didn't he just say so: I have no clue where it happened, because the day's a complete blank.

Leith wondered about the stranger, Parker. Bosko had told him to hold fire. What did that mean? Was Parker a member of some covert Internal Affairs unit, to be unleashed when Bosko had enough evidence? Or a private investigator? Which raised all kinds of questions.

In the afternoon, he and Dion had sat in the incident room with the MVA file folder, as promised, and Leith had found the accident report from Cloverdale, last July the 1st. He had given the road numbers to Dion. Dion wrote them down. He then asked if he could flip through the file briefly, to see what was in there. Leith had said no, his authority didn't extend that far.

"What authority is that?" Dion asked.

"You should probably okay that with Bosko."

Dion had thanked him coolly and left.

Alone, Leith had gone through the file and found the usual traffic analysts' diagrams, pathology and toxicology reports. He saw the time of the crash was approximately 2:00 a.m. Photos depicted the two vehicles mangled to scrap metal. Gory photographs of Luciano Ferraro, dead. The driver of the red Corvette, a young man with jetty sunglasses smeared into his skull. *Who wears sunglasses at 2:00 a.m.?*

There was Dion, too, like a black-and-blue loser hauled away from a boxing ring. He had been shaved for surgery, taped for broken ribs, masked for breathing, and strung with cables for all other bodily functions. He had been heavier then. On his solid right shoulder was a tattoo of black wings. That he had survived was miraculous, considering he hadn't been wearing a seat belt.

Then there was the damage to his right hand. Leith had looked at a close-up. The split skin and grazing over the knuckles sure looked to him like scars from a fistfight, not an MVA. He had seen plenty of both kinds in his career.

The evidence tallied: Dion's claims of amnesia around the day of the crash, doubtful. His presence in that place at that time, mysterious. Returning to the scene seemed important to him, yet his reason rang false. Add to that evidence of a possible fistfight. And wrapping it all like a bow, there was Bosko's lose-lose investigation.

Intuition told Leith that a crime had been committed, serious enough to warrant the steps he had taken tonight. He happened to have in his possession a GPS tracker, and at day's end he had attached it to the wheel well of Dion's car.

Why? Being proactive. If this turned out to be a legitimate murder investigation, then the tracker data could prove critical. If the investigation went nowhere, so would the tracker data. Simple.

He turned out the lights. He was doing the right thing. He was doing his job, nothing more and nothing less. So why did he feel so sick about it all?

Sixteen

KNOTS

DION'S SECOND VISIT TO Cloverdale had focus. The crossroads of 56th and 168th looked like so many other intersections in the farmlands. Night was falling, his workday was over, and he was on the shoulder looking at the road from this end to its vanishing point; 56th was a minor highway, fields all around. Fairly busy now. A cube van sped by, breaking the limit, raising dust. This was where Looch had died, right about where he was standing. That side road marked with railroad signs and low bushes was where the red car had torpedoed out and slammed into him, hurling him and his car somewhere along this ditch.

But he wasn't here paying his respects to Looch — who didn't deserve it — or to curse the dead boy in the Corvette. He was here to reconstruct the night of the crash so he could relocate the gravel pit. They hadn't come far, after leaving that driveway in the pursuit of their lives, so it was just a matter of casting his mind back, reversing the trip, and looking for landmarks.

He got back into his car and drove south. He took the first left off the highway, then the first right, then sped up along the paved two-laner for two, three, four kilometres. An overpass told him he was near. He slowed, slowed further, and pulled over. *This is it.* The pull-off he stared at was wide enough to allow oversized equipment through. The weeds grew wild here. A soft wind brought that same stink of ditch water into the car. The same gate was swung shut but unpadlocked, and the same "no trespassing" sign in faded paint was stuck up on a post.

But there was also a startling difference. He stared, as he nosed his car against the gate, at the large white-and-blue Re/Max sign erected in the weeds. "God," he said. He read the smaller print. Eight-plus acres, commercial zoned. A realtor's smiling face and the number to call. The sign looked new.

He left the driver's seat once more, pushed the gate open, drove through, shut the gate, and drove half a kilometre into vaguely familiar territory. Other than the realtor's sign, little had changed. He parked the car amongst sand-and-gravel canyons, and stepped out onto asphalt chewed up by time. Hands in his jeans pockets, he looked around. Getting dark. Ghosts were out and about, rustling through the small bushes and leafy trees that lined the pit.

Other than the ghosts, he was alone. Just like then, he might as well be on the moon. He walked to what he believed was the location of the grave, and looked beyond for something he had tossed into the bushes back then, a ragged scrap of plywood, the makeshift shovel. He couldn't see it, but maybe with a high-powered flashlight …

He stood unsure, staring at the ground, scanning about. Maybe this wasn't the spot at all. Maybe it was over there. He walked the perimeter, using his phone flashlight to illuminate the place. The light was too weak to tell him much, but he remembered the ground as lumpier, earthier, more scrub pushing through the crust. It was neat and flat now, rubbly and rough but somehow tamped down.

Had the backhoes been in, shoving the dirt around? Why? Owners considering what to do with the land, finally deciding to sell? How long would it take for a buyer to move in and start ripping it up for construction? What would they build? Another warehouse, probably. Never enough warehouses in the valley.

One thing was for sure: once the machines started tossing the ground, life as he knew it would be over.

He didn't stay long. The place was as dead and desolate as he could hope for, and maybe it would stay that way for another year or two. Maybe that was all he needed, or wanted. He returned to his car and steered it in a loop, back to the gate. What had he achieved from this trip? Nothing but another knot in the gut.

Seventeen

SINKER

"HEY," JD TEMPLE SAID, as Leith got to work this morning. It was always *hey* with JD. Never *sir*, like with most of the other younger constables he worked with. Or *Dave*, which he would have expected, as they worked so closely together. But, *hey*?

This particular disrespectful *hey* wasn't a slack-assed *hello*, he noted. She had something to say.

"Joey Liu said something to his grandma Zan last night," JD told him. "She left a message on my machine. Want me to swing over there and check it out?"

Even key names in cases didn't always instantly snap into Leith's mind, because the lists could be long and his mind could be overtaxed. But Joey's he knew on the spot. Cute as a duckling, sad, dark eyes, the lone survivor found hidden in a kitchen cabinet. "I thought she took him back to Calgary."

"They're in town this week to visit her brother, make funeral arrangements. She was going to leave Joey in

Calgary, but she says he doesn't want to part from her, so she brought him along. Which is a good thing. We can see him in person, and they're not far. Blueridge."

After listening to the message with JD, Leith drove out with her to the home in the cookie-cutter suburbs above the Seymour River. Zan admitted them into a living room with Asian decor, scented with incense. The boy was not present, but Leith could see him through the living room's window, out in the backyard, playing with a large, bouncy black-and-white dog.

"I should get him one," Zan said. "He's four, young enough that a dog will help him mend. But something smaller. A Border Collie's a bit much. Maybe a Jack Russell, I think. I had a Jack Russell once. Smart as a whip."

"Can you tell us how it came about," Leith said, "that he disclosed?"

She shook her head. "It wasn't dramatic. I've enrolled him in Sunday school, which is new to him. He enjoys it. Takes comfort from the teachings. I believe that's what gave him the courage to remember. I have not urged him to speak. I believe it should come at his own pace. Well, after the last class he just said it to me, very simply, as we sat down for dinner. But I'll go bring him in, and you can ask him yourself."

The boy was in a better frame of mind now. Out of breath, but in a good way, like a typical four-year-old who's been running and jumping and wrestling with an energetic dog. He sat in the armchair, wriggling a bit because he wanted to get back to his new friend. Only when JD addressed him did he freeze and stare at her. Maybe her voice and face reminded him of the terrible blackness that was still so close. His eyes widened; his mouth shrank.

But JD smiled and talked to him about the dog, and other pleasant things, until he began to relax. She said to him in the same soothing voice, "Your grandma says you remember something and want to tell us about it. I'd like to know, too. Can you tell me?"

He bit his lip. She told him he was absolutely the bravest little boy she'd ever met. He looked guardedly pleased. She said, "Somebody was in the kitchen when you were hiding in the cabinet, hey? Can you tell me who that was?"

He shrugged and kicked restless heels against the base of the armchair. "An oga."

The mystery word Zan had relayed to Leith and JD, the word they needed to hear straight from the source. JD said, "An oga, eh? Was it a male or a female? Could you tell?"

"I don't remember."

"What was it doing?"

"I don't know."

"What did the oga look like?"

Joey didn't know that either, so he said it again. "Like an oga."

One of JD's brows went down as she looked back at Leith. Leith looked at Zan, who only shrugged at him. *Ogre*, all the adults were thinking. But nobody wanted to say it and taint the boy's memory. In case it was not an ogre, but an *oga*, something altogether different.

"Maybe show us what it looked like. Pretend you're the oga," JD said.

Joey grimaced and flailed his arms in mimicry of whatever it was he was recalling.

JD complimented his acting abilities. "So what was it wearing, the oga?"

"I don't know," Joey said again. He hugged his arms around himself and went silent. Then spoke again, viciously. "A hat."

JD asked for details of the hat, but Joey couldn't say, except it was dark. Maybe black. Neither could he recall what else the oga was wearing, or its face or hair, or whether it had on any jewellery. JD asked if he could draw the oga. He took the pad and pencil she gave him, and drew a blob with big round eyes and a big round mouth. An oga indeed.

"Can you draw what it wore on its head?" she said.

He drew a large shape on the oga's head that might have been a ten-gallon hat.

"Did it see you?" she asked. "Was it looking at you?"

Joey blinked, squeezed his eyes shut, said he didn't know.

"Did it talk to you?"

Joey thought about it, and said in a strange blurting monotone, "Give us food and give us sins and save us from temptation and save us from the evil one."

"It said that?"

"Yeah," Joey said.

"Did it say this loudly or quietly?"

Joey didn't know. Leith suspected it was composite false memory. JD said, "Was this oga there before you got in the cabinet, or after?"

Joey said nothing for a moment, then, "Mama said to hide. I went inside there. I saw him."

Ah good, Leith thought. *The oga is a he.*

Joey sat up straighter in a listening mode, but probably only because the dog outside was barking, eager to play. Leith was distracted, too; something had caught his eye on the wall beside him, a framed photograph of Cheryl and Lance Liu.

JD said, "Can you tell me again what he said?"

"Save us from temptation," Joey said, heels banging. "Our fodder who art in heaven."

Leith divided his attention between the photograph and the boy.

JD was looking stumped. She said, "Did you shut the cabinet door, Joey?"

Without warning Joey began to cry. Uncontrollably.

Later, after Zan Liu had comforted the boy and he was once again outside at play, she said, "I'm sorry. He didn't say anything about the Lord's Prayer before. He must be getting confused. I wanted him to know his mama is in heaven, so we talk about that a lot. We pray. My son and daughter-in-law were not churchgoers. So it's quite new to him."

Leith could understand Zan teaching Joey about a sweet afterlife. He had seen children traumatized or dying, in the course of his career, and yes, he would prefer them to believe in heaven. He wished he could believe in it himself, as he once had.

"Do you think he means ogre?" he asked her.

"No doubt. Lance used to tell him monster stories all the time. I told him not to give the child nightmares. But Joey liked them. He didn't have nightmares. Now he does."

"How long are you in town for, ma'am?"

"Lots of family to visit, so probably a couple of weeks."

"Okay, good. If he says anything else of interest, please let us know right away."

"I will, sir," Zan said to Leith, and bowed her head at JD.

Leith beckoned JD over to the photograph on the wall and pointed out what had snagged his attention. Not the attractive couple, Lance and Cheryl, but what stood on the table behind them. A squarish, repurposed liquor bottle sporting a sprig of dry flowers, snapping into place Dion's missing vase — barely noted, quickly buried, and completely forgotten, till now.

This bottle was blue. Bombay Sapphire.

* * *

They drove away from the little house in the suburbs, considering what they had learned. The Bombay Sapphire bottle had been at the Lius', then. Not a vessel for booze, but a vase. That was something. And then there was Joey's cryptic tale.

"Well, you predicted he'd have something to tell us," Leith said, studying the drawing the boy had provided, a portrait of a killer, but not something he could very well post on the Wanted board. "And you were absolutely right. I'm just not sure what it is."

Behind the wheel, JD looked disappointed. "Ogres," she said. "In cowboy hats. Spouting the Lord's Prayer. Good start. Weird, though. Who shut the cabinet door?"

"I'm betting it wasn't the ogre," Leith said.

"And who took the baby bootie, put it in the bottle, and threw it in the ocean?"

"Again, not the ogre."

JD agreed. "There was a second person there. A person with a conscience."

"A person under duress, maybe. Who's under this guy's thumb. Tossing the bottle was his or her only opportunity to send us a message."

"And one way or another, that person under duress was on or near the water at some point. Or else ..." JD held up a finger, "... he or she dropped it off the bridge."

Leith had sent the Stubbs' coordinates to the tech department, which had consulted an oceanographer of some sort who could best line up tide and current and provide at least a good guess as to where that little blue gin bottle had been dropped in for it to turn up where it did, in the middle of Burrard Inlet, just off Deep Cove, not far from Indian Arm. With several variables taken into account, the options had been highlighted in a preliminary report, telling Leith the drop had likely occurred from one of the far shores, Port Moody to the south or Burnaby Mountain Park to the west, but most likely somewhere in the middle of the inlet, which could mean from a boat, which had given him some hope of narrowing the equation. But with a bridge thrown in ...

"Or a small plane," JD added.

Leith made a mental note to add the possibility to the exponentially expanding list.

"That's what I want to be when I grow up," JD went on, looking moodily at the heavy grey clouds on the horizon rising upward into the silvery skies like a slow-motion explosion. "A bush pilot."

"You are grown up, and you're a detective, and a damned good one," Leith said.

His compliment seemed to unsettle her. "You don't even know me. Trust me, I'm not a good detective. I don't like puzzles, never have. I don't like anyone I work with, especially the white-shirts. And sorry, yeah, even the motto gets up my nose."

Leith bridled. He loved the motto, *Maintiens le Droit*, which he believed meant *uphold the law*. And he admired the commissioned officers, and aspired to be one, someday. Maybe he didn't care for some of his coworkers, particularly, but he still considered them all family. As for puzzles, like JD, he had never much cared for them, but that wouldn't stop him trying to bang in the pieces, even if they were the wrong ones. He said, "You knew Luciano Ferraro. Was he a good friend?"

She made a rude squirting noise. "Looch? No. Loud, opinionated class-A asshole, good riddance to him, may he rot in hell."

Leith didn't pursue it. He watched the skies, cloud heavy. He thought he saw lightning, way over there where the darkness began.

On return to the detachment, he told JD to go ahead, he had forgotten something in his car, and initiated Stage 2 of his unendorsed, possibly illegal undercover operation. He crossed the lower level of the parkade to his personal vehicle. He opened the glovebox, rummaged, took out an old gas receipt for authenticity, shut the glovebox, locked the car, and headed back to the stairs. Passing Dion's car, he crouched as if to pick up a dropped pen, and grabbed the tracker from the wheel well while he was at it. Then he was on his way again, blushing and edgy, a bad actor, a terrible spy. His act would be caught on surveillance video, but if all went well, it would never come to light.

In the hallway upstairs he found JD talking with Jimmy Torr and Cal Dion. They didn't look happy. They spotted Leith and summoned him over, as if they had a score to settle and he was the appointed judge.

"Sigmund Blatt's gone," JD told him. "Employer reported he wasn't showing up for shift."

"Disappeared from his digs in Calgary," Torr said. He held a paper cup in one hand, Starbucks logo, a little drift of steam escaping from its sip hole. "Calgary's on the BOLO for him. I'm thinking we better get over there. If he's not dead, he's maybe being held captive. All I'm saying is we should be there when it hits the fan, right?"

Dion spoke up now. His hands were stuck in his trouser pockets in a carefree way, but there was nothing carefree about his face, overheated and damp looking. "He'll show up," he said. "He's scared, that's all. He's gone into hiding."

Torr said, "And how d'you figure that? Some real hardass terminated the Lius, and this Blatt dick told us he'd be next, which is why he skipped town. So he's got something to hide, and maybe this thing is bigger than we think. Maybe we're talking hit list. Maybe the hit's followed him east. What's to say he's not already dead?"

"Because he took the bird with him," Dion said.

Leith said, "Bird?"

"What bird?" Torr said. "What the fuck you talking about, bird?"

"His pet bird, the one in the cage he had when we talked to him." Dion was staring at Torr as if he wasn't quite possible. "You think the hitman took it, too, in case it talked? Or not to separate them, maybe? Out of the goodness of his heart?"

Something dawned in Jimmy Torr's eyes. "The parrot? What d'you mean he took it with him? I talked to Calgary, you didn't, and nobody mentioned anything about a parrot."

Dion was raising his voice, too. "Because you didn't ask, so I did. I called 'em back and asked, and they said there was no bird in the townhouse when they searched it, but there was a stand and birdseed scattered around. So he either delivered it somewhere or took it with him, which means his disappearance was at least partly planned, so it was voluntary, so he's probably fine. Not too bright, but fine."

"Be nice if you told me all this at the time," Torr snapped.

"I did," Dion snapped back. "You just didn't hear. Too busy listening to that weird buzzing sound between your ears."

Torr opened his mouth to answer, but Leith flagged both men to silence. "Hold it. I didn't see anything about a talking bird in any of the reports. Let's hear a bit more."

"Some fucking noisy parrot Blatt had in his apartment," Torr said.

"It's a cockatoo," Dion said. "I Googled it. Blatt took good care of it. It had a clean cage, lots of toys. It looked happy."

Torr said to Leith, "Whatever it was, however it *felt*, it was a pet bird, and it wasn't relevant to our enquiries."

"It is now, isn't it?" Dion said.

Pissed off, Torr shot out an arm — maybe just an over-elaborate gesture — and it was the hand with the Starbucks Venti. The lid popped off and coffee splashed out. Dion stepped back, but not fast enough. Possibly he was hit in the face by some of the hot liquid, which was possibly why he stepped forward and shoved Torr in the chest.

The details of the skirmish that followed lost distinction in Leith's mind. Torr staggered and his cup flew. JD yelped as she was sprayed. Torr came back with a grab at Dion's necktie, whereupon Dion's arms went up to defend himself from strangulation, after which the situation became messy and ridiculous. A crowd gathered to enjoy the show. Watch Commander Corporal Paley appeared, not to enjoy himself so much as put an end to things fast.

Half an hour later, Leith was obligated to describe the hallway battle to Mike Bosko. He did so, and added in his frustration, "Grown men in suits bashing each other like kids in a playground, be lucky if this doesn't hit the press. They should both be given the boot."

"Not the boot," Bosko said. "But I'll have a talk with them."

As he returned to his desk, Leith thought over what he hadn't told Bosko. That in his opinion Dion knew that the coffee hadn't been tossed with malicious intent, that he hadn't been scalded or injured in any way, and it was just an excuse to fight. Neither had Leith told Bosko anything about the war of words Dion had exchanged with Sean Urbanski earlier this week. This worried him. What if Bosko heard about it through the grapevine? He wouldn't like being kept in the dark, might lose his trust in Leith, with reverberations all down that wobbly ladder of promotion Leith so wanted to climb.

"A" Watch left for the day, but he remained at his desk, in a pocket of silence. He was looking at his computer screen, at the map that the tracker provided, the route Dion had taken out to Cloverdale, the route Leith should probably not follow himself, on his first day off, if he had any sense.

Where was Dion now? Sent home, but was that where he had gone? After the fight was quashed he had calmed down, looking at his knuckles in wonder. Then wrapped his arms over his head like an athlete who had just flubbed a gold medal competition. Paley had lectured him on professionalism and self-control and told him to go home, report in tomorrow first thing for further discussion.

With Dion gone, Paley gathered those who had witnessed the fight to talk it over, to see if anyone was going to make noise about it. Leith sensed it was more a question of getting their stories straight than a disciplinary exercise. Torr said he didn't care, JD said she didn't either, and Leith didn't foresee anyone else here making waves. But he did see rough waters ahead.

Eighteen

ZEPHYR

DION DIDN'T SHOW UP IN the morning, but it wasn't Leith's problem. He went back to brainstorming with the others about the missing parrot. Or cockatoo. JD suggested that if someone had kidnapped Blatt, they might have taken the bird in case it got noisy as it got hungry, and the noise would alert the neighbours. Leith didn't think so. Those birds were noisy round the clock, in his experience. JD said the hitman might not consider that. Leith told her no, he just didn't see a hitman carting off a full-grown man along with his pet bird in a large cage. He believed Dion was right, that Blatt had taken himself, and bird, AWOL.

Leith made some calls and learned from Blatt's townhouse neighbour in Calgary that Sigmund Blatt was "kind of a paranoid weirdo," and yeah, he had this cockatoo that talked pretty good English. It could sing "O Canada," but other than that, pretty well all it had to say were taunts, one-liners, and profanities. The neighbour wasn't surprised that Blatt had vanished. "Like I said, he was paranoid. He wasn't about to tell me where he was headed, was he? I'm just a neighbour, not a friend. But he was spooked."

"Did he seem to have any friends?"

"One rude cockatoo. How sad is that?"

Leith spoke to Blatt's employer as well, a Mr. Ray Duhammond, who ran an electrical contracting firm in Calgary. It was the same firm Blatt had left last year, to move out here to the coast to start his own company with his now-dead partner Lance Liu. Duhammond had taken Blatt back because he was short of linemen. He had already been grilled by the Calgary police and was fairly snappy with Leith, saying he didn't know where Blatt was now. He ended the call, "When you find him, tell him if he wants a third chance he can kiss my sparky ass." Which Leith had to assume was electrician lingo.

He promised to pass on the message, hung up, and went on to the next task. It was going to be a long day, and they were short a man — damn it.

* * *

Sometimes morning brought answers and fresh starts, but not today. Dion stayed in bed and inspected the congealed blood on his right fist. It stung. The knuckles had ripped across Torr's metal cufflinks, that's what had done it. Ripped the skin. He had sabotaged himself yesterday, taking a crack at Torr like that, but it was a good thing, in the end. It took the guesswork out of his future. It put him on the road.

Sun flares skewed by traffic slid across the ceiling. There had been no alarm clock beeping this morning, no texts or phone calls, because he had turned everything off. The sleep meds had dazed him but not knocked him out.

Now it was nearly eleven, checkout time. He rolled out of bed. He showered and shaved and got dressed. He went downstairs to the hotel's restaurant. The place had character, but it was empty. It was probably empty because the food was bland, and the food was bland because the cook no longer cared. He no longer cared because his days were numbered; the hotel was slated for destruction by the end of the year, and another high-rise would stand here soon, adding more pressure to the Earth's crust. The vertical growth in North Van was causing traffic jams, bottlenecks, and road rage. Home, to Dion, was feeling less like home every day.

Over a cup of coffee he knocked his notebook flat with a fist and tried to list his options.

The paper remained blank, and his eyes filled with tears. The heavy old waitress was eying him from her resting spot behind the counter. He palmed away the tears. He knew nothing except police work. He had joined up straight out of high school, gone to training depot in Regina alone, and come back to the coast as a member of the largest family in the world.

Probably leaving like this, abruptly and in disgrace, would bar him from working in any police force. Security guard was out of the question — nothing in a uniform. Suicide seemed logical, but he had thought it through, and knew he wouldn't. Mechanics, computers, clerical, service industry, mining — nothing fit. Some ex-cops got into the consulting business or opened security firms, but those were the ones with their faculties intact.

Maybe he could go out to the oil fields of Alberta, where a man like him could learn on the job and make good money while he was at it. Even with the slump in the gas industry these days, there would be something for him there if he pushed hard enough.

"You all right?" the waitress said. Though he'd seen her often during his stay, all he knew of her was the name pinned to her frock, Raquel.

He realized how he must look. Dreadful and red-eyed. He said, "I lost my job."

She had a bulldog face, breathed like an asthmatic, never smiled. She nodded. "Yeah, that's tough. But you know what? You're young and healthy, so don't you forget to count your blessings. Okay?"

It sounded like an order. She refilled his cup and walked away, wheezing.

Dion paid his bill and handed in the key, telling the desk clerk of his plan, to set it in stone. "Going east. Alberta, probably."

He hauled his two oversized duffel bags of belongings out to his car, feeling jittery. He still had furniture and appliances in storage, and some personal items Kate was holding on to for him, but he would deal with it all another time. Now that his mind was made up to go, he wanted to put the miles down fast. A gentle, warm wind blew in from the west and rippled his T-shirt. He had the trunk open and was stuffing in the bigger bag when a low-slung silver car entered the lot behind him with a throaty purr. He stopped packing and watched it slip into a slot not far from where he stood. A man and woman stepped out.

He knew them all — the car, the man, and the woman. The woman wore a filmy red dress with fluttering kimono sleeves. She was tall and curvy and managed to hold herself in a way that was both careless and photo-worthy. Jamie Paquette. The man with her was Jon York, and that was the Nissan that had been parked in the York driveway in Deep Cove.

York had his hand on Paquette's hip as they talked and seemed to lean in toward her, maybe to whisper something in her ear but more likely to plant a kiss. But Paquette spied Dion, stepped back, and said something. York turned to look at him with surprise. He left Paquette by the car and approached with a grin. "Wow, this is awkward," he said. Hands up, *don't shoot.* "I can guess what you're thinking, but you're all wrong, I swear, Officer." He stopped as he spied the giant duffel bag half-crammed into the trunk, and his brows went up. "You've been slumming? *Here?*"

"Just leaving," Dion said. He slammed the trunk and looked pointedly east, away from the ocean he had once considered his lifeblood, toward the Rockies and Alberta beyond. "I'm quitting the force. Going to find work in the oil fields."

"You're shitting me. Why?"

Dion shrugged. "Time for a change." The woman in red was dragging at his line of vision, spotlit in the sun. So he angled his body away from her, asking York what brought him here. Though he could pretty well guess.

York jerked his thumb toward Paquette, who paced at the side of the sleek car. She had her back turned to the grubby brickwork of the Royal Arms and was watching the entrance to the parking lot. "She's got a meeting with an agent. That was a good-luck kiss you saw. I'm just her chauffeur."

"Oh. What sort of agent?"

"Talent. It's a euphemism, but don't tell her I said so." York laughed. "We were all hoping she'd change her ways, go back to school and become an astrophysicist, but it's not going to happen. With Oz dead, she's decided to go back to the stage. Not the thespian type."

Another car pulled in, an older-model Corolla with a crunched rear panel and duct-tape over the door frame, and parked next to the Nissan. A heavy man struggled out from behind the wheel and stood straightening his suit.

"God," York said. "Don't tell me that's him."

The man strode around to Paquette, firing his index finger at her. Dion could overhear the conversation, but barely. "Wow, you've changed," the man told Paquette. "Man, you're hot. Hot, hot, hot. Tssst, ouch!"

"You say that every time, jerk." Paquette was grinning.

"But this time you're hotter. And fatter, but I like it."

Fatter? The two walked toward the hotel lobby, and the conversation faded, with more compliments from the agent: "And what'd you do with your hair, kid? No, it's fab. You're going to have lineups 'round the block."

York cupped his hand and shouted, "Jamie. Going to call?"

Paquette turned and waved at him. "Yeah, I'll call."

Dion watched the talent agent open the glass doors and Paquette step inside. The door eased shut. "She's not staying here, is she?" He couldn't imagine anyone transitioning from the Roth house to these rooms, with their rattly mini-fridges and bar music thudding up through the floor.

"No, she's staying with us, till her life gets sorted. They're just meeting for coffee, talk over the percentages. She wanted me to drive her to his office on Richards, but I said no. Give an inch with that girl, she'll take a mile. I said meet at the mall. No, she wanted to come here. It's quiet, she says. She's not keen about crowds. So I gave her a lift."

"Then how's she going to cope with dancing? That's all about crowds." Dion thought about Jamie Paquette under the black lights, up on stage and snapping the bands of her G-string. The image was vivid, and lust did not mix well with depression.

York shrugged. "Oz is gone and she needs money. I guess she'll have to get over it."

Dion said, "You've got a stage. Is she going to work for you?"

"That was the original plan. That's how Oz met her. Saw her in a club in Vancouver, got all possessive, told her he was opening a club pretty soon, promised her a long-term gig, with perks. But he fell for her long before opening day, and he wouldn't have let her dance even if she wanted to. As it happens, she pretty well stays clear of Diamonds. Not sure why."

"Well," Dion said, and jingled his keys, a man with important places to go.

York said, "Hey." He had a freckled, open face, an easy smile, and about the kindest blue eyes Dion had ever seen, the kind of kindness that made him wary. "Tell you what," the club owner said. "I'm heading over to the joint. Come on down and I'll buy you a drink. I'm fascinated with this seismic shift you're making. I want to hear more."

By *the joint* he meant Diamonds.

Tempting, if only because Dion had been wanting to take a look around inside. But it wasn't going to work. The last thing he needed was to be distracted off his chosen path. "No, thanks, Jon. I appreciate it, but it's late. I gotta hit the road."

"How about if I insist?"

A slight hesitation sealed Dion's fate. York smiled and clapped him on the back. "Great, see you there in ten."

* * *

The entranceway was low key, just a black metal door with *D*I*A*M*O*N*D*S* stencilled across it. At the top of a flight of stairs was a foyer with sofas and a coat-check counter. Then, through swing doors, the dance floor itself, silent now. On the water side were floor-to-ceiling windows and doors leading out to a covered deck. Out here the air was heavy with brine and slightly rank. The view at night, York said, was spectacular.

He pointed out at stairs leading down to a dock. "That's our white elephant. Phase II. We were going to have a dance boat, barge-sized — well, mini-barge-size — for charters. Or special events."

"What happened? Why isn't it going ahead?"

York smiled, though something like annoyance flickered in his eyes. "Seems we overreached a bit. Kind of hard to offer dance boat cruises without a cruise boat to dance on, isn't it? We ended up scaling back. Maybe next year."

Back inside, Dion saw a nightclub much like any other nightclub he had ever visited. Maybe it was the hour, or the silence, or his own low mood, but he didn't find the place inspiring. It was just a businessman's daydream of what a nightclub ought to be. Its theme, to go with the name, was plenty of mirrors and glitter and twinkly LED stars strung everywhere. When the lights went down, probably the lasers would start to flash and the disco ball would rotate. He took in the elongated S-shaped bar for serving drinks, two diamond-shaped stages with brass poles. A glassed-in DJ booth. There was purple upholstered seating along one wall, barstools and counter along another, with several table-and-chair sets around the periphery. The best feature of the place was the large, open floor space. The floor tiles were translucent Plexiglas, no doubt underlit.

"Great place," he said. "Is this some kind of millionaires' club?"

"Not millionaires, but a deep pocket helps."

"Where does the elevator go?"

"Unfinished."

"Unfinished what?"

York took him up to show off what he called the second white elephant. A short elevator ride took them to an upper level, and they stepped out onto raw plywood. The room had a wraparound view of harbour, city, and mountains. The walls were Gyproc'd but not taped or mudded. From the layout, Dion guessed it was set up to be a luxury living space, and York confirmed it. "Our guest suite, for celebs and oil barons. But again, we put the cart before the horse. You want to hear the story?"

"Sure."

"In a word, overextended. The residential permits wouldn't go through without a lot of expensive structural rejigging. So instead, we're going to convert it to offices, maybe a rental boardroom. Which was probably a better idea to start with."

A fine leather sofa set was arranged in what would have been a living room, incongruous against the raw wood and unfinished walls. Also incongruous were shimmery blue drapes covering windows that still bore factory decals. People had been making themselves comfortable here, Dion realized, with or without a permit. He said, "Wow, I could live in a place like this."

York shrugged. "I've let friends stay here a time or two. Bending the rules a bit, but hardly a federal offence. Looks like I've spoiled your travel plans, so if you end up with nowhere to stay tonight, you're welcome to camp out on the sofa."

The offer was generous, strange, and startling. Dion said, "Well, thanks. I appreciate that. But I'll figure something out."

They returned to the empty club. Dion was still thinking about the highway. He asked what time the doors would be opening.

"Two," York said. "Today is Friday, we have the girls till nine, no cover charge. At ten the DJ's in. We run till about 3:00 a.m. on weekends. Weekdays are slower than we expected, so we're closed now Monday to Wednesday. But Sunday bookings are making up for it. It's like any new venture, a learning process, you know. Win some, lose some."

For financial wizards, Jon York and Oscar Roth seemed to have done a lot of overshooting and scaling back. But they were just getting started, and like York said, it was a process. The city was growing fast, and true, there weren't enough choices for late-night entertainment on this side of the bridge.

York was looking up at one of the two silent stages with what looked like moodiness or maybe regret. "Oscar wanted to get the ladies in," he said. "Start a tradition. So we're planning an inaugural ladies night, next month. Seems like a gamble to me, but maybe he's right. It'll be a hit."

"Probably will be a hit," Dion agreed, though he wasn't so sure.

After an awkward silence, he said again what a great place it was. He hadn't made a move toward the purple booth seat with low table that York was gesturing at. "Thanks for the tour, but I better shove off now."

"No, you're not shoving off," York laughed. "You haven't told me your life story yet. Sit down. No, sit down, that's an order."

A man arrived, said hello to York, and stepped into the DJ booth. A microphone screeched. Bar staff were also arriving. Music began, a suspenseful beat that said *sexy flesh pending*. Dion looked at his watch. Not quite

2:00 p.m., which meant the girls would be onstage soon. He took a seat in the purple booth York had indicated. A brass plaque on the wall above the upholstery said "VIP."

"What'll you have?" York said.

Dion asked for anything on tap. His mood was lifting, maybe because he really didn't want to hit the highway tonight, and York was making it impossible. Or maybe it was a lot baser than that: the girls were on their way.

York brought over an ice water for himself, and for Dion, a bottle of Sapporo and tall, frosted glass. He relaxed back and said, "So tell me why you quit. It's just that it really pisses me off, because who's going to solve my good friend's murder now?"

"Everyone who hasn't quit, that's who."

"I don't want everyone who's not quit working on Oscar's case. I want you. I could tell, the minute I saw you, that you're a good, serious cop, and you'd get things done."

Dion told York that he was changing his career path, and there really wasn't much more to say about it, sorry.

He expected things to wrap up fast, now that he wasn't being a sport, after all York's hospitality. But York seemed unoffended, and switched the topic back to the girls. He described who was up this week, their particular charms and special features. "Not top-of-the-line," he admitted. "This batch. But they're real." He grinned and winked.

Waitstaff were setting up the tables nearby with snacks and cocktail napkins. York bantered with them, and they bantered back.

The waitstaff, Dion could tell, liked their boss. He, too, was beginning to admire York, considering what he was going through, and how he was handling it. York was running what looked like an impossible show, single-handed. He had an easy relationship with trouble, something Dion could use lessons in. And to top it off, the man had dashing good looks.

A dark-skinned woman approached, a flashy dresser, maybe a dancer. York stood to talk with her on some scheduling level, her hand on his arm in sympathy or affection. York introduced her to Dion, and Dion stood to shake her hand.

This was Ziba, not a dancer but stage manager. Ziba made a show of checking him out. "Auditioning? Nice hire, Jon." She gave Dion a smile and walked away. When she looked back, he smiled at her, too. What did it take to get back in the flirting game? It was nothing. It was muscle-memory, like riding a bike.

He turned his smile to York, minus the suggestion. York had brought another Sapporo, on the house.

A mostly male audience began to fill the tables and bar stools. York sat next to Dion, closer than any fellow police officer would dream of doing. But that was that culture, and this was this, and body contact was permitted here, even expected. "What I'm going to do," York said — he had switched from water to hard liquor — "is show you a good time tonight, then you're going to go out into the world and tell everyone how fantastic my club is. Is that fair?"

Dion said it was fair.

York left him to go speak with others, friends or staff or customers, Dion didn't know. He was fine with that. With a drumroll and DJ intro, Girl Number 1 walked onstage.

She was too young, trying to look haughty but failing. He could see her blush behind her makeup, and he could see her fear. York was right, she wasn't top-of-the-line, but she was real. York kept busy with his crowd of friends or fans, and some of those friends and fans came to keep Dion company. They were entertaining, too, and the drinks kept arriving. Dion began to forget his troubles and spent much of his time enjoying himself. Hard to believe, but that person he could hear laughing out loud was himself. From time to time he sought York out with his eyes, keeping tabs on him, for no particular reason. Last week he had written off York as a suspect. This afternoon he had come to wonder if he had written him off too soon. The question was, did he care?

Nineteen

HEAT

EARLY MORNING, NOT QUITE seven. The sun had climbed the mountain ranges to the south and was flaring its rays across the flatlands of Surrey. Leith was following the course of Dion's travels those few days ago, out along straight roads through farmers' fields into serene Cloverdale. He had a doughnut and a cup of dark-roast coffee along for the ride. CBC played on the radio, a talk show about the wolf cull. He stuck to the speed limit of eighty, though these roads that spanned out like runways begged a driver to floor it.

There were no witnesses to his passage but cows and flocks of starlings. He turned up 168th and pulled over. He sat regretting the doughnut, for his fingers were now sticky. He wiped them on a napkin dampened with the remains of his coffee, then stepped out to study the scene. Cars and trucks tore by on 56th, everyone going over the limit. He walked up and down the roadside. This was where the crash had occurred. The fool in him expected blood and car bits, but of course there was nothing here but grit and dust.

In the car again, he looked at the tracker's path. The path didn't end here and didn't circle around and head back home, either. It led that way. He restarted the car and drove, turned off busy 56th onto a quiet side road, and from there onto an even quieter side road that beelined between fields and train tracks. He drove for a distance until the tracker told him to turn again, up that rough driveway. He parked facing a metal swing gate. A sign told him not to trespass. Another sign said the place was for sale. He walked over and found the gate unlocked. He pushed it open and drove through. Got out, shut the gate. Back in his car, he checked the tracker info and saw that Dion had driven about half a kilometre along this gravel road before the trip had come to its end.

He followed and found himself at a large plateau of busted asphalt overshadowed by heaps of sand and gravel. The heaps were old enough to host several generations of dandelions and shrubs. An old shed stood over there amongst the saplings. He stepped out. Underfoot, the weeds were discovering cracks in the blacktop and taking back the land. Above, a hawk circled. He listened to the silence. Great place for a nefarious meeting. Or for disposal of a body. Plenty of loose grit. Ideal. He trudged about, kicking at the earth and drifts of gravel.

Maybe it wasn't a body at all, but loot of some kind, or damning evidence. Maybe the thing was already scooped and taken away.

None of Leith's searches had turned up any unsolved crime that he could remotely tie to the timeline that began last July, to Dion, to Luciano Ferraro, nobody and nothing had gone missing around the day of the crash, no big heists, drug busts. But that didn't mean it didn't happen.

He returned to his car. As he drove the desolate road back to Highway 99, his phone rang. *Alison.* That name flashing on his phone always made his heart race. Had there been an accident? Was Izzy hurt? Or stolen? Or *dead?*

He pulled over too abruptly, tires skittering against the shoulder grit, and slapped the phone to his ear. "Ali?"

"Good morning to you, too," Alison said.

Her tone was normal, and the blips of his heartbeat slowed. "What's up?" Already he was moving on, impatient, fingers drumming at the steering wheel as the engine idled.

"You left an urgent message for me to call, is what's up," she said.

"Did I? Sorry, yes, I did. It's just last night I got to thinking, we should hold off on the sale till I decide what to do here. Maybe we'll rent the house out for a year or so. Maybe we'll end up back there. You know?"

She gave it a moment and said, "Walking backward is harder than it looks."

Leith's window was down, and somewhere a red-winged blackbird shrilled its distinctive cry, urgent and forlorn. Another answered from across the field. From where he sat, the city seemed galaxies away. He said, "You're probably right, babe. I'm glad you'll be in my arms again soon. Even if it's just for a few days. Really glad."

Another pause. She said, "Something's bothering you."

"Well, yes, something's bothering me." He gestured so wide his fingers cracked against the steering wheel. He sucked the knuckles. "This whole housing fiasco," he said. "Why didn't someone warn me? Why didn't I warn myself? Do a little research? Maybe put an iota of thought into this move beforehand?"

"No. It's something deeper I'm hearing. Like you're really, really troubled."

What was troubling was Alison knew him better than he knew himself. Joey Liu bothered him, and Oscar Roth bothered him, but right now the gravel pit bothered him most of all. He said, "I missed breakfast."

She was unconvinced. "Go get something to eat, then. I've booked the flight. Call me tonight?"

"I sure will."

He left Surrey behind and joined the heavy traffic pounding toward Vancouver. Alison was right, he was troubled, more than he even realized. Frankly, there was only one way to unload that trouble and get back to normal. It was high time to talk to Mike Bosko, give him the lowdown. Dust his hands and walk away.

* * *

Dion woke to brightness, not sure at first where he was. The air smelled like drywall dust. He was stretched out on a leather sofa, fully clothed but no shoes, with a Mexican-style throw blanket over his lower half. The sofa wasn't quite long enough to accept his length, but it was comfortable. One window was partially uncovered, and he watched a lone gull cross the sky. Thick glass didn't quite mute the shunting crashes of trains down by the wheat silos; otherwise the room was silent.

He recalled what had put him here. Too many drinks and Jon York's generosity. It hadn't seemed weird last night, but now that he was sober he had to wonder. He tilted his head to test for the mind-splitting headache that usually came with heavy drinking. Not too bad. He ran a palm over the flatness of his stomach and realized he had missed dinner. What a night, though. Hanging out with Jon York in the purple VIP booth for hours, watching the action.

Conversations came back to him in muddled bytes. York went on and on about a project he had going in West Van. The house of his dreams, under construction, almost to lock-up stage. Had photos on his phone, endless photos. Even brought over a laptop to Google-Earth it, show everyone how his new property sat like a barnacle over the inlet waters.

But even with York going on about his dream house, it had been a great night, great music, nonstop fun. The VIP booth never slowed. People crushed up next to Dion with drinks, and wild stories that didn't always climax. Somebody kissed him. Melanie York had shown up at some point. In retrospect, he understood why. She had come to chauffeur Jon home, because he wasn't fit to drive.

He recalled her waving at him, and couldn't remember waving back.

He returned with an effort to the scary question of what next. On his phone he found two text messages from Mike Bosko, separated by several hours, asking him to call ASAP. He switched off the phone and stuck it in his pocket. He would deal with it later.

Twenty

A TURNING TIDE

LEITH CALLED ZAN LIU TO let her know they were making progress in the murder investigation of her son, daughter-in-law, and granddaughter. He didn't tell her the progress was pathetic and the leads were probably false, and that, in fact, Lance's partner and friend, Sigmund Blatt, was now missing, which only complicated the file. She didn't need to know all this. She thanked him for keeping her informed. He thanked her for her patience.

Immediately after disconnecting from Zan Liu, he turned back to the Roth case, reviewing the witness statements, Cleo Irvine's in particular, the dead man's ex-wife. On his first talk with her, she had not struck him as moved by Oscar's death. In fact, what had she said? He looked up the verbatim quote. Oz was a "walking waft of bad karma." Too touchy for his own good, and he rarely thought twice. About anything.

Besides that bit of spiritual slander, she had little to

offer. By the end of the interview Leith had her summed up as cool but not complicit, and JD agreed.

That was several days ago. Now he collected JD to go and speak to the ex-widow — if that was the correct term — once more. Now that she had possession of the luxury home and the disturbed little girl, Dallas, what were her plans? Would she trench in and try to control Diamonds, or sell the shares? If she sold, who would buy? Jon York? Would he then become the King of Diamonds?

And was that his motive? Had he killed his partner and good friend to gain full control?

"What do you know about corporate structure?" Leith asked JD as she drove up to the gates of the Roth home and rolled through.

"Nothing."

Neither did he. The plateau at the end of the driveway was busy with vehicles. There was a bright red Kia that probably belonged to Cleo Irvine, and a couple of vans with contractor logos on their sides. A man on a ride-on lawn mower burred along the green. Window washers were setting up a scaffold. JD said, "Already fixing to sell, I guess."

Up by the front door, Leith rang the bell. Cleo greeted them, looking not like the lady of the manor but part of the cleaning staff, with her fine brown hair in an untidy bun, no makeup, and clothes fit for scrubbing floors. But instead of a mop and rubber gloves she had a businesslike camera around her neck. She didn't seem to recognize Leith from their first meeting, but he wasn't surprised. She had been digesting some big news then, and no doubt in her eyes he had been nothing but a large blur asking questions.

"How long is this going to take?" she asked now, as she led them inside. In the spanking-clean foyer, every article picked up light and bounced it back in starbursts. "Not to be rude, but I'm in the middle of documenting this place for the ad. The agent took some snaps, but low-res. Figure I'll get better offers if people can actually see what they're getting for their buck." She reviewed her last shot, and grimaced. "I've never been here before, you know, until today. Knowing Oscar, I expected ostentatious with a capital O, but this is ridiculous. Have you ever seen such an overgrown fungus?"

She paused to peer through her viewfinder at the broad staircase, her body welded into a living tripod. "D'you think using wide angle is false advertising?" she said. But she didn't expect an answer. Snick, snick, and they moved on, past the dining room and into what was probably called a breakfast nook next to the showroom kitchen.

Leith and JD took chairs by the window. Cleo sat across from them, removed the camera from around her neck, and said, "First of all, thanks for handing over the crime scene so quick. I know it wasn't easy for you people. I just hate things hanging over my head. I'm anal that way. Second, let me tell you about Oz and what makes him tick, because I'm sure you're interested. I got to know his parents before they died. They're old money, I mean really old money, and they cherished Oz. So he grew up not knowing there's such thing as adversity. Or the word *No*. Always got what he wanted. But for all that, he could be a nice enough guy, when he wasn't being an unholy idiot. Smarter than you'd think, too. What went wrong in our marriage?" she tacked on, as Leith opened his mouth to ask his first question.

Speeding things along, and doing a good job of it too, he thought, impressed.

"Probably Dallas," she answered herself. "What Dallas turned out to be, that was the first time in his life he couldn't get what he wanted. She was meant to be perfect, you see. His perfect little princess. He had her life plotted out from first birthday party to grad to wedding day to business partner. You should have seen him when he first got to hold her. He was weeping with joy. Pretty quick we realized she wasn't reacting as a newborn should, and the specialists were called in, and bingo, everything went sour."

Leith irritated her by interjecting a question. "Did you know Melanie, his sister? Was she spoiled in the same way he was?"

"No. Being a girl, she was pretty well left to go find a rich husband. That or get a job. She didn't do so well with the job, sounds like, but the husband was a perfect score. Jon, what a peach. Anyway, if I can continue. It's a bit of a shock for me, having Dallas. I would like to love her. Many of those kids are lovable, but not Dallas. How can you love someone who won't even look you in the eye? I have hired help for now, but I will be setting up a more stable long-term arrangement for her. Yes, she will live with me, unless I find it's detrimental to either of us. If invested even semi-wisely, the money I receive from the sale of this place will cover her expenses, not into perpetuity, but until she reaches eighteen, when her trust kicks in."

Leith held up a hand for permission to speak. "I understand that along with everything else, you've got Oscar's shares in the nightclub. Where will you be taking them?"

"Unless you're charging me with something, I don't believe that's any of your business. Is it?"

JD said, "Actually, it is our business. Just think of the club as a suspect right now. You've got forty-two percent Class A shares, right?"

Cleo stared at her. "Well, two things. Thanks to the shareholder's agreement, it seems Class A reverts to Class B upon death of a major shareholder, meaning I don't have voting rights. Unit price is stipulated in the articles. Jon can't afford to buy my shares, so he's looking for other options."

"Are you giving him a deadline?"

"Not at this point. I like Jon. I'm not going to push him. Second thing, the forty-two shares are divvied up to Oscar's heirs, meaning me, his sister Melanie, and his daughter in trust." She looked at Leith. "Anything else?"

Leith didn't have anything else at the moment, but JD did. "Do you know Jamie Paquette?"

"That skinny hooker half his age with brown hair?"

Leith almost interrupted, not sure they were talking about the same woman. Paquette's skinniness was subjective, of course. Personally, he would call her slim verging on voluptuous. Age-wise, she was younger than Oz, true, but not by half, and seemed older than her years. Cleo's "half-his-age" was probably spousal exaggeration. Hair colour was another matter; she was definitely blond, not brunette. But of course hair colour can come from a bottle. He kept his mouth shut.

"No, that's not fair," Cleo contradicted herself. "Not necessarily a hooker. I only met her once, at that restaurant, when Oz and I got together to talk about Dallas. That was just a few days after Jamie moved in with him. Last May or June, I think it was. I got to observe her a bit. She's not shallow, just does a good job of looking it. Well, he was mad for her, and I could see why. She was … alive. A good fit for him. Better than some of those other showroom dummies he took up with after he and I split."

As Cleo showed them out, she said, "He brought all this on himself, you know."

Leith expected it was a general comment on Roth's lifestyle, but asked, "How so?"

"When we met at the restaurant he told me something. It was supposed to make me madly jealous, I guess. When he first got the boat, he called it *The Cleo*. That's me. It is now, wait for it, *The Jamie*. Or was. Seems it's been purged from his list of assets. Sold or sunk, I don't care, it wasn't worth much to me."

Leith recalled the empty boat trailer in the dead man's garage. He still wasn't sure what this had to do with bringing on trouble.

JD was losing patience, too. "So why does this matter to me, ma'am?"

"Well, it's bad luck to change a boat's name," Cleo said, lifting her brows at her. "And Oz knew it. Just wasn't thinking straight, I guess."

* * *

"I don't like her, but that's because I don't like anybody," JD said.

Leith was finding JD to be quite a liar. She did know something about corporate structure, and she did like people. For some reason she preferred the negative slant on anything that was remotely personal. He wondered if she had been violently disappointed at some point in her life. Possibly way back in the formative years?

She wasn't done. She said, "Although I don't like her, I bet she's not responsible."

Leith agreed. He and JD were restudying the crime scene photographs from the Roth residence. They were in the Oz case room, but the Lius were here too, photographically speaking. Up on their own board, keeping an eye on matters. Not forgotten, by any means, a team on their case full-time, but Leith wanted them present in his own mind, always.

He checked his watch, jounced a knee. He watched JD study a photograph with a loupe, cross-reference it with the Roth floor plan, and move on to another one, back and forth, as if weaving together a specific concept. He had no idea what that concept might be. He said, "What's up?"

"Quite a struggle," JD said. She centred the floor plan on the table between them and pointed out the trail of havoc. "Here, here, here. They're all over the place. Pull a drawer, topple a bunch of chairs, break a dish, scatter knives. This is not a fight. This is Kaiju versus Kong."

"What it is, is two big guys duking it out," Leith said. "Or three, probably." The team believed it was two against one, considering the damage and apparent control the home invaders had over the burly Oscar Roth. The fight was charted and timed, from bloodstains and scuff marks, and there was nothing staged about it.

Except to JD. She said, "It looks fake to me. For one, with that kind of struggle there would be DNA all over the place, from all parties. Or something, some shred of themselves left behind."

"They might have been tossing the place, too, with gloves on. Looking for something. Or just causing malicious damage, for the hell of it. Or to send a message."

JD burst out laughing in her annoying way, loudly and with mouth wide open.

Leith frowned. "What?"

"Maybe they were looking for something! A pillowcase. Ripped the place apart and finally found one in the upstairs linen closet. These guys are clowns!"

Leith didn't think they were clowns, and he didn't think any of it was funny. "You're making a story out of nothing. This was a scary scene. We don't know why things happened the way they did, but a man died."

She pushed a photograph at him, one of the most graphic shots: Oscar with the pillowcase removed. He was banged and bruised. His face looked melted and grotesquely coloured, the resting cheek purple with pooled blood, the drained side like pale wax. She said, "And once again, why cover his head, these two big guys, if they're going to kill him?"

The team had worried about that. Had the struggle begun with a bag over his head to subdue him, then progressed organically from a beating to murder? Not with those signs of struggle. A hooded and subdued man wouldn't have left a trail like that. So the bagging had come later on.

Was it sadism, to increase the victim's fear, a form of torment?

Certainly it wasn't remorse or empathy, considering the way he'd been shoved headfirst into his car and left to die.

Another theory was he was being led to the garage with plans of kidnap, and he was hooded so he wouldn't see the route they would be taking. But he had tripped and knocked himself out, and the kidnappers had decided it was more trouble than it was worth to cart him away. So they had found the car key and decided to gas the man instead.

Chaotic, yes. But one thing Leith knew was that people committing violent crimes don't always read like manuals. People are on booze, meth. They're psychotic. High on adrenaline. Sexually charged. Confused. He had wasted too much time over the years looking for logic in scenes like this, and these days didn't agonize over it except as a last resort.

"You know what I think?" JD said. "I think this is a bullshit crime scene, that two people he knew well took him by surprise, bagged his head to render him helpless, and killed him. Tried to make it look like a home invasion, or a revenge killing, with that *die asshole* schtick. Why do we think there was someone after him? Because Oscar was apparently paranoid that someone was after him. Why do we think that? Because those two say so."

Leith followed her eyes to the board on this side of the room. Melanie York and Jamie Paquette.

True, other friends and acquaintances of Oscar Roth had been questioned, and nobody else thought he had been particularly antsy lately. No more than usual, anyway, hard to say with the hyper type. Leith pointed out that Jon York had corroborated that paranoia. "He said Oz worried he was being followed, right?"

"Yes, he did," JD said. "So maybe he's in on it. I'll put him in the mix, dig some more, and see where it goes."

Leith nodded, feet thumping nervously. Again he checked his watch face, and again he was disappointed. Still a ways to go.

"Getting married?" JD said.

In a way, he was. Alison would be arriving tonight, and he felt edgy as a blushing groom-to-be.

Twenty-One

GOLD

THE SKY WAS BLACK, THE windows open. A breeze gusted through Leith's apartment. He wandered restlessly, selected music, a pop band Alison liked. He checked his face in the mirror again. He sat and tried to read *Maclean's*. Tried to work his case files.

Finally he sat on a hard-backed chair by the window and smoked a cigarette, his last for a while, probably, because Alison would once again be after him to quit. He was always quitting and always sneaking one final puff, it seemed.

He worried about the plane. *What if it goes down? Of course it won't go down. But what if it does?*

Or another one: what if she arrived, and their time apart proved them incompatible? What if incompatibility led to divorce? How could he bear it?

And finally: why was he thinking these thoughts?

He sucked harder at his cigarette and lit another.

He had wanted to pick them up at the airport, but things got too complicated as he was on call, so in the end he had told her to grab a taxi. Now he wished he had damned the consequences and driven out there, to Richmond, to greet them as they came through the gates.

Around 1:00 a.m. a noise like garburated metal ejected him from his chair. The chair capsized, and then its legs caught his and tried to capsize him, too. The noise was the intercom buzzer; his family had arrived. He crushed the cigarette and fanned the air. He jogged out to meet them, down the carpeted stairs, past fake ferns and a dry fountain. He found her standing in the lobby, two suitcases at her feet, child in her arms.

Leith grabbed the suitcases and showed her the way up. She stood in the dark living room looking around. Her sandy-brown hair was shorter than he recalled, and styled differently. Her pretty, full face seemed to be trying to smile, but something held her back. "Where should I put Pumpkin?"

Together they laid Isabelle down on Leith's bed. He stood staring down at the child, and thought about little Rosalie Liu, and how blessed he was to have Izzy here, safe and whole. He turned to Alison, who was watching him patiently. He went to hug her but recalled the front door — he had almost forgotten — needed deadbolting.

"Always do this," he told her, as he snicked the lock shut. "Both locks, always. Right? This isn't Prince Rupert. Remember that."

"You gave me the same lecture in Prince Rupert," she reminded him. "Except you used my hometown as a comparison. 'Always lock the door, this isn't Parksville,' you said."

She still had her coat on, he realized. He rushed to help her out of it, and with the coat fallen to the floor, they finally were standing together. She held him tight. He held her tighter. They swayed to the pop tunes. He came a little undone, his tears wetting her hair. He knew he had missed her, but hadn't even guessed how badly. Not even close.

* * *

Under the black lights, dancers looked like fireflies. Up on the stage the go-go girls undulated like deep-sea creatures. Dion should have been long gone by now, should have been over the Rockies and in a motel room somewhere between Calgary and Edmonton, resting up before the next leg of the trip. But he wasn't over the Rockies. He hadn't even left the building. Partly because he couldn't seem to get off the penthouse suite sofa today and had dozed through to dinnertime.

But it was more because he wanted to see Jon York. He had a question for him.

After dinner he returned to the club to see if York was around. He wasn't, but staff said he would be in soon. So Dion waited with a beer. York arrived and seemed pleased to see him. Just like last night, Dion was invited to hang out and relax. York himself couldn't stick around quite yet, he had things to do, but would be back later.

"I thought I'd stay one more night, if it's okay with you," Dion told him. "I'll pay, though."

"You can stay all week, and you don't have to pay a cent," York said, with a cheery salute.

"How come you're so nice to me?" Dion called after him.

"I'm nice to everyone," York assured him. "If I like them. I like you. Is that so hard to believe?" And he left.

Dion's phone had been vibrating on and off all day. Several of the messages were from Mike Bosko. They had started out as simple texts — *call me* — which he had answered with, *Sorry, will be in touch when I have time.* This hadn't satisfied Bosko, who began leaving voice mails instead. *You have to do this by the book. Consider your future. Don't want a mark like this on your record, do you?*

The last message was a soft-spoken threat that he had listened through twice: *If I don't hear from you tomorrow, I'll take measures to bring you in.*

Now it was past ten at night. York had returned, joining Dion at the purple VIP booth. Again the place was a zoo. Not jam-packed, like some of the Vancouver clubs Dion had visited in earlier years, but what he would call hopping. Again, people glommed around York to talk. This time Dion stayed at the edge of the conversation. He watched the go-go dancers on the stage, but today they seemed unreal, and nothing to do with him.

No time so far was a good time to ask York the question. Not a terribly important question, but he needed to know.

Finally he took his beer bottle outside to the deck for a bit of cool, some lower decibels, and a cigarette. He didn't lean on the railing and stare outward — he still had that mysterious aversion to the sea — but sat on a bistro chair facing into the club.

As he half expected, York joined him, taking another chair on the other side of the table. None of York's royal subjects followed, and Dion was glad. York had his own cigarette pack out and was fiddling with a lighter.

"I haven't formally quit my job," Dion said. "I just walked out. My boss says he's going to have me arrested. I've been procrastinating. That was stupid. I wrote a resignation letter this evening and dropped it off. Hopefully that's good enough."

"Wow," York said. "You really like to burn your bridges."

"I *bomb* my bridges. There's something wrong with me."

"You don't say."

York's smile came from a level place. Not up, down, or sideways. He heard, got it, but wouldn't try to fix it. Instead he shared his own news. He spoke of the extraordinary shareholders' meeting he had been to today, and the brass-tacks sit-down with his financial team. "The power's back in balance," he finished. "Numbers are looking good."

But he spoke in a quick, nervous way that made Dion wonder if it was, to some degree, wishful thinking. "That's great," he said.

"Yep, they don't call me Midas for nothing." York flicked ashes into the night, and a bit of silence followed. Which meant question time had arrived, now or never.

Dion said, "What's Jamie up to lately?"

York looked at him, and slowly he smiled. "You want me to hook you up?"

"Too soon. Her boyfriend just got killed."

"I don't think she's got any kind of moral compass to worry about there."

"She's bad news, is she?"

York was still considering him, with too much inter-est. "The worst," he said. "But maybe that's what you're looking for."

Maybe. Dion thought of Kate, who was so different from Jamie. Kate was good news, and he wanted her forever, but she wasn't his. Probably any relationship he pieced together with Jamie, if York managed to rig it, wouldn't last. But it was worth a try. He said, "That's what I'm looking for. You said she never comes to the club. Why not?"

York was making attempts to blow smoke rings, but the wind coming off the water ripped them up and dis-persed them. "Don't know," he said. Then, "Tomorrow morning we're going boating. Me, Mel, and Jamie. You could join us."

No. Not out on the waves. The thought was sicken-ing. "Thanks, but no thanks."

York ignored him. "Come over around ten. Mel will pack a lunch. We'll spin along the shore, and I'll show you the Sea Lane house I told you about. If all goes well, we can dock, step inside, you can tell me how fabulous it is. What d'you say?"

"Not crazy about boats," Dion said.

"It's not a boat. Just a tub. Eighteen-foot outboard. But goes like stink. After that we're having a wake, at my place, Deep Cove. For Oz."

A boat ride, followed by party, Dion realized, rad-ically upped the odds of getting to know Jamie Paquette. And as for the waves, maybe facing them would be just the medicine. "I'll think about it. Did Oscar know Jamie's bad news?"

"What d'you mean?"

"Was she fooling around on him? Who with? Anyone you know?"

"You, my friend, are nuts," York said.

Their cigarettes were done. They stood to return indoors, and to Dion's shock, York slung an arm across his shoulder as they made their way back into the thud of music, the strobing lights and milling crowd. Like they were friends, had been for years, and would be forevermore.

* * *

When he'd had enough partying, which wasn't much past midnight, Dion sat on the sofa in his unfinished temporary living quarters above the club — the sound-proofing here was amazing — and wondered about that Midas reference. He had never been a big reader of fiction, hadn't aced anything in high school, and it wasn't love of learning that had got him through to grad and onward into the RCMP. What got him through was a fierce determination to be free of his father. So he had studied, cheated, and memorized — whatever it took to get his B's and C's. A side benefit of his determination was that it kept him out of trouble. Still, even working doubly hard, anything English lit–related had slid right past him, and he had just squeaked through with a passing grade. So tonight, when York said "Midas," it had rung only a faint bell in his mind.

Sitting here now, he knew Midas was more than just a muffler shop — it was a fairy tale, a myth about some bigwig with magical powers. He opened his laptop and after a short search, learned that King Midas was supposed to have turned everything he touched to gold. So that's what Jon meant.

But if that were true, if Jon York was King Midas, then he, Dion, should be inert right now. Valuable but immobilized, and he wasn't either. His nerves still jangled from the sensation of York's arm lying heavily across his shoulder. It was presumptuous and weird, but probably not a sexual come-on. It had felt like friendship at the time, but now he wondered if it had been more of a threat.

But why would York threaten him? It made no sense. Maybe it was time to accept that plain and simple friendship was possible outside of the force.

He stared into the glow of his laptop screen and read further. In one version of the legend, the most logical one, in his opinion, King Midas in the end had starved to death. Because — and this made sense — you can't eat gold.

Twenty-Two

SHEER

BAD DREAMS HAD DION ON the run all night long, chasing him to exhaustion. Then somebody said something, and he woke fast. It was Looch, somewhere, saying his name, *Cal....* He propped himself swiftly on an elbow and stared down a hall that wasn't there, breathing hard because it was impossible, because Looch was dead. Then a noise from the far end of wherever he was snapped the room into focus, and there was a stranger silhouetted against the light from a window. He tried to remember where his firearm was, but recalled he no longer carried one.

"Cal," the voice said again. "Sorry about that, didn't mean to scare you. There's no intercom in this place, so I let myself in."

Jon York came into one eye's focus. Dion blinked to clear the other one. "What's going on?"

"Wanted to call but realized I don't have your number," Jon said. He wore clothes fit for the beach, white tank and easy-fit canvas trousers. "Was in the neigh-bourhood anyway, so just thought I'd swing by."

Dion looked at the folding alarm clock he had placed on the coffee table, set to go off at nine thirty. It said eight thirty-nine. He wasn't supposed to be at the Yorks' till ten, he had thought.

Jon said, "Early, I know. It's a gorgeous morning, but rain's in the forecast, so we thought we'd bump up the schedule, get out a little earlier. But, hey, if you want me to buzz off —"

"No," Dion said. "I'm up." He dropped back and closed his eyes.

Jon said, "Good, then. We'll grab you a coffee on the way. Get dressed — dress for the water, it's coolish out there, and bring along a change of clothes for Oscar's party. C'mon, make it snappy. Might as well take my ride, which you've been eying. If you're ready in five, I'll even let you drive." He stood by the window, waiting, looking outward.

Dion pulled on cargo shorts and T-shirt for the boat ride. Into his overnight bag he packed clothes for the wake to follow. He couldn't find his phone, not on the windowsill, not in his coat pocket, not in his pants. Not in the ensuite, either. He stood before the mirror, ruffling his hair. Had he lost the phone? Before the crash he had never lost anything.

Before the crash he had been an early riser; 6:00 a.m., get up, make coffee, jump back in bed and harass Kate for sex, then out the door. He used to hit the gym before work, if he could fit it in. Pound the treadmill and press weights. Where had all that energy gone?

He returned to the main room and told Jon he had lost his phone. Jon was still by the window, still contemplating the strait waters. He turned. "When's the last time you used it?"

"I don't remember."

"Is the phone finder turned on?"

Dion didn't know of the option.

"Maybe you left it in the bar."

Downstairs, Jon unlocked the dark and silent nightclub. He flicked on the lights, and Dion checked the VIP booth while Jon looked through the lost-and-found box behind the counter. A couple of Samsungs, but no BlackBerry.

"It'll turn up," Jon said. He held out his car fob like a consolation prize.

Dion took the key and followed him out to the street, toward the silver Nissan parked at the curb, and thought how crazy this was. He had been gotten up too early, had lost his phone, his life was in shambles, but somehow none of it mattered now, as he was about to drive the car of his dreams.

* * *

On Leith's first day off he took Alison and Izzy to a child-friendly restaurant for lunch. Izzy was given a high chair and drawing material. She promised to behave, and for the most part did, till disaster struck: the blue crayon snapped in half as she scribbled over the duck's face, the two halves flying out of reach.

Disaster is a relative concept, Leith realized. His daughter yelled her outrage, but to his relief, Alison dealt with the crisis swiftly. She had a good rapport with Izzy, who was turning out to be quite a card. If Alison said *shush*, Izzy would thrust her arms in the air and open her mouth and eyes wide as if to scream even louder, but she'd just be kidding. With a mischievous smile, she would shush.

They performed this beautifully choreographed little act now before Leith's astonished eyes. Alison tweaked Izzy's nose and gave her back the blue crayon. Izzy continued to scribble over the duck's face.

The touching vignette got Leith worrying that he was too wrapped up in his workaday world to appreciate what he had in this child of his. It was so fleeting a time. Would he blink and find it was gone?

Must slow down, leave work at the office, he told himself.

He said so to Alison as the food arrived. "Later, I'll tour you around," he said. "We'll go to Capilano Canyon, show Izzy the rainforest." Would Izzy care? Probably not, but she would love the fresh air and the closeness of family. "It's going to be better here," he told Alison.

"Oh, no, it's going to be worse," she replied, matter-of-factly. Not blaming him, just saying. "Big city, more pressure. I'll never see you. Ever."

"Not true." Leith bit into his buffalo burger, munched, and swallowed. "Less travel, for one thing. No overnighters, 'cause it's a smaller territory. I've learned the hard way, I can't let the job take over my life. I have duties and obligations, but I also have some say over my workload."

The waitress stopped by to see if everything was all good here. He said everything was great, and could he have a coffee? The phone in his pocket buzzed, the

BlackBerry. "It's nothing," he told Alison, taking the call. "I'll delegate."

Alison rolled her eyes. Doug Paley was in Leith's ear, saying he was looking at what was probably Cleo Irvine right now. She was lying on the grounds at the Roth house, and she was definitely not alive.

"How?" Leith said, staring blindly at the messy, mangled blue duck in front of Izzy. "What happened?"

"I dunno," Paley said. "But you better come see, quick."

Leith banged down the BlackBerry and swore, the F-word and the S-word in combination for maximum impact.

"Dave!" Alison said.

He apologized to Alison, and to Izzy. "I didn't just say that," he told his daughter. "It's a bad word. Don't you ever say it, sweetie, okay?"

She offered a bit of fish stick on her tiny palm and said "fiss."

He stood, pulling on his jacket. "Get that burger wrapped for later," he told Alison. He asked if she had enough cash for a cab, and was too distracted to hear her answer. He leaned and kissed her forehead, and said bye to Izzy, and jogged past the puzzled-looking waitress bringing the coffee he had just ordered.

* * *

If it wasn't so tragic, it might have been funny how the death of Cleo Irvine came with its own virtual diagram called *this is how it happened*. Leith was with JD upstairs in Oscar Roth's office, the spacious room with the expensive but abused desk, the lewd posters, the dart-board. Leith looked at one feature of the place he had taken little note of on his earlier visit: the high, bay-style window in four parts, with a broad sill painted silky white. The two side sections were fixed, but the central two were casements, swinging outward.

Both casements were flung open. A gold velveteen drape hung half off its hooks and flopped sluggishly outside like a heartbroken flag. The desk had been moved, Leith saw. Somebody had pushed it close enough to the window that it could be stood upon, to reach the rod, presumably. But the person doing the hanging would have to stretch.

JD said, "She was wearing one-inch pumps with zero tread. And apparently taking the drapes off. Why was she doing that? They look new."

"If she was doing anything at all with the drape, she was putting it up," Leith said. "It was missing when Roth died."

"Oh." JD thought it over, nodding. "So she was hooking it up, leaning forward, slipped, and out she went. Why would she have the windows open?"

"Place stank of cigarettes," Leith said, recalling clearly that day here with Dion. "Probably she was airing the place."

"So she stands on a slick desk in slippery shoes, leans toward an open window over a thirty-foot drop, and fiddles with curtain fasteners," JD said. "She's like the reasonable man, except the exact opposite."

Leith gave her a warning glance not to be flippant. He had edged past the angled desk to stand by the window and look out and down. Not exactly a dizzying drop to the smooth lawn below, but a deadly fall. He saw it was busy down there, like a garden party in progress, all those people milling about in the sunshine, talking, pointing. A party with an odd dress code: baggy, white coveralls. Her body lay as found, crooked, busted, sad. Unlike the day he had seen her last, she was dressed for business today in a black skirt and sleeveless white blouse. Her one-inch, zero-tread pumps had fallen wide and were marked with evidence pins. He recalled something about a phone found on the scene. He said, "Where was her phone, and who was she talking to?"

"It was on the grass next to her," JD said. She, too, was looking down. "We could add that to her unreasonable-man mistakes; she's hooking up drapes, leaning over an open window, and making a call, all at the same time."

"I'm starting to think you're wrong," Leith said. "And you don't know she was talking on the phone."

"She must have had it in her hand, anyway. No pockets." JD shrugged. "Anyway, battery was in the red zone, so we did a data-dump first thing. She'd last placed a call to someone listed as 'Pearl.' We haven't been able to reach her, but we're tracking her down."

JD had already given him the rough outline of the events of the morning. The 911 call had come in at just before noon, when a prospective buyer and his realtor came by to view the Roth residence, and had instead found a body. Paley and JD arrived at 12:22 p.m., along with the coroner. At twelve thirty the coroner guessed the victim had been dead between two and four hours, which nailed it down to between eight thirty and ten thirty, but JD had it narrowed down even further, thanks to the disconnection of the call to Pearl at eight forty-one.

The question remained: had Cleo been speaking to Pearl when she fell, and had Pearl then disconnected? In which case, why hadn't Pearl, hearing the scream, immediately called 911? Probably, then, the call had ended without incident at eight forty-one, and sometime afterward, Cleo had fallen.

Leaving the room to the Ident team — JD telling them to pay particular attention to the desk for prints and shoe marks — she and Leith went downstairs and outside to talk to Doug Paley. Paley turned near-black shades at Leith and said, "What's the verdict?"

"Appears to be an accident," Leith said, looking at the body still *in situ* on the grass, her limbs outspread but for one snapped arm that angled toward the torso. The woman's fine brown hair had fanned out, the trimmed ends lifting and falling. Her face was crooked toward him, her eyes half shut, her beauty destroyed by a broken jaw and the explosion of blood from her nostrils. "Unless we find out she wasn't alone," he said.

Paley nodded and removed his glasses to stare at Leith. "You okay?"

"Of course I'm okay."

He wasn't, really. He had talked to Cleo the day before last. She had been so solid and seemingly in control. Her death was a nasty reminder to Leith about who or what really was in control, and that scared him.

Paley lowered his shades over his eyes again, and turned back to the business at hand.

* * *

Leith sat on the steps and wrote down his questions and tasks for his team to get started on. Where was the child, Dallas? Study the phone's recent calls and text messages. Talk to the two individuals who had found the body. Track down Pearl ASAP. Likewise, get the name of the real estate agent Cleo would have been dealing with on this, who would be different than the buyer's real-tor. Search for answers as to why Cleo was apparently attaching that curtain herself, instead of getting some kind of housekeeping service to do it. And where had that new drape come from? Was it ordered specially, or had it just been at the cleaners? If so, get in touch with those cleaners. If not, find the outlet or service that had supplied the curtain. Was anybody else scheduled to be at the estate this morning, housekeepers or yard main-tenance? If so, get their contact info. Canvass neigh-bours and Cleo's closest friends.

And then there was the question of Cleo's other latest windfall acquisition — her shares in the nightclub, Diamonds. This meant Leith would have to interview Jon York once more. He dangled pen and notebook be-tween his knees and looked into the distance, thinking about York, and how he really didn't like the man. Just plain didn't.

Twenty-Three

THE BRILLIANT BLUE

DION WASN'T ENJOYING THE drive as much as he'd expected. He stuck conscientiously to the speed limit along the Dollarton Highway toward Deep Cove, more evidence of his degradation. Before the crash he would have been thrilled at a chance to peel asphalt with a sports car like this. Before the crash he had risked a ticket a few times, taking his Dodge up to 140 through Manning Park's hundred zone, and he would have pushed it higher, except he really didn't want to lose his job.

But the crash had killed his need for speed.

Also, he had lost his touch with manual transmissions, and he worried about fouling the gears. He worried about reaching their destination, the high-density, hilly neighbourhood where Jon lived, parking badly and putting a scratch on the thing. Now Jon was piling bad news onto his anxieties: Jamie had changed her mind, he said, and wasn't going boating with them.

"What?" Dion said. "Why?"

"Well, sorry. It's because you're coming. Don't take it personally. She's lived on the wild side and doesn't like cops. Or trust them."

"I resigned. I'm not a cop."

Jon smiled at him. "Yes, well, we had a talk last night, Mel and Jamie and I, and we agreed you're working undercover. Just so that you know that we know, and we're okay with that. Well, Mel and I are okay with it. Jamie doesn't want to have anything to do with you, I'm afraid."

"I'm not working undercover," Dion exclaimed. "How could I be working undercover? You're saying I set up the meeting in the parking lot? I was there first! You invited me for drinks. I said no. You insisted. If you hadn't insisted, I'd have gone on my way. How could you possibly think —"

"Us showing up in the parking lot was just one of those lucky strikes for you. And if I hadn't insisted, you'd have turned up anyway, one way or another. Flat tire in front of the club, something like that."

Dion stared at him, not sure he was serious.

Jon said, "I told Jamie, relax, even if our Cal is working undercover, he won't find any dirt on us. We're much too smart for that." He laughed at his own joke — if a joke was what it was.

Dion remained stunned. At the accusation, at the joke, and at the news that Jamie, the whole point of this expedition, wasn't going out on the water. "Then I won't go," he said. "Tell her that. She can go, I'll stay, no problem."

Jon fluttered the notion away with his fingers. "You're going boating. It actually took a lot of convincing to get her to agree to join us to start with. She's not keen about the water, either."

They arrived at the house in Deep Cove. Dion parked, carefully, without incident, his heart still beating hard from the undercover allegation. Jon hopped out, saying, "Come on in. Mel's just putting a few things in the cooler."

Dion followed him inside and glared at Melanie, who was preparing food in the open-concept kitchen. Even if she didn't think he was a spy, it might have been awkward, meeting like this, considering the last time he had spoken to her, she was under investigation, and he was the one investigating her. Or at least taking notes. She waved hello with a smile. She didn't seem bothered by his presence. Jamie was nowhere to be seen, but it hardly mattered, since he was on her blacklist.

In the living room, he sat on the sofa and looked around, wondering if they were right, the three of them. Why was he here? Was he checking out Jon York, trying to resolve some vague doubts? Or did he have it all flipped around, and Jon was checking him out? Or both, or something else altogether?

The place was much as he remembered, but tinted now by his new, permanently off-duty status. The colour scheme was pale and earthy, muted but picked up with gold, softened with plant arrangements. A mantelpiece was lined with artefacts; centrally placed was an old-fashioned clock with a dark, wooden body and an audible tick-tock, and on either side of it were framed photographs.

He stared at the photographs for a moment before getting up to study them.

Most of the photographs were of Jon and Melanie. A group of children, maybe the class Melanie had once taught. Hadn't she said she was a teacher? Photos of an older couple — relatives, he assumed. Photos of what he thought were Jon as a child and Melanie as a child. Photos of the Diamonds staff on opening night. It had been a big group. And finally one shot of Oscar Roth giving Jamie Paquette a bear hug.

This photograph Dion studied closely, surprised by the changes Jamie had gone through in a relatively short time. Her face was thinner in the photo, her hair longer, straighter, and darker. Her makeup seemed less elaborate, too. Oscar had met her only a year ago, so it had been a swift transformation. He recalled Paquette's talent agent saying she was fatter. If Jamie Paquette was fat now, she must have been a beanpole then.

She looked happy in the photo, being squeezed silly by her new boyfriend. The Jamie he knew didn't seem happy or carefree. But then he had only seen her across the interrogation table, and her boyfriend had just been violently dispatched. He turned and saw, through doorways and obstructions, something he probably wasn't meant to see, a moment of husband-and-wife playfulness, Jon hugging Melanie from behind, nibbling her ear. She laughed and pushed him away.

Minutes later, Jon collected Dion from where he stood by the mantelpiece, ushering him out the door, not to the sporty car in the driveway, but the roomier SUV in the garage, and not to the driver's seat, but the back. Melanie sat in the front, passenger's side, texting somebody about something. Dion sat and fastened his seat belt. Jon forgot something in the house and had to run back in, leaving Dion and Melanie to make small talk.

"Well," she said, turned around so they were somewhat face-to-face. "I hear you quit the force."

Maybe she was smirking, or maybe it was just the light. "I did," he told her explicitly.

"Big decision." She faced around front, and the conversation was over. Jon jumped in behind the driver's wheel, apologizing for the delay, and they were off to the docks in West Vancouver.

The boat that Jon had described yesterday as a "tub," Dion soon discovered, was a showy speedboat, a length of fibreglass muscle bobbing at the wharf. He followed Jon aboard, then grabbed coolers and gear bags from Melanie below. Finally he gave her a hand up, and she smiled her thanks, though she didn't seem to need help climbing aboard any more than he did.

* * *

He had to make this day out into a good thing, he decided, as the boat ploughed slowly out of the harbour. Therapeutic. It would force him to confront his uneasy feelings about the ocean. Where those feelings came from, he couldn't fathom. He had grown up on these shores, had always taken the Pacific for granted. It was just *there*, part of life. But since his return from the north, it had taken on a sinister persona, like an old friend he had fallen out with, someone he'd rather avoid.

As they entered open water his depression intensified. He sat in the seat next to Jon York and didn't look ahead, or behind, or over the side, but kept his eyes fixed on whoever was speaking, Jon or Melanie. He held tight to the seat railings as the jet boat picked up speed and bucked and slammed across the heavy green water. Only when one of the Yorks pointed at something would he dutifully stare out across the waves, at Siwash Rock, or some famous luxury cruise ship, or any other point of interest they thought he would appreciate. The motion was tougher to ignore, and he began to feel ill. *Pukey* ill. He shouted at Jon to please slow down.

Jon slowed down. They were cruising along gently now, passing the slower yachts, gaining on the *Queen of Whatever* surging her way across the straits toward the Island. Tour time, Jon said, and looped the boat back toward the calmer shore, giving Dion a bit of a reprieve. Jon chugged the boat past the homes of the wealthy, around an arbutus bluff, until a rocky point came into view, jutting out and taking the waves like the prow of a ship. Here he idled the engine and pointed up to a house under construction. That was his dream home on Sea Lane, peeking over boulders and wild grasses, its windows reflecting the horizon like melancholy eyes.

"Wow," Dion said. "Gorgeous."

"I would moor and show you around, but we don't have a lot of time," Jon said, and steered back out to the open. "I'm going to speed her up." He grinned. "Don't worry, you'll get used to it."

He sped up. Dion remained miserable, but no longer felt about to throw up.

Melanie, who had sat between them for the first while, moved to the back — the stern. She wore a bathing suit and some kind of wrap. Jon, at the controls, wore swimming trunks and a fluttering Rayon shirt with a palm tree motif. Dion felt overdressed in cargo shorts and T-shirt, with an added long-sleeved denim shirt over top, to protect himself from the spray. Like the Yorks, he wore dark sunglasses.

Jon gestured out at the waves. "Oz loved the water. Loved the rush. But he wasn't smart about it. Hit a deadhead last summer, doing upwards of eighty knots in his little Stingray, but lucky bastard was skipping like a stone, just clipped it and bounced right over. Still totalled the boat, got a big hole ripped in the hull, had to hightail it for home before it sank. If he'd hit that thing head-on, he'd be crab meat."

Dion said, "Eighty knots, what's that in KPH?"

"It's fast," Jon said. "Especially in the chop he was pushing. You need glass for that kind of speed. Flat water. Couldn't do it in these conditions, say, bit of rock and roll. In fact, I wouldn't do it in the best conditions. Value my neck too much. Must be getting old, but these days I'm more of a cruise-along type, pop a beer and throw out the line."

"Is that why Jamie doesn't like boating, 'cause of the crash?"

Jon shrugged. "Unlikely. She wasn't out there with him that day. But he told us all about it that night, when they came over for dinner. And he's a good storyteller. Scared her, possibly, and she decided boating definitely isn't her thing. Truth is, she finds it a bore."

Jon went on to talk about boats, which led to the sport of fishing, which led to sports in general, which Dion knew was inevitable in a way because Jon was athletic. Dion was not athletic, mentally or physically. It was a temporary setback, he told himself. He would get back on top of it again soon, get active, get interested, as he once had been. Be avid about who won the Stanley Cup, as he had once been. Or FIFA. But for now, the sports world was like a stranger's wedding, some big event happening down the hall, nothing to do with him. He braced himself for the questions, and they came at him now, a pop quiz he was bound to fail.

Are you a hockey guy? Follow any of the big games? What about soccer? No? Football?

Dion told Jon the truth: he had once cared, had jumped around like every other sports fan when a goal was scored. But just didn't have time, lately.

York asked what games he had played.

"Floor hockey, as a kid. Then the RCMP beer leagues, whatever was up. Some soccer, but mostly baseball. I played baseball quite a bit."

Jon took the lead and tried to run with it, to turn the conversation that direction, but Dion had little to add. To him, baseball had been easy fun, when Looch was alive. He had stood where he was told to stand and did his best to catch the ball, or swing and hit it, if he was up to bat, and if he hit it he'd run fast as he could. Skidded into base or missed it. In the end, who won or lost didn't matter to him, so long as there was a party afterward.

He explained all this to Jon. Jon said he understood but sounded wistful. "Not into racquetball, by any chance? Oz and I had a weekly game." He had steered the boat into a long, slow curve toward a small island, a dot in the distance. "He was *bad*," he added. "I won every time, even when I tried to lose, but it never stopped him trying."

"I haven't played racquetball," Dion said, another fail. It didn't matter. The relationship was some kind of false construct anyhow. He had been brought out here as a joke. Even if he wasn't a joke, Jon was from a higher plane of life, they were spectacularly mismatched, and this outing was going to be their last, he was sure of it.

The salty wind and harsh sun began to rasp at Dion's face, and his mouth felt chapped. He pretended to relax back and watch the ocean, but closed his eyes instead. He had a plan: get through this nightmare, then civilly part ways.

"So what d'you do for exercise?" Jon asked, still at it. "Work out?"

"Not a whole lot these days."

"Run marathons?" Jon asked. "Wrestle crocodiles? Climb rock faces without a rope?"

Dion didn't bother answering, because the questions were no longer questions, but rhetorical insults.

"Xbox? Chess?" Jon said. "*Collect stamps?*"

Dion's patience snapped. "My job was all I needed for fun," he said. "Now I'm not working, so I'll probably take up rock climbing without a rope. And Xbox, and racquetball. It's just a matter of learning how. Piece of cake."

"Great. I'll teach you."

"*What?*"

"Racquetball."

Dion stood, grabbing onto the seat back for stability as the boat swayed. "Think I'll have that beer you offered. Want one?"

"Nope, H_2O's fine." Jon raised his water bottle.

In the back of the boat, Melanie York sat, apparently meditating on the view, legs stretched out, ankles crossed. Dion pulled a beer from the cooler, and she pointed at the padded bench next to her. He sat and twisted the cap off. The beer he chugged was cold, bitter, and refreshing.

"You don't look like you're having a great time," Melanie called out over the ruckus of the wind. Just as in Diamonds, this boat in motion was a noisy place to talk. "But don't worry about it. Hedonism doesn't come naturally to everyone. You gotta give it time."

"No, I'm just boring the hell out of Jon. My life is about this big compared to his." He showed a small space between finger and thumb.

Behind her dark glasses, Melanie smiled. "I doubt it. You're good for him, someone real to talk to. All his friends are businessmen and snobs. You're more down-to-earth, like Oz. Who he misses fiercely."

"I'm not real," he said stiffly. "I'm just an undercover cop. Remember?"

She laughed. Her laughter made him feel foolish, but her words made him feel better. He was oversensitive and too serious, and it was time to lighten up. He said, "I'm sorry I scared Jamie off. You probably wish she'd come along, so you'd have someone to talk to."

"I'm talking to you," she said, and added, "No, stay a while," as he made to leave.

The boat picked up speed, began to batter the water again as it came out of a curve. It seemed to Dion they were going to crash into that little island, a little island that wasn't a dot any more. Uninhabited, nothing there but trees and rock and surf.

"I'm wondering," Melanie called, drawing his attention away from approaching catastrophe. He moved closer so she wouldn't have to shout. "If what you say is true, then you just left an incredible career. Why? Jon says you're very mysterious about it, but since you *are* going to tell me everything sooner or later, might as well be now, right?"

Her words added to the slow-building shock of the day. He tried to study her expression, but her eyes were hidden. He said, "How d'you figure I'll tell you everything sooner or later?"

She removed her sunglasses. "Because I'm honestly curious, and you're dying to unload. You're savvy enough to know I'm trustworthy. We're love at first sight. Do me a big favour and take 'em off."

Not his clothes, he realized, but his shades. She was wheeling and dealing. He took off the sunglasses and stuck them in his shirt pocket.

"Lost somebody, didn't you?" she asked.

"Yes," he said, to his own surprise. He had meant to say *no*, because it was nobody's business, especially hers, what he had lost.

"Good friend?" she prompted. "On the job?"

Just like the *yes*, he went on without hesitation to tell her. "We got smoked by a car coming off a side road. The guy must have been doing one-sixty. My friend Looch, we worked together for years, he was in the passenger seat. He was killed on impact. I survived."

Melanie nodded, waiting for more.

"I got a little dazed," Dion said. "Wasn't sure I could keep the job, but scraped through. I'm not myself, probably never will be, but I think whatever's wrong with me doesn't register on their machines. It's deeper than that. I figured it was time to leave."

Melanie's reaction, as he replayed it later, was perfect. She moved over till she was right next to him, put an arm around his shoulder in a firm embrace, with none of the subliminal menace of Jon's yoking arm last night. This body contact was different. It was like they were soul mates, and he leaned into it, giving back, his right arm around her waist because it had nowhere else to go, and how could he not be aroused, breathing in her lotions and sweat, after losing Kate, and his job, and all self-respect, to be drawn so close like this?

He pulled away, catching Jon looking back toward them, just a glance. Jon didn't seem upset. Melanie didn't either. She sidled back to her end of the bench, reaching into the cooler, and for the first time he took in exactly what she was wearing, the white one-piece bathing suit with chrome accents, pale-blue sarong splitting at the side to show her two-toned thigh, the imperfect tan lines left over from shorts. Her gold-brown hair was tangled with the wind and dampened into tendrils against her throat and temples. Her eyes when she returned his stare were clear and confident. "Well, my dear," she said. "This calls for something a little more serious than beer. I'm going to make you the perfect Harvey Wallbanger. Bet you didn't expect a full-service bar on board, did you?"

She shouted at Jon, "I'm keeping your guest for a while."

"Have him, he's a total dud," Jon shouted back.

His words were a one-two punch but just a tease, a signal that all was okay.

Breathing became easier for Dion, and the sun less harsh as clouds smeared in from the west.

Melanie mixed vodka and OJ, adding a dash from a long, tall bottle of lemon-yellow liqueur that she told him was the secret ingredient, Galliano. Dion's drink came to him in a tall plastic tumbler instead of a high-ball glass — to avoid spillage, she said — no garnish.

The drink was nice, citrusy, more refreshing than the beer. He gave Melanie the okay sign, and she blew him a kiss.

Jon called out that it was time to make tracks, and the boat picked up speed again, nosing high into the chop. With vodka and OJ like cold fire in his system, Dion could hear and feel the rising RPMs, and could taste the flapping wind, briny and sweet. The sun found a gap in the clouds and beat down, and he stripped off his long-sleeved shirt, letting the solar energy and spray hit him, hot and cold, the water dashing against his bare arms as intoxicating as the Wallbanger. "Next time bring swimming gear," Melanie told him, shouting again because they were skimming now, just gunning around that little island like they were lassoing it for keeps. *Next time.* He stood gripping the railing with his heart beating fast and faced the panorama of ocean without the protection of sunglasses or shirt, and it wasn't just speed they were wrestling with here, he realized, but dominance, and he was right there in the middle of the fight. In smashing against water and wind, they were killing something, he wasn't sure what, but it didn't matter, because he'd been inducted, by Jon's arm first and then Melanie's, and as they circled that island at breakneck speed, York on his feet at the controls bellowing like a hooligan and Melanie braced against velocity but laughing hard, when the 150-horsepower roar was sure to drown him out, he let go of some inner straitjacket and shouted into the turbulence his rage and triumph. Somehow the day had shifted violently into beautiful, and he was no longer lost. Definitely, he was back in the swim.

Twenty-Four

TANGLES

WITH A STRAIN OF DARKNESS in his genetic makeup, Dion didn't burn easily, but he could feel the ominous sting on his unprotected neck and the backs of his arms as he climbed down to the dock, joining the Yorks. The dock seemed to bob up and down, but it was just his sea legs, Jon assured him. Dion told Melanie it wasn't sea legs; it was vodka. She had had a brief swim when they anchored by the small island for some fishing. No fish were caught, and she was still wet. She had climbed back on board after her dip, and Dion watched her pull a thin T-shirt over her bathing suit. She had small breasts, what Looch used to call tangerines.

He was trying not to imagine her shirtless as they stood on the dock. Jon had his phone out and was switching it back on with a grimace. "I always kill it when I'm on the water," he explained. "No crisis on earth is going to ruin my sea time." He made faces as he listened through the messages, to amuse Melanie. Mock disgust, mock boredom.

Then he stopped being funny and said, "Damn." Melanie raised her brows at her husband as he pocketed the phone. "Cops want to talk to me again," he said.

"Maybe they got the guy," she suggested.

Dion knew they weren't calling because they got the guy. Notifying family on case progress was on the list of priorities, but not super high. If anyone, they would be contacting Melanie directly, the blood relation. Not the brother-in-law.

Jon said, "Let's hope so. I better call 'em back. Sounds important."

He phoned the RCMP number as he stood on the pier, surrounded by luxury craft. Dion sat on a bench and waited, listening to rigging hitting metal softly, like wind chimes. There was the smell of rotting kelp, the kiss of water against hulls. The threatening clouds had evaporated, and the sun was directly overhead, glaring down and obliterating Jon's face.

Dion wondered who Jon was talking to at the office. Leith, maybe. "Out for a boat ride," he heard Jon saying. "We're just back on shore." Pause. "Not really," he said, and Dion knew he had just been asked if it was convenient that he come to the detachment right away. Anxiety began to knuckle harder in his gut. "We've got a memorial service to get organized," Jon said. "Honouring Oz." Pause. "No, it's quite a production. It's an Oz-style memorial. Live music, a magician, the works. We can't cancel. People will be arriving soon." Another long pause, and he said, "That would be worlds better. We'll be home in half an hour."

Jon finished the call and was talking to Melanie, their heads together, too low to hear. Watching them, Dion felt a chill, in spite of the sun. Probably he had known all along and should have paid heed to his own intuition. Should have steered well clear of Jon and Melanie York.

* * *

Leith didn't like the way JD dealt with traffic. Obstacles meant nothing to her. She simply wove around them without braking. She was ballsy and efficient, but hair-raising. But as always, she had won the keys today for the ride out to Deep Cove.

Trying to relax, he told her what he had learned. "They've been out boating all morning, and now they'll be throwing a party in memory of Oz. There's going to be magicians, York says. Some version of grief I'm not familiar with, I guess."

"It's a version of grief you couldn't afford," JD said. "You think he did it, don't you?"

"Jon York? Did I ever say that?"

"You growl slightly whenever you say his name."

The sky was turning a pale ultramarine as JD knocked on the Yorks' front door. The door opened. Melanie York was barefoot, dressed for summer, and unless Leith was wrong, she had been drinking. She led the way to the living room, where Jon York rose from a leather arm-chair. Another man was present, a stranger seated over there on the sofa, but Leith focussed on Jon York, intent in catching every nuance of expression.

York seemed wry but friendly. He shook Leith's hand, and JD's. "I'm sorry to rush you, but I'm hoping this will be ultra brief."

"Just a few minutes," Leith promised. Melanie York had disappeared, which was good, as he wanted to talk to husband and wife separately. He could hear her talking in another room, to another woman. Jamie Paquette? Now he looked at the young man on the sofa, drink in hand — casual, like he belonged here, a friend of the family. He wore shorts and a grey T-shirt. He was dark haired and clean cut, watching Leith with what looked like faint annoyance. Leith did a double take. Far from dead, as he'd begun to believe, Constable Dion was alive and well, and, wouldn't you know it, hanging out with Leith's own favourite murder suspect.

* * *

Standing by the window with grey-blue ocean and grey-blue sky as backdrop, Leith kept his information to York simple: *Regret to inform you that Cleo Irvine died this morning.* Then waited for reaction. York looked confused, searching Leith's eyes for the punchline, checking JD's face, too, then exclaiming, "*What?* What d'you mean she died? How?"

"All we know at this point is she fell out a window, so we're just trying to fill in —"

"A window? What window? Where? At False Creek?"

That was where Ms. Irvine lived, in a million-dollar condo on 1st Avenue. Leith ignored the interruption.

"We're trying to fill in her activities of this morning and yesterday. Have you seen or spoken to her at all recently?"

"No," York said. "Or, yes. Not this morning, but yesterday morning, we had a short discussion. On the phone. About Diamonds."

"And?"

"Told her I'm looking for two partners to buy her out, have one in mind, need one more, how long will she wait, that kind of thing."

"Were you happy with the agreement?"

"No," York shouted. "Apparently I was so pissed off I went over to her condo and shoved her out the window. Yes, I was happy with the agreement. Not nearly as happy as I'd be if Oz walked in the door and said this was all one giant bad dream. Which, by the way, any progress finding *his* killer?"

"We're on it," Leith said shortly.

York became silent and thoughtful, studying Leith as Leith studied him. "Was it an accident? Or you think someone pushed her? You wouldn't be here if it was an accident, would you?"

"You say you were out boating today," Leith said. "What time did you leave? Just tell me about your day. In detail, if you could."

"In between pushing Cleo out her condo —"

"Right, why don't you just try and be straight with me, okay?" Leith said. "Jokes don't help either of us at a time like this."

To York's credit, he seemed to get the message. He ducked his head like a scolded child. "Sorry. Let me think." He moved to the window and frowned outside.

With the lights turned up in the residence, the view was marred, overlaid with the ghosts of Leith himself, JD standing at his side, York maybe pondering his own reflection.

"First Oz, then Cleo." He was shaking his head. "It's got to be connected." He turned again to face them. "My day. I'll do my best. I was up early, about seven, reading the news. Mel got up. We had a light breakfast. I went to town, saw Ziba. Then picked up Cal, since I was in the area. Came back to collect Mel and the sandwiches, and off we went to the docks."

"Picked up Cal from where, and why?"

The Cal they were talking about had been told to wait his turn elsewhere in the house. He would be downstairs, he said, in the den.

"From the club," York said, with a careless rush that Leith saw as evasive. "There's a room upstairs, unfinished offices. That's the where. As for the why … well, I had to step in to Ziba's place to discuss something. She's my stage manager. She lives in an apartment on 3rd, not far from the club. And since I was in the area I decided to pick up Cal. I know, nobody's supposed to be there, no residency permit and all that, but it's just a crash-pad till he finds an apartment, just a day or two."

Leith stashed these bizarre fragments for later. "Discuss what with Ziba?"

Almost imperceptibly, York rolled his eyes. "There was an incident at the club last week between a girl and a guest. Drinks thrown and whatnot. I needed to talk to Ziba about it, see if anybody was going to make a stink, figure out how to settle it without getting the authorities involved. Anyway, she can fill in the details for you. She's a busy woman, so I wanted to catch her early."

"What time?"

"Can't remember exactly. Had to be eight thirty, thereabouts. Was there for ten minutes, max. She'd gotten the girl settled down, got the guy to apologize, it's a nonissue. Then thought I'd pick up Cal. He was going to be at our place at ten, but I wanted to get out on the waves nice and early. So I went over, rousted him out of bed, and away we went. Again, it was around eight thirty, eight forty, eight forty-five, in that neighbourhood."

Leith considered the man's face. Pale, but that was his normal complexion, typical Anglo-Saxon right down to the freckles. Distressed, but he'd just found out Cleo Irvine was dead, so why wouldn't he be? But there was something else, also a fixed element of his persona, the part Leith didn't care for, just below the surface. Chronic amusement.

"I have to say," he told York. "I'm surprised to find out Calvin Dion is living at the club and boating with you. And hanging around your house. Sounds like you've struck up quite a friendship."

Did York's mouth twitch? "Nothing mysterious," he said. "I chanced to run into him in the parking lot at the Royal Arms the other day. He told me he was leaving town. I was curious, so I bought him a drink. I like him. He likes me. I invited him to tonight's party, and since we were going out boating, I asked him to come along. Turns out he's not nautically inclined."

"Your phone was switched off this morning. Why's that?"

Now a grimace. "That's my self-imposed rule. Sometimes all this worldly connectedness is deafening. I'm sure you know what I mean. My gift to myself is I shut off my phone when I'm on the water, always. Keeps me sane."

Leith nodded, and thought *hogwash*. But it was something he could hopefully check with collateral sources. He had run out of questions, so he threw in a filler. "What kind of boat have you got?"

"An old eighteen-footer. Glastron bowrider."

"And where did you go?"

York described the route in more detail than Leith needed. Just a slow ride around Passage Island and back past the Grebes. But first an idle along the shore, past his house under construction in West Van. To show Dion.

"Huh," Leith said, taken aback and disliking York even more. "Right on the water?"

"To die for," York assured him.

JD said, "Made any phone calls this morning, Mr. York?"

York looked at her. He seemed to see her for the first time, and his face crinkled in a broad smile. "I called Mel, asking if there was anything she needed picked up. She said fancy mustard, which I promptly forgot, so in the end she had to use the plain stuff."

"Didn't call Ziba, let her know you were on your way?"

"No. We'd fixed that the night before, at the club."

"Didn't call Cal?"

"Didn't know his number, actually. Never thought to take it down. So other than Mel, no, I guess that's it." He drew an iPhone from his pocket, called up its log, and handed it to JD.

She made a note in her book and showed the phone to Leith.

The call, he saw, was logged in around the time of Ms. Irvine's fatal plunge, eight forty-four. But without location attached, it didn't mean much. He would need phone company records to narrow it down, and for that would need either consent or a warrant. He wouldn't get a warrant, not based on instinct, so he tried for consent. "That's helpful. Would you agree to us obtaining your phone records?"

"What d'you mean?" York said. Surprised, irritated, but not alarmed. "I just don't see why."

"Process of elimination, sir."

"What, you really think *I* killed her? Well, I didn't. And I don't want you snooping in my phone records either. I've got a lot of sensitive stuff in there."

"Only the relevant —"

"No."

"We can narrow it down to just records from this morning."

"Doesn't work like that, does it. Since you're there, you'll try to turn my whole life inside out."

"No, sir, we would only —"

"Forget about it. Sorry. Get a warrant."

"I suppose we'll have to do that," Leith said coolly.

York was wincing again. "I don't like to be difficult, but honestly."

"Sure."

Next, Leith and JD spoke to Melanie York, a woman JD had been investigating for the past two days, finding nothing to sink her teeth into; Melanie didn't have so much as a speeding ticket to her name. She had changed from her casual beachwear and now wore white — interesting choice for a wake, Leith thought — white mesh over white mini dress, and flat, beaded sandals. As he spoke to her, he found her a different woman from their first encounters. More relaxed, though maybe it was the drink or two she had apparently treated herself to. Not drunk enough to drop her guard, though, he noticed. Wariness showed in the tilt of her face and the hardness in her eyes.

Her story lined up with her husband's, dead on. He had gone off quite early to see Ziba about an incident at the club. About eight thirty. He had called some fifteen minutes later — no, she couldn't remember the exact time — to ask if she needed anything from town. Dijon, she had requested. "Instead he came home with *Dion*," she said to Leith, deadpan. "I told Jon he must be dyslexic, but I don't think he got it. Jon's crazy about his boat, gets me out there whenever he can, even happier when he's got a guest to show off to. So he was running circles around us, wanting to get out on the water before the rain."

"What rain?" JD said.

Melanie seemed to find the question too silly to answer. Which it was, Leith thought. Unless JD had caught something he had missed. He made a mental note to ask her about it, later. First he had to deal with the reprobate, though, and he decided it would be best if he did it alone.

* * *

The den where Dion waited was the same room he and Leith had occupied to question Jon York and Jamie Paquette, seemingly so long ago. Cozy and warmly decorated, the perfect nook to deck in for the night with a glass of brandy and read a good novel. Dion was slumped in an armchair with no drink in hand, no reading material to entertain him, and no enthusiasm in the lines of his face. Leith took the adjacent armchair and made himself comfortable, because he intended this to be less an interrogation than a brother-to-brother chat. "You never returned my calls. Or Bosko's. What's going on? He's holding back the firing squad for you, but he's about to let them lock 'n load."

"I dropped off my resignation letter," Dion said. He had unslumped to sit straighter. There was a new cast to his eyes, softer and harder, lazier and meaner. "What else does he want? Dock my severance? Charge me with something? Tell him fine, go ahead."

A resignation letter, Leith knew, changed everything. Probably for the best. But all the same ... "The Yorks are smack in the middle of our radar. Could you find any worse place to hang out?"

"That's one good reason to quit. For once in my life, I can socialize with whoever I want."

Apparently they were no longer brothers, so there was no further need to chat. Leith pulled notebook and pen from his breast pocket, checked the time, and wrote down the particulars of the interview. "I understand Jon York called on you this morning. Recall what time?"

Dion answered promptly. "Eight forty. Or one minute to."

"You know that for sure?"

"He woke me up, scared the hell out of me. I looked at the clock."

"Maybe your clock was wrong?"

"No. Other clocks said the same thing."

Police training still ticking away in there, Leith thought. He said, "I understand York picked you up earlier than agreed. Why the change of plans?"

"Not sure. He said something about wanting to beat the bad weather."

"It was a nice day. No rain in the forecast."

"I don't know, then."

"And you're staying at Diamonds," Leith said. "Upstairs. How did that come about?"

"That came about 'cause I'd left the Royal Arms and was heading to Alberta, but met Jon and we got talking. He ended up letting me stay there a couple nights. It's not finished, but it's livable. I'll be leaving soon."

"You'll be leaving now. Tell me about your day. You went out motorboating, you and Jon and Melanie. How was it?"

The lazy, mean eyes drifted away, not to the window but the vague shadows of the room. "Brilliant, actually," Dion said, and surprised Leith by firing out some stats. "Glastron GTS 180 with 150-horse merc, speed you wouldn't believe. Why?"

"Why what?"

"Why the questions? What happened?"

Leith told him, in the same minimal way he had informed Jon York, that Cleo Irvine was dead. He waited for reaction, saw none, so gave a little more. Dion would hear it from his new best pal anyway. "She fell out a window, died on impact."

There was a flash of interest, the briefest glimmer. "Where?"

Leith shut his notebook and rose without an answer. If Dion's demeanour was saying loudly *go to hell*, his own was just as rude: *Damned if I'm telling you more*. He walked out.

Twenty-Five

SQUALL IN A BOTTLE

TO BE SURE THAT LEITH and JD were gone, Dion stayed in the den an extra few minutes. The house was well built, and he couldn't tell by voices or car engines, so he had to wait, counting to a hundred. When he lost count he sat trying to remember who exactly Cleo Irvine was.

Oscar Roth's ex-wife, that's who. She lived over the bridge, in False Creek, if he recalled right. But the afternoon was slipping away, and he heard music coming from upstairs. He changed into the clothes he had brought for the party, the clothes he had been hoping to impress Jamie with, dark jeans and a button-down shirt, black-on-black vertical stripes with a bit of sheen.

Upstairs, he found a few guests had already arrived. In the dining room, Jon and Melanie were chatting with a heavy man in a flowery Hawaiian shirt. Introductions were made. This was Bob, the first of the guests to arrive, a friend of Jon's and Oz's from way back when.

Some low-key music played, and dozens of amazingly realistic fake candles flickered their gentle flame on tables and shelves. Bob and Jon were loudly reminiscing about an Oz who was both lovable and exasperating. Melanie languidly arranged snacks and decorations on a long table brought out for the occasion. Dion assisted, mostly by watching. He could smell marijuana and wondered what he'd say if the joint passed his way. *Hey, thanks,* probably, now that he was a free agent. Melanie beckoned him over, telling him to help himself to the bar, beer or wine or whatever else he could find.

A photo album on the counter distracted him from the liquor, and he found within its covers assembled memories of Oz. He flipped through some not-so-cute baby pictures, then glum, three-quarter-profile posed school shots. Snapshots of a rowdy-looking teenager. One of more current interest showed Oz not so long ago, with buzz cut and beard and catty shades, maybe in some kind of biker-wannabe phase. He had a good-looking, dark-haired woman at his side, infant in her arms. The couple looked happy. As Melanie was walking by, he called her over and asked if the woman in the photo was Cleo.

"That's Cleo," Melanie said. "I can't believe she's dead, too. And that's tiny Dallas before she shocked us all with her silence. Happier days."

He found a trio of photos of Oz and Jamie, all taken around the same time. There was the bear-hug photo he had seen on the mantelpiece, a shot of Oz and Jamie kissing in a nightclub, and the two of them in a motorboat, looking back at the camera. "The Stingray Oz totalled," Melanie said.

"When were these taken?"

"Last June, I'd say."

Which made the photos about one year old, yet the Jamie in the photo looked more than a year younger, to Dion. Maybe it was the size of her grin, big and carefree.

The last photograph was more recent, no bear hug this time. Jamie as a blonde, unsmiling, and Oz looking at the camera with doleful eyes. Maybe doubtful eyes. He shut the album. "What happened to Cleo? All I was told was that she fell out a window and was DOA."

"I was going to ask you the same question," Melanie said, teeth crunching on a carrot stick. "I was hoping your friend there would give you the inside scoop."

Leith, she meant. "Hardly. Far as he's concerned, I'm a traitor."

"And are you?" She winked at him as she opened the bar fridge, pulling out orange juice. She set down a bottle of Absolut and a tall, skinny bottle of Galliano and two fat tumblers. "Should we stick with Wallbangers? Our friends and relations will start arriving soon, and I, for one, need a boost."

Dion took a tall chair and said yes to the drink. He spun a coaster and saw that one of the bottles lined up before the bar's mirrored shelf was squared off, blue, and he couldn't help thinking of one small, pink-velvet baby bootie.

Melanie was dispensing vodka like a mixology pro. She smiled at him, but he realized that however close she got, she remained remote. And she drank too much. He spun the coaster again.

"How come you don't have a date?" she asked, slapping the coaster flat and putting the drink on top. It was properly presented this time, in a highball glass, complete with swizzle stick, maraschino cherry, and orange slice.

There was no point dancing around the issue, and he had the feeling she knew anyway. "I thought I'd have a shot at Jamie. But she doesn't like cops."

"But you're not a cop, are you? I'll talk to her. She's in her room, laying low, not looking forward to this party. I'll take you down there. Break the ice."

Melanie stood next to him where he sat, stood too close, placed her arm around him. He felt her palm on his lower back, not just resting against him, but feeling his structure. And Jon in plain sight.

But only for a moment. Now she beckoned and took him downstairs.

* * *

A vicious night wind had scattered litter and pine branches all over the North Shore, but the late afternoon had become calm and unnaturally bright. A ship in a bottle sat in front of Mike Bosko, setting sail in the sunshine that flared over the desktop. Bosko told Leith and Doug Paley that he had found the treasure at a garage sale. He told them to go ahead and take a look up close.

Paley had a look, seemed unimpressed, and tried to hand it to Leith.

"I'd rather not," Leith said. "I'm pretty good with not dropping stuff, unless it's valuable. This looks pricey, so I'll just look from here, thanks."

"Oh, I don't know about pricey," Bosko said. "Somebody made it in their workshop. Maybe they followed DIY info on the Internet, or maybe it's a lifelong passion. Just take a look, though, at all that work. It's not your typical ship in a bottle. Look at its tilt, like it's driving into the headwinds. Quite a little masterpiece."

Leith picked up the bottle, gingerly, and peered. The boat was embedded in green gunk of some kind, to mimic the briny deep. What at first he'd thought was exquisite detailing was quite crude, now that he saw it up close, and the tilt was maybe the creator's failure to set the thing straight before the gunk dried. He murmured his appreciation, then passed the bottle back and said, "Sir, I found Dion."

Bosko's brows went up. "Yes?"

Leith went on to recount his visit to the Yorks' Deep Cove home yesterday, and what he had learned. How Dion had taken up with the King of Diamonds, was actually living at the club. "So he's finally resigned, I hear."

Bosko's brows either went up again or hadn't gone down yet. "Hm," he said. "Really."

And with that, Leith's unofficial involvement in the unofficial case was over. It was out of his hands. He was glad. He returned to the matter at hand, reporting on the major cases. He referred to his report and summarized. "No luck getting a production order for Jon's phone records, but still trying. Ziba Farzan has corroborated Jon York's evidence; he stepped in for a few minutes between eight thirty and eight forty-five. I found her credible. JD found her theatrical. So there's that. Ident found shoe scuffs on Oscar's desktop that weren't there before, and some grit, along with Cleo Irvine's fingerprints. But they couldn't match the scuffs to Cleo's shoes. The desk had been pushed about three feet out of alignment, for a climbing surface. It's a heavy desk, but Irvine looked like a strong woman. JD's following up on Irvine's last communications. Irvine had finished a call at eight forty-one with someone named Pearl. JD tracked Pearl down. She's Irvine's housekeeper, and Irvine had hired her to take care of a few things at the Roth house. She was supposed to have hung a drape. *The* drape, we suppose. And had forgotten. Pearl says Irvine called to harangue her about it. They were going to discuss the question of if and when Pearl would go and take care of it, but she says she had the feeling Irvine was just going to do it herself. Pearl says Irvine ended the call abruptly, before any decision was made, and said she'd call back in a couple minutes. Irvine didn't give a reason for the interruption, and never did call back."

"And that was the last call on record?"

"Yes. Irvine pretty well lived on her phone, by the way, so there's a lot to check up. Piles of online info on her too, social media, blogs, so on. She's an art dealer, has a lot of plates spinning. JD's exploring that side of her life. We're thinking that because on the day of her death she was dealing with the house as well as an artwork sale, she might have had other calls coming in, is why she ended the call with Pearl. No evidence of it, but it could have been an incoming that wasn't completed. Anyway, like I say, Irvine's call with Pearl ended at eight forty-one, and that lets Jon York off the hook. Because he was downtown, talking to Ziba, then picking up Dion. Dion says York came to collect him at eight forty, and he, too, is certain on the time."

Unless he's lying, Leith didn't add. He looked at the ship in the bottle. He thought of the gravel pit, and the cadaver dogs, ground-penetrating radar, soil analysis, all those things he might have had to consider putting into motion, if he had found one bit of corroborating evidence. Thankfully, he had not. He had one final task to check off in that regard, and then he would shelve the matter.

"The Lius," Paley said. "This one's eating me alive, sir. Every tip that's come in so far has hit a wall. And we're still looking for this Sigmund Blatt individual. I'm starting to think Jim's right, he's dead, and what got Lance, Cheryl, and Rosalie is a vendetta hit of some kind. I'm even taking another look at Phillip Prince."

Leith swung the talk back to the Oz Roth case. "Jamie Paquette and Melanie York are still in the frame, but I can't imagine how they pulled it off. It was a messy scene, and both of them were processed soon as we brought them in. Paquette was clean, no injuries, not a hair out of place. Melanie York had a bruise on her arm and seemed more dishevelled, which she couldn't or wouldn't explain. She does seem to be a bit of a drinker, so maybe it's just clumsiness. I don't see how she could overwhelm Oscar without major help, in any case. So some external muscle would have to be involved, and that's a link we haven't been able to make."

Bosko thanked Leith and Paley, and they stood. Paley walked out, but Leith hesitated in the doorway. "Whatever his faults," he said, "I thought Cal loved the job."

The BlackBerry near Bosko's elbow on the desktop lit up. Leith had noticed it flickering throughout the discussion, like a silent Fourth of July, with messages, alerts, and prompts. Bosko had ignored some and glanced at others. "Oh, for sure he does," he said. He picked up the phone and brought it to his ear. "That's why he left! Sorry, I have to take this."

Leith took a last look at the little ship in the bottle, leaning against the gale, and followed Paley back to the grind.

* * *

Melanie leaned in the doorway to a large bedroom. It was a half basement set-up with high windows that allowed little daylight through. The walls were painted mauve. The decor was cluttered and feminine, the air rose-scented. Jamie Paquette sat centrally on the bed, her legs drawn up. She was half naked, wearing a filmy black shirt and nothing else, by the looks of it. She had been painting her toenails, and her kohl-lined eyes gazed past Melanie, straight at Dion.

"This guy really wants to meet you," Melanie told her. "He's okay, promise. I've totally vetted him for you. No wires."

Jamie unfolded her slim body, sat on the edge of her bed, and tilted her head at Dion, taking his breath away, much like before, only better. "Okay," she said. "Let's talk."

Twenty-Six

WALL BANGER

THE BOY NOW HAD A DOG of his own, Zan told Leith and JD. The dog's name was Louie, a sweet little Jack Russell rescued from the pound.

"It's so good to see Joey smiling again," she said.

"Wonderful," Leith said. "Where is he now?

"In the kitchen, having lunch. Thank you for coming so fast. I'm not asking him any questions, like you said not to. He's been busy with Louie. In fact, I think it's because of Louie. He talks to the puppy, tells him things he won't tell me."

"What did you hear him saying, as close as you remember?" JD asked.

"Something about the noisy man, and about Cheryl — mom — having a fight. That's all I caught. Noisy man, mom, fight. That's when I called you. I'll bring him over now."

Once again Leith sat quietly off to one side in the living room, while JD sat on the other with the little boy, asking carefully framed questions. "You were telling Louie about what happened to your mom, Joey?" she said. "You remember some things that happened that day?"

Joey nodded.

"That must have been tough to talk about."

He nodded.

"But it felt good, too, to tell somebody, didn't it?"

Joey shook his head.

JD said, "Yeah, I guess nothing really makes it any better, does it? Can you tell me what you told Louie?" Her digital recorder was on, and Leith's notebook lay open on his knee, ready to take down what would probably be another patchwork of unhelpful semi-false memories. He hoped this would be more than just ogas this time around.

Joey spoke softly, barely audible. "The man came up the stairs."

"Up the front way?" JD asked.

"The back."

The back door, as Leith recalled it, at the Liu home on Mahon, led out to a deck, entered via the dining room. There had been a clothesline hitched to a post on the deck, a pile of damp laundry, and the door had been unlocked. Unfortunately people weren't as vigilant about locking back doors as front, even in the big bad city.

"Did he say anything as he came in?" JD asked.

"No, he just came in. He was loud. Mama said we'll play hide-and-seek. She said to go hide and not come out or make a noise till she says so, and she went to go get Rosie."

"Where was Rosie?"

"She was on the floor, by the television."

Leith could see it all playing out before him. Cheryl was maybe in the kitchen with Joey. The man barged in, placing himself between Cheryl and Rosalie. Cheryl wanted to run to pick up the daughter while protecting the son, so she did the only thing she could think of, told Joey to hide, then made a dash across the room. She scooped up her daughter, but now here was this terrifying stranger, asking questions she couldn't or wouldn't answer. She was backed into a corner. And Joey was in the cabinet, staring out at the man, the oga with the big eyes and big mouth, until somebody saved his life by shutting the cabinet door.

"I was hiding," Joey went on. "I was scared. I heard Mama …" He ground to a stop, huddled into himself, sucked his thumb, and his eyes filled.

The silence continued. Leith could see JD thinking. Should she make more small talk, press him to go on, or sit and wait? She did none of the above, but got up, beckoning to Zan, and they left the room together. Moments later, they returned with a small dog trotting behind them, lured by the dog biscuit JD held. She gave the biscuit to Joey. He smiled down at the dog, and the dog smiled up at him.

"Louie," the boy said. "Sit," and gave the dog the biscuit without waiting for it to obey.

The dog sat munching biscuits at its new master's feet, and JD took her chair again. "I thought it might be easier to tell us both what happened. D'you think so, too?"

It went marvellously from then on, and Leith's notebook began to fill up.

"Mama told him to go away," Joey said. "She shouted at him. She went aaaaaah nooo. He said …" Joey pitched his voice high, doing his imitation of someone yelling, "*Noon, noon, noon….*"

Noon?

Joey went suddenly silent and then began to talk, quoting the big, noisy man who was shouting at his mom. He no longer shrieked the words but carefully pulled them from memory, one by one, like a string of awful beads, each bead logged into Leith's notebook.

"You bits."

You bits, Leith wrote.

Joey said, "Rosie was crying. *Shut up shut up shut up.*" He had pitched his voice into a scream again. And again to imitate his mother. "Mama went *noooooo, pleeease.* I went like this." Joey demonstrated how he went, head ducked down, clapping palms over eyes, then ears. "Then it was dark, and lots of noise, and then I didn't hear anything."

JD said, "Could you try to think of him again, Joey, the man, and tell me what he looked like, please?"

He shook his head. "I don't know."

"No? He had something on his head, you said before. Do you remember what that was? Did it look like one of these? Which one, d'you think?"

She had drawn several styles of hats in her notebook and was showing him, like a four-year-old's version of a photo lineup.

Joey shook his head. He was looking at JD with something like brewing resentment. Why was she pulling him back to that dark place? Could any adult be trusted, ever?

She closed her notebook. She said, "Did you hear any more voices after it went dark, any more words?"

Joey suddenly shouted, making Leith jump, and out came a flood of weirdness. "*Wuvvadun, wuvvadun? Bang bang bang, bang bang bang,* walking and walking and walking. He walked close, and I was scared. *Bang.*" Again Joey demonstrated something he couldn't have witnessed but must have visualized, lashing out a fist at an imaginary wall. He fell silent, frowning down at Louie the dog. "Baby," he added. "*Wuvvadun* baby."

* * *

She was perfect. Dion had thought Kate was perfect, but Jamie was up on another level. She was from another world. She was magic, and she had cured him, in one night of talking, and sex, and more talking. As far as conversation, they had spent most of the night together, up at the party and then down in this room. She had been careful in the beginning, answering no questions he put to her. So he learned to ask no more, and only tell her things, whatever came to mind. In time she met him halfway. Which was approximately when they'd had sex. After that, once she decided she could trust him, she opened up and talked. Which was exhilarating. Not deep talk, but deep wasn't what he wanted — not yet. Finally at 4:00 a.m. she fell asleep beside him. They were now what he would call a couple.

He had slept barely an hour, yet he woke feeling good. The house was silent now, the guests had gone home, Jon and Melanie were asleep upstairs.

He wouldn't wake Jamie. He could sit here forever on this chair by the vanity, next to her clutter of cosmetics and junk jewellery in this dim mauve room, watching her sleep. She lay somewhat on her side, naked, partly exposed, a long leg twined in bedsheet, one arm crooked over her head, the other across her stomach. Her face was beautiful. Her elbows, hands, fingers. Her thigh, her calf, her foot. She breathed almost imperceptibly.

She was more than what most people thought she was, not just a streetwise ex-stripper with nothing much on her mind, but for whatever reason, that was how she wanted to be seen. It was a disguise. She had invented her own kind of force field to keep the world at bay.

He had a plan, of sorts. He would dismantle her force field, bring her out into the light, save her from her own defences.

She told him she was afraid, that Oscar's murder terrified her. It made her a refugee in this house. It was why she stayed away from the city. The men who had killed Oz would get her next. But not only that; if they spotted her, they could follow her to the Yorks', and then Jon and Mel would be in danger, too.

"I doubt that," Dion had told her.

"How come?"

"Oscar was the one in trouble. Not you. If you were in trouble, you'd know about it. You said you don't know who these people are or why they did it."

Here he got hung up on doubts. He had a feeling she knew exactly who those people were and what they were after.

She asked him about the investigation into Oscar's murder, the way the cops kept wanting to ask her more questions. "It's like they think I did it. How could that thought even possibly cross their minds? Why would I want to hurt Oz? After all he'd done for me?"

They had been sitting in bed at that point, with the lights off. The house around them was silent. The window was slid open and a breeze flowed through, scented of ocean and lilac.

"No way in fucking hell would I kill that man," she told him.

He had believed her then, and he believed her still. He looked at the pile of gems on her vanity. Lots of glass glimmering in the dark, tangled chains, different colours. Last night she had gone upstairs with him when the party was in full swing. He had sensed her anxiety as she took in the scene. Before relaxing, she had to case the place, looking for assassins in the guests the Yorks had invited. Whether she was looking for some kind of subtle indication of danger or a face in particular, he couldn't tell.

The party had been loud and long. People had taken the floor to talk about Oscar Roth. Jon had talked, and Melanie. Dion watched Jamie's reactions to the eulogies more than the eulogies themselves. She seemed touched, and laughed at all the jokes, and shouted out comments, but gave no speech of her own. Later, a woman banged on a drum kit, another on guitar, and someone sang the blues. He thought the music was good, but it wasn't, if he was to believe Melanie's remark in his ear as she came to sit beside him. There was also a pushy man talking at him, demanding something of him, *pick a card, no, not that one. Any card but that one, bud.*

And fire. Had there been fire?

Jamie shifted on the bed, still asleep. Her eyelids flickered. Her lightly curled hand resting on the pillow overhead clenched into a fist, and released again into childlike innocence. He watched her, a part of him hoping she would wake, but a bigger part of him hoping she would stay asleep a while longer, and let the dream continue.

Twenty-Seven

DEEPER

THE HOUSE WAS A MESS, like a Mardi Gras parade had marched through. Dion collected dirty dishes, scraped leftovers into the garbage, helped Jon move furniture back into place. Jamie made a show of wiping down surfaces while Melanie gathered beer cans and wine bottles and rinsed them out. Music played, the doors were flung open to air the place, and outside, birds twittered and flitted.

Jon and Melanie were deep in conversation. About Dallas and what would happen to her now, after Cleo's sudden death. "I'm her aunt," Dion heard Melanie say. "It should be just a matter of signing a document, right?"

Jon's answer was inaudible. Dion rested against the counter and watched Jamie. She was chatting to him as she worked, about the nice things people had said about Oz last night. She wore no makeup, and without mascara her eyes looked less exotic. Her complexion wasn't actually all that great, in broad daylight, with every freckle and blemish showing. On her feet were rubber flip-flops and on her ass, slack blue joggers. She wore a pink tank top with an iron-on transfer of Tinkerbell stretched over her breasts, the emulsion chipped and fading.

She caught his admiring stare and smiled at him. He loved her style of smiling, with just the corner of her mouth lifting and one eye narrowing almost into a wink. She thrust out her chest, stretching Tinkerbell, and said, "Hey, Cal. Will you teach me to drive? I gotta get out of this town, like, for good."

* * *

The early morning light was brilliant, the traffic along the flats thick. He switched on the vehicle's AC, dropped the shades over his eyes, and thought how other drivers spying him in this smashing white Lexus would think him a millionaire, driving to town with his girl. He said, "How did you get through life not knowing how to drive?"

She shrugged. She had changed to go out, but not by much. Cut-offs instead of joggers, and oversized sunglasses. "Greyhound took me everywhere I needed to go," she said. She had a cigarette in hand and was flicking ashes out the window rolled down partway. "Then I met guys, and guys had cars. I wanted to learn how, but couldn't count on anybody to teach me. Till I met Oz. He went over the manual with me, but we never got to the point of me taking the test. And now he's dead, and I can't live with Jon and Mel forever. Got to get mobile. Get back on stage, make some money. Hey," she said. "You missed the bridge."

"No point writing your test in Vancouver when we've got a perfectly good services centre here."

"I told you I want to go to Vancouver."

He looked at her and saw that she was genuinely upset with the change of plans, and her upset, he knew, had to do with killers. "There's nobody lurking around waiting to jump on you," he told her. "Sure, someone is out there, but what are the chances that, A, you're on their hit list, or B, they'll chance to spot you and start tracking you down? And if they do, good. I'll see them, and I'll deal with them, and you can stop worrying."

She didn't look convinced. She stared at him thoughtfully for several moments before answering with a shrug. "Yes, you're right. I'm an idiot."

Minutes later they entered the grey government building on Esplanade, where licences were applied for, complaints were launched, taxes paid. The place was busy, and they had to stand in line. Jamie put her hand through the crook of his arm as he described the lengthy procedure of getting permission to drive. First came the "L" licence. She couldn't drive alone till she got her "N," the next step up. And there were restrictions on that, too, till she was fully licenced. It wasn't going to happen overnight. She would need a qualified driver to ride in the passenger seat for a good long while. "A qualified driver like me," he told her.

She smiled at him. She turned to look around, as she did from time to time. She looked toward the glass doors at the entrance, and she lurched.

It wasn't much of a lurch, more a twitch, but Dion felt the shockwaves transfer from her arm to his. She returned her gaze casually forward, and he turned to see what had startled her.

The threat appeared to be four young Asian men idling in the lobby, looking around.

Jamie, he saw, wasn't actually gazing casually forward, as she would have liked him to think, but hiding. Hiding her face from the men and hiding her fear from him. He saw that the men had gone to an information board and were studying it. He knew how to spot fakes, and these men weren't faking anything. At this point in their lives, they cared about nothing but those governmental brochures pinned to the board.

"This is going to take forever," Jamie said. "We'll come back later, okay?"

"The line's moving. Just another few minutes."

She held his hand, swinging it carelessly.

It was almost funny, the way she was surreptitiously checking out the men and hoping he wouldn't notice. The men were talking amongst themselves. Dion watched them. They weren't checking out the other visitors to the centre. They didn't once look toward Jamie. They weren't on the hunt for anything except information — on property taxes, or building permits, or immigration help. All the same …

Jamie gripped his hand tighter, squeezing till it hurt. "Don't stare at them," she hissed.

He continued to stare at them. He wanted to memorize their faces. Oscar Roth had been afraid of strangers dogging him, threatening him, and maybe eventually killing him. Were these them?

"Look," he told Jamie. "You can quit bullshitting me.

You know something, and you'd better tell me all about it. Look at those men. Look at them. Do you know them?"

With an effort, she turned to glance at the men directly. Two from the group were maybe feeling the heat of scrutiny on their necks, for they were now looking this way. If anything, they seemed puzzled.

"Do you know them?" he asked her again.

She was still trying hard to be invisible. "I don't know them," she whispered.

He and she faced around front again.

"Then what's the problem?"

"I just don't like Asian guys lately," she said. "They freak me out. And I told you, I don't like being here. I'm leaving. You can stay, I don't care."

She clamped her handbag under her arm and started for the exit, giving the Asian men a wide berth. The men stared after her, but probably because she was attractive from every angle. Dion gave up his place in line and followed. The Asian men stared after him, too, but probably only because he had been staring at them. He guessed from their faces and accents they were probably Thai. He added this clip of information to his mental *Jamie* file.

* * *

Back in the vehicle, she told him he was an asshole, putting her through that like he did, and he could go to hell. She wanted him to drive her home, now.

"Tell me who they are," Dion said. "If they've got anything to do with Oscar's death, you've got to say so. Now. We're going to sit here till you talk."

On Esplanade, with traffic stopping and going around them.

"Then we'll sit here forever," she said.

"Fine," he said.

She pushed open the passenger door. "I'll just get a cab. Thanks for nothing."

She was out, banging the door shut. He saw her in the rear-view mirror, standing on the sidewalk, watching for taxis. A taxi buzzed past, but she didn't flag it. He watched her walk back to the passenger door and climb in.

"How are you going to prove it to me, you're not a cop, you actually quit, this isn't some fuckin' sting?" she said. "How can you possibly prove that?"

"I guess my word is all you've got," he said.

She blew out a breath, then dug into her handbag and took solace in about all she had left to count on in life, the hit of a fresh cigarette.

* * *

She did feed him a little information. The men following Oscar were Asian, she said. Oz had told her so. He owed them big money that he couldn't repay fast enough, and they were going to harass him about it until he paid up. But in one way or another, he was going to suffer for what he'd done.

All of which sounded to Dion like something straight from Hollywood. He asked her why hadn't she told all this to the police, after Oscar's violent death?

Because that would only make it worse, wouldn't it? They would know she had ratted on them, and they'd redouble their efforts to find her, kill her. He told her he found that highly unlikely. She seemed to run out of patience with him, and when they were back at the York home in Deep Cove she disappeared downstairs. He heard her bedroom door thud shut.

From the kitchen Melanie called out, "Come and keep me company."

She was stirring noodles in a pot. "Guess what," she said, smiling at Dion through steam. "I've made inquiries. If all goes well, we're getting Dallas. We're going to adopt her!"

"Wow, nice, congratulations!" Dion looked into the pot. His plans to take Jamie for lunch on Lonsdale had fallen through, and he was hungry, enough to distract him from what else he might have blown. "What are you making?"

Melanie scooped a noodle with a spoon and chewed it experimentally, wasn't satisfied and kept stirring. "Kraft Dinner. Jon ate practically nothing else as a kid. He says that's why his hair is orange. Sometimes he misses the taste. I never learned to cook, but this I can handle. So I see you've upset Jamie. What happened?"

"Nothing, really," he lied.

Melanie looked at him doubtfully. She nibbled another noodle. "Still *al dente*. This dinner in a box isn't as easy as it looks. Now that I'm going to be a mom, I guess I better learn a few kitchen tricks, hey?"

Dion was too troubled by his thoughts to listen much. If she was making Kraft Dinner for Jon, it meant he was close by and could walk in any minute. He had resolved to ask no questions in this home, to prove himself not a spy, but this he needed to know. He said, "Tell me about Jamie."

Melanie gave him a stare. "Tell you what about Jamie, exactly?"

"Everything. Every little thing."

Twenty-Eight

MURK

JD WAS SPEAKING IN TONGUES: *wuvvadun ... you bits ... wuvvudan baby,* while she worked at her side of the table. On his side, Leith tried blocking the sound with a thumb in the ear as he once more read over the pathologist's report detailing the horrific damages to Cleo Irvine's body. JD was trying different pitches now, higher, lower. "*Wuvvadun, wuvvudun.* What have you done, or what have I done?" she asked no one. "You bitch. Baby ... Noon."

Leith leaned back in his chair and studied the wall-mounted timeline stretching across the width of the case room's corkboard. JD had told him she didn't like puzzles, but had put together a fine bird's-eye view of the morning of Cleo Irvine's fall. She had detailed every call and text the woman had made in the days leading up to death, with lines radiating out to boxes which represented the key points from those conversations.

Most of it was work for nothing, he guessed, but buried in the data might be a pearl. Pearl, the housekeeper who had failed her mission to hang the drape. Jimmy Torr had come up with a theory: following the heated phone conversation between employer and employee, Pearl had stormed over and tussled with her boss by the open window, and out Cleo had gone. Leith had scoffed at the idea, but now he wasn't so sure.

"Would you shut up," he snapped at JD.

On parallel lines JD had marked the activities of Jon and Melanie York, every documented communication they had made, every place they had been, or claimed to have been, highlighted in different colours to indicate whether or not that event had actually been corroborated.

Dinner time had come and gone. Between studying, writing, and speaking, JD was eating something salad-like out of a reusable plastic container. She wore a shapeless dark blazer and skinny jeans, and to Leith she looked like a scrawny homeless youth devouring a soup-kitchen handout. He had purchased a sub, stuffed with a variety of cold cuts, and he unwrapped it now to take a bite.

She pointed her fork at the sub and said, "Good choice, David. Those nitrates will blow up your arteries and finish you off nice and quick."

Munching, Leith retaliated. "You look like a boy. Did you know that? Everyone we meet gives you a double take, trying to figure you out."

JD ignored him, eyes downcast at the little bucket of rabbit food in her hand.

Leith gestured at her wall chart. "I see you're spending a lot of time on the Yorks. Don't know why, since they're pretty well cleared. Unless you're saying they hired someone. You have any evidence of their involvement?"

It wasn't the brightest question, since all her evidence was on display in front of him. JD continued to ignore him, continued to eat. Leith focussed on his nitrate sandwich. His veins felt odd, that's how suggestible he was. JD said, "It's the kid. You realize she inherits everything?"

Dallas, the little girl who didn't speak. "Yeah, I know. You've mentioned it about sixteen times."

"And who's the kid's closest relative? Aunt Melanie. And guess who's making noise about getting custody of the kid?"

"Aunt Melanie?" Leith guessed.

"And Uncle Jon, who already filed the paperwork. What d'you think the Ministry will say to the application? They won't say anything. They'll stamp it, sold. So suddenly Jon York's a lot closer to Oscar's millions, plus he's got the final controlling shares in Diamonds. Oh yes, Mr. York's got motive galore."

"He's also got an alibi," Leith said. "The alibi's name is Cal. So unless Cal is lying …" he stopped, because there it was again, the doubt. He didn't know Dion, or what he was capable of.

JD kept chewing. Last week she had told Leith she wasn't a good multitasker, and by now he knew she was not just being modest. Once she fixed on an issue, she stuck to it with blinders on. Right now her mind was not on Cleo Irvine, but little Joey Liu and his oga.

Leith was a so-so multitasker, so he tried to help her out. "*What have I done, baby.* Maybe he was blaming Rosalie for all this, 'cause she was crying, she made him do it? Or addressing his partner at the scene?"

"I'm thinking the latter. Makes more sense. Only those close to a child would call her *baby.*"

"Which means they were a couple. A man and a woman."

"Not necessarily a man and woman. Time to join the twenty-first century, Dave."

He gave her the eye. "Yes, I know, not necessarily, but probably, right?"

Hadn't Dion presupposed there was a woman on the scene, back when he was still part of the team?

JD agreed. "Probably, yes, a man and a woman."

A faithless couple, if the better half had scooped the baby bootie, and the gin bottle vase, combined them for some wacky reason, and flung them out to sea. A betrayal, or a statement of some kind, or a meth addict's illogical head game?

"But Joey only mentioned a man."

"She maybe came in later, when he was already hiding."

Leith left JD to her Liu mystery and turned his thoughts back to Cleo Irvine. Melanie's alibi wasn't so tight. She had been at home that morning, she said. Alone. She could have run out and done the deed. But he doubted it. It was a simple matter of power balance; Cleo was the tall, wiry, athletic type, and Melanie … well, not so much. Even if Melanie came with a gun and said "Get up on that desk and jump," he imagined Cleo would have outmanoeuvred her.

He tried to imagine a hitman walking into the mansion, finding Cleo there. Maybe she had been standing by the open window, preparing the curtain for others to come along and install. Maybe she turned, mistook the hitman for the potential buyer arriving early for a look-around. Maybe he had taken advantage of her surprise, strolled up to her, hoisted her up, and tossed her. But if she'd been manhandled, she would have acquired at least one small bruise or scratch that would stand out as inconsistent with the fall. There was nothing like it in the pathologist's preliminary reports.

Maybe the intruder had cajoled her at gunpoint up onto the desk and given her the choice of a bullet or a leap, and she'd chosen the latter.

Frankly, Leith didn't buy the hitman theory, either. Accidents did happen, even within the murk of a murder investigation, and it was quite possible their imaginations were firing off unnecessarily.

"Anyway, I'm outta here," JD said, cleaning up her dinner and paperwork with sudden zeal. "Brain is stuck in a loop, and it's time to get back to real life. Bye."

"See you tomorrow."

She was gone, and Leith dug into the Oscar Roth file, viewing the attack through the lens of new developments.

Could little Dallas be the prize?

The child would be a dependant all her life.

Whoever controlled the child controlled the money held in trust for her.

It would be a slow payoff, but a payoff all the same.

But even with the shares thrown in, was it worth killing for? Really?

* * *

Jamie and Dion sat side by side on the sofa in the den, brushing up on the rules of the road. Jamie was surprisingly literate. She took notes, and her handwriting was loopy and childish, but not hesitant. Her spelling, grammar, and punctuation were good, too, better than Dion's. When he quizzed her, she was more often right than wrong.

"Lookit, they're talking about a four-way intersection," she said, and fell back, laughing. "How kinky is that?"

He tried to turn the page, but she was bored with lessons. She leaned to turn up the music, then crawled to the soft Persian rug to lie beguilingly before him, giving him his own private, professional, and irresistible floor show. "Ever done a four-way intersection, Cal?"

"No. Have you?"

"Three-way, four. Once I did five."

He didn't want to hear of her record-breaking orgies or who she had done them with. He hoped it was a thing of the past, but wouldn't ask. He was too afraid of the answer.

She said, "Come here."

And he did, there in the Yorks' living room, when Jon or Melanie could walk in on them any moment. Not that it mattered. They would just step around the couple on the carpet and carry on with whatever they were doing. The nightclub mentality of "anything goes" was all around; like the pull of a strong current, wade in too deep and he'd never see shore again. Like it or not, soon it would draw him in, too.

Twenty-Nine

SINKER

PROGRESS ON THE OSCAR Roth/Cleo Irvine case was showing the first signs of decay, yet another day passing with no new leads. But on the other major file that was also growing colder by degrees, the death of the Liu family, Lance, Cheryl, and little Rosalie, there was news. Not much, but some. On a Tuesday afternoon, Leith's last day before his weekend, a constable from Drumheller, Alberta, was patched through to his desk. The constable said he had found Sigmund Blatt. There in the Alberta badlands, of all places.

"Guy got in a fight outside the Dollarama," the constable explained. "No bloodshed, no big deal, but after we broke it up we had a look at him, figured he's a little dusty-looking, a little on the vagabond side, and so we engaged him in conversation. He said he's in the process of moving, no fixed address, lost his ID. Said his name was Dean Broadfoot from Portage la Prairie, out job hunting in the promised land. Sounded credible enough, but I didn't believe him. Probably 'cause the *a la*."

"The what?"

"Portage *a la* Prairie, he says. For his alleged hometown. Should've picked something easier, like Newton. Anyway, ran his plates, belonged to a Marcia Tannenbaum ..." he spelled it out for Leith "... from Airdrie. He says it's a friend who lent him the truck for his job hunting. I poked around. He seemed to be living out of the vehicle, by the looks of it. And by the smell. Carting around a big, ugly bird in a cage, too. Fucking thing told me to kiss its tail feathers. In perfect English, would you believe it? Anyway, the guy was reasonable enough, after we bought him lunch. Convinced him to take us out to his campsite down the 840 around Rosebud there, a pretty good little hideout in the bluffs by the river."

"How did you figure he was Sigmund Blatt?"

The constable's voice remained deadpan. "How many homeless types haul around parrots? I read my bulletins, sir. I asked him straight out, your name's Blatt, right? And he fessed up. So what do you want me to do with him? He's cooperating so far, seems happy sitting in the holding cells eating jail food. But can't very well hold him overnight, can I? Even if he's okay with it, I'm not. The bird's here, too, and he's a noisy bastard."

"Can you put Blatt on the line?" Leith said.

After some background mumbling, Sigmund Blatt said, "Hello." He sounded tired, fed up.

Leith said, "I told you to remain in contact. Instead you disappear. What are you afraid of, Mr. Blatt? Time to tell the whole story, don't you think?"

"You'd be scared, too, if your best buddy and his family got massacred practically before your eyes," Blatt said.

"And you have no idea who's behind it, but you believe this killer's after you next, no particular reason?"

"It was no random act. He was after something. Maybe something I have."

Leith tried out Joey Liu's verbatim words. "Do you know someone named *Noon*?"

"No."

"Anyone that sounds like Noon?"

"No."

Leith made a note. He said, "Can you hazard a guess as to what this thing he was after could be?"

"No, sir, I have no idea."

"Something you've seen? Something you know? A password? Top-secret microfiche?"

He could feel the dusty refugee glowering at him over the line. "No clue," Blatt said. "And I'm not going to hang around like a sitting duck and wait for it, either."

"Did you do something to piss this guy off? Is that what this is really all about?"

"No, I did nothing. Nothing at all."

"So let me get this straight. You didn't feel safe, even fifteen hours away from the scene of the crime, way over there on the other side of the Rockies, so you took to the hills, living rough. Sounds kind of extreme. I'm thinking you must have got tipped off. Did you hear something? See something? Get some kind of message?"

"No, sir. Just a bad feeling."

Leith rolled his eyes. He went on to give Blatt the

lowdown, that he couldn't detain him, couldn't even order him to stay in touch, but was asking him, politely, to please keep him, Leith, apprised as to his whereabouts from now on. And not to leave the province without saying so.

For what it was worth, Blatt swore to God he'd stay in touch.

Leith spoke to the constable once more, then hung up and added a note to the Liu file: contact information for one Marcia Tannenbaum of Airdrie, Alberta. If Blatt disappeared again, this time Leith would have someone to harass about it.

* * *

Dion's cellphone had turned up at Diamonds, lodged in the VIP booth seating. Odd. Checking it after several days of being misplaced, he found it not as loaded with messages as he expected. The force had given up on him, then. They had received his resignation letter, and that was that. He'd been cut loose. Good.

He went to Hami's for a trim. The barber had switched the radio station back to Persian Pop, Dion noticed, and he remarked on it. Assimilation shouldn't be rushed, Hami said. Hami noticed changes, too. "Nice neck-chain. Never seen you pimping heavy metal before."

The slang startled Dion. The silver around his throat was an impromptu gift from Melanie. She had taken it from Jon's collection and put it on Dion, so he would show proper respect for Oscar at his wake, she said — he wasn't sure how serious she was — and afterward Jon told him to keep it. *Looks better on you, anyway, man.*

Hami stood with scissors and comb in hand and again suggested Dion might relax the FBI look a bit. Either go longer or shorter. This time Dion agreed. Longer.

"I quit the force," he told Hami. "I'm looking for an apartment." He no longer believed he had the courage to move east, start over in the prairies. He had Jamie now, though he already saw their relationship as a rough road in dense fog. With a washed-out bridge somewhere ahead. But Jon had made him an offer he was considering, working security at the club. "Know of any leads?"

"I got an uncle, owns the Belleview Apartments up here," Hami said. "Bit of a waiting list, but I could maybe pull some strings."

Dion went to check out Hami's uncle's apartment. The pad was on the second floor of a blue-collar low-rise up on 14th, with no view whatsoever, and he couldn't move in till June 1st, which was still over a week away. Another week living with Jon, Melanie, and Jamie, who seemed to expect him to stay forever. He said yes to the apartment.

His days were empty, but not peaceful. Jamie had her learner's licence, and he was taking her out on the road, teaching her to drive. He was also learning more about her, filling in what Melanie hadn't been able to tell him. Melanie spoke of the changes Jamie had gone through, from a thin but gregarious brunette to a hot but reclusive blonde. Happened pretty well overnight, Melanie said, and not long after Oz picked her up.

How long was not long, Dion wanted to know.

Maybe a month, Melanie said. She attributed the shift to sudden wealth and the pandering but possessive reins of Oscar. Such a new lifestyle, both liberating and stifling — who wouldn't go through a dramatic metamorphosis?

What Dion discovered from Jamie herself, in their stop-and-go conversations as she learned to drive, was that she was an only child; she had grown up in South Vancouver; she had been Little Miss This or That from kindergarten onward. Cosmetics and pretty dresses, subjected to perms and pedicures, being touched and stroked, put on a stage, turned around, taught to wiggle her butt. "So, yeah," she said. "Pretty early on I looked in the mirror and went ugh." Soon as she grew gangly, she was in high heels and push-up bras. Riding in parades, waving at people. When she was in her teens, her mom started to hate her, and her dad started to love her. It got so weird, she had to leave home. Right away she was snapped up by an entertainment agency. Out of one weird and straight into another.

On Friday morning Dion also learned she had a mean streak. The driving challenges were getting tougher, and today she was learning to merge onto the highway. She happened to not merge fast enough, causing a Chev truck coming up behind to step on the brakes. The Chev blasted its horn at her. "Don't worry about it," Dion told her, but with a flare of temper she floored the gas, passed the Chev, cut him off. More horn blasting. Dion bellowed at her to pull over. She did, and so did the other driver, the two out of their vehicles, balling up their fists. They fired words at each other, from insults to threats of bodily harm, and if Dion had not stepped in fast to calm the situation, it would have ended in tears. And a police report, as he told them both.

The Chev driver backed off, swearing all the way back to his cab, and pulled out. Jamie slipped behind the wheel. She was no longer cursing, but laughing like it had all been a spin on the tilt-a-whirl. "What an asshole," she said.

Dion began to worry about the day she would receive her full licence and be set free on the roads. If she lived that long.

On Friday at noon Jon York texted him, telling him to drop by the club; he had momentous news. The news wasn't so momentous, as it turned out. The club wasn't open yet, the overhead lights on, and Jon only wanted to tell him of plans he was hatching for tomorrow, for Melanie's surprise birthday party. "We'll move those tables out to the edges, set up a buffet along there. I've got Darcy doing up a birthday soundtrack with all Mel's favourite dance tunes."

Ziba joined them, telling Jon with delight, "Hey, I've got Tony lined up."

"Tony, you know Tony, right?" Jon asked Dion. "Was here the other day, flashing his headshots around?"

Dion didn't know who Tony was, but was starting to guess.

Ziba said, "Professional boy-toy with tear-away cavalry stripes."

"And," Jon said, "a *fabulous* cake from Thomas Haas. I'm really stretching the budget for my Mel, but you only turn forty once, right? This is a special occasion. And we're doing good, financially-speaking."

"Really?" Dion was pleased. Maybe he was wrong; the place wasn't in trouble. The future was solid. His new life was secure.

Ziba said, "Yes, and that's because, all due respect, Oz has stepped down. I'm sorry, Jon, but much as we all loved him, he had his ideas. Didn't he?" She smiled at her boss, with a message behind the smile that Dion couldn't read. "Once Oz had his mind set, you couldn't budge him with a bulldozer. Which is a virtue, Jon. I'm saying it's a good thing, just a little too much of it."

"Bulldozers or dynamite," Jon agreed with a laugh. "We're also going to have a little guest of honour tomorrow," he told Dion. "Dallas. Just got the word, the adoption's going through. Big relief. Mel and I couldn't imagine that kid in an institution. Couldn't bear the thought."

Dion congratulated him on the good news. Ziba and Jon then went on to discuss last-minute logistics around the birthday bash. When Ziba left, Jon picked up where he had left off, describing to Dion what would go where and who would do what tomorrow night.

Dion listened and nodded and watched him talk. He was fairly certain that somewhere along the line, something had undone Jon's good mood. The sunniness had cooled by several degrees, hadn't it? And the enthusiasm was now false. Working back through the conversation, he could even pinpoint at what point the clouds had moved in: right around the word *dynamite*.

* * *

Leith was in the middle of his three-day weekend and fast asleep when his BlackBerry woke him with an urgent buzzing. He pushed himself off his pillow, reached for it, noted the time — 1:15 a.m. — and rasped, "What?"

JD Temple was in his ear, saying, "Sorry, did I wake you?"

"No. Just wait a second." He put her on hold and looked at the curvaceous mound of blankets beside him. Alison was a light sleeper, and he didn't want to bother her. He took the phone to the living room and dropped heavily to the sofa. "Why aren't you asleep?" he asked JD.

"Because the Internet's more interesting. I found something. I think it's a game-changer."

Leith rubbed his eyes till they could stay open on their own. "Fire away."

"I did some trolling," she said, "since I don't trust those financial docs that the Diamonds' CA dump-trucked on us following our warrant. Want to hear what I trolled up?"

"Yes, please, tell me."

"This is one nightclub operation that threw it all in and crossed its fingers," JD said. "Well, the wheel's about to stop spinning, and the number's off. The strip-bar dance-club combo idea, jazzy but not so wise. Strip bars are a thing of the past, 'cause guys get their rocks off at their computer screens these days. Tourism's down, staycations are in. Nightclubbers are young, and the young don't have jobs, so they're not dancing much, and if they do, they go across to the big city where the in-crowd goes. So it's pretty grim."

Leith wasn't impressed. "So what? He'll scale back the dancers and raise the cover charge. Anything else, JD?"

She sniffed, maybe disappointed that he wasn't excited by the breaking news. She said, "York's cancelling contracts for a courtyard extension at the dock-front, and sounds like he sank a lot of money into some charter yacht scheme for nothing. The rumour mill says he's firing staff left, right, and centre, trying to recoup. But too little, too late. The big payees are waiting, and they're hungry." She paused, probably for dramatic effect. "No doubt about it, Diamonds is sinking."

Thirty

BLUE SPARKS

SOME NIGHTMARES WERE SMALL-scale and disturbing, and others were larger-than-life and terrifying. Tonight's was epic. Dion stood on the tenth-floor balcony of his old Seacrest apartment, transfixed by an eerie glow on the horizon, against which he could see the furthermost buildings crumbling to dust. Destruction spread like spilled ink toward him and toward the RCMP detachment he could see from where he stood. He knew those within wouldn't know it was coming. They would all be crushed in seconds if he didn't do something. So he climbed onto the railing and leapt, waking himself with his own frightened yell.

He sat up. Jamie was not in bed beside him, and upstairs he could hear a woman's laughter. Then silence. He spotted an item on the floor. It wasn't a tidy floor, but the item stood out to him as though it was flashing for attention. He left the bed and picked it up. A small black matchbook, partially used, with the Diamonds logo on it.

Jamie used a lighter. Melanie didn't smoke. He himself had never picked up matches from the club. Which left only Jon. He wasn't as shocked as he wished he was.

* * *

Inside, the place was looking more gymnasium than dance club, with its fluorescents on full. Dion helped move tables and chairs. Then he strung up decorations, what seemed like a billion foil stars lit with LEDs that were to cascade from the stage frameworks, with bunches of purple helium balloons on the fringes. "The last of the helium reserves," Jon said. "But my baby's worth it."

Up on his ladder, Dion stuck up another streamer of stars, and asked if Melanie was actually going to be surprised.

"Not hugely," Jon admitted. "She knows I've got something planned, just doesn't know what. It's not what I'd call mind-blowing, but it's better than our humdrum old dinner parties. This'll be a night to remember, promise."

"You're lucky to have her," Dion said, looking down at Jon.

Jon smiled up at him. "I know it."

The stars were up, and Dion climbed down. Jon dimmed the lights and switched on the psychedelics, and all stood back to admire the effect. To Dion it looked old fashioned, but nice. Jon said, "Party goes till about midnight. Then VIPs will cruise around the bay a bit. Buddy of mine has a yacht. We're going to end the night with champagne and waltzes. What d'you think?"

"Melanie will be thrilled," Dion said.

But Jon was looking at him seriously, with something to say. Dion couldn't imagine what and braced himself. "Now, I know you've got a thing about the water," Jon said. "Mel told me about it after we took you out on the Glastron. I didn't know. You should have told me, and I'd have taken it slower, or whatever. You could have worn those inflatable armbands, say. We wouldn't laugh."

He was laughing now, though, and Dion didn't care for it. "It's not a big deal."

"It is, once you hear what they call it. *Thalassophobia.* Fear of the sea. Which is just plain cruel, considering where you live."

"It's not that. Really."

"But a yacht's different," Jon went on. "Steady as a rock. You'd think you were on terra firma. Just stay indoors and you'll be okay."

"Sure. Is Jamie coming tonight?"

"Of course." Jon slapped him on the shoulder and went back to supervising the surprise party that Melanie was half expecting. Dion stood with a beer bottle in hand, looking up at sparkling tinfoil stars. Convictions, he was thinking about. Looch had once said, *Just because you got yourself a conviction, Cal, doesn't mean it's right.*

* * *

About nine that evening Melanie walked into the darkness, baited in with a lie about signing more adoption papers. A little girl in a blue velvet jumper was at her side. Melanie had on a flowered wrap over a slinky black dress, and looked beautiful, Dion thought. He also thought that for two individuals not expecting to walk into a party, they were superbly decked out. They stood silhouetted a moment before the lights came on, along with the opening strains of "Kiss You All Over." The guests shouted "Happy Birthday!" Melanie did a good job of looking shocked, and Dallas seemed indifferent.

Soon the disco ball was churning, spitting pink and blue sparkles across the floor, and people were dancing to the mellow playlist the DJ was blasting, loud oldies mixed with the latest hits. Dion had been drinking beer all evening, but Jon told him to grow some class and handed him a mixed drink, gin and tonic. "It'll grow on you," he promised, as Dion pulled a face.

Dion tried to open himself to the fairly turpentineish taste. "What's the gin?"

Jon's hand signal in response, *I'm watching you,* was serious but facetious. "Yes, it happens to be Bombay Sapphire, Detective. But you won't find any baby booties in here."

"No, I was just wondering," Dion said. The reference had alarmed him, until he recalled that the message-in-a-bottle clue had been all over the media. Pretty well the only thing that had been suppressed in the Mahon Avenue case was the survivor, Joey Liu.

Dion kept an eye out for Jamie, but he knew she wouldn't show. People danced around him. He raised a toast, smiling, feeling the buzz.

An echoey and seductive song played, and Melanie was at his side, saying, "'Face the Sun.' I love this one." Dion was far gone enough to grab her hand and pull her into a dance-floor embrace. They hung on to each other and swayed artlessly, more like long-lost lovers than friends. Dion could see Jon York deep in conversation, but looking their way now and then, unconcerned, even grinning. This was the new romance, he realized. This was how it would be from now on. No rules, no convictions.

Melanie noticed the time and said, "Jesus, I forgot." Dion followed her out to the foyer, where Dallas was being overseen by a staff member. Not that there was much to oversee. The little girl sat in a chair, a toy in her hand, a white plastic horse. The plastic looked almost luminescent, like weathered glass. The girl was murmuring in its ear.

"She loves horses, especially this one," Melanie told him. She had phoned for someone to come and pick up the child, take her home, put her to bed. "She won't watch TV unless there's horses running about the screen. The wilder the better. Keeps her captivated for hours. People say it's sad. I'm not so sure. I guess I have a lifetime to figure it out."

Dion couldn't imagine having to care for any child, let alone one with special needs, but he could see no fear in Melanie's eyes. She said, "I tiptoed into her world the other day. I brought another horse and lay on the floor, and my horse grazed in a nearby field. Her horse eventually came over to check mine out. It was the closest we ever got to a conversation."

"She never talks?"

"She tried it out for a while, but seems to have abandoned the effort. She's been to specialists, had tutors, all sorts of tests. They've given up. But I haven't, and won't. I love her as is."

The music filtered through the walls, a thump-thump heartbeat. Dion and Melanie picked up the slow dance where they had left off. Dallas wandered, running the little horse along mouldings and coffee tables. Sometimes the animal cantered and sometimes it flew.

The care aide arrived and took Dallas away, and moments later, Jon came striding out from the double doors of the club, calling them over. "Is Dallas gone?" he cried out happily to Melanie, taking her hand. "Good, 'cause we've got some grown-up-girl entertainment 'specially for you."

Tony, Dion thought, following along. Walking wasn't easy, either because the ground was slanted or because he was laughing too hard. Everything was funny now, and a male stripper just about topped it.

Inside, the MC was wrapping up her intro, and an electric tom-tomming of suspense began. The partiers hooted and whistled, and Tony the male stripper power-posed onto the stage. Women shrieked with laughter. Dion used his hands for a megaphone and added to the noise with a wolf howl. He turned to seek Jon out in the crowd. Jon gave a wave and thumbs-up. He had said this would be a night to remember, and it was turning out to be just that.

* * *

Afterward, there was the yacht. A bigger boat than Dion expected, and the VIPs numbered only about fifty, so there was plenty of room on board. He stood in what somebody called the stateroom, a curved lounge with a window viewing the waters chugging past, a dreamy parade of lights from anchored cruise ships. There was no waltz music, as Jon had promised, but meandering jazz. Conversation was lively. Dion was glad to see Jon and Melanie leaning against each other like young lovers, kissing often.

Definitely, though, someone should cut off Melanie's drinks. She was getting loud, and he knew how easily loud could slide into obnoxious. Himself, he had switched from liquor to sparkling water with a twist of lemon. He joined the group on the foredeck to watch the fireworks. The boat was now in the middle of the great corridor called the Georgia Strait, idling as the ignited rockets whistled. Whistled and torpedoed and exploded into curtains of gold. VIPs gasped and cheered. Melanie's eyes reflected the sparks, and she leaned so far back as if to embrace the sky that Dion stepped behind her to break her fall.

"This is so perfect," she told him, not falling but leaning, and she raised her glass to the atmosphere. "Isn't this perfect, Cal? Aren't you glad you came along?"

He gripped her arm as she went to the railing and leaned on it, out over the cold, black water. "Look at that, it's so deep and powerful and wise. How can you not love the water? How can you be *afraid* of the water, Cal? What happened? Did you nearly drown? Let me cure you. Let's go swimming."

"Let's just watch the fireworks," he said.

"My glass is empty."

"Time to do like me and stick with water," he told her. "Or you'll regret it tomorrow."

She stared at him, then laughed aloud, and he noticed that however drunk she became, she never quite lost touch. "You're right," she said, and turned and flung out her arm. He watched her champagne glass sail out over the waves and fall in a glittering arc. It swirled for a moment then was sucked into the deeps.

She said, "I drink too much. Pay attention. I'm going to blurt out something I shouldn't."

"Like what?"

She laughed. She hit at him but missed. "Nice try, Detective." She leaned into him, and he had his arms around her again, if only to keep her from slumping to the ground, and he had to correct his earlier assessment: she *did* lose touch. Another round of fireworks popped off, quite a blitz. He watched with the rest of the crowd as Melanie seemed to doze against his chest. The last bang was the biggest; the show had orgasmed, and was now winding down. The guests drifted back inside. Jon stood alone, watching the last of the blue sparks spiral out of the sky. Getting his money's worth.

Dion helped him get his money's worth for a minute, then roused Melanie and took her inside to get some tea or coffee into her. People were leaving, going out to bid Jon goodnight. They gathered their jackets and wished Melanie a final happy birthday, and she blew a few kisses. Dion watched the stateroom empty and grow quiet. The jazz still playing now seemed sad. Melanie lay on the cushions with her head on his lap, and outside Jon York stared out at the water, watching his night to remember coming to an end.

Thirty-One

JIBE

JAMIE PROWLED THE HONDA down the avenue. Dion was in the passenger seat, praying his car would get through this lesson without a fender-bender. The windows were down, and the warmth and fragrance of a warm spring night after a rainfall filled the car's interior. He had instructed her for an hour in an empty elementary school lot, working on the fine art of parallel parking, using a couple of plastic milk crates to mark out the driver's allotted space. Now, past midnight, they were looking for real-life obstacles to practice on, parked vehicles on a quiet residential street.

Jamie knew just about everything. Windshield wipers, high beams and low beams, emergency flashers, tire pressure, and the alerts on the dashboard that should never be ignored.

"Try these two," Dion said.

She parked perfectly in the space he had pointed out, and told him she was tired of this exercise. "I want to go back to the highway," she said. "Let's go bully another asshole into a coronary."

"No," he said. "Let's just talk."

"What?"

"Shut it off."

Reluctantly, she killed the engine. He said, "With an 'L' you're going to need a passenger with you for a whole year. Someone with a licence. You realize that? Who's going to supply the car when I'm not available? Who's going to ride with you?"

Her stare was not quite blank. There was the creeping stain of anger in her eyes. "You're planning not to be available?"

"I'll help for a while, but I've got a life. You'll have to find someone else."

She stared at him, and stared harder, as if he might be intimidated into changing his mind.

"What about Jon?" he suggested, with some edge. "Or Melanie?"

"Too busy. They've got Dallas now. I was going to tell you today, I'm leaving town, and I want you to come with me. But you've changed. I can tell. So if you're going to fuck off, then maybe I'll just pack up and go on my own."

He and she were similar in a way; they both kept threatening to fuck off and leave, and then never took that important first step. He crossed his arms. "Getting someone else to teach you to drive won't be easy. You have a bunch of friends I don't know about?"

"I have friends."

He didn't believe her. "If you're thinking any guy on the street will take one look at you and offer to help, you better remember he'll want something in exchange. And that guy won't be as nice as me, that's for sure."

Her face was tilted up slightly, facing him directly, but she seemed distant.

He said, "You told me you're in trouble, but you're not telling me what matters. If you told me, if I knew, then maybe we could do something about it, and you could stop running."

"Like do what?"

"Find these Asian guys. Put 'em away."

He expected her to step even further back now, one way or another. He could see her mind ticking. She was thinking hard, of what she had to gain, what she had to lose, and in a way, he was doing the same. With sudden clarity he realized who they each were: she was an incubating menace, and he was still a cop, manoeuvring around a suspicion.

She occupied herself tying her hair back, checking her face in the visor mirror before answering, a simple but icy admission. "I know who they are, and I know why they did it, because I'm part of it all."

She checked his face, but he was giving nothing away. She said, "They want to kill me for what they think I did. They were going to, once. She had her guys put a gun to my head and pull the trigger. I fuckin' wet my pants. But it was just a warning. They weren't sure it was me. They let me go. I dyed my hair and figured no way I'm going outside again. Next time they won't let me go. They're going to make it hurt. I'm not going to the cops, because I can't, so I'm going to do the next best thing, leave town. That's all I'm going to tell you. I thought you and me could go together. I think we're made for each other. I still think we should do it. Well? Will you come with me?"

With all of that, she had supplied him with several answers, and a whole bunch of questions, too. The biggest was her use of the word *she*.

No perceivable connection existed between Oscar Roth and the Liu killings, but the possibility had planted itself in Dion's mind from the day he had walked into the Roth residence and stood behind Jimmy Torr doing his investigator's squat. He had looked at the body and the scene. The nexus was right there for anyone to see: time and space. Two violent deaths in one week, in one relatively safe city, was enough to draw a line between them. The madness of both crime scenes was another. They felt the same to him. Then along came Jamie, with her fear of Asians. And now she was telling him there was a *she* in the mix. An Asian *she*, he supposed. Which all but finalized it for him.

The best plan of action, he decided, was to ask her outright, ask it fast, and word it ambiguously. He said, "Did you go to a house on Mahon with Oscar last month?"

He saw a flicker in her steady gaze. She wanted to come across as confused by the question, maybe bewildered, but she overdid it slightly. Ever so slightly, but enough for him to know. He had her. She said, "Mahon? What's that?"

"I think you know what I'm talking about."

"Oh good, 'cause I sure don't."

"You don't have a criminal record, that's why they couldn't ID you. You're not in the DNA databanks. But you know what? Everyone leaves something at a crime scene, no matter how clean you try to be. One long blond hair is all FIS needs. Or an eyelash, for that matter. They had nothing to compare it to before, but when I give them your name, they will. Your sample matches up, they've got you."

She was busily tamping down her outrage, lighting a cigarette, looking out the side window as though she couldn't bear the sight of him. Her hand trembled.

He said, "Why did you do it? Were they the stalkers?"

She said, "You told me to trust you, so I did. Everyone's a fucking liar."

"I never lied to you."

She shrugged, letting him know she was writing him off forever. "For all I know, you're lying about finding a hair, too."

There had been no long blond hair at the scene, nor an eyelash, but even so, he had told her no lies. "No, I'm not."

"So you've been after me all along."

"I didn't think so," he said bitterly. "But I guess I was. I started to wonder."

She pulled on her cigarette and kept her focus out the windshield. "The Asian guy was following us. Oz took him on. He went nuts, went overboard, because he was just that mad. He was protecting me. It's what men do when their girlfriends are in danger, protect them. Or *most* men."

"How did he track down the guy's family?" Dion asked. He had unclipped his seat belt, for two reasons. One, to be able to sit at an angle, back against the door, the better to see her. Two, to be able to defend himself if she should decide to do away with her enemy.

"Oz got the guy's phone. He looked through the contacts and ended up trying Siri. He said *home*. And then went where the phone told him to go."

"And?"

"And you know the rest."

"Did you go in the house with him?"

"No, I waited in the car."

"No, you didn't. I told you, there's evidence you were inside."

She hugged herself and puffed on her cigarette, the window open to let out the smoke. She said, "There were toys in the yard. I couldn't stand it. I went in. I saw."

"Saw what?"

She managed to put the cigarette to her mouth, but it was a struggle. Tears filled her eyes. She wasn't faking her distress.

Dion said, "Okay. You have to go to the police. This is going to end here."

"No. I can't."

"If Oscar did it, if you were just there, if they know you were there, the best thing you can do is turn yourself in, right now."

"Bit late for that."

"No, it's not. You were scared. They'll get that. You'll explain that you thought about it. Or tell them I counselled you, and you realized it's the right thing to do."

She sucked nicotine and billowed smoke. She had managed to calm her shaking hands, but her face was still wet.

Dion said, "If you run — and that won't be easy without a driver's licence, will it? — the police will catch up to you. Guaranteed. And then you can kiss leniency goodbye. They'll figure you're just as guilty as Oscar, and they'll put you away, probably for life. Turn yourself in now, at worst you'll get probation."

Her next words, softly spoken, were a sign of progress. "What if they don't believe me?"

"If it's the truth, they'll believe you. You're way better off walking in there today and telling them what happened than letting them catch you trying to get wherever you're going."

Nearly a minute passed. She said, "I'll tell you what happened, what I remember. It's a blur, but I'll try."

"Better if you go in and make a statement. I'll drive you there. I'll go in with you."

"No, I'm not going in there. I'll tell you, and you can do what you want. Go tell 'em. They can come and arrest me, whatever. I don't care."

He didn't want to be an intermediary, and told her so. But now that she was telling all, she went on to tell all of the all: "First he got the guy in the truck, took him down a hill and smashed the fuck out of him. Then got his phone, went to the house, killed that lady and the little kid. I think the kid was an accident. He didn't mean to do that, and it really, really bugged him. I had left the house pretty quick when he started strangling the lady. I sat in the truck, scared out of my wits. Then he jumped in and started driving south, said we'd go straight to the border, jump across. Then freaked that they'd be waiting for him, and pulled a U-ey. Then started worrying about the dead guy's phone, and figured he had to ditch it. He said it had some kind of chip the cops could track, even if it was off. So he pulled down this little dead-end road so he could rip out the battery. It's something he saw on TV, right? Without a battery it couldn't be tracked, he said. But he couldn't figure out how to take it apart, and I said just chuck it. But he had it in his mind he needed to remove the battery."

"Where?" Dion said. "Where did he ditch it? What's the name of the dead-end road?

"I don't know."

"Did he get the battery out?"

She crushed out her cigarette and lit no more. "No. There was this metal bar lying on the side of the road, and he got out and used it to smash the phone open. That didn't work, either, so he got back in and spent, like, five minutes on that phone, wiping it down. Then got out again and threw it into the ditch, and the bar in after it, and then rocks and gravel and shit, yelling and crying. I mean, he had a total meltdown. Which is great, isn't it, when you're trying to lay low after you've just killed someone. Lucky for him nobody drove by. I yelled at him to get in the fucking car, let's go. So he pulled it together, and we went home. He had a hit of something from his medicine bag and calmed down. 'We're just going to play it cool,' he said. 'We'll get through this if we both just keep our mouths shut.'"

She shook her head. "But we both got it wrong. That guy wasn't following us. I didn't figure it out till I saw the toys, but Oz was too steamed to step back. It was just a big mistake. Just a big fat stupid mistake."

A four-door sedan was driving slowly past where they sat parked on this quiet street, distracting Dion from his next question. A ghost of a face looked out from the passenger window. Slow-cruising cars were always a worry. He tried to make out the occupants, but they were too murky. The sedan rolled by without incident, and he returned to his next big question, the bootie in the bottle. Like his first shot in the dark, this would be another, one chance, now or never. Investigators could try it later in the interrogation, but either it would be too late to be meaningful, or it was a meaning they would miss. He said, "Did you take something from the scene?"

"Huh?" she said, still refusing to look at him.

He wished she would look at him. He wanted to see her eyes. "The Liu home, when you were leaving. You took something from there?"

She stared down at the hands in her lap, laying so peacefully one on top of the other, and she nodded. "Yeah," she whispered. "I did. I took one of the kid's little booties."

Motion in the periphery. The lurking car had backtracked. It had done a U-turn at the intersection and was heading this way. One cruise-by was worrisome; two was alarming. The car pulled alongside and idled. Someone stepped out of the driver's side.

"Jesus," Jamie said, recoiling. She and Dion were both staring at the dark figure approaching. The street was badly lit, and Dion wasted no time analyzing what little he could see. He shoved open his door as the person leaned down toward Jamie's open window, and he saw that it was an older man in a short-sleeved plaid shirt, silver hair, glasses. The man straightened as he saw Dion.

"Oh, hello," the man said. Not a gangster, not Asian, not armed.

"Hello," Dion said.

"I'm sorry," the man said. "Saw you sitting here talking. Are you looking for them, too?"

"Looking for … what?"

"The Almonds. The Almond house." The man looked at a piece of paper in his hand. "At 4241 Cloverley." He looked harder at Dion. Dion tensed. The man said, "Are you by any chance little Marty Almond?"

"No, sir, you've got something wrong."

"Ah," the man said. "Sorry. Family reunion, you see. Wife and I just flew in from Ottawa. I haven't seen Martin since he was this small. Thought you might be him."

"I'm not, sir."

The man looked again at the piece of paper. "We've been driving around, and there doesn't seem to be any 4241 Cloverley. Somebody got something wrong."

Dion could guess who.

The man said, "Don't want to phone the family and ask for directions. It's late. Don't want to wake 'em, this time of night."

"You'll be waking them when you arrive, won't you?"

The white eyebrows went up. "That's very true." He smiled at Dion. "I used to give you shoulder rides, back when you were this little."

He went back to his car, and away they went.

Dion returned to the passenger seat of his Honda Civic, feeling a little knocked off course, thanks to the man from Ottawa. He pulled a map from the glove compartment and opened it to the section showing the North Shore streets. He presented the section to Jamie. "Whereabouts did Oscar ditch the phone? Show me."

"It matters?"

"It matters a lot. Point it out."

She studied the map, her eyes travelling around, and he wondered, what was she seeing in her mind's eye as she searched for the route they had taken after killing a young woman and a baby girl? What memories was this pulling up? *How can she be so cool?*

"There," Jamie said. "This little road here, I think that's it."

She folded the map and handed it back at him. "You mean it, right?" she asked, not threatening but pleading. "About probation? I did nothing except follow him around. I know I should have stopped him. I should have tried."

Dion said nothing, too busy burning into his mind the location she had pinpointed on the map, in case she changed her story. He got out of the passenger side and told her they were switching places. "We'll go there now," he said, when he was behind the wheel and firing the engine back to life. "Gotta find that phone."

Thirty-Two

SHADES OF BLUE

LEITH WAS HEADING UPSTAIRS to the main office when his work phone rang. He stopped to look at the caller ID. It was a personal number, not dispatch, and nobody from his list of contacts. He put the phone to his ear and answered brusquely. "Leith."

The voice was male, young, not immediately recognizable, and rough-edged. "Could you meet me? It's important."

"Dion?"

"I'm down on Orwell Street, off Bond. I'll wait for you here."

"I'm on my way to briefing," Leith said, and continued walking to prove it. "I'll be at least an hour."

"Cut it. Get a recap later. I'll bet this is more important."

"Business or personal?"

"What?" Blast of impatience. "Business. See you soon." Dion disconnected.

The morning had started out brisk, but the forecast said to dress light. Leith ditched his jacket in the back seat of his unmarked and keyed the coordinates Dion had given into his GPS. He arrived on a quiet dead-end road, houses on one side, brambles on the other. The brambles looked formidable, and the houses were mostly blocked off by high shrubs, tall fences, or drawn curtains. It felt like the kind of place a drug deal could go down in peace and quiet. He pulled in behind the sporty blue Honda Civic with tinted windows. Dion stepped out of the car and walked to meet him, no smile, no formalities. "I've got some info for you on the Liu murders."

Leith stopped at a neutral distance and gave a neutral nod. "Yes?"

"I got this from Jamie Paquette. You'll have to get the details from her. She says Oscar Roth murdered the Lius, and she was with him."

Leith crossed his arms, the better to contain his surprise.

"These bushes here," Dion said. "You're going to have to get Forensics —"

"Hold it a moment," Leith said. "This is spinning my head, considering you've just not only solved one of our biggest files, but linked it with the other. Oscar Roth killed Lance, Cheryl, and Rosalie Liu?"

"Seems so. And what I'm trying to tell you —"

"Hey, this is breaking news," Leith interrupted, hands out both to embrace the information and slow it to a manageable level. "You get that, right? You can see I'm not taking notes or recording this. So we can either carry on, you go ahead and tell me what you know, then we go over it again at the station, or we can stop now and drive there and do it right. I appreciate what you're telling me, but I'd rather get this firsthand on the record, Cal."

"I just want to finish this."

Dion was sounding adamant, and Leith knew better than to push his luck. "I'm listening."

"Because you'll need to get going on this part. When they were driving back from the Liu home, Oscar pulled over, found a metal bar on the road, and tried smashing Liu's phone open to remove the battery, because he figured — I don't know what he figured, if the phone was located it would be traced back to him. He wiped the phone clean of prints and tossed it in the bushes, and the bar, too. Somewhere along here." Dion pointed at the brambles, and Leith turned to take in the length of them. They seemed to go down the block and into infinity. "I tried to get her to pin down the spot for me, but she couldn't say, except it was on this road. She mentioned the dead end, so I guess it would be here somewhere. She says he threw it far."

Again Leith studied the bushes. Even narrowed down to this stretch, there were a lot of them. He said, "Does Paquette know you're telling me all this?"

"She knows."

"You should have brought her in."

"She refused. I wasn't going to manhandle her. That's your job. She's at the Yorks'."

Dion waited while Leith called in instructions to Doug Paley to have Jamie Paquette detained for questioning. Leith pocketed his phone and said, "Why did she tell you? Or why did you ask? Far as I understand it, you're off the force. You've become a PI, have you?"

"We got to be friends," Dion said, with arms crossed.

"Uh-huh," Leith said. "You, Paquette, and the Yorks. You're in bed with the whole lot of them, are you?"

A flush of wind tore by, ruffling their hair and blowing dust in their eyes. "How about you just find Liu's phone," Dion said. "Or at least the piece of metal he used to smash it with. Maybe that'll help."

"Piece of metal …" Leith said. Then realized: it was a matter of fingerprints. He called out to his informant, who was walking back to his car, "So what about that statement?"

"You'll be busy a while," Dion shouted back. "Just call me when you're ready."

He got into his Honda. The engine fired up, music thudded from the open windows, and Leith watched the car pull out and accelerate off Orwell, back toward wherever he was hanging out these days.

* * *

Jamie Paquette was brought in and interviewed. Her confession was astonishing. JD had been assigned solo conduct of the first round of questioning, in hopes a female investigator would get more out of the woman. It seemed to work.

JD related the story to Leith late Thursday afternoon, following her interview and before it got transcribed. "Paquette saw toys in the yard. She believed they'd made a mistake, this wasn't any kind of gang house, or even if it was, if there were kids involved, she had to try to stop

Oscar, so she went in. She didn't mention a little boy, or trying to protect anybody. She says it was so traumatic, she can't remember any details. She remembers picking up one of the baby's booties, with some vague idea of holding on to proof of what had happened. She recalls something about a bottle, but not what she did with it. Oz had gone rogue, and she was afraid of him. She didn't seem to have much of a plan, though."

"She doesn't remember Joey? Kind of a big deal, isn't it?"

"Her memory is scrap metal. And when you think about it, everything she remembers she could have picked up from the press. So she could be feeding us what we want to hear."

"A false confession," Leith said. Why would Paquette confess to something she hadn't done? It went into the mystery box of why would anyone confess to something they hadn't done. Happened all the time.

"But then there's this," JD said. "There are these Asian guys who were after Oscar, and I asked her, what, south Asian, east, north? She said they were Chinese. I think that's her umbrella term for anyone from that side of the world. She can't say how many, or describe them, except they were not kids and not old guys. She couldn't give any names or pick anyone out from the mug gallery. But you know what?"

By now Leith knew that when JD said *you know what*, she had something interesting — and probably complex — to tell him.

"What?" he said.

"In going through the shots, Paquette picked out a

couple, and said one of the bad guys stalking Oz looked kind of like this guy here. The guy she pointed to looked south Asian. Vietnam, Laos, Cambodia. It was obvious, at least to me."

"Okay."

"So I'm saying he wasn't Chinese. She keeps calling them Chinese. If she's wrong —"

"Not everyone can see the differences, JD. Sometimes the differences are pretty hard to make out, unless you're some kind of anthropologist who specializes —"

JD made a noise, losing patience with him. "That's not the point. If you'd let me finish. The point is Joey Liu said the ogre — who we now know was Oscar Roth — was yelling at Cheryl Liu about *noon*. Right? Get it? *Noooon*."

"Okay," Leith said again. "And?"

"How about *win*?" she said, with a smug smile.

Or *win* was what it sounded like to Leith. "Huh?" he said.

"The Vietnamese name. N-g-u-y-e-n. Someone who didn't know how to pronounce it might say *noon*. Or *nooyin*."

Maybe Leith was looking more stupid than usual, for JD reached up and gave his forehead a disrespectful little rap with her knuckles.

"Oh," he said. "I see." Possibly they now had a name for whoever Oscar Roth was looking for. Nguyen. Sometimes Leith wondered why he was in this job, when he could be combing a beach somewhere, looking for lost change.

* * *

All male Nguyen mugshots from the Lower Mainland were separated out and shown not only to Jamie Paquette, but to Jon and Melanie York, and even to Zan Liu. No Nguyen was pointed out as meaningful to any of them.

Two days after Dion had met Leith on Orwell with his breaking news, a battered iPhone 5 was found in the brambles. It had been located with the help of city crews and their giant side-mower, metal detectors bought and borrowed, high-powered lights, and a crew of auxiliary officers in bushwhacking gear. The piece of metal was found, too, an old L-shaped tire iron, its chromed surface going patchily to rust. The phone itself had been wiped of prints, sure enough, but the tire iron had a nice fat thumbprint belonging to one deceased ogre: Oscar Roth.

* * *

Leith's more formal interview of Dion took place at an Internet café on Lonsdale. Dion wanted to meet offsite, and Leith had considered refusing — the information was sensitive, and the walls have ears, especially at Internet cafés — but he had submitted in the end. The café wasn't half as popular as the Starbucks just up the block, was nearly empty, and he decided the risk was low enough.

Dion arrived looking like a stranger, in jeans and dark T-shirt, silver chain around his throat, plain black baseball cap straddled with sunglasses. He looked like a man with criminal intent, the type Leith would eyeball if they met on the street and mentally file away for future reference.

Sitting in comfortable armchairs across a low table, jazz playing quietly overhead and Leith's digital Panasonic set to record, Dion gave much the same story as he'd given roadside, but with times and dates and further explanations attached. He described how exactly he had become friendly with Jamie. He was visiting the Yorks, and she was living there, so they got talking. She needed driving lessons, and he had helped out. That was all. Leith asked if they were dating.

Dion said no.

"It still doesn't make sense to me, how you got her to tell you."

"I guessed there was a connection, and told her so, and she knew she was up against a wall."

"But how did you guess?"

"Just a lucky shot in the dark," Dion said. "She was afraid of Asian men, so I got her to tell me why. She said Asian men were after Oscar. The Lius are Asian. Somehow Oscar latched on to Lance Liu as a stalker and went after him. It was all just a possibility I put to her. I put it to her that she had been to the Mahon house, and I could tell I hit a nerve. She denied it, but I bluffed. I said I had evidence, and she bit. So I gave her a couple of options, and she was smart enough to know the only good one. I told her if her involvement was nothing more than just being there, she'd probably be let off light, maybe just do probation. Finally she accepted that. She told me about the phone and showed me where it was tossed. That's it."

Leith was watching him closely, puzzled by the simmering discontent he saw in the younger man's face that didn't quite fit the scenario. "Well, you did good," he said. "You broke it wide open."

Dion continued to look discontented.

"And you're right, she'll probably get off light," Leith said. He saw his interviewee frown, as though he'd been slighted by the comment. "Especially considering it sounds like she protected Joey from Oscar."

Dion heaved a sigh, ducked his face so his eyes were hidden by the bill of his cap, and said, "Yeah."

Leith said, "Is there a problem?"

"Can you shut off the tape recorder?"

Leith did.

With face still ducked, Dion said, "I'm sorry that I bragged that I'm better than you."

To buy time and look unamazed, Leith sat back in his armchair and crossed his arms. The apology was long overdue; it went all the way back to the Hazeltons, to one of their several confrontations. "I've been told worse," he said.

He was ignored. "I used to be smart," Dion said. "But after getting spun 360 degrees and a crack on the head, I'm pretty well useless. I can't stand it. I can't stand me."

A phrase popped into Leith's head, two words that neatly described Dion: *pugnaciously depressed.*

"So I can't draw lines between my thoughts anymore," the depressed man carried on, still looking down. "Sometimes it all just disappears. And it's getting worse. Next year at this time I might be a vegetable. Hopefully I'll be dead before then. But sometimes things are clear, and

I know everything, and then I grab the moment. That's why I called you, before it went up in smoke. That's why I can't figure out what I'm supposed to do right now. It's why I quit."

Finally he looked up, catching Leith's eyes, holding them.

I have something more to tell you, he was saying, without saying it.

Leith waited a beat before answering all these startling revelations of disintegration and death. "I didn't know it was that bad. You were right to leave. You did the right thing."

Dion's eyes glinted darkly. This wasn't what he wanted to hear.

"But it's not over," Leith told him. *Now for the good news.* "You're smarter than the average Joe, that's for sure. Maybe some counselling —"

"Fuck no," Dion said. He was straightening out, rotating his shoulders, already leaving the confessional and changing topics. "Still haven't got my termination paperwork from admin," he said more briskly. "What's the holdup?"

"You'll have to ask Bosko. What're your plans for the rest of the day?"

"Got an apartment. Just moving in, actually."

"Oh?" Leith was curious, if only for selfish reasons. "Whereabouts? How's the rent?"

"On 13th. Rent's okay, pretty standard for this area."

"One-bedroom? Two? I need a two-bed. Any vacancies?"

"I don't think so. We're done?"

"Yeah, we're done," Leith said. "Unless you want to know how Joey Liu's doing. He's the little boy on Mahon who survived the blitz."

"I know who Joey Liu is. How's he doing?"

"Not bad. Does the name *Noon* mean anything to you? *Noo-win*? Nguyen?"

"Nguyen? No. Why?"

"Joey heard the killer asking Cheryl Liu about somebody named Noon, is how he said it."

"What's the context?"

Leith wasn't sure about the wisdom of sharing insider information with an outsider. But in this case, it was definitely worth a try. He quoted the hearsay as he recalled it. "Noon. You bits. Which is you bitch, we're thinking. And what have you done, or what have I done? That's pretty well it."

Dion stared at him, maybe thoughtfully or maybe blankly, hard to say. He shook his head. "No clue."

"Okay, then. Is there anything else you want to tell me, Cal? I get the feeling there's unfinished business between us. Tape recorder is off. Something you wanted to say?"

"Yes," Dion said. He took a breath and plunged on. "It's just that I might be totally wrong, except I know I'm not. I'm thinking Oscar Roth didn't kill Cheryl or Rosalie Liu. I think Jamie did it."

The team had considered the idea and all but dropped it, because Oscar was the aggressor, and the muscle, and the paranoid madman, not Jamie Paquette. "Why? Why do you think that?"

Dion's mouth was crimped in frustration. "I don't know. That's just it. I don't know why, but I think I'm right."

"Okay, then, let's backtrack —"

"I *have* tried backtracking," Dion shouted, making the barista look over her counter with raised brows. Leith signalled to the woman that all was good. Dion stood, digging in his pocket for change. He dropped a couple of quarters on the table for a tip and said, "I'm going."

Which he then did, and that was that.

* * *

The apartment came partially furnished. It had a queen-sized bed, three-piece sofa suite, tables and chairs, all looking like a 50 percent sale at The Brick. The place was small but not insanely so, a one-bedroom with a decent, modern kitchenette with marble-like counters, pale-blue walls. It had a narrow balcony damply shaded by evergreens that grew like a wall around the adjacent complex. The only view was branches.

Dion washed down the counters, thinking of Jamie in custody. She was safer inside than out, for sure — and the world was safer from her. He wouldn't visit her. He couldn't trust anything she said or did, and he couldn't trust his own impulses. She would get to him, if he gave her half a chance. She would own him.

He thought about how he had barked at Leith, who only wanted to work together to get at something important. But something *what?* Even that was hazy now. Whenever he thought of Jamie, he saw her naked, lying back on the bed, nearing climax. Which was hardly productive. A sheet of foolscap sat before him on the coffee table, proving how far downhill he'd gone. They were notes he'd written in pencil and pen, words crossed over, lines radiating from one thought to another. Reading it now, it disgusted him. Jon York drank G&Ts, and the club stocked Bombay Sapphire. That was nothing.

The dirt under Melanie York's fingernails that first time he'd seen her, that was probably nothing, too. Before the crash, Dion hadn't cared much about dirt under his own fingernails. Now he did. Now he noticed and scrubbed them clean every morning. Melanie was the nail-scrubbing type, too, so something could have been on her mind the night of Oscar's murder, but she could just as easily have been on a bender.

Now there was Noon. *Nguyen.* A common Vietnamese name, but did it ring a distant bell? He thought maybe it did, until he tried to pin the thought down.

He added the name to the notes, and the brief quote Leith had given him. His phone buzzed in his pocket. He read the text: *Time to man up and try rqtball. Court's bkd and my usual foe stood me up. Get yr ass down here!!!*

Dion texted back to Jon York that he was quite busy.

Jon wrote, *Sure? B fun!!* With a happy face wearing shades attached.

Dion smiled at the happy face and texted back, *Ok WTF.*

Which made him wonder again, what did it all matter who did what? He was no longer much of a crime solver, but that left a whole new world open to him. What did Melanie call it? Hedonism. That was something he'd been fairly good at once, something he might try to regain.

As he changed into sportswear for the one o'clock racquetball lesson he saw the dingy little apartment around him had picked up character. Not so much like the fire-sale section of The Brick now. Blue, sun-dappled walls, a pleasant layout. With a little love and attention — and a coat of paint — it might just start to feel like home.

Thirty-Three

FLIER

MAYBE IT WAS BECAUSE SHE was under the gun, but Jamie Paquette had got herself a job. The day before her arrest she had secured herself a position serving drinks at the Royal Arms. Leith had to wonder about the timing. He also wondered how she managed to get assigned a Legal Aid lawyer who happened to be a human terrier fresh out of law school. The terrier lawyer had it in his mind that Jamie, an oppressed woman without a criminal record, guilty of nothing more than subservience, should be released on a recognizance pending trial, in spite of the serious charges of aiding and abetting, conspiracy after the fact, obstruction. The lawyer made application and pushed up the hearing date. Another surprise: Jon York stepped up as surety, agreeing to the bail amount, set at twenty thousand dollars. Jamie walked.

She didn't walk far, of course. She needed to remain at her address on record — which was the York residence

— to report in to a bail supervisor daily, and was subject to a strict curfew and a dozen lesser conditions. But still, she walked. It helped to have that job; courts don't like disrupting income streams.

Leith had shared with the team Dion's disturbing but baseless belief that Jamie, not Oscar, had killed Cheryl and Rosalie Liu. The idea had been thrown around once or twice, but dropped. They examined it once more in consultation with the Crown, and again agreed there was nothing to it. Crown counsel seconded the doubt, and the allegation sank.

Submerged, but not forgotten. Leith decided it was time to agitate some of his persons of interest. He picked up the phone once more.

York showed up an hour later. He wasn't looking quite as handsome as usual. Tired, with shadows under his sparkly blue eyes, and his skin seemed paler so that his freckles stood out like a rash. Leith asked him about his relationship with Jamie Paquette, about which he had to wonder, considering that risky bailout, was it more than convivial?

York said, "Jamie is a bit of a number. But then so was Oscar, wasn't he? Why am I looking after her like this? She's part of Oz, and that means she's part of my family. I'm not afraid of losing that money. She won't run. How can she, without a car?"

Leith could think of a lot nastier things to call Oscar and Jamie than *numbers*, at the moment. But York had only just learned of the charges levied against Jamie, which he considered some kind of ridiculous mistake. *Oz killed that family? Are you nuts?*

"It's a lot of money to risk," Leith said.

York shrugged. "Not really. Anyway, I had a good talk with her. She promises to be good. And she's living with us, so she's under my eye. She's got zero resources, so she can't bribe anyone. A bus wouldn't get her far. She's pretty well grounded."

He seemed to believe himself wholeheartedly. Leith wasn't so sure. "Do you know Cal Dion is giving Jamie driving lessons? What d'you know about their relationship?"

York seemed mildly surprised, not by the driving lessons, but the question itself. "They're friends. Maybe there's benefits attached, but nothing serious. He's got enough brains to know she's trouble."

"She is? How so?"

"She's the tin man," York said, with a hand held gravely over his heart. "Nothing there."

What a strange pile of souls these were, Leith thought. He still believed that whatever else she had done, Jamie had at least protected Joey, which meant she wasn't any kind of tin man. And what about Dion, sucked into their midst? Would he have regrets about turning her in? Would he now pack up his car with his belongings and hers, and together they'd take to the hills?

In fewer words, he put the question to York, if only to see how he'd react.

"Cal wouldn't do that," York said, smiling warmly. "He may like Jamie, but he likes me more."

"And you like him?"

"I love him," York said. "Like the brother I never had."

* * *

That night, when Dion learned through Jon York that Jamie had been released, he had to blink back his surprise. He excused himself from Jon's presence in the VIP booth, walked to the quietest spot he could find in the foyer, a set of sofas between coat check and the Keno machine, and called Dave Leith's cell number. It was past midnight, and Leith's voice was thick. "What's up?"

"You let her go?" Dion said, not so much a question as an expression of disbelief.

"I didn't let her go," Leith snapped quietly back at him. "The courts did. Why?"

"Why? This isn't a shoplifter we're talking about. Amongst other things, she maybe killed a woman, in cold blood. And a baby. I told you that. She's disturbed. Why didn't you ask me before springing her?"

Leith had gone silent. Except for the sound of breathing, heavy, as if building up steam. Or maybe he was walking. A door squealed and thumped shut, and now he was back on the line, speaking at volume. "Like I said, I didn't spring her. If it was my choice, I'd hold her. But in the circumstances, the judge deemed her not a flight risk or danger to the public."

"She's both," Dion exclaimed at his phone. "Did you even testify? Did you look for witnesses? Someone who knew her character? Me, for instance?"

"No," Leith said, coldly. "Anyway, she's got no history of violence. She looks to me like a not-so-smart woman who just got into a bad situation with a bad man. Also, by the way, she just landed a job, and the judge didn't want to jeopardize her chances of becoming self-sufficient."

"Job?" Dion said. "What job?"

Leith told him, and Dion checked his watch, and saw that it wasn't quite twelve thirty, and the Royal Arms pub would probably still be up and running. Too angry to thank Leith, he disconnected without a word, digging into his jacket for his car keys.

* * *

At the Royal Arms he learned that Jamie's shifts were noon to 8:00 p.m., but she hadn't been scheduled to work today. He had already called Melanie, and Melanie said Jamie wasn't there, either. He now stood at the Royal Arms bar, wondering what to do next. A game was on the TV monitor, loud, though nobody was watching. Dion leaned across the counter to get the bartender's attention.

The bartender explained how Jamie got the job: she asked to see the manager, and she'd smiled at him. That's how. Whatever, she was a pretty girl, knew the ropes, could look after herself, and she snagged the job easy.

Right now the bar sat almost empty, just a few doped-looking older guys slouched in corners. "Has she hooked up with anyone that you know of?" Dion asked. And because he didn't like shouting, added, "How about turning down the scores?"

The bartender turned to lower the TV volume, answering the question with something that sounded like *Polly Tompkins*.

"Who's she?" Dion asked. In the quiet now, he didn't have to lean. He took a barstool.

"He," the bartender said. "I've seen you around. You a cop?"

"No."

"So you want a beer?"

"No, thanks."

"Paul," the bartender said. He yelled out, "Last call."

"Paul …?" Dion said. "Paul Tompkins?"

"Yeah. Paulie Tompkins."

"Are they romantic, him and Jamie?"

The bartender pulled a beer and shrugged. "Guy's old enough to be her gramps, but decent-looking. Like whatshisname, Han Solo. Except more in his *Airforce One* days. Retired, widower. Nice guy, though. Nicest you'll ever meet. He's got a way with people. Got her talking."

"Was Paul giving her driving lessons?"

"You know I hate beer? Hate the taste of it, the smell of it."

"Was Paul giving her driving lessons?"

"The sound of it, even. Weird, eh?"

Dion squeezed his eyes shut.

"What were you saying?" the bartender asked.

"You have his contact info by any chance — Paul Johnson?"

"Tompkins. I think he's down near the Superstore. That's about it."

Dion wrote it down, the name, the area. The bartender watched him with doubt. "Sure you're not a cop?"

"Anybody else around here might know how to get hold of him?"

"I doubt it. Why? Is she your squeeze? Because let me tell you, if anything happens to Paulie —"

"No. No trouble. I just need to talk to her."

"Good on you. Crazy about Jamie myself, but look at me. What are my chances?"

"If you see her, or Mr. Tompkins, will you give me a call right away?"

"Can do."

Dion gave the bartender his number. He drove to Deep Cove, in case she had shown up at home. Jon was back from the club by now, but had gone to bed. Melanie was in the living room with the TV on. She watched him pound downstairs to check Jamie's room.

The room was empty. Melanie was in the doorway behind him, her hand to her face. "What's the problem?"

"Where is she?"

"I don't know. Please don't tell me she skipped bail."

Melanie left to call her husband, tell him what was happening. Dion looked around for any evidence of where Jamie might have gone. He got back on his phone and woke Leith for a second time to give him the news. "Your low flight risk's taken off."

* * *

Leith joined him in the messy room with the mauve walls and king-sized bed. Jon York was up now. Dion could hear him upstairs, fretting about his money and what he'd do to that bitch if she had taken off.

"How many times have you been down here?" Leith asked, and since he was standing by the foot of the over-sized bed, the question was loaded.

"Several."

"See anything missing?"

"About half her clothes. She took her peeler costumes. Makeup seems to be cleared out from the bathroom, mostly. And the ashtray's gone."

"Ashtray?"

"One of her first gigs was at the Cobalt," Dion said. "It's an East Van strip bar. She swiped the ashtray as a memento. It was glass, had some logo printed on it. She gave me its history, and seemed to care about it. It lived here, bedside. It's gone."

Leith's phone buzzed. He spoke into it for a minute, mostly saying "uh-huh." He tucked the phone back in its pouch on his belt and said, "Paul Tompkins. He's not home, either. I've got a bulletin out on his vehicle, for starters. You really think he's in danger?"

"I think he's dead," Dion snarled.

They glared at each other. Leith said, "If she's such a menace, why didn't you flag her for me right off the bat?"

"I told you I thought she killed Cheryl Liu. You need a bigger flag?"

"You were vague as shit. If you were just a little more forthcoming, maybe I'd have told the Crown to fight the bail app."

"I thought she was in custody, and I thought she'd stay in custody. Since when have major suspects been set free on bail without massive hearings?"

Leith crossed his arms. "There was a massive hearing. It was just shorter than usual. Let's stick to the issue. Where d'you think she's gone?"

They had moved to the bay window to argue, a pleasant nook with a bench seat and houseplants. Neither sat down. It was almost 3:00 a.m., and the world was silent. Upstairs the Yorks had gone silent as well. "I don't know, but I'm guessing north," Dion said. "She told me once she'd make a ton of money if she went north."

He was thinking about the province, so long and wide, so many options. Even if he was correct about north, that didn't narrow it by much. Jamie had a good head start, if she had left this morning. She had reported in to her bail supervisor at 10:30 a.m., as ordered, so he could only assume she had been tearing up the highway since then. Fourteen hours made for a wide radius.

Beside him he heard Leith talking to his phone again. "What, already?" he was saying. "Okay. Be there soon as I can."

News. Dion looked at him, not sure he wanted to hear it.

"Where the hell is Brohm Lake?" Leith asked.

"On the Sea to Sky Highway, heading to Whistler." Fists in his pockets, Dion calmed his voice. "Why? What about it?"

"It's where Paul Tompkins happens to be. Squamish found him."

By Squamish Leith meant the Squamish RCMP. Dion nodded, numbed. He could see it all playing out, the stark white body of an older man, looking a little like Harrison Ford, nicest guy you'd ever meet, lying face up in the rocks and weeds by Brohm Lake, belly and chest criss-crossed with ribbons of blood, eyes already clouding over, flies already feasting.

"Going to be a long night," Leith said. "For me. Not for you. Let's go." He ushered Dion out of the bedroom, upstairs, saying goodnight to the Yorks and refusing to answer their questions.

Out on the silent Deep Cove road, Dion said, "At least that narrows it down. You know she took the 99, right? Up to Lillooet. From there, she'd have her options. Could cut west to Bella Coola or east for the mountains. But I'm still betting north, in which case she'd be well past Prince George by now, if she didn't make any stops. Of course, at Prince you've got more junctions. She'd figure there'd be money to make in McKenzie, Dawson Creek, Fort St. John, and they're a lot closer than the Yukon cities. For sure, if you want a focus, go north, then east from Prince to the Rockies."

Leith jingled his keys. He had come rousted out of bed, and stood by his vehicle in baggy cords and an old sweatshirt, looking more like a hard-working farmer than a cop. "Good, thanks," he said. "I'll keep all that in mind. First I'll have a talk with this guy, though I'm not counting on much from him. Totally shitfaced, apparently, hardly knows his own name. Might have to dry him out for a few hours before he can make a statement."

"Shitfaced?" Dion said. "What d'you mean?"

"It means drunk. Whacked, smashed, bombed, pickled, soused. Which sounds kind of tempting right now, frankly."

"I know what it means. Who are you talking about? Paul Tompkins? He's drunk? He's not … dead?"

Leith burst out laughing. It wasn't a happy laugh, but the hysterical noise of a sleep-deprived man, tired beyond care. "No, Mr. Tompkins isn't dead. He was sitting by the lake with an empty Scotch bottle. He's half frozen but quite alive. No keys, no car, no cash in his wallet. Fill in the blanks."

"Naked?" Dion asked and half hoped he'd gotten at least that part right.

Leith stopped grinning tiredly. "Naked? Why the fuck would he be naked?"

Dion forgot why, but it didn't matter. The nightmare was over. He couldn't stop from beaming. "Good. I'm glad he's alive, that's all."

"So am I," Leith said, more kindly. "Go home, Cal. I'll keep you posted."

Dion watched the Ford Taurus drive away, a rental sticker on its bumper. Gradually, like warmth creeping back into frozen veins, he began to feel the redemption. Tompkins wasn't dead, and Jamie would be rounded up soon enough. She was dangerous, but not yet a full-fledged psychopath. Still, until she was brought back safe and sound and locked up, *for good this time,* he wouldn't rest easy.

But what were the chances of that, he wondered, as he sat in his car and turned the key. Paul Tompkins was okay, but Jamie was out there, sailing along through unknown territory. Her stolen car was packed with tearaway miniskirts and strappy spike heels. She had barely learned to drive and had canyons, oncoming traffic, freight trucks, merge lanes, hairpin turns to deal with. She had no experience with any of it. Sheer madness. And what about these chilly late-spring nights? How would she stay warm?

He climbed the stairs to his apartment and let himself in. He was certain, as he stretched out on the bed and before he flicked on the radio, that Jamie would not make it home alive. The late night/early morning radio chattered about a shooting in Richmond, and a new weight-loss trend, and the forecast for today — rain. But no highway catastrophes. Yet.

Thirty-Four

THE LOWEST TIDE

FRIDAY, LATE AFTERNOON. Rain pattered on the huge awning, cooling the world after a blistering week. Dion sat alone on the patio at Diamonds, overlooking the defunct pier. He had before him a glass of water with a twist of lemon. Life seemed unutterably bleak. His severance paperwork, along with his final auto deposit, had not come in yet, and he could use the cash. He had said no to Jon's job offer. York was probably glad. With his surety money gone, he would be seeing Dion as nothing but a jinx.

In his mind, Dion was halfway to Alberta, this time for sure. He would know nobody there, and he could stop pretending to be something he wasn't. In the flatlands, far from this city and the sea, he would build up a new social life, limited but solid. Find a girlfriend of sorts, get work, carve out a living. His plan paralleled Jamie's in a way. Just the more realistic, less extreme version of escape.

Which brought him back to Jamie. Why didn't she stick through it? If she went through trial and closed off this chapter of her life — at least as she perceived it — she could start clean. Maybe the interrogators had frightened her. They had hinted they suspected her of far worse than collusion just to rattle her, see if she'd fess up to anything further. Which would have been fine if they hadn't then gone ahead and released her so she could put Plan B into motion.

He didn't want to think of the mistakes he had made with her himself, but listed them anyway. He should have kept himself together better, insisted he stay by her side throughout. Go into the station with her, reassure her after the interviews. Maybe she wouldn't have run.

Nothing startling came at him in the morning news. No wreckage in the canyons or capture of a fugitive. His phone didn't light up, but he didn't expect it to. Leith might get back to him as promised, but not this quick. Even if the case had closed. He wasn't in that brightly lit GIS office anymore, central and relevant, the first to know what was happening in this city of his.

His throat felt constricted and the corners of his mouth weighted by stones. Only his ability to hear the world seemed more acute this morning. The banging trains, the tapping water and dashing traffic. Gulls screamed, pigeons flapped. Striptease music issued from the club, and rap music came and went from a passing car. He heard every noise, separated out and supernaturally loud.

A shadow fell over him, and he looked up as Jon pulled a chair close, saying, "Hey. Did they get her yet?"

"Don't know, sorry."

Jon sighed. "Trust me to put my faith in that lying little … well, whatever." He sat back in his chair, crossed his arms tight, and looked worried.

"Why did you?"

Jon grimaced. "I can't live without her, is why. I mean, I can, but …" He shrugged.

"How long have you been seeing her?"

"*Seeing* her? What d'you mean, seeing her? We have sex. From time to time. In lieu of rent. I'm not *seeing* her."

"*Rent?*"

"Grow up. I'm kidding. She likes it as much as I do."

"Yeah? Were you having sex with her when Oscar was alive? Did he know? Does Melanie know?"

Jon stared at him. "It really disgusts you, doesn't it?"

Dion shrugged.

"I never had sex with her when Oz was alive. I wouldn't do that to him. And Mel knows. We have an understanding, me and Mel. She knows she's my best girl. She knows I've got appetites she can't keep up with. For her, it's a break."

Dion looked down.

"Do me a favour and bless me with your ever-so-precious forgiveness," Jon said.

"It's really none of my business."

"Don't be an asshole."

"I'm not."

They both sulked quietly, until the full force of Jon's troubles hit him again. "Damn," he cried, sitting back, looking at the sky. "I never for a moment thought she'd blow the scene."

Dion ignored him.

York became practical again, almost businesslike. "So am I in any kind of trouble over this?"

"For what? Posting bail? No. You're not expected to read the future."

"If they catch her, do I still pay the penalty?"

"Depends, I think."

York was looking into the club through floor-to-ceiling glass. Reflections confused the image, but just visible was a girl on stage, her pale body flashing in the laser beam, rotating languidly down the brass pole. He looked irritably at Dion, who was feeling gloomier than ever. "What's up, Cal? Sitting out here alone in the rain. You look like the poster child for dejection. You're bad for the image. We're all about fun here. I could sue you, if you don't watch out."

Dion shrugged. "It's nice out here."

"It's not nice out here. You're hurting. I hope you're mourning my blown cash."

Dion searched his mind for a good excuse for his mood, and found one that might do the trick. "Racquetball, that's what troubles me. Who invented that dumb sport?"

He had chosen his excuse well, and York was back in a place he understood. "I told you," he said. "The first game's always a fail. Takes tons of practice to get the hang of it. Actually, you did good, for a newbie."

"I could spend the rest of my life practicing, and I'll never get the hang of it."

There was a moment's quiet. Or not quiet, with the banging of the trains and the strip-bar tunes pulsing through. When York spoke, he sounded sad and genuinely sympathetic. "Not a natural-born jock, are you?"

"Not these days."

"Funny. Every cop I've ever known has coached little-league something or other. But you don't even know which end of the hockey stick hits the puck."

Dion knew very well which end hit the puck. But it was true: when it came to sports, he had a one-track mind. The job had provided all the challenge, excitement, and satisfaction he could ask for. The losses were devastating and the wins glorious. Who needed floor hockey with a career like the one he had just given up?

York slammed the table and said, "Fuck it, let's go boating."

"I'm really not up for it."

"Not now. I'm talking tomorrow. Supposed to be a nice sunny day, not too hot, not too cold. Take the day off. We'll pack some beer and sandwiches and hit the waves. In honour of Oz. I'm thinking we'll take the ass out of thal*ass*ophobia, teach you to love the water. You're living in North Vancouver, water all around you. It's falling on you. You're drinking it. You depend on water. You really should accept it in your heart. Like Christ."

"Some other day, maybe."

Another stretch of silence told Dion that he had successfully severed his ties with the King of Diamonds. "Some other day, sure," York said, glum again. "*Maybe*. Catch you later, then."

"Right. See you."

With a final searching stare, York got up and returned to the club. The crowds were just flooding in, and he liked to be there to watch. Or trickle, lately, Dion had noticed. However cocky York was, business was slow.

Two of the bouncers had been let go, and the next ladies' night was cancelled. He thought about York's emphasis on *maybe* just now. The threat of a cut-off, as he had been cut from the force.

Odd to think that no matter what he did, the city he loved would carry on. It carried on now, booming and droning, amplified like a monster machine in his ears, and the rain continued to fall slantwise, drizzling off the awning into the ocean at his back, water joining water.

Nguyen, he thought. A name as common as Smith. He had been looking at the name from all angles, some time ago, but like Smith, it came up a lot.

Still. He said the name aloud, pronounced correctly and incorrectly. Nothing clicked. He was here to drop into Diamonds and socialize a bit, one last time. Now he felt torn between doing that or heading out and not looking back. He took a final sip of lemon water, bitter now with rind, checked his watch, and headed inside.

* * *

From what Leith heard through the grapevine, Mike Bosko was inviting everyone at the detachment over to his place for tomorrow's Victoria Day, a bit of a do. The weather was supposed to clear by then. He would have the barbecue going all day, an open buffet, beer and wine. As people were on different shifts, it would be casual, just drop by if and when you can, no RSVP required. Families and friends welcome. Leith had not personally received an invite yet, but suspected it was coming. He didn't care. His heart wasn't into parties of any kind, not with Jamie Paquette on the run.

"I'm starting to like this Bosko guy," Doug Paley was saying, also awaiting the invitation. He and Leith and Jimmy Torr stood on the main-floor corridor between the General Duties pit and the elevator, eavesdropping on a group of female civilian staffers talking about the party, and whether they were going, and what they should wear.

"He gives me the creeps," Torr said, when the staffers had moved out of earshot. "And what's he thinking? Nobody will show up except a few hot-crotch secretaries."

"Not true," Paley said. "I'm not a hot-crotch anything, and I'm showing up. I want to see how he lives. I want to see if he really has a wife, and what she's like."

Torr said, "If she's as weird as he is, I ain't going near the place."

Paley said, "What about you, Dave? Going to drop in, scope him out?"

Leith worked up the enthusiasm to say his bit. "I'm wondering what he's putting on the barbecue. Isn't he some kind of vegetarian?"

"Tofu burgers and kelp chips." Torr placed a finger in his mouth and pretended to barf.

Paley said, "I hear he's renting a real shack bungalow on Heywood."

"He's renting?" Leith was interested. "How come? He could afford to buy something pretty decent, surely?"

But a group of white-shirts were heading their way, Bosko amongst them, and the three men fell instinctively quiet.

"Dave," Bosko said. "Have a moment?"

The other brass moved on, and Leith joined Bosko. They went along to the Liu/Roth case room, the cases now forged into one monster mystery, partly solved but mostly baffling. Who was Noon/Nguyen? Why had Oscar Roth gone overboard, killing a family? Then there was the corollary mystery of Cleo Irvine's fatal fall. But what Bosko wished to discuss at the moment, as they took chairs at the long table, was Jamie Paquette's escape.

Leith still felt ill about the blunder. He owed it to Zan Liu and to Joey to solve this case, not allow vital witnesses and/or suspects to slip away. He told Bosko what actions he had taken to catch the bail-jumper and where the file now stood. "We're compiling a list as fast as we can. If she had a huge and supportive family, we might have somewhere to start. But she's got nobody that seems to care, much. Her parents are divorced. Mother lives abroad, isn't answering her messages. We're having her checked out. Nobody showed up for Paquette's hearing except her dad, and he sounds delusional. He's been on the news already, talking about his baby girl — his words. But doesn't appear he's been in touch with her for years."

Bosko had jotted down notes, nodding. He looked across at Leith and said, "And then there's Cal. Do you have any idea how he got so much background on Paquette? Was he personally investigating her, off the books?"

"I asked him the same thing. He says they became friends. He was helping her learn to drive, if you can believe it."

"It's just like up north," Bosko remarked. "He's getting at the truth from his own particular angle. I'm not sure it's deliberate, but it certainly is amazing."

"He's got a knack for getting in the middle of things," Leith agreed. "I meant to tell you, he's anxious to get his severance docs. He's wondering why they're not coming through."

Bosko said, "Oh, yes. That's my fault. I'll deal with it." He smiled as they left the case room, saying, "Oh hey, by the way, tomorrow, if you're not too busy, I'm having a barbecue down at my place...."

* * *

The experienced guys behind the bar who could juggle martini shakers while delivering witty one-liners were gone, and in their place were mute students fresh out of bartending school. But as Jon York told Dion, bartending these days was 99 percent pulling beer, right? "Now and then someone orders a mojito, well, all you need is a recipe book and one of those muddle sticks."

The penthouse upstairs remained closed down, barred now from all entry by order of the city. Dion had learned some of the truth about that room; it was a place where couples had gone when they just couldn't keep their pants zipped or skirts lowered, with permission from Jon and a few bucks passed his way. But those days were over. Jon had reached an agreement with the city and would be re-opening it soon as a legitimate conference room, which should pull in some serious cash. The pier he was also leasing out now to a charter boat company. He was cutting back the strippers from six to two and reducing the hours they'd be up. The Sunday bookings were picking up, and the dance-club numbers were holding steady, at least on Fridays.

All the same, Dion knew that Diamonds was dying. Looking around, he wondered: if Oscar Roth had stuck around, with his mad but feisty plans, would the place eventually have grown roots? He stopped York on his way by and told him he had finally got it together to leave. He would be in town a while longer, had a few things to take care of, but this would be his last time at the club.

Jon laughed, not at Dion's announcement but the glass of water he was still holding. "When's the last time you had a real drink in your hand? Let me get you something. What's your favourite, again? G&T?"

Dion said, "No," but Jon was already shouting out an order to the server buffing beer steins. The server went to consult his cocktail book, and Dion said, "I'm actually quitting drinking, too."

"Sure you are," Jon said. "Cheers."

Dion's least favourite drink arrived, heavy on the gin. Jon said, "I miss Oz. It's that stage of grief they failed to mention. I've angered, bargained, felt guilty, all of that. Now I just plain miss him. He was funny, smart. Sure, I got tired of him, and he pissed me off, and we fought. But in the big picture, he was the best kind of friend I could wish for. And now he's gone, and there's this big yawning … gulch where he once stood."

"I know what you mean."

"I feel so old."

"You're forty-six."

"Which is at least fifteen years older than you. Trust me, you get to a certain age, and you lose all flexibility of spirit. Hard to make friendships as solid as the ones you made when you were growing up. You'll find out."

Another gin landed in front of Dion, this one on the light side. To avoid a third, he told Jon that he really didn't care for G&Ts. Jon sent the drink back and ordered him a beer instead. Dion wrapped his palm around the cold bottle. He was beginning to realize just how bad his timing was, leaving Jon just when Jon was feeling abandoned. He didn't want to end it like this.

"Hey," he said, pleased with himself as an idea popped to mind. "I'm sorry I didn't answer your last text. You asked if I wanted to play another game of racquetball. I'm up for it. Totally. One more game, name the time, I'll be there."

"You know what I think?" Jon said, and he sounded angry. "I think another racquetball lesson is the last thing in the world you want. I think you're just trying to make me feel better."

"Sure I am. It's that or going out on your fucking boat, and I figure racquetball's easier."

Jon was not just angry but cold. "Sorry, pal. I have to get this off my chest. You're a good person. But a coward."

Dion blinked.

Jon said, "A rank, chicken-shit coward, and I don't run with chicken-shit cowards."

Dion had set down his glass and was opening his mouth to defend himself, but Jon interrupted, wrapping a palm around his neck to pull him closer, and he should have known it was all just a lead-in to another invitation.

Jon said, "So we're going to cure all that. I'm not taking no for an answer this time. Tomorrow's Victoria Day, and we're going to celebrate. First thing, out on the waves."

Dion pulled away. In fact, a boat ride was preferable to the racquetball court. It was actually not a bad idea at all. A good way to leave this friendship on a positive note. "Is Melanie going? I'm only going if Melanie's going."

"Mel, Dallas, anyone who wants to come along. We'll throw in the line, catch something for dinner. Remember that island we circled last time?"

Dion did, very well. He remembered the rush, the embrace. Jon said, "This time we'll pull in. Spend the day on the beach. It's the only way to confront your phobia, my friend. You want to hear the prescription?"

Dion laughed. "No, I sure don't."

"You go at it in stages. Up to the ankles, reward yourself with a shooter. Up to the knees, have another shooter. Up to the waist, wow, that calls for a double. Plus, by then it's probably time for lunch, fresh salmon on the grill."

"I could get used to that," Dion said.

He sorely wished he hadn't told Melanie about his hang-up with water. She had passed it on to Jon, and Jon had made it a pet project, curing the thalassa*whatever*. But it didn't matter. Tomorrow he would talk to them both. He would explain to Jon it wasn't a phobia, wasn't even a fear. The ocean was just some kind of ego-crusher that he was working at getting over, but at his own speed. Maybe in the bigger picture, talking to Jon and Melanie would put his own topsy-turvy life in some kind of perspective.

Maybe everything would be all right.

Thirty-Five

DEADHEAD

TO CELEBRATE QUEEN VICTORIA, or at least the national holiday in her name, Leith was up early with pancakes on his mind. He turned on some bluesy rock and roll — volume down low — and began preparing breakfast from scratch.

There was a sadness to this day, for Alison and Izzy would be on the plane tonight, back to Prince Rupert. Much had been accomplished over their too-short visit. A home had been found. Not a genuine kiss-the-ground freehold with a backyard and a spot to plant sweet peas, because there was no such place here within their means, but the bottom floor of a largish house which they could rent until they figured out where to go next. They had put in their application and been approved. Alison would return to Prince Rupert and arrange for a moving van, and next month, on the move-in date to the new place, she would be back here in his arms, permanently.

A message pinged on his BlackBerry.

JD: *Big news. Call me.*

He called her. "Two things. Isn't this your day off, and how big?"

"Big-big," she said. "The lab messaged me. You know the bottle, the bootie bottle?"

Of course he knew the bootie bottle. "What about it?"

"One of the bright new lab girls had a second look. She checked the bottle neck, *inside*, something the wise old guys before her failed to do. And she got a print. And the print's got a name."

"Holy," Leith said. "Who is it?"

"His name's Alex Caine, and I've actually seen him around. He's sixty-eight, lives in a home-share kind of set-up. He's got a history, a record, some violence, but he's been good since his last release. Struggling alcoholic, perennial AA attendee. Perpetual walker, too. I talked to him."

"You talked to him?"

"I didn't want to bother you last night, and didn't want to wait, either. To make a long story short, he found the bottle. He'd sat down to rest on the steps of the *North Shore News*, up on 15th, and saw a little cardboard box tucked in a corner there. Inside the box was the gin bottle, with something inside. He tried to fish the thing out but couldn't, of course. Left that precious print, though. He says there was something else in the box. A note. He doesn't recall what it said."

"But fortunately he kept it," Leith said, gloomy in advance.

He heard JD sigh. She said, "He took the bottle, thinking it was kind of nice, and went walkabout. Crossed the bridge. Got tired of carrying it and for fun dropped it off the apex, into the water below. But not before whittling a makeshift cork out of a piece of wood he also happened to be carrying along with him. Because who doesn't walk around with pieces of wood in their pockets?"

Leith thought of *Winnie-the-Pooh*, which he had been reading to Izzy just last night. The little poet bear dropping things off bridges. *Poohsticks.*

JD said, "Which was damned reckless. What if he'd hit a boater? I gave him a lecture. But as for the note, he's not sure what he did with it. Maybe left it in the box, or maybe stuck it in his pocket. The newspaper hasn't got it. He promised he'll search his room thoroughly. He's a bit of a collector, I hear. That's all. I'll follow up with him, of course."

"Of course," Leith said. He thanked her and disconnected. He thought about the note, but not for long. The pancakes needed his full focus.

The pancake was his one culinary specialty, and he wondered as he measured out flour how long he would be allowed even this minor act of devil worship. Refined carbs, syrup, and fat, that's what pancakes were. Composite evil.

He could guess what the note said. *Here's your evidence. My boyfriend killed those people.* Jamie Paquette trying to assuage her guilt.

Or was it something else altogether?

Pancakes. He knew Alison would eat only one, and only to be polite, and would suggest he limit himself as well. Izzy could only have a small one on the side, along with a healthier breakfast of fruit and yogurt. Reasonably enough, Alison didn't want Izzy getting hooked on empty calories.

Leith enjoyed empty calories. Back in his lanky days, he ate whatever the hell, whenever the hell. But Alison was right; if he wanted to keep fit into his older years and avoid becoming pear-shaped like his dad, he would have to beware. Two pancakes, max. But big ones.

While he mixed the batter (he was starting to resent the batter, for what the batter had done to him, making him crave it, only to reject him), he thought through a certain irony that had occurred to him lately. Possibly Bosko knew *who* Dion had killed — if it really *was* murder — but not where the body lay, while Leith possibly knew just the opposite. He knew the *where*, but not the *who*. They each held one half of a broken key, and only needed to put those halves together, like in the best adventure films, to unlock the possible crime.

He turned to prepare the coffee maker. So far, his own research hadn't turned up any possible victim. There were persons reported missing in the Lower Mainland around the time of the Cloverdale crash, and he had checked all leads. Nothing. So if not murder, what then? Maybe contraband of some kind. Drugs, weapons, the fast proceeds of a heist or the slow sapping of embezzlement?

The problem with those theories was they all pointed to premeditated criminality, and maybe he was wrong, but he didn't believe Dion had it in him. Dion was more the series-of-unfortunate-events type.

He still didn't know who or what the man called Parker was.

He heard the bedroom door squeak and Alison pad out. She was barefoot, mussed, wearing an old dressing gown over a Walmart nightie, and Leith looked almost as ravishing in his favourite faded T-shirt over pyjama pants. She hugged him, and he was back to his frying pan while she set the table. "Pancakes on Victoria Day," she said. "Better make a heap."

* * *

Victoria Day. Dion felt like a beach bum in board shorts, T-shirt, and flip sandals, with his favourite ball cap to keep the sun out of his eyes. With wine in one hand, beer under his arm, he climbed the driveway and stairs to ring the bell at the Yorks' Deep Cove home. Jon welcomed him in with a smile. He, too, was dressed for the outdoors, but the house behind him was silent, not the hustle and bustle Dion expected of a family getting ready for a day out on the water. Jon explained, as they walked to a living room fragrant with fresh-brewed coffee, that Melanie wasn't well.

"How not well?" Dion asked.

"Headache," Jon said. And then admitted, "Well, she's got the spins."

"She drank too much."

"You could say that."

"Why? What's the occasion?" Dion could guess what the occasion was; it was called stress. Jamie Paquette was still evading capture, and a lot of money was swirling down the drain.

"Melanie doesn't need an occasion to drink too much," Jon replied, with a wry smile.

Dion didn't smile back. "It's a problem, isn't it? The drinking. She should get help."

"You should mind your own business. Have a seat and I'll get your cup of joe."

Dion sat on the sofa on one side of the fireplace. There was no fire in the grill, just a bouquet of dried wildflowers. The hard morning light reflected off the water of the outdoor Jacuzzi and danced on the ceiling. It was the most beautiful home he had ever set foot in, and he realized he coveted it, in a hopeless way, as he coveted most things these days. A time or two he had mentioned his envy to Jon, who answered that this house was nothing special. *Just wait till you visit Sea Lane.*

Dion wondered if Sea Lane was slowly but surely slipping out of reach, too.

The promised coffee arrived. Jon said, "Suck it up fast. Then let's go."

"Go where?" Dion asked. The trip cancellation had disappointed him more than he expected. He didn't want some alternative walk on the beach.

"You're not getting out of it that easy. We're going anyway."

The disappointment lingered. Dion wanted Melanie to be there. He wanted a replay of their last ride. He called out to Jon in the kitchen, "We can postpone till she's feeling better. How about tomorrow?"

"I have meetings lined up from here to the blue yonder," Jon called back. "Today's my only window, and I plan to take it, Cal."

The little girl Dallas appeared, tousle-headed and in

pyjamas. She stared plaintively toward the kitchen and made a noise that wasn't quite a word.

Jon came to greet her with obvious delight. Dion could see him almost scooping her up in his arms. But she wasn't that kind of human being. She was the kind who turned away from touch. Jon knew better than to try, and instead, crouched down and held out his arms, if only symbolically, saying, "Hey, good morning, teddy bear. Hungry?"

She looked at him with faraway eyes. She nodded, and then, to Dion's surprise, she stepped toward her foster father where he crouched and tapped one of his open hands with an outstretched finger. Just a touch, and she then drew back, and for some reason he thought of Jamie, the way she begged for attention, only to then repel it. Jon glanced up at Dion and winked. "Progress," he said. And to the girl, "C'mon, then, kiddo. Let's find your favourite cereal."

Dion watched the girl follow her surrogate dad off to the bright little breakfast nook next to the kitchen. If Melanie had the spins, he wondered, who would look after Dallas while he and Jon were out motorboating? Maybe the care aide was scheduled to show up soon.

Jon reappeared hauling a cooler, which he set on the floor. "Just in case we don't catch anything, I've prepared for the worst," he said. "That's what separates men from bears. We make hoagies!"

He placed the six-pack Dion had brought into the cooler and went off whistling to gather the rest of the gear for the trip. Minutes later he showed up with Dallas at his side. She was dressed for a day in the sun, in shorts, a tank top decorated with blue flowers, and a floppy hat. She was clutching her little plastic horse. Jon carried a netted sack of beach gear, and spilling out the top, Dion could see the answer to his question of who would be looking after the kid today: a tiny orange life jacket.

"Let's go, bud," Jon said to Dion. And to the little girl, "Onward ho, cap'n."

* * *

The morning was perfect, fresh and cool. The water was choppy but not wild. Clouds lay across the horizon with airbrushed perfection, slowly drifting, not a threat but a promise of an ideal day. Light rain in the forecast, but not till evening. Dion sat in the co-pilot seat, keeping both a forward and aft lookout. Forward to the marine traffic floating dreamlike along the strait, and aft toward Dallas in the U-shaped passenger area. He worried about her safety, though Jon had told him she was a competent little sailor, had been out many times without a problem. But there would have been more adults on board then, Dion thought. More supervision.

"She's okay with speed?" he asked. "Doesn't get scared when you go too fast?"

Jon laughed. "If this is your way of getting me to go slow —"

"Fuck off," Dion answered, the kind of *fuck off* that only true friends could get away with.

Jon didn't answer the question about Dallas's fears, so Dion kept an eye on the girl, checking how she responded as the boat throttled up and began to cleave through the waves. But he didn't need to worry; Dallas sat on the floor in the cozy well formed by the back seating. She appeared comfortable, even in the confines of her life jacket. She sat on the air mattress covered with a plush beach blanket, where Jon had lodged her with all that her little heart might desire close at hand, juice container, bag of snacks, colouring book, crayons, and toys.

She sat upright, sometimes gazing about at the passing scenery, her hat brim flapping and her short hair lashing. Not that she would see much from down there. Blue sky and gulls. What if she got restless when he and Jon weren't watching? What if she climbed over the seating onto the back deck, where only sober adults should sit?

He said, "Melanie was okay with her coming along today?"

"Right now Melanie's okay with anything, so long as there's no light, noise, or sudden movement involved."

"If she's that sick, somebody should be with her."

Jon said, "Cal, believe it or not, we've managed so far without your guidance. I think we've got life more or less figured. She's not on her deathbed. She's got friends nearby and a phone beside her. She'll be fine. D'you think you can have fun now? Is that even remotely possible? Get yourself a beer and breathe."

Dion relaxed in the passenger seat and watched the world through the wraparound windscreen. Droplets of seawater spattered across the Plexiglas, caught the sunlight and gleamed like travelling strings of diamonds. Something nagged in the back of his mind, the image of a speedboat smashing into a deadhead at eighty knots. Another collision sat even more heavily in his heart. If he was edgier than the average man, he had every right to be. One high-speed collision in a lifetime is plenty.

He tried making conversation. He asked Jon about the nightclub — not its future, but its past, one of Jon's favourite topics. But today Jon seemed touchy about it. He wanted to talk about boats instead. Dion asked about Melanie's teaching career. Why had she left it? Why didn't she go back to it?

Jon veered the conversation back to sports fishing.

Dion stuck with his topic of choice. "It's just she seems kind of restless. Maybe that's why she drinks so much. Far as I can see, she does nothing all day except hang around the house or plan parties."

"Well, now she's got Dally to take care of," Jon said.

The ocean was wide open in front of them. Unlike driving a car on the highway, there were no white lines, or oncoming traffic, or speed limits. A driver could smash through the sound barrier or set the controls to cruise and just lounge. But Jon wasn't in a cruising mood. He stood like a sailor heading into a gale and upped the speed another notch.

Dion looked back again. Dallas lay on her side now, her body joggling with the boat's ups and downs. Her hat lay discarded, and her little toy horse was meandering through the peaks and valleys of the blanket. He said, "She doesn't need a lot of supervision. Won't she be going to school, special ed? A nanny could take care of her the rest of the time."

Jon made a choking noise. "Have you considered the economics of that? After paying a nanny, Mel's take-home pay would be minimum wage, at best."

"So what? It's not like she needs the cash. It's about doing something with her life."

"You're projecting. Mel's lazier than you think. Maybe she likes hanging around the house, getting drunk and planning parties. Ever consider that?"

"I've considered that and I've rejected that."

"Well then…." Jon swigged his alcohol-free beverage and gave Dion a searching, sidelong stare. "Tell me about your family."

He knew Dion didn't care to talk about his family, or the accident, or his dead friend Looch, and the question was a blatant attack, an eye for an eye. Dion went back to the cooler and picked out his first beer of the day. He popped the tab, sat again next to Jon, and said, "Okay, you win. Tell me how to catch a salmon."

Jon fell silent. He steered effortlessly around a floating log that had blipped on his radar. Dion watched it go by.

"We wanted kids," Jon said, finally. "She did especially. Went to the doctor, doctor says it's not going to happen. Mel's always been a trooper, and she decided to accept the situation, move forward. The only logical direction for a human to go in. It still bothers her. She's lost a bit of, I dunno, *life*. Gave up teaching. Gave up reading and writing. She's got Dallas now, but …" He leaned sideways, though there was no danger of Dallas overhearing. "Between you and me, with that kid, I think you'd get more emotional response from a hamster. But Mel knows what she's getting into. We've known Dallas all her life."

Dion thought of the glow in Melanie's eyes as she told him of her attempts to communicate with the girl through horse talk. But if the latest drinking binge meant anything, the happiness hadn't lasted. He thought of her open marriage, and who got the benefit of that openness. He thought she deserved better. "Maybe she hoped she could change Dallas. Maybe she's finding out she can't."

Jon shook his head, dismissing the idea.

"How do you feel about it? You're going to have Dallas with you for a long time. Most kids grow up and move on. Dallas will never do that, will she?"

"No, she won't. Yes, it's scary. And you're right, too, I wouldn't have the courage, myself. If it were up to me I'd have said no, I can't do this. But Melanie never doubted for a moment that we'd take her, after Cleo died. She doesn't regret it. It makes her happy."

"But not happy enough to quit drinking."

"It'll take time. There's our island, just in time to shut you up. Hold on to your hat."

Jon shifted the throttle forward, and Dion did as told, gripped the brim of his cap to keep it from blowing away. He checked his watch and saw that it was just past twelve o'clock.

Noon, he thought. And then it clicked.

Thirty-Six

ONCOMING

JAZZ PLAYED IN THE SUNSHINE, and the large backyard was festooned with lanterns and crepe streamers from Chinatown. The aromas that drifted to Leith's nose were gourmet and enticing. With Alison at his side and Izzy in his arms, he introduced his family to a casually dressed Mike Bosko, and Bosko introduced his wife Sarah.

Sarah was nothing like Leith had imagined her. Over the months he'd known Bosko, Bosko had rarely talked about her, which seemed unlike him; he talked about everything, at length. So Leith had created his own composite image of the woman. For whatever reason, he had Sarah as subservient, a beautiful but tragic figure, buxom and sad-eyed, with long, oak-blond hair, her spirit withering in the shadows cast by an overwhelmingly cerebral husband.

The Sarah he met looked a few years older than Bosko, who was forty-two. She wasn't what Leith would call beautiful, tragic, or buxom. She was short and skinny and wore her brunette hair in a bob. Like her husband, she stared out at the world from behind wire-rimmed spectacles, which made her look a lot smarter than Leith felt.

"Hi," he said, grinning down at her, "Nice to meet you."

"David Leith," she said, smiling up at him. "Likewise. I've heard much about you!"

And now, zing, he was afraid of her too. What had she heard? And why? But already she had moved away, gone to greet new arrivals.

The yard was semi-full of people standing or sitting around on lawn chairs, eating and drinking. It was a bigger crowd than Leith had expected. He had expected to see dozens of familiar faces, but saw none. Bosko took him on a social tour, and he learned that few of these people were local flatfeet like himself. Some were associates of Sarah's, who he now learned was Dr. Sarah Bosko, a psychiatrist. Some were colleagues from Bosko's previous CCS posting in Vancouver — Commercial Crimes Section — and seemed a different class of shark than Leith was used to swimming with.

We won't stay long, he promised himself, somehow cowed. Still, he did his best to mingle and hobnob. He had never been a great social butterfly, more a social moth, but he could cope, so long as he could source out talk on a level he could fathom. He was glad to see that Alison was engaged, sitting with Izzy on her lap and surrounded by admirers.

The food was good, too. Vegetarian was an option, but not mandatory. Leith had loaded his plate and was seated at a patio table, munching on an onion-smothered smokie in a bun when Paley and Torr arrived. They were soon followed by JD. Leith was happy to share his table with people he knew. They sat with drinks in hand like the nerd-pack in high school.

Paley swigged beer and peered sideways at Bosko across the lawn. "You know, I've never seen him in anything but a frickin' black suit and white shirt. I was starting to wonder if we're all part of the matrix, and he's the evil Agent Smith. Just the shabbier version. But lo and behold, flip-flops, and what are those red things all over his shirt?"

Torr surprised everyone by knowing what they were. "Hibiscus blooms."

JD gazed across the lawn at their boss having a deep but amiable conversation with strangers. "How d'you know the motherboard didn't reprogram him into those cargo shorts, just to fool dumbshits like you?" She bared her teeth and hissed, "I for one don't believe. I *am* the glitch."

Leith stared at her unladylike profile, and then at Torr as Torr burst out with, "This is the best fucking burger I've ever eaten. You're telling me this is fucking *soy?*"

"Who says it's soy?" JD leaned to check out his plate. "That's not soy. That's genuine dead cow."

"*I* told him it's soy," Paley said proudly, his fat cheeks bulging with food. "That's the joy of Jim. You can tell him anything and watch him make an ass of himself. Endless fun."

"You're a twat, Paley," Torr said.

Leith sat wondering what Bosko had told Sarah about him, if anything. Had she just made it up, as the polite thing to say? Would a qualified psychiatrist lie without cause? He didn't think so.

JD said, "You look like you're thinking, David. Or is it indigestion?"

He told her that Sarah was a psychiatrist, and what she had told him. "'I've heard much about you.' What on earth would he tell her about me?"

JD answered promptly. "That as dudes go, you're a good one. Happy?"

The sunlight sparkled through her brown crewcut, and her eyes had almost smiled. He decided yes, he was happy. For the moment, he was feeling pretty good.

Which was never a good sign.

He watched JD answering her phone, and he could see it in her eyes: the party was about to end. She put away the phone and told them, "Guess what? Ziba Farzan has recanted."

* * *

"I have been covering for Jon a lot," Ziba said at the station, the tension in her face marring her elegance. "Little innocent things. So when he dropped by that morning and asked me to lie about the time, I thought it was just another of those. Of course, when you police came by, I had my doubts. Yet I was taken off guard, and on the spot made a bad decision and lied as he asked me to. But then I found out about Ms. Cleo Irvine, Oscar's ex-wife, and I put two and two together. I mean, I feel terrible about this, because I'm not certain. But I couldn't in good conscience not tell you. Not if there's a crime involved."

Leith wondered what "little innocent things" she had covered him for previously, but could guess.

"So he wasn't at your place at eight thirty," JD said, keeping it nonconfrontational, even friendly. Even grateful. "What time *was* it?"

"Nearer to nine. Five to, probably."

Ziba was arrested, if only to keep her from contacting Jon York, and Leith rushed to the case room to study JD's carefully constructed timeline again. She stood beside him, looking troubled.

"That makes no sense," she said. "Cal swears he was with York at quarter to nine. An airtight alibi."

"Maybe his alarm clock was running slow."

JD checked the file notes. "Except he confirmed the time from Jon York's car dash," she said. "And also Melanie's SUV."

Leith stared at Dion's name on the board. One alarm clock and two dashboard displays. Add to that Dion's lost cellphone, and what did you get? A dupe. A sense of cold disbelief washed over him as he looked at JD. He could see the same thought crossing her mind.

"Jon York changed the clocks," she said. Her voice took a fast hike from amazement to outrage. "The fucker changed the clocks. Jon York pushed Cleo Irvine out that window."

And smiled through his teeth as he denied it, Leith thought.

JD was out the door, on her phone, gathering the team for an emergency meeting. Leith followed, wondering where in the world was Cal Dion.

* * *

Nguyen. It came to Dion with a bang. He had interviewed a witness, an informant, who kept talking about a "Mr. Noon." That Mr. Noon had turned out to be the mispronunciation of a Nguyen. It was a loose link in the last case he had worked on before the crash. In his rounds he had heard rumours that an individual nicknamed T.T. Nguyen, a shadowy figure in the contraband trade, was out for revenge for something lost. Not money, not drugs, but a sister.

Dion had been only just starting to tie the rumour to the girl washed up on the rocks by the Neptune shipyards — which was troublesome because the girl had been determined to be Caucasian — when he had been smashed out of orbit, and Looch was killed, and everything else went on the back burner. Now, nearly a year later, was it possible to put the theory back together? He considered getting in touch with Leith again. But there was nothing to present, not even a full name. Leith would just brush him off.

To hell with Leith then. To hell with Jane Doe, even. And to hell with the phone in his pocket, which had buzzed a couple times at length before giving up. He was free of caseloads and complicated lines of inquiry, now exploring a small, uninhabited island and enjoying life.

The day was pleasant. No other visitors to the island except a bunch of gulls and some kayakers stopping by to shake out their legs. Dion had followed Jon in a tromp through the woods. Easy exercise, because they had the slowest hiker in the world in between them, Dallas.

No fish had been caught, so in the afternoon Dion sat on the rubbly beach next to Jon, and they unwrapped the hoagies Jon had packed. "God, I love it out here," Jon said. "I think I missed my calling. I should have been a hermit."

Before them Dallas plodded barefoot along the flat, wet sand, in and out of the rolling surf. Not a wild, rolling surf, just playful wavelets. She held a mini sandwich in one hand, a flying horse in the other.

Dion couldn't put Nguyen out of his mind. And the dead girl with the short blond hair and wide-spaced eyes. He didn't know the colour of her eyes, because they were gone, but the reconstructionist suggested brown or hazel, to match the natural light brown of her hair. He had checked for boating misadventures after she washed ashore. None reported. Had never gotten Nguyen's full name, had never been able to put a face to him. He asked York, "Did the police talk to you about the men who were stalking Oscar? Because they're real. It wasn't all in his head."

"They did ask me about it, and I didn't have a clue what they were talking about, and still don't."

"Was Oscar a good swimmer? That time he hit a dead-head and had to race back to shore before the boat sank. If he'd sunk, way out there, would he have drowned?"

Jon looked at him. His face didn't seem to fit him right, all those fine laugh-lines sagging. "Oscar could swim okay, and he could float great, especially with a life jacket on. Where is this going?"

"He never reported the accident, right?" Dion asked, between bites of sandwich. "What happened to the boat?"

"He scrapped it."

"Wasn't fixable?"

"I guess not."

"No insurance claim?"

"Christ," Jon said.

Dion gave it a bit of a rest, but he had one more question. He stood, dusted sand off his rear, and looked out to sea. "Who was with him that day?"

Jon wrapped half his meal and stuck it back in the cooler. He unscrewed a flask and swigged, then offered the flask up. "Nobody."

"Jamie?"

"Nobody."

Dion took the flask and drank from it, and handed it back. "There was a case I was working on last summer, before I got transferred north. I'm wondering if it's connected. Is that around the time he started getting paranoid, after he totalled his boat?"

Jon didn't answer. His eyes were tired and his mouth was a thin line.

"Sorry," Dion said. "Old cases. They can haunt you."

"I see that."

Motion out of the corner of his eye distracted Dion, and he saw Dallas down in the lapping surf, leaning over and thrashing her hands about in a panic. Her sandwich floated away, but it wasn't the cause of her distress. He was about to jump to her rescue when he saw her grab at some floating object and stand upright again. She looked pleased, her world back in balance.

So her horse could fly just fine, but apparently couldn't swim.

Now she turned and made her way up the sands toward them, to Jon, pointing at the sky, at the animal-shaped clouds drifting over the sun and cutting the glare.

They packed the boat and cruised northwest instead of southeast, since Jon said he couldn't face returning inland just yet, back to the bastard straitjacket called life. The daylight was ebbing away. Along with the clouds came spatters of rain, and the water ahead looked rough. Dion pulled on his windbreaker. Jon left the boat idling and made his way back to put another sweater on Dallas. He re-zipped her life jacket, placed a blanket over her, and returned to the controls.

Dion had stopped worrying about Dallas. She wasn't a child who made sudden moves. He had watched her running on the sands, and even chugging along at full throttle she was a slow mover.

They hadn't left the island far behind when the outboard motor choked and sputtered. Dion stared back at it with concern. "What if it fails?" he asked. "Way out here. You have Plan B on board, I hope?"

"My Plan B is in the shop for service," Jon said. "Don't worry. There's nothing I can't fix."

The motor had only guttered briefly, and was growling away again as if nothing had happened. Dion forgot about it, until some minutes later it choked again. Now there was no nearby landmass in sight, and no sign of other boaters on the horizon. "Just needs a tweak," Jon said, standing. "Take the wheel, if that makes you feel better."

He left Dion at the controls and went back to deal with the motor.

Dion had never operated a boat before, and steered nervously against the waves, on the lookout for the dreaded deadheads. But nothing happened, and soon he heard a shout of triumph. He turned and watched Jon clambering his way back, stepping over the child and untidy piles of picnic gear. Cheerfully cursing technology, Jon took the driver's seat once more and started putt-putting them forward again.

Dion sat back in the passenger seat. "Everything's okay?"

"Perfect," Jon said. "Everything's perfect."

But he was quieter now. Maybe having his doubts about coming out here without Plan B on board, his name for the secondary fifty-horse motor that he had assured Dion he kept tucked in a storage box. Now he stared toward a distant opening between what had to be the northern flank of Vancouver Island and another jut of land that might be mainland, or maybe the peninsula of Sechelt. The opening looked narrow, but Dion knew it was a matter of perspective. It would take hours to reach that passage, and then it would be vast, an ocean in itself. Without explanation, Jon gunned toward this space with purpose.

The boat was bucking now, smashing the waves. "What's up?" Dion asked, his shout ripped apart by the wind. "Where are we heading?"

Jon's finger traced an arch, due east. The sky was dimming toward evening, and his intentions seemed illogical. "I'll take you along the coast," he shouted. "Show you the inlets. Some great kayaking. If you weren't such a wuss I'd lend you Mel's Delta and take you for a tour."

The heart-to-heart conversation Dion had prepared hadn't happened, much. He hadn't talked about his long-term plans, or suggested Melanie deserved a faithful husband. And he hadn't told Jon how he felt about water, not a phobia, not even a fear. But it didn't matter anymore. Their mysterious friendship seemed to be dying a natural death.

He stared forward anxiously, and then back once more, checking as he did every so often to make sure Dallas was safely lodged in her nest of cushions.

She wasn't.

Thirty-Seven

CRAWL

SHE WASN'T IN THE SNUG cabin below, wasn't anywhere. Dion knelt on the back deck, gripping the rail, and scanned the sea for a dot of orange. Jon had sent out an SOS, cut a turn, and was retracing their path, not too fast — she could be missed too easily in the rise and fall of the turbid waves.

"There," Dion shouted. "There, to the left," he cried, pointing, not knowing boater's lingo. "See her? *Go, go, go,* that way."

Jon throttled up and started the sharp turn, and the motor revved too high maybe, too fast, because instead of shifting audibly to the higher RPMs, it gagged and spat and went silent. It was the coldest silence that had ever hit Dion. The boat lolled like a dead whale. He stared over his shoulder at the man at the controls, who was cursing and fumbling, trying to get it going again.

Instead of going again there came a horrible, impotent whirring sound. "I can't restart her," Jon called out.

"She's flooded. It'll take a minute to dry out." He left the driver's seat and came stumbling back, stepping up onto the deck beside Dion. "Where is she? I can't see her."

"Way over there, the orange." Dion tore off his jacket.

York stood peering outward, hands clasped to face. "Call for help, Cal," he ordered, and turned to do something, strip down or remove his shoes. "I'm going — *what the hell are you doing?*"

Dion was barefoot already, T-shirt discarded, and now it was just a matter of taking aim.

"Hey man, don't be crazy, you can't swim!" Jon reached for him. "Cal, you can't — *don't!*"

The words blew away on the wind. Dion steepled his bare arms toward the horizon and swung them down toward the grey-green water. He sucked in air, as much as he could hold, and dropped his weight forward and outward, launching for speed with a push-off kick against the boat's flank.

He was inside the ocean. The cold gripped him like an electric shock, but he had propelled as far forward as the subsurface control would allow, aiming for where he hoped the girl would be. Surfacing, pulling in air, he was rocked and shoved by the waves. He saw her, was hit in the face by a falling elephant — not an elephant, but a wave. He flailed, blinded. He sank, kicked to rise back up, spat out brine and pulled in air.

He would need to stay calm, avoid thinking. *Don't imagine the depths.* He needed to predict the roll of the water. He would crawl, breathe, predict, crawl, to get to her, climbing and falling on this swell that was so much wilder from down within it than it appeared from the deck.

He located the dot of colour once more, what looked like a mile away, flashing in and out of view. He wheeled an arm back, plunged it forward, and began to kick with all his might toward it.

* * *

It seemed like an hour to reach her, but time was distorted. His flesh was numb. His ribs ached, and his muscles were starting to seize. He clutched at the girl's life jacket and pulled her toward him. Her face tilted back to the smacking rain, shiny white skin, mouth open, eyes half-closed. She looked dead, but he was in no shape to check. He began to crawl right-armed back toward the boat, double the trouble, hauling her dead weight with his left.

He heard an engine. Jon had got it going again. He bobbed a moment, thanking God as his lungs wheezed like broken bellows. The boat came into view, far away, toy-sized, but that was okay. It would be roaring toward him now. He was blinded again by another wave. When the view cleared he saw the boat was ... smaller. Not bigger. It was receding.

Why?

Why wasn't it speeding toward him? The waves kicked up by the vanishing boat began to course faster, washing over him with watery muscle. He stopped swimming and treaded in place, gasping, thrown around like a cork, trying to understand. Was it a trick of the light, a mirage? The waves dropped away, and he blinked hard and stared. The boat was just a pinprick on the horizon now.

And now it was gone completely.

Jon had just murdered him.

* * *

The rain was coming down now, mingled with the light of the setting sun. The road to the airport seemed endless. The world was flat here. A sociopath was out there somewhere, at sea, along with a mentally challenged child and Leith's mentally challenged ex-colleague. But it was beyond him, out of his control. The planes were huge in the evening sky, one surreal structure floating down, another drifting away. The sun sat low, harsh on the eyes, making him squint. The ambient airport roar seemed to distort sound, and his ears felt plugged, like he was climbing a mountain.

He wasn't climbing a mountain but was sitting behind the wheel of his rental Taurus, with Alison beside him and Izzy behind in her car seat. He followed the directional signs to the airport's drop-off zone and parked. He unloaded family and suitcases, helped them inside, and in the lobby gave Izzy a squeeze that only made her protest. Then he and Alison embraced. The drive had taken longer than they had expected, and Alison would need to rush off directly to Departures. There was no time to sit, no time to add to what they had already said. Probably that was a good thing; the sooner she was gone, the sooner she'd be back.

"What d'you think about what I said?" he asked her, as they broke apart.

"I'm still not sure. I don't know if I could get used to the horizon. And I've got so many connections here."

"It's not the moon."

"Oh Dave, it is. But I'll give it some serious thought."

"That's all I ask," Leith said.

Driving back through Richmond, he cast his mind back a few days, himself and Ali standing in their prospective new apartment, two-bedroom, exorbitant rent, signing the lease. Awful. Depressing. To be truly happy he would need to get away from this boxed-in living. He'd go home, if it took a year or more. Back to Saskatchewan, buy a place close to his parents.

It was a romanticized picture, of course, the open door, the fresh air and dazzling sun. A world without barricades, bottleneck bridges, bumper-to-bumper traffic. To hell with the spectacular mountain trails that now surrounded him, and the endless drama of the crashing sea. He would trade it all for the simple freedom to walk for miles in any direction, stretch out his arms, turn in circles and not hit anything. Or anybody.

As a boy in Saskatchewan he had run everywhere. Not walked. His legs had been long and his head full of wonder. Probably he linked that time in life with the land itself, something he couldn't get back, innocence and optimism.

But face it, he was a man now, and a fairly sedate one. Even if the terrain stretched out invitingly before him, he wouldn't run. He would just get his chores done, then climb back in the ol' truck and speed home to the hockey game on TV.

"She's right, it's the moon," he said. He zipped along for a while, until traffic bunched up. He didn't know, but could guess: another accident on the bridge.

Traffic crawled, then came to a stop. His phone was silent. He idled a minute more, then shut off the engine, and like everyone else on the planet he was trapped in a lineup to nowhere. An ambulance charged by along the shoulder, wailing loud, then a police car. One by one in front of him, the tail lights switched off, and in Leith's mind the prairies continued to beckon.

Thirty-Eight

COLD BLOOD

DION FLOATED WITH THE strapping of the child's life jacket still hooked in his left fist. She was in and out of the water, submerging and rising at the whim of the sea, definitely a corpse by now. So was he. All he had were the depths below and the sky above. He was cold beyond shivering now, and his thoughts were going haywire, but not so haywire as to not know what was what. York had not gone for help, had not sent out an SOS. This was deliberate.

He eyed the darkening grey skies with wonder. There was no heaven up there. No angels were going to pull him to safety. Cold pellets of rain hit the water and struck his face. No cosmic house party, no reunions. He would be nothing, nobody, alone forever. Fish food. He cried out in anger and fear, but only in his head. He had no spare energy to even sputter.

He tried to estimate his distance from all points of land, but knew there was no hope. This would be his final resting place. Here. Down there. He knew why, too. This was the punishment he had been in line for, for what he had done, and what he meant to do. He could still taste the blood spatter, and he could still feel the thrill of the chase.

Thrilling was his sin, and for that he was drowning. *Good*, he told himself. *No more searching. No more worrying. It's over.*

He woke with a start. He thrashed and began a mad kicking crawl toward what he believed was the closest point of land. The heat of fear thawed the freeze of the ocean and spurred him on. He strained toward an imagined goal, but with every foot of progress the sea gripped him and dragged him and his cargo two feet back. He looked again at the dark dome of the sky. No stars, smothered clouds. No sun, ever again. He would go down raking at the air and rain, lungs flooding with seawater. The water would turn the lights out slowly on him. The fish would watch him descend, doing slow-mo jumping jacks, however many miles it was to the ocean floor.

He heard a motor. He saw a pale speck on the blue-black horizon. Maybe a hallucination, or maybe a passerby teasing him with a glint of light. It disappeared below a wave, and reappeared.

And it was coming this way. Definitely heading closer.

The shock of hope nearly filled his lungs with water, nearly sank him. He spat again, kicked harder, tugged Dallas closer. The speck got bigger, became a beam of light. A boat, throwing white froth behind it, and now he knew. It slowed and shut off its engine. York was clambering down the ladder toward him, leaning forward and extending an arm. "Drop her," he commanded. "Grab my hand."

Dion was an iceberg. He couldn't crank an arm or splay his fingers. He couldn't stay afloat. Definitely couldn't respond, or even keep his eyes turned up toward the confusing play of light and darkness that was salvation. He was spent. He was aware of York climbing further down the rungs, swearing, slipping into the night waves, and approaching in clumsy strokes. A rope encircled him, clipped to a cable. York swam away, left him there. Dion was tugged like flotsam toward the boat till he bashed against the ladder, his fist still attached to Dallas's life jacket.

York was shouting down at him. "I said let her go, you fucking idiot. You're going to have to climb up yourself. She'll float. I'll get her once you're on board, but I can't haul both of you up at once. Let her go! *Now!*"

The words worked through Dion's frozen brain, and they made sense. He let go of Dallas. He hooked the rungs with stiff fingers and could see but not feel them connecting. The rope harness helped him climb, tugging steadily until York could grab him by the arm and haul him the rest of the way.

Onboard, Dion collapsed. He struggled to roll onto his front, for more control, in case he needed to launch himself up again. From here he intended to keep an eye on York. He would make sure the man descended those rungs as promised to collect the child before she was carried back out to sea.

Maybe he blacked out, and sometime later he heard someone say, "I'm sorry."

He shifted onto his side and looked up. York stood with his arms full of a limp little body in an orange life jacket. Dallas's head and arms and legs dangled. "I couldn't see you," York said. "I panicked. I went to flag down help." He laid the child in a heap on the dark deck. "She's dead, Cal. I killed her."

Shut up and try to revive her, Dion said, or thought he said. But York had sunk into the driver's seat and was bowed forward, arms wrapping his head.

Dion pushed himself into a kneel, which made him cough, lung-scorching hacks that nearly put him back on the floor. An abandoned flashlight lay within reach, its rays sliding this way and that. He managed to grab it and used it to look Dallas over. She was a sopping wet miniature human, and York was right, she was dead.

Dion's CPR training was stale but not expired. He struggled to get her life jacket off. He pressed on her chest with the heels of his hands, not too heavily because she was so small, but hard enough to hopefully jump-start her back to life. He tilted her face back, clamped her nose shut, leaned, and puffed breath into her, twice, slow but steady. Then checked for response. Nothing. It was over.

York was steering them toward the mainland, glancing back often but saying nothing. *Strange silence,* Dion thought, with fury. The occasional shout of encouragement would be appreciated. He repeated his efforts and again checked for signs of life. Still nothing. He tried again.

And again.

And again.

He saw York rise from the driver's seat and approach, staggering as the floor sloped side to side. The boat kept chugging forward without a pilot. He gave York a warning scowl, the man who had steered away from him instead of toward him, when every fraction of a moment counted, but York kept coming, rasping "No. It's too late. Let her be." He sounded careful, like a man approaching a mad dog. "Even if you bring her back, she'll be brain-dead. It's not fair to her. Or to us."

"She's alive," Dion replied. He pushed the words through pain and fatigue, and they sounded distant, unreal. "She's got a pulse."

"Then stop, now, before you send us all to hell. Let her go."

A burbly choking sound made Dion look down. Dallas coughed. He cradled her head in one palm, gave her face a light slap with the other. He told her to breathe. She sucked in a rough inhalation, then coughed again, violently. He rolled her to her side, and she spewed water and vomit. When he was sure she was breathing on her own, he wrapped her in a blanket, and for more insulation added the windbreaker York handed him. Now he stood with her in his arms, his own legs like rubber, to keep her away from Jon Fucking York. "You sent an SOS?" he said. His voice quaked. "Did you?"

"I did," York said.

"Send it again."

He followed York to the cockpit and sat in the passenger seat with Dallas in his arms. She was shivering as bad as he was now, which was a good sign. It was better than good, it was fabulous. York took the radio mic, yanked hard, snapping the cable, and threw it sideways, into the ocean. Dion blinked.

"We'll get to land okay without the coast guard," York said. "You saved her life. I can't believe it, but you did. So this isn't going to end well, obviously, and I have to ask you something. I really want to know. Do you believe in life at all costs? Or do you believe in dying with dignity?"

"Don't give me that line," Dion said. "This has nothing to do with dignity."

"It's all I want. For her and for Melanie and for myself. There's going to be no dignity in our lives. Have you seen these challenged kids when they grow old? Have you seen their parents growing old trying to care for them? Is that what you want for me? For Mel? For Dallas?"

"I can think of a million better ways —"

"No," York interrupted. "You can't. You're not torn in half like I am. Look into my future for a moment. Dallas is cute now but won't be for long. She's going to wind down early and need constant care. And you know where I'm coming from, because you asked me about it yourself, how I'd cope. I told you I was scared, but I didn't tell you the half of it. I'm frantic, Cal. I'm out of my wits. I won't cope. I'll leave Melanie, in the end, and she'll be alone. She doesn't even realize what she's getting herself into."

"So you threw Dallas in the ocean and hoped I wouldn't notice till it was too late. Was the engine even stalling, or did you set that up, too?"

The lights of the city were visible now, blurred by the rain on the windshield, still far too distant for comfort. The boat chugged toward those lights, but slowly. York shrugged. "You can blame me for bringing her along and not keeping a closer eye on her. But I didn't throw her in the ocean. She fell in herself." He snapped his fingers. "In fact you saw her there, remember? We lost power. I went back to deal with the spark plugs. You were at the wheel. You turned around, and I was making my way back to you. She was there behind me, safe and sound. You recall that, right? I did *not* throw her in the ocean."

He was right. Dion recalled it distinctly. He had turned to watch York stepping around obstructions, coming back to take over. Dallas had been one of those obstructions, just sitting there. She was looking toward the back of the boat, though. Which was odd, but no warning of what she would do next.

She was wakening now, in his arms. She whimpered and twisted, an awkward bundle starting to protest this unwanted physical contact and the pain of her abused lungs. She arched her back and growled. He needed to unload her. He had to get her to the warmth of the little cabin below.

He looked down at her slack but troubled face, at her small hands trying to hit out at everything in anger. With an effort he contained her, held tight. She only squirmed harder.

The night air felt warmer, now that the chill was seeping out of his muscles and tendons, but he had a new kind of struggle ahead, a rebellious little girl who refused to be cradled. Where was that coast guard hovercraft? The thing travelled at 130 k, if he recalled right, and should have been sprinting within view minutes ago.

"You didn't call SOS," he told York, as it dawned on him it was just another lie. "They should be here by now. Where are they?"

York kept chugging them toward land. He said nothing.

The little girl bleated a near word as she slithered and kicked.

"You're looking for your horse?" Dion asked her. He gathered her close and stood, fought for balance, and made his way back to the pile of blankets where she had been playing. He set her down so he could search for her damned toy, and instantly she was up on hands and knees, too weak to stand, shedding her covering and crawling single-mindedly toward the rear deck. Exhaustion slowed her, but it slowed Dion, too, and he had to work hard at recapturing her. She squealed in a panic, stretching both arms to the wake churning its pale line in the darkness behind them.

"Jesus, Dallas," Dion shouted, trying to collect her limbs into a manageable package. He'd had enough. He carried her down to the cabin, locked her in, then clambered back up, breathing like a marathon runner on his last leg, to keep the menace York under surveillance.

There was nothing menacing about York now. He was slumped tiredly at the controls, maintaining his route for the coastline, not too fast, not too slow.

"I get it," Dion said, with ragged anger. He stood behind the killer, adjusting his stance with the motion of the boat. "You didn't throw Dallas overboard. You threw her horse."

York's shoulders juddered, as if he was laughing or crying. "How d'you figure that? Probably was in her hand when she fell. Probably that's why she was up on deck in the first place, leaning over, trying to give the thing a dip in the ocean."

"No chance." Back on the island Dion had watched Dallas scoop the fallen animal from the surf, gripping it to her chest in her relief. She would never risk its life as York suggested. "You threw her horse. You knew she'd go after it."

"Never."

Dion heard the catch in York's voice. In profile, he could see the man's eyes fill with tears, and he could feel his own heart shattering. "I'm your alibi," he said, pounding in the spikes. "Problem is, I'm smarter than you think."

York laughed. "I *know* how smart you are. I just thought you couldn't fucking *swim.*"

"I can swim," Dion said, bitterly. "It's the one thing I do well."

"Why didn't you tell me?"

"You never asked."

York sobered up. Dion sat next to him in the passenger seat once more, knowing that if he had any say, this would be his last boat ride ever. "I didn't throw her horse out to sea," York said. "I put it on the edge of the deck, and it blew away. Which is as good as throwing it, I guess, 'cause I knew it would blow away. I shouldn't have done that. I don't know why I did. Just being mean."

Something banged against the hull, a deadhead or sea monster, but they kept going. York said, "I honestly didn't think she'd jump after it. I honestly really truly didn't, I wish you'd believe me. My only crime was hoping we couldn't save her."

Dion almost believed him, that this had been a spiteful act toward the little girl, but not attempted murder.

Except he knew York. He was a planner. In business, he was the logic, and Oz had been the impulse. But for all York's planning, he lacked luck — and definitely a fully developed conscience. Maybe intent had only formed when he picked up that horse, looked down at that little girl, and his soul had flooded with new hope.

"You didn't think I'd jump after her," he told York. "But when I did, you decided to let us both die. I'm not going to let it slide. What d'you think, I'm going to take pity on you? What's it all about, really? Money?"

York was deflating before his eyes, as if he no longer cared. "To save Mel from a life of sorrow," he said. "To save myself from a life without Mel. But sure, the money that would pass to Mel would be nice. Not enough to save Diamonds, but enough to get Sea Lane up to lock-up stage. That's all I want. Once I'm in Sea Lane, I'll rebuild. That's what I'm good at, turning shit into gold. I've got ideas, Cal. With that location, forget the nightclub biz. Imagine that setting, take out the go-go girls and install a world-class chef. Live music, fine dining, one-of-a-kind view. What d'you think, hey?" He grinned at Dion, saw Dion was not looking impressed, and glared again at the oncoming harbour lights. "Before you jumped in, I was going to myself. Make every effort to save her, and fail, and we'd all forgive ourselves and live happily ever after, knowing it was just a tragic accident. But then you fucked it all up, didn't you? You dove in like a pro. The man who's afraid of water."

"Is it the same with Cleo?" Dion asked, as it occurred to him that pushing a woman to her death was not so far from letting a little girl drown.

York appeared shocked, amazed, hurt. *"What?* No!"

Because of the money, Dion thought. The fall meant the full inheritance moved from Cleo and Dallas to Dallas and Melanie, and now a tragic drowning, and once the dust settled the money would be Melanie's, and what else would Melanie do with the cash but prop the falling timbers of their lives. Sure, it was all premeditated. Pressuring Dion to go boating today was part of the plan. It had nothing to do with friendship.

"How the fuck could I have killed Cleo?" York exclaimed, throwing a hand out, like a man on stage proving how dismayed he was. "I wasn't even there at the time. I was picking you up."

In a way, Jon York had just confessed.

"Yeah?" Dion said. "So how d'you know what time she fell?"

York closed his mouth in a tight grimace.

"You know because you were there," Dion told him.

"No. I know because it happened early that morning, because your detective friend said so. And I was nowhere in the area, because I was talking to Ziba, and from Ziba's I went straight to Diamonds to pick you up. When I say I wasn't there, I mean generally, not specifically, and you're a real bastard, you know that?"

"You showed up in my room. Walked right in. You wanted to get away early. To avoid the rain."

"Sure."

"There was no rain in the forecast. That was just an excuse."

"My God!" York shouted it out, a man falsely accused. Railroaded. Betrayed. "I looked at the sky. I saw clouds moving in. I'm a man of the ocean. I can read the skies. Now and then I get it wrong. I got it wrong. You're going to hang me because I didn't predict the weather right?"

A new thought hit Dion, so outrageous he had to rise to his feet. He stood bracing against the dash panel, staring down at York's profile. "You took my phone," he said. "You changed my alarm clock. You changed the time on your vehicle. Every clock I looked at confirmed what time it wasn't."

York grinned up at him. "You're crazier than Oscar," he cried, and with sudden enthusiasm spun the wheel to veer them away from the oncoming shore. Dion lost balance, but grabbed at the dash, gathered his wits and swung a fist, cracking York on the side of the head. York sprawled against the controls. He righted himself, swearing, and punched out sideways. Dion dodged the blow, and both men grabbed at the wheel. York shoved blindly at the shift and throttle by his knee, and again the boat swerved out to sea, nosing up and cracking down. Dion's feet went up and he went down, smashing a hip against something, shoulder against something else. He struggled back to his feet and dropped on York so they shared the pilot's seat like a vaudeville team, gripping each side of the wheel and tugging. The boat swung in circles, tacking wildly to centre, bringing in an icy spray of seawater.

Weakened by his swim and losing ground, Dion fought dirty and used his elbow to bloody York's nose. Which did wonders. He climbed across the writhing body and pulled down the lever. The boat settled, and York, in surrender, moved to the passenger seat, palm over nose and mouth.

Dion was in control now and only had to figure out how to work the machine, as a bleeding York wasn't going to give him lessons. He took a breath and looked forward, through windscreen into the rugged distance. He would be okay, he felt, with the glimmering prospect of land in sight, but in so many ways he was still so lost at sea.

Thirty-Nine

ROCK BOTTOM

"OKAY." YORK WAS MUFFLED-sounding as he used the hem of his shirt to staunch the bleeding. He sat in the passenger seat, looking not as beaten as Dion wanted him to be. "You've got me. I don't know what came over me. It was just there, like a sign from God. Door was open. I went up, and Cleo was in Oscar's office. She was on the phone. When she saw me she told whoever was on the line that she'd call her back. She was right there by the window, like an accident waiting to happen. I walked over, and it was the last thing she expected. Barely a touch." He brayed another laugh, through all the wetness on his face, blood, rain, ocean spray. "Sick, I know. And then I had to think. I set the scene. Pushed the desk over to make it look like she'd climbed up on it. There was a drape on the floor that looked like it was waiting to be put up. So I put it up, partway. Blame it all on being so close to perfect. If it wasn't so close I wouldn't be such a maniac, I swear, swear to God, this is not me. I wouldn't keep killing everyone in sight, except I was always this fucking close."

"You rigged my clock. And you swiped my phone, too, because you couldn't change the time on that so easily, could you?"

York nodded. "Yes, I rigged your clock and swiped your phone. If you'd made a fuss about the phone, I would have magically located it on the counter, or whatnot, and the gig would be up. But you were like, oh well, must have left it somewhere, so I went with it. Kind of clever, right? Both vehicles, too. Easy to change the time. I really had you in a little time warp there. Actually, it's the oldest trick in the book, if you read the classics."

Dion had never read the classics. He thought back on the deception. Later all the clocks got set back to normal, except his little alarm clock. But if he had noticed, he blamed it on the batteries. He just wasn't so sharp anymore.

"I bet you killed Oscar, too," he said, only to be nasty. He didn't mean it, and didn't believe it. Oscar's death was one that York couldn't have done, since he was in Victoria at the time.

"Actually, yes," York said. "I did."

Dion wasn't sure he could stand another surprise. A hired hitman, then. He was steering them back to land, and not doing so well. The engine was choking up again, gagging as he tried to pick up speed. He was starting to wonder if he would ever step on that wharf again.

"Inadvertently," York said. "Chain reaction, really. There was this electrician, Sig, who I had working on the dance-floor lighting. At Diamonds. I hired him cash under the table — but that's a long story, has to do with my binding contract with the firm that won the bid. Anyway, one night I caught this guy Sig walking out with a bottle of something in his tool bag. Scotch, I think, not even the high-end stuff. We had a good talk. He begged me not to turn him in, said he was just getting started, the rap would ruin him. All those liquor bottles, he said. They put him in a trance."

York smiled as he recalled the confrontation with the electrician Sig — Sigmund Blatt, that would be — and in spite of his damaged face and flapping wet hair he seemed to be enjoying himself, like this was just another day on the water. "It's the fuel-line connector," he said. "I jinxed it, then guess I didn't fix it so well. Don't worry, you'll make it.

"So," he went on, "I did this guy Sig a favour, absolved him of the crime, and asked for a favour in return. Plus I'd drop him a buck or two if it worked out. I didn't want to tip Oz over the edge. I just wanted to get him put away for something, just for a while. He sells drugs, I guess you figured that out, too. Just grass. Just on a social level, amongst friends, wouldn't get much more than a slap on the wrist. Few months plus probation, max. So I asked this electrician Sig to follow him around, gather some evidence. If nothing else, it would cool Oz off a bit, distract him. I'd have leverage, if he was in trouble. I could roll back his plans. It might even break the partnership. That would be best-case scenario. Oz was a great guy, a visionary, but he was a businessman's nightmare."

Dion didn't know Oscar Roth had dealt drugs. If he had, it was on such a small scale that it had never set off any alarms in the RCMP's drug section. "You tried to frame him? So you could nix his plans for Diamonds?"

"Don't give me that look. I know it sounds crazy, but you never met Oz. He's relentless, when he wants something. I needed a break from him and his big ideas. Diamonds needed a break from Oz. Our shareholders needed a break. *Oz* needed a break from Oz. His ideas were fabulous, if your funds were too. Philosophically there, we differed. He says go for gold right out of the gate, I say go for break-even for a few years. We were getting debt-heavy, Cal. Oz just didn't get it."

So York had strong-armed the electrician Sigmund Blatt to tail Oscar Roth with some hare-brained idea of getting Oscar straitjacketed for a bit of a reprieve. But Oscar was paranoid. Something had happened, involving Jamie — probably *because* of Jamie — and he was seeing Asian killers in his rear-view mirror. Not Sig Blatt, but Blatt's partner, Lance. Blatt had delegated the tailing job to Lance, and Lance got killed for it. Along with his wife and child. It was one hell of a rogue bullet York had fired, knocking out an innocent family and orphaning a small boy.

"But how did that get Oscar killed?" he said. Because here the chain broke. If the Asian gang was real, not imaginary, it seemed likely they had done the deed. Mr. Noon, maybe. Nguyen. The dead girl on the rocks with the ligature marks and "Jane Doe" on her toe-tag tied in with Oscar's totalled Stingray, he was starting to be sure of it. And if that was the case, York's prank had nothing to do with it.

"I don't know how," York said. "But one way or another, I got him killed. And I'm sorry. For everything I did. But at least I came back for you. Didn't I? You know what? You really want to know why I came back for you?"

Dion kept his mouth shut. The dock was coming in sight. He saw water traffic, too, some nighttime boaters heading in, and one or two heading out.

"Because I admire you," York said. "You're what I wish I could be."

Dion didn't care what York wished, because he was starting to panic. "What do I do now? I'm going to crash!"

"Slow down," York said. "You're going to have to swing around and ease in. I'm sure you'll figure it out."

Dion slowed the boat till it puttered. He was staring through the darkness, and if he wasn't tensed to breaking point already the pistol blast might have jolted him overboard. He glanced sideways at York's body slumping from passenger seat to deck.

There was blood everywhere, and York's handsome face was gone.

Dion looked at the dock structure ahead. He stood to see better. He passed too close to a yacht that was nosing out to sea, and somebody shouted angrily down at him. The wharf ahead looked huge, crowded and complicated, now that he was alone. The pilings loomed, the passage too narrow. Lights shone down, creating visual confusion to add to the noise in his head. He steered toward the opening. His heart banged in his chest cage like it was trying to break free.

The boat thudded hard against wood and pitched him forward. He fumbled at the controls till he had the motor shut down. Silence followed, except for the clanging of sailboat masts. Someone far off was laughing. His hands were gripping the wheel so tight they hurt. He had no phone, as he had drowned the thing in his shorts pocket. He would have to use York's. First he would check on the girl in the cabin, make sure she was all right down there, then he would get a hold of the police.

Except he couldn't move. He heard excited voices. People were standing up on the dock, staring down at him, at the blood, at the lifeless body lying between the two seats. He lifted his hands to show he was unarmed, but the people on the dock shouted and scattered, leaving him alone. The boat had crumpled its nose against the piling, and now sloshed gently at rest.

"Fuck," Dion said, with loud and helpless passion.

But at least he need do nothing further. The police would be here soon enough.

Forty

LEEWAY

DION WASN'T SURE WHAT Sergeant Mike Bosko was going to do to him, skin him alive on the spot or just have him thrown into barracks. He knocked on the open door and stepped into the room, and Bosko stood, smiled, and gestured at the visitor's chair before his desk.

Dion dropped into the chair. "Sorry I didn't answer your calls. I was pretty busy."

"Oh yes?" Bosko said. He had shut his laptop cover, and his phone was nowhere in sight. There was nothing hooked to his ear for hands-free communication, no paperwork on his desk ready to be filled. "So how are you? Got a touch of pneumonia, I hear."

The only lingering effects of Dion's frigid swim were a gravelly voice and an ache in his chest when he inhaled. "I'm okay now. How is ... Dallas?"

A name he could barely say, it was so wrapped in shame.

"They're holding her in hospital for a few days, but they expect she'll be fine."

"That's good."

"They say she must have been in the water for a lot longer than a couple minutes, as you said in your statement. Maybe as much as forty-five minutes? If the water had been a couple degrees colder, you'd both be in caskets now. Or a couple degrees warmer, for that matter. Sometimes the cold is what saves you. Also her passivity, her lack of panic, helped. Did you see her go in?"

"No. Jon and I were both looking forward. Really didn't expect her to leave her spot."

Dion had not made a statement yet, about what really happened, what Jon had done. Jon had brought a gun along, which made him wonder what the alternate plan was. But maybe the gun was only there as a tool of last resort. As for the attempted murder of Dallas, he considered downplaying it, letting what happened lie as an accident, even if it meant shouldering part of the blame. Negligence. Because what would the truth accomplish? A whole lot of hours of questions and answers, with the pointless objective of proving Jon was even more a bastard than anyone imagined. So what? Jon would be damned for everything else he had done, with the murder of Cleo Irvine all over the front pages. And he was dead, and how much post-mortem punishment did he deserve?

Something else made Dion sit on the truth, though. If the child welfare people learned that Jon had tried to drown Dallas, might that affect Melanie's custody?

"A terrible experience for you, all around," Bosko was saying. "I've read your statement. You've managed to put a lot of questions to rest. It's just too bad Jon York isn't around to answer the rest. But we've got Cleo Irvine at least half sorted out, and the motive behind the Lius. It would be a comedy of errors, if there was anything remotely funny about it. I'm tempted to say good work, except I don't know it really was. More like you turned a blind corner, and there you were."

"No, you don't have to say *good work*, 'cause it sure was not."

"So what's next? What do you want to do now?"

Dion's arms, which he had crossed over his chest, tensed. "What do I want to do about what?"

"As far as a return date."

"Return to what date?"

"You can't keep idling forever," Bosko said. Odd, the way nothing in his manner signalled a topic change. It was disconcerting. Dion had heard staff saying Bosko wasn't human. Rubber stretched over a manifold, engine oil for blood. Which made him impossible to gauge, except for some superficial facial expressions, angry, pleased, or indifferent, the evidence just wasn't there. "Your short-term sick leave is running out. And LTD," long-term disability, "of course is a whole new ball of wax. You haven't done the paperwork yet, so I can't keep the funds flowing. About how much longer do you think you'll need? Just so I can fill in the blanks and send in my very late report?"

"I'm not on *sick leave*," Dion enunciated. "I *quit*. I sent you my letter of resignation."

Bosko's brows went up. "That's right, Dave did mention something about that. But I haven't seen anything come in. Did you mail it to me directly or send it to admin?"

"I wrote it out by hand and put it in an envelope and left it with reception. But it specifically had your name on it. Attention to you."

"Well, it must have gone astray," Bosko said. "My fault, no doubt." He didn't seem upset. He scrounged in his desk drawer, and placed pen and paper invitingly in the middle of the desk. "Never mind. You'll just have to write another one, then we'll get the wheels in motion, properly this time."

Dion looked at the pen and paper.

Bosko rearranged the pen, putting it on top of the paper and pushing both forward, in case the offer hadn't been clear enough.

The letter had gone missing? Dion swallowed and reached for the pen. It was one of those that click open and closed, so he clicked it open and closed a few times. "I'm really on sick leave right now?"

"That was my understanding," Bosko said. His black suit was crumpled, as always. Today his necktie colour of choice was sky blue. "Oh dear, did I get something wrong? Hope I didn't mix up my docs and send some other poor constable packing." He grinned to say that wasn't the case. He was only joking.

Dion drew the paper close. "What do I write?"

"Same thing as you wrote before, I'm sure. Standard resignation, short and simple will do the job."

Dion clicked the pen open and couldn't breathe. Three days ago he was in the ocean, swimming for his life. The ocean wanted to pull him in, but he'd fought back. Maybe just because of Dallas, her survival interlocked with his. But even without Dallas in tow, he didn't want to go. Just as he didn't want to quit.

"Take your time," Bosko said. "Just not too much of it."

Dion realized how he must appear, sitting here frozen, staring at blank paper. He edged his seat forward, the better to write, and scrawled the date at the top of the page. But his hand shook, and the letters were wobbly. He said, "Probably better if I type it out. My handwriting's not so good right now."

"You said you handwrote the first one, didn't you? The one I misplaced?"

"Maybe 'cause of the pneumonia, just can't seem to hold the pen straight."

"Doesn't have to be a masterpiece in calligraphy," Bosko said. "Long as it's legible." He looked at his watch. "But I've got something coming up pretty quick here, Cal. So just put it down, any which way. You know the language, dear sir ..."

Dion wrote *Dear Sir/Madam* ...

Then he looked at Bosko. "I'm really just on sick leave? Till when? Because maybe we could just hang fire for a day or so on this. I'm actually feeling better lately."

"Oh, are you?" Bosko said. "Good to hear."

A short staring contest followed, ending when Bosko reached to retrieve the paper. He folded it and dropped it into the recycle basket next to his desk. "That's fine, then," he said. "We have a bit of a window here, thanks to my *dis*organizational skills." He leaned back in his chair. "A lucky thing, perhaps. Probably you just needed some time to think it through. As I had suggested."

The last remark had an edge to it. Dion nodded. His veins felt fizzy and his throat had seized up. He was afraid if he tried to speak, he would sob instead.

Bosko said, "Either way, there's going to be repercussions. You were still on the payroll when you were talking on a social level with witnesses — which we'll have to have a good talk about shortly. But discipline hearings are expensive, and there's nobody as far as I can see who would push for your dismissal. So we may be able to cut costs and avoid a lot of bureaucracy, for now, as long as we're straight-up and honest with each other. And remain *meticulously* in contact."

"Right," Dion said. The dizziness was all over him, and he was afraid Bosko could see his heart punching through tank top, button-down shirt, suit jacket. He smoothed his tie to conceal it, but Bosko was on his feet now, reaching across the table to shake hands, making it clear this meeting was done. "Welcome back, Cal. Just email me the day of expected return, and we'll have to have another discussion, plus finish up that sick leave paperwork. Which you still need to sign, by the way."

He winked.

Forty-One

CAUGHT

LEITH HAD HIS OWN PAPERWORK to fill out. Jon York's suicide left a mess of unanswered questions. Where he got the gun was answered — a grandfathered licence to possess passed down from his dad, certificate attached. Why he had taken it boating was another question. Was suicide the intention all along, or had he meant to shoot beer bottles on the beach? Or other people?

Along with those troubling questions, the progress reports Leith was delivering were starting to look like Incompetence Central. According to Dion, York had hired Sigmund Blatt to gather evidence on Oscar Roth to put him away, no bloodbath intended. What was the motive for that little gaffe? Because Oscar was a pain in the ass? *Really?*

A dazed Dion had given his statement to Doug Paley from his hospital room, where he had been held for forty-eight hours as a precaution. Swallowing water could have potentially fatal after-effects, and pneumonia, too, was a real concern. Apparently he would be okay, though.

Leith and Paley had talked off the record and not too seriously about the possibility that Dion had shot York and set the stage to look like suicide. But the crime scene analysts nixed the idea. The only hand that held that gun and pulled the trigger belonged to the dead man. The blood spatter said it all. Lucky for Dion, he had been photographed, seized, and analyzed by investigators before he'd had a chance to move around much or mess up the spray of blood that had caught him on face and body, on upholstery and mechanisms. The pattern clearly showed Dion had been in the driver's seat, just as he stated, looking ahead and slightly to starboard when the shot was fired.

The mystery of the suicide would be hopefully explained through Melanie York.

She had been crying when Leith and JD arrived. They were calling at her home in Deep Cove to spare her having to come to the detachment, a woman in mourning.

"He's been so depressed lately," she told them, as she served coffee. "But I didn't know he'd do this. I didn't realize what kind of hell he was going through."

Leith let JD do the talking. Whatever tomboy image JD portrayed off the record, as soon as she needed to soften her edges and treat witnesses with delicacy, she was a pro. *It just gets the damn job done,* she had told Leith once, as if she didn't want to be accused of having soft spots for anyone, as if hardened criminals, children, and fuzzy little kittens were all the same to her. Like he'd believe it for a moment.

"Would the inheritance have saved the business, if Dallas was out of the way?" JD asked.

Melanie shook her head. "It might have finished the Sea Lane house, but even that would have to go sooner or later. To pay off the debts. Diamonds has become a sinkhole."

"There's a sizeable insurance policy on Oscar's life. That would go to Dallas and to you, am I right? Again, you would get Dallas's share if she died."

"It's all just pennies in a wishing well," Melanie said. "Oscar didn't put insurance on the mortgage. Now, that would have been a windfall to whoever inherited. Me, as it turns out."

JD said, "Even so, looks like you'll end up with a small fortune, Mrs. York."

"Yes, I guess. I'll be able to pay everyone off, sell the business, sell the houses. I'll set up a trust fund for that little boy, Joey. What a nightmare. What a damned nightmare Jon has caused."

"And then, any long-term plans for yourself?"

"I'm thinking of teaching. In South America. Dallas will come with me, of course. If I'm allowed to keep her."

"You won't be leaving the country right away," JD warned. "Now, I have to go back to the morning of Cleo Irvine's death. Have you been able to pin those times down any better now that you've heard Ziba Farzan's version?"

"No, sorry."

"Jon didn't ask you to lie that morning? At any time?"

"That day we all went out on the boat," Melanie said — *Dreamily*, Leith thought — "it was a nice day. Out on the water, the three of us. Cal's so sweet. If I hadn't had such a godawful headache, I would have gone with them again. And none of this would have happened."

All of this would have been postponed, Leith thought.

She said, "I hope he's okay. Cal, I mean. I hope this hasn't put him off friendship for life. And the ocean. No. Never in a million years did I know what Jon would do. Never in a million years would I believe it."

"But you believe it now," JD said.

Melanie nodded, and she was in tears again, unable to carry on. Leith asked if he could arrange for her to see a counsellor, maybe somebody from Victim Services. She assured him she would be all right, and Leith believed her. He and JD left the woman to deal with her complicated grief alone.

* * *

Late in the afternoon, Sig Blatt came in to give Leith a statement, and more loose ends were tied. Blatt agreed he had been more or less bullied by Jon York into tailing Oscar Roth. To a supposed drug house, where he was supposed to take photos, which were supposed to get the guy in hot water with the feds. But Blatt wasn't much of a spook, didn't have the patience, and he'd gotten Lance Liu to share the task, promising they'd also share the take. A disastrous move that he would regret for the rest of his life. Blatt worried he would be charged with something now. Leith didn't think so. Blatt thanked Leith for letting him know the danger was over, that the man who had killed Lance, Cheryl, and little Rosalie was dead, and he could stop looking over his shoulder. Leith didn't mention that there was still a group of Asian men out there who might have killed Oscar Roth, because in no way did he think Blatt would be their target, and sharing the thought would only put Blatt into another tailspin of worry.

Blatt asked how Joey was doing, and was redeemed to a degree in Leith's eyes. "Joey's lucky to have grandparents and an extended family who care for him a lot," he answered. It sounded formulaic, but it was true.

Blatt was gone, and Leith was left unsatisfied. York's relatively innocuous scheme had triggered a landslide of tragedy, but it didn't answer a big one: who killed Oscar Roth, and why.

Bosko arrived in the detectives' room to let everyone know that Constable Dion would be back next week. From sick leave. There was scattered applause from the team. Even Sean Urbanski and Jimmy Torr seemed pleased. Only JD kept her arms crossed.

Leith wasn't pleased. Maybe he was being selfish, but an absence of Dion would make his own life easier. He visited Bosko in his office. Rules were being trifled with, and if nothing else, he wanted to make his position clear. "With respect," he said, invited to take a seat, and taking it, "Cal was clear he was quitting. You can behead me if I'm out of line, but I think you're rewriting history here."

Bosko's answer came only after a maddening pause. "I went on a diet once," he said. His fingertips were touching, a signal that this wouldn't be brief. "It was tough, but I was determined. And it worked! The pounds came off. I began to feel lighter. In a month I had lost a few inches around my waist. I really believed I was on that regimen for life. It's what I told all my friends, anyway. A couple months later I found that I wasn't. Dion believed with all his heart he was quitting, but he was mistaken. He was really just taking some time off."

He checked Leith's face to see if he got it. Leith did, but he still didn't like it. "Seems to me you should have seized the opportunity and let him go. I like him, but I don't like working with him. I don't know who he really is. He's like … like a confused terrorist with a bomb strapped to his chest, and I for one don't want to be around when he pulls the pin. Or trips over his own shoelace and the pin gets snagged, more like. I want some distance between me and him when that happens. That's going to be a problem."

"What do you suggest?"

"Place him away from the front line. Let him blow up amongst the file cabinets. Fewer casualties."

"I can't do that," Bosko said. "I need this fellow on my investigative team. He's pure gold, Dave."

Leith said nothing, but maybe Bosko read the set of his expression and went on to explain, "We've talked about this before. I don't know how he does it, but he gets at the truth like some kind of human homing device. I've put him back on the case of Jane Doe, and we'll call it a test. Leave him alone and see if he comes up with an answer."

"Which Jane Doe?"

Bosko put a memo in front of him with the details — a girl washed up on the rocks, bloated beyond recognition, never named. "Cal tells me he had been looking into something he had heard on the streets last year, but he didn't get it verified before his accident. The case has since gone nowhere and remains open. Cal's now seeing how Oscar Roth and Jamie Paquette tie into the story, if at all."

Leith hadn't heard of the drowning. He had been working in Prince Rupert when it happened, and he'd had his own John and Jane Does to deal with. He said, "I'm still not sure how you're going to avoid this blowing up in your face. It'll all come out in court, how he was mixing with the witnesses. If that's not contaminated evidence, sir, I don't know what is."

"*If* it goes to court. And it will only go to court if Jamie Paquette turns up, and if she pleads not guilty."

There came an interruption. With unbelievable timing, Constable Urbanski stuck his head in the door and shouted, "Fuck yeah, they got her. It's on BCTV, live, car chase along the Yellowhead. C'mon and see!"

* * *

The rest of the evening was like movie day in Sex Ed. class — paperwork and phone calls abandoned, everyone glued to the monitor as the chopper followed the insect-like progress of several police cars and one sedan, zooming in, zooming out. And then cheers as the sedan was successfully boxed in and the driver stepped out, her hands in the air. Jamie Paquette's run was finally over.

Forty-Two

THE EMERALD WAVES

LATER, LEITH HAD TO WONDER how much Dion's advice had influenced him. If not for his firm but unsubstantiated belief that Jamie had killed Cheryl Liu, would he, Leith, have interrogated her so hard? Long into the night, pushing her for answers, shoving at her denials, tripping her up, and circling back to catch her from behind.

He grilled her on the bootie she claimed to have picked up. Why had she done so? What had she done with it? Why couldn't she describe it? And why did she not recall picking up a second object? He didn't describe the gin bottle, as the holdback could come in handy later on. And then there was Joey, the little boy — had she seen him or not? How could she have seen him, shut the cabinet door, and not remembered any of it? Other details she was clear about, so why not this one? Jamie admitted she had been stoned that night, her and Oz both. She had a bit of weed and coke, as had Oz. Not crazy high, but enough to lose it a bit.

Leith was up half the night, sweet-talking her, commiserating with her, but in the end what worked was a persistent harangue. It came down to stamina. She was strong, but he was stronger. So he asked, and asked again. How could she have attacked a helpless woman holding a small child? How could she with any stretch of the imagination justify such a horrendous act? Did she really fear that woman? Even high on whatever she was on, couldn't she see what she was doing was insanely wrong?

His questions were calculated to knock her off balance, and they worked. She oscillated between ingratiating, frightened, and angry. She lost track of which emotion would serve her best, and foundered. She tried tears. Tried insults. Then crossed her arms and refused to speak.

He kept talking in the face of her silence. He asked if she was religious, and how would her God want her to deal with this now? Lie, or come clean? He told her she could turn her life around. She could still do well in the world, but only in truth.

Then he let her eat dinner, which she left barely touched, then let her rest, then went at it again, chipping away at her story and her patience until, in the eighth hour, the dam broke.

Yes! She screamed it at him. Yes, she had attacked the Asian lady with the kid. Oz hadn't done it. She had. Why? Because the Asian lady had attacked her, tried to kill her, for something she didn't do. It was called self-defence. It was an eye for an eye. Last summer that Asian lady had snatched Jamie off the street, took her to a basement suite somewhere. The lady and some Chinese guys had questioned her for hours, just like in this room, but with a gun to her head. The gun was fired, too. It had no bullets, but she had died on the spot. She really did.

"What did she think you did?" Leith asked.

"I don't know. It was some big mistake."

Lot of big mistakes happening here, Leith thought.

Jamie went on. The lady let her go, but her guys followed her everywhere, until she was afraid to set foot outside. She knew the Asian lady's name, because she'd seen it in the paper, because the lady was arrested for running a dial-a-dope operation. Jamie saw her name was Nuyn, or Noon, something like that. Later she saw that the Noon lady had been found not guilty, and released, and so much for her peace of mind. And no, she didn't go to the police, because she didn't trust them. But she wasn't going to live in fear anymore. So when that Chinese guy started following her and Oz, she told Oz to stop running away like a fucking dick and confront him.

Oz did. He beat the shit out of the guy. Yes, she saw him do it, and yes, she saw it later, on the news, that he was dead. Oz got the guy's phone, as Jamie told him to do, and Jamie checked out the photos on it. Sure enough, there was a picture of Lady Noon, and as far as Oz was concerned, Noon was doomed, too.

The phone led Oz to the house, crazy little GPS voice calmly telling him to turn here, turn there. At the house they found their way up the back stairs, and Oz confronted the lady. But he wasn't sure of himself. He wasn't sure Jamie got it right, because of the kid, all the toys around. This didn't look like a drug-selling type to him, and he asked the lady if her name was Noon. He was getting frantic about it, too, coming apart at the seams.

"So I took over. Her baby was screaming so loud I couldn't think. I took it from her, and it fell. I didn't mean for that to happen. I really, really didn't mean it."

Jamie was crying, and they were real tears. Whether her tears were for what she was remembering or what she was predicting, Leith couldn't say. But the camera picked it all up, every sob and sniffle. Which would work well for her when it came to trial. Especially if her lawyer recommended trial by jury. Which he would.

Leith said he understood, and he knew Jamie hadn't meant for any of this to happen. He asked if she was ready to continue.

She nodded. "Then the lady started screaming even louder than the baby, and I tried to tell her to stop, to be quiet. I just wanted to let her know I wasn't going to put up with her people following me around anymore, to lay off, leave me alone. She grabbed a bottle and tried to hit me with it, but I took it from her, and I was going to smash her with it. But I didn't. I thought I was in control. Except she kept screaming, and I was so mad at her, for what she'd done to me, and to Oz, and to her little baby. I grabbed a towel thing there, wrapped it around her neck. I just wanted her to shut up and listen. But I killed her."

After another fit of sobbing and ripping tissues from the box, she calmed down. She said, "Oz tried to stop me, eh, but I'd just totally fuckin' lost it. He went stomping around, going, *What have you done, what have you done, oh my God, what have you done?*"

She closed her eyes.

"So how did this all start?" Leith said. "Why was this Lady Noon after you?"

"Like I said, I don't know."

"Oh, I think you know very well. I think you might as well tell me."

She shook her head. "No idea."

"Then I guess we'll have to find out, won't we, Jamie?"

She said nothing to that, but he thought she looked just a tad worried.

* * *

Dion was on the Jane Doe cold case. He now had plenty to work with, following Jamie's interview. It was easy. There weren't too many dial-a-dopers arrested and released in North Vancouver last year, and only two named Nguyen, and only one Nguyen who was a female. Her westernized name was Lisa, and she was thirty-five years old, and if he squinted, she looked a bit like Cheryl Liu. He pulled her up on PRIME. She was arrested, brought in, and he questioned her. He showed her the police artist's rendering of Jane Doe, and he showed her Jane Doe's distinctive earring, little round pendant, red background, and two arms of a yellow star, which he now realized was an artistic interpretation of the Vietnamese flag.

Lisa Nguyen studied the evidence and said, "Sunny. My sister. She's dead."

Later, Dion would work what she told him into what he managed to dig up himself: Sunny's name was Vu Thi, with the given name Bian. She was not Lisa's blood sister, but was informally adopted, and she had been in Canada on a work visa. The visa would have expired next month, except she had expired first. The question was how.

He presented photos of Jamie Paquette to Lisa, before and after her transformation.

Lisa nodded, pointing at the picture of the thinner Jamie with long brown hair. "She did it."

"Did what?"

"Sunny had very pretty necklace, made in Vietnam. This woman, her name is Paquette, she wants to buy. Sunny is in Vancouver, at a dance club, and my brothers are there, too. My brother, he hear this woman talk to Sunny, want to buy her necklace from her. Sunny say no, her boyfriend give it to her. She will not sell. Later Sunny and this woman walk out together. We never see Sunny again. This woman kill Sunny."

Dion asked Lisa what she had done about it.

"Nothing," Lisa said.

Soon Lisa Nguyen would become an open file in her own right, along with her brother, T.T. Nguyen, and others, to be investigated for kidnap, assault, uttering threats, and obstruction. But that would come later. Now Dion paused to catch up on his notes.

In a separate but related investigation, he had established the date of a certain boat crash. Inquiries at the marine scrapyard had led him nowhere, so he had gone at it the long way, picked up the phone, and made some calls, until he found a gardener who had worked for Oscar Roth last summer. The gardener recalled Mr. Roth hauling the damaged boat home one day. He had seen a great crack along the bow, and he had asked Mr. Roth about it. He clearly recalled Mr. Roth laughing as he answered, "My dumb bitch sweetie-pie dead-headed my favourite boat, man."

Soon after that the boat had disappeared off the estate, and Mr. Roth didn't seem to think it was funny anymore. He also told the gardener he was no longer needed. Coincidence? Maybe.

Fortunately, the gardener could pin down the crash date quite accurately, thanks to being fired exactly four days later.

Dion asked Lisa Nguyen for the date that Sunny had disappeared. She knew that quite accurately, too. Later that day, he applied the date she gave him to the date of the Stingray crash, typed it up into a report, and handed it in to Constable David Leith.

* * *

"It was an accident," Jamie told Leith in light of the new information. "We hit something, and Sunny fell overboard. I couldn't save her. Are you going to arrest that lady for what she did to me?"

She meant Lisa Nguyen.

Leith said, "Let's just stick with Sunny. Tell me about Sunny's necklace."

Jamie stared at him. "Who told you?"

"Just tell me the story."

"Oz was away. I was out partying. I met her on Richards. She was with a bunch of Asian guys, and she said they were supposed to keep an eye on her, and she wanted to ditch them and go have fun. Fine with me. She was a fun girl, super pretty. She'd never been on a motorboat before, so I took her out on the Stingray."

She reflected a moment. "She didn't drown like you see in the movies, lots of shouting and splashing. She went under, then came up, and she just lay there. I was so scared. I was going to try to pull her on board, see if I could save her, but water was coming in fast. I knew if I didn't get back to shore real quick, I'd be in there, too. So I left. Those Asian guys she was with, they must have tracked me down. That's when everything started going wrong for me. I told Oz I wrecked his boat. I told him I was sorry. I thought the cops would come and throw me in jail for what happened, but they didn't. I told him not to tell anyone. He took the blame for me. He didn't know about the girl, though. But even if he knew about her, he would have taken the blame. He was like that."

She looked sadly at her own hands. "I didn't treat him good. I took him for granted. I hurt him, a lot. I wish I could just back step, back step, back step to the day we met. I'd have done it differently. I'd be a smarter girl, and all those people …"

Leith nodded. He and Jamie had spent so much time together over the last two days that an odd rapport had developed. She tilted her head to one side, her eyes softly reflective, and gazed at him across the table. "You ever see something, and you think to yourself, if I only had that thing, I'd be okay? I'd never be sad again?"

Leith had never seen such a magical object, but he understood the power of longing. He murmured that he knew what she meant.

"It was like that," she said. "Emeralds on silver, like a million little sparkling leaves. I offered her a thousand dollars, but I guess it was worth a whole lot more, because she wouldn't sell it to me. But that's nothing to do with anything. If you're thinking I wanted to steal it from her, I didn't. I've had enough shit stolen from me, and I hate thieves. I don't steal. But I thought she'd change her mind, if I showed her some fun. But she didn't. Maybe I was a bit mad. Maybe I tried to scare her a little, going so fast. But that's all. Just a little tiny payback."

Leith thought she was probably telling the truth. He also thought there was a darker side to her truth. Her anger was probably not tiny at all, but huge and impotent, and if she didn't intend on killing anybody that night, she did intend on terrifying the girl for what she had done to her, making her want something she couldn't have.

Leith had one more item to put to her. The alcoholic wanderer Alex Caine had gotten back to JD. As requested, Caine had searched his apartment for the piece of paper he had discovered tucked in the box and left on the steps of the *North Shore News,* along with the blue bottle. He had found it. The note pointed the finger directly at Jamie.

Leith wasn't sure how useful the note would prove to be. Even if it wasn't excluded in court, which he suspected it would be, it did nothing to help solve the crime of Oscar's own death. Except to say, in a PS, that Oscar felt his life was in imminent danger, which in retrospect went without saying.

He placed it before Jamie, and she read it to herself, slowly, carefully, and sadly.

*To the North Shore News/Police. Enclosed please find
proof that Jamie Paquette killed the lady and her baby on
Mahon Street,* the note said. *Also please find enclosed the
bottle she grabbed to threaten the lady. It's got her fingerprints all over it. She's pure evil and you should arrest her.*
That was the main part of the note, with some elaborations. It went on: *She also made me beat up Mr. Liu,
but I didn't kill him. I solemnly declare I just hit him a
couple times and he was okay when I left. I told him I was
sorry, and I don't understand what happened, but I take
full responsibility for his death. PS. Some guys are after
Jamie for something she did last summer, and they're after
me, too, and I fear for my life. That's why I want to come
clean. I plan to leave town and never come back. I want
her put away for good.*

Jamie subsided in her chair and looked at Leith.
"Okay, so I'm pure evil. What about it?"

"Nothing, really. Just hoping it might refresh your
memory, and give you some idea about who killed
Oscar."

"Well, after reading this, yeah," she said. "It's kind of
obvious. *He* did."

Leith sat forward. "He *who?*"

"Oz. Oz killed Oz."

He charged Jamie formally with the first-degree murder of Cheryl Liu and Rosalie Liu. Maybe she eventually
would also be charged with complicity in the murder of
Lance Liu. That one would take a lot more work, but it
was a job Leith was determined to undertake to the best
of his skill and ability, so help him God.

He called the guards to remove Jamie to the cells.

"Oh, and tell Cal I'll get him for this," she said, and gave him a final smoky-eyed smile.

* * *

The beach in front of Jon York's Sea Lane home was a narrow, rocky strip that disappeared at high tide. This evening the tide was low, and Dion stood, dressed against the chill, boots in the grit, facing the water. The water looked rough, but not wild. To get wild water, he would have to travel by ferry and car as far west as one could get from this corner of the world, to Tofino, where the breakers rolled in high and strong.

Still, the sea before him was far from flat. He stepped onto a barnacled rock and watched the waves swell and subside. Water slapped the shoreline and spat at him where he stood. He turned to look up the slope behind him. From here he could see only the eaves of Jon York's dream house. The place would go on sale now. Unfinished, priced accordingly, it would sell fast.

Still on the boulder, being knocked almost off balance by the wind, he bit the bullet and phoned Kate. When she answered, he said, "I'm thinking we should go to Tofino and learn how to surf, what d'you think? I don't mean now. I mean when you're through with the guy you're seeing."

Kate was good enough to say yes, learning to surf at Tofino sounded like a great idea. The phone call finished, Dion stared down the water, his reason for being here. He cupped his hands to his mouth to hoot out contempt at the waves that had tried to kill him.

Another reason for his visit to the beach was to get closer to Jane Doe, Sunny. He had a name for her now, and stats. An orphan, Vietnamese father and French mother, both killed in a plane crash. He had a photograph of her for the file, but he still pictured her as an artist's initial rendering, pre-3D model, soft pencil lines and a playful gleam in those dark eyes. Not that it added much to the file, but Sunny's boyfriend was also a known entity now. Tran, a young police officer in Vietnam, with whom Dion had spoken on the phone. Struggling with his English, Tran had described a necklace he had bought for Sunny, which she cherished. Green emeralds? No. He didn't know the English word, so he had consulted a colleague. Glass, he told Dion. Bought in Biện Hòa for a hundred and thirty-five dollars.

Crazy. Dion hugged himself, and thought about Melanie, who he had come so close to calling last night, because he missed her. He had convinced himself that maybe with Melanie there was a chance to build something out of the carnage. But a memory kicked in, stopping him cold. The clock on the mantelpiece at the York home. That was one timepiece Jon had no chance to rig, yet it had been rigged all the same. He recalled that day, clearly, looking at the clock face, noting the time, habitual from years of note-taking. The clock jived with all the other lies. So who had turned back its hands? Guess.

And if she had done that, lied to his face, what else had she participated in?

He didn't believe her role was anything deep or malicious. Probably she was only doing her husband's bidding, and probably she didn't have a clue what it was all about.

But later, hadn't she guessed? He wouldn't report her, but he wouldn't get in touch with her either, for anything.

His phone rang. It was Doug Paley, wanting him to get down to Rainey's, on the double.

"Why?"

"Because we're here cursing ourselves soundly, and we need help."

Good enough. Dion thrust the phone in his pocket, said goodbye to the emerald waves, and left the beach for his car.

He learned, as he took a seat at the crowded table at Rainey's, why they were cursing themselves. Because Oscar Roth had killed Oscar Roth, that's why, a truth which snapped into place so ridiculously well that they needed to get drunk, fast.

"We should have seen it," JD said. "Oz killed himself and set it up like a murder so the insurance would pay out. We're Keystone Kops, is what we are."

"We oughta be issued a new uniform," Doug Paley agreed. "Rubber billy clubs and long, flat shoes that patter when we run." He reached over and ruffled Dion's hair consolingly, because Dion had learned he wasn't going to get off so easy for his insubordination. This morning Bosko had informed him that sorry, it was beyond his control. Back down to the general duties pit he was going, gun, uniform, and street patrols, for the foreseeable future.

"Well, all the same, how could we know how crazy this Oscar guy was?" Sean Urbanski asked. He looked more biker than ever today, and now Dion knew why. Not an incipient identity crisis, but a perfectly healthy unit transfer. Sean was moving to Surrey to take part in undercover operations. Dion didn't want Sean to leave, but that was how it went. People transferred in, and then they transferred out.

Leith was coolly answering Urbanski's question. "How could we know Oz was crazy? Maybe because everyone kept saying so?"

"'Course that snort of coke didn't help," Paley said.

"Yeah, Doug, you really gotta cut down on the white stuff," Urbanski remarked.

There were more jokes along that line, and some laughter, until JD spoiled it with her crabby morality. "One life, just one puny life you get, and you want to fuck up your brain with drugs. I just don't get it. Even this," she held up her beer. "Even this is stupid."

Leith had a question for Dion. "Any chance you recall why you suspected Jamie? Without that heads-up, I'm not sure we'd have squeezed a confession out of her."

"You've got Oscar's note," Dion pointed out. "That would have done it, without my heads-up."

"Not necessarily. Oscar's note could have been Oscar covering his own ass. And you didn't answer my question."

Dion finally had an answer to that question. He had found it only this morning, as he stood on the narrow deck of his apartment, looking at his view of branches. "Jamie and I were talking," he said. "I asked her if she had taken anything from the Mahon home after the crime. She drew a blank, just for a moment, and I could see her thinking. Then she recalled it, but only because it was in the news, the missing bootie, and she's a quick thinker, and she's smart. She said yeah, she took the bootie. I almost didn't catch it. But in that moment, bang, I knew I'd got it the wrong way round. She was the one we were after."

"And Oscar was the ogre with a heart," Leith said. "And then he couldn't live with himself for what he'd taken part in."

Or live with what his girlfriend was doing with his best friend, Dion thought. Because Oscar had known. One way or another, he had figured out what this friendship was really worth.

Epilogue

TWIST

LEITH LOADED HIS LONG-handled shovel into the bed of his Tacoma under bleak afternoon skies. No more rental car, no more bachelor suite. He had his truck back, and his family. He didn't tell Alison where he was going; she assumed it was work. Which it wasn't.

He wondered as he sped along how he would explain himself if caught digging holes in an abandoned gravel pit in the middle of nowhere. He would flash his ID, say it was police business, and whoever was harassing him would hopefully buzz off and leave him alone. If worst came to worst, and that person reported him as a suspicious trespasser to the Surrey RCMP — whose toes he would be treading on — he would just have to tell Bosko everything and hope Bosko bailed him out. What if Bosko only raised his brows and looked surprised?

It was a terrible thought that he decided to forget. For now.

Leith almost missed the turnoff to the Pacific Highway. A plane passed overhead, another jumbo jet lowering belly-first into Richmond's YVR. Further out, another sailed off to some other key city. Soon Melanie York would be on one of those planes, maybe already was. Down to South America — he'd forgotten the specifics, but had it on file — to teach disadvantaged children the valuable art of everything. She had taken Dallas with her, along with the new toy horse Melanie had bought for her.

Leith had asked Melanie how Dallas was accepting the replacement toy, and the answer surprised him. "She doesn't like it," Melanie told him. "She puts it aside. She's still in mourning."

Ironically, the fact that Dallas mourned her lost horse somehow cheered Leith. Her mourning meant that within her impenetrable skull was a regular human being, which meant she might one day emerge and be part of the world. He also learned she had spoken a word, as she lay recovering in her hospital bed, to Melanie.

Leith guessed what the word was, but asked all the same.

"*Horse,*" Melanie quoted, with a shine in her eye.

Strange woman. She had sobered up and looked about ten years younger, as if maybe the end of her marriage was the best thing that could have happened to her. That she was leaving bothered Leith, with so many questions unanswered. Some people fought to the bitter end to stay home; others fought to leave. Melanie was unequivocal, and there was nothing he could do about it.

The wheels of his Tacoma hit the on-ramp, taking him southwest on the dead-straight highway to Cloverdale.

He worried about the logistics, which were easier to deal with than the bigger question of why.

What if he found nothing? All he would have proven was that he might not be digging in the right places. The gravel pit was huge, with a dozen eroding hills and valleys intertwined with dirt-bike paths and overgrown with weeds. A body could be buried anywhere, and he would need a crew and a week of man-hours to properly excavate it.

On the other hand, with the little information he had, he suspected the event had been unplanned, followed by a hasty burial, somewhere on the flat grounds where the trucks had come and gone in the years before the gravel pit finally locked its gate and posted its Re/Max sign. He guessed that he could further narrow down the spot to somewhere close to where Dion had parked his car, according to the tracker device. Which gave him at least an X for a starting point.

About a year had passed. Would the dirt have recompacted itself by now? Wouldn't local dogs have dug up a shallow grave? Maybe not. Maybe the two men — he assumed Luciano Ferraro was a partner in crime — had dumped the body into an existing crevice, then loaded dirt on top. Maybe they'd had time to bury it deep enough so its smell wouldn't attract scavengers.

What he would do was take his shovel and tease the soil here and there, check if any earth was looser than the rest. That was all.

Would that ease his conscience?

Probably not.

Worry was making him speed. He eased off to eighty.

What if he should find disturbed earth? Would he dig deeper? At what point would he stop and take it to the authorities? Who were the authorities? What would Bosko do with the information?

Which brought him finally to the why.

"Because I like you," he said, to his own surprise, and the clouds cleared.

He liked Dion. Or at least cared for him. Dion was in trouble. And if the trouble was as super-sized as Leith was almost sure it was, that meant Dion was going to be caught, sooner or later. Why not take his concerns to Bosko, then? Because he didn't trust him, and he didn't trust that man Parker. He didn't know what kind of tricks a man like Parker might pull, but he had a feeling it might hurt worse than a leghold trap. If anyone was going to catch Dion, he wanted it to be himself, and when he turned him in, it wouldn't be to Bosko, but a higher authority, one with no shady hidden agenda.

He turned onto the long, straight road with farmers' fields on either side, hedges shrill with birds, the rumble of distant machinery, and not much else. Closing in on the crash site, he saw a plume of grit and dust ahead, obscuring the road as though a stampede of wild horses was charging at him. He slowed to fifty, and out of the dust came not horses, but a pair of headlights. A large dump truck roared past, and Leith discovered seconds later where its dust trail led from: the entrance of the gravel pit. He braked and peered to his left. The RE/MAX sign was gone.

The pit had been sold, and the gate stood open.

He drove down the half-kilometre lane and arrived at the marshalling grounds for machinery in the past and machinery in the future. The place was as desolate as ever, but different, and it was one hell of a difference. It sat him back in the driver's seat as if winded, staring at the scene before him. No people here, no vehicles, just clouds of debris swirling up from a recent dump-load of blast-rock.

Where had the rocks come from? Trucked in from the nearest quarry and stockpiled to sell to local contractors and homeowners. Leith knew something about quarries and pits. Soon the whole plateau would be covered in mounds of this stuff, in varying grades from fine sand to boulders.

He stepped from his pickup to gaze at the grey mountain of crushed rock that had obliterated yesterday's flat land, just about exactly where Dion had parked his car two weeks ago. A shovel was no longer what he needed. He'd need a stop-work order, for one thing. And an excavator. And a sit-down meeting with IHIT, and a whole ream of warrants. All of which meant it was no longer a private mission. This was the point of no return.

"I don't believe it," he said. "I just don't believe it."

He winced at the sunrays cutting through the billows of rock dust. Before leaving the Pacific Highway he had turned off his phone, to prevent triangulation, to prevent tracking. Which showed just how ambivalent he really was. The temperature dropped suddenly in the gravel pit, like a heavy cold front had just bullied out the warmth. He shivered and returned to his truck. Not until he was crossing the Fraser River did he turn his phone back on and become once again connected to the world. The bridge supports chopped the view as he sped along, creating a fluttery image of his new home territory. He was beginning to feel it, the pull of the Lower Mainland. Strange days were coming, indeed.

Acknowledgements

I ACKNOWLEDGE IN A HAPHAZARD way today, because the help I have received since publishing *Cold Girl* is amorphous and amazing. Dundurn did a fabulous job of getting *Cold Girl* out there to be read. Many people read and many people reviewed and/or took the time to write me personal notes to let me know they loved the novel and wanted more. My thanks go to them especially. Writers at any stage need that vote of confidence.

I have made friends in the writing community, too many to name, all excellent writers who are putting character to B.C. crime and placing its stamp on the world. In particular I'll just say *Noir in the Bar*, thank you, all, for those best days and nights on the road! And the good people who ran CUFFED International Crime Festival in Vancouver last March — Alma Lee, Lonnie Propas, Sue Ogul, Irene Lau (accomplice), and writer Robin Spano (panel moderator) — for introducing me to the wider world of writing, all the while making me feel like one of the family.

Thank you to Judy Toews, my up-and-coming crime-writer friend, who read and remarked on *Undertow*'s first draft, which led to many improvements; to Allister Thompson, editor, for guiding me through some pivotal questions; and to David Warriner of W Translation, many thanks for stepping in to help with some eleventh-hour edits.

Finally, my gratitude goes to the RCMP member who gave me tons of insight and technical advice when I asked. Anything I've messed up in that regard is completely my fault!

RMG

Some geography and places in this novel have been treated with some degree of artistic licence, particularly the Royal Arms, which does not exist, except in composite form pulled from memory.

IN THE SAME SERIES

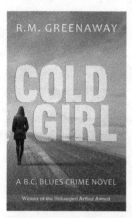

Cold Girl
R.M. Greenaway

*2014 Unhanged Arthur Award
for Best Unpublished First Crime
Novel — Winner*

It's too cold to go missing in northern B.C., as a mismatched team of investigators battle the clock while the disappearances add up.

A popular rockabilly singer has vanished in the snowbound Hazeltons of northern B.C. Lead RCMP investigator David Leith and his team work through the possibilities: has she been snatched by the so-called Pickup Killer, or does the answer lie here in the community, somewhere among her reticent fans and friends?

Leith has much to contend with: rough terrain and punishing weather, motel-living and wily witnesses. The local police force is tiny but headstrong, and one young constable seems more hindrance than help — until he wanders straight into the heart of the matter.

The urgency ramps up as one missing woman becomes two, the second barely a ghost passing through. Suspects multiply, but only at the bitter end does Leith discover who is the coldest girl of all.

OF RELATED INTEREST

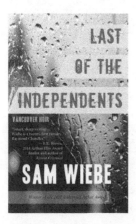

Last of the Independents
Sam Wiebe

2015 Kobo Emerging Writer's —
Winner, Fiction

2015 Arthur Ellis Award —
Nominated, Best First Novel

2012 Unhanged Arthur Award —
Winner, Best Unpublished First
Crime Novel

What do a necrophile, a missing boy, and an unsavoury P.I. have in common? Private detective Michael Drayton is about to find out....

Twenty-nine-year-old Michael Drayton runs a private investigation agency in Vancouver that specializes in missing persons — only, as Mike has discovered, some missing people stay with you. Still haunted by the unsolved disappearance of a young girl, Mike is hired to find the vanished son of a local junk merchant. However, he quickly discovers that the case has been damaged by a crooked private eye and dismissed by a disinterested justice system. Worse, the only viable lead involves a drug-addicted car thief with gang connections.

As the stakes rise, Mike attempts to balance his search for the junk merchant's son with a more profitable case involving a necrophile and a funeral home, while simultaneously struggling to keep a disreputable psychic from bilking the mother of a missing girl.

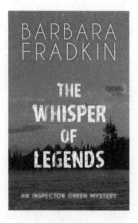

The Whisper of Legends
Barbara Fradkin

An empty canoe washes up on the shore of the Nahanni River — has the river claimed four more lives?

When his teenage daughter goes missing on a summer wilderness canoe trip to the Nahanni River, Inspector Michael Green is forced into unfamiliar territory. Unable to mobilize the local RCMP, he enlists the help of his long-time friend, Staff Sergeant Brian Sullivan, to accompany him to the Northwest Territories to look for themselves.

Green is terrified. The park has 30,000 square kilometres of wilderness and 600 grizzlies. Even worse, Green soon discovers his daughter lied to him. The trip was organized not by a reputable tour company but by her new boyfriend, Scott, a graduate geology student. When clues about Scott's past begin to drift in, Green, Sullivan, and two guides head into the wilderness. After the body of one of the group turns up at the bottom of a cliff, they begin to realize just what is at stake.

Cold Mourning
Brenda Chapman

Nominated for the 2015 Arthur Ellis Award for Best Novel

When murder stalks a family over Christmas, Kala Stonechild trusts her intuition to get results.

It's a week before Christmas when wealthy businessman Tom Underwood disappears into thin air — with more than enough people wanting him dead.

New police recruit Kala Stonechild, who has left her northern Ontario detachment to join a specialized Ottawa crime unit, is tasked with returning Underwood home in time for the holidays. Stonechild, who is from a First Nations reserve, is a lone wolf who is used to surviving on her wits. Her new boss, Detective Jacques Rouleau, has his hands full controlling her, his team, and an investigation that keeps threatening to go off track.

Old betrayals and complicated family relationships brutally collide when love turns to hate and murder stalks a family.

MY GREENAWAY, R. M. 10/17
Undertow /